Will tried to remember how well Gilly and Amy knew each other

They hadn't been friends—nothing like that, but Amy was part of the crowd he'd introduced Gilly to. They had looked a little bit alike. Both five-eight or nine, leggy, boyishly slim, naturally blond. Neither blue-eyed. Gillian had had pale, almost sea-green eyes, Amy... He couldn't quite picture them. Brown? No, not brown. Flecks of yellow and green.

Dead. Because, like Gillian, she was tall and blond and willowy? But their killers weren't the same man. Couldn't be the same man. Mendoza was guilty, guilty, guilty. A scum who had no business hitting on Will's girlfriend in the bar, becoming enraged because she'd rejected him, raping, murdering, taunting.

Had Amy been chosen precisely because she looked like Gillian? A copycat crime required a copycat victim. But who in hell would imitate something like this? Could Elk Springs really have spawned two monsters?

It made no sense. Gilly's murder by a man who'd hot-wired cars and fenced stolen goods but never committed a violent crime. This one now, six years later. Why Amy? Why now? A stranger, killed like Gillian, would have been bad enough, but Amy! Less than a week after they met again, talked about old times, flirted a little.

He went cold. Was *that* why she'd been chosen? Because he'd flirted with her? Because she'd once meant something to him?

Dear Reader,

It's hard to believe that the Signature Select program is one year old—with seventy-two books already published by top Harlequin and Silhouette authors.

What an exciting and varied lineup we have in the year ahead! In the first quarter of the year, the Signature Spotlight program offers three very different reading experiences. Popular author Marie Ferrarella, well-known for her warm family-centered romances, has gone in quite a different direction to write a story that has been "haunting her" for years. Please check out *Sundays Are for Murder* in January. Hop aboard a Caribbean cruise with Joanne Rock in *The Pleasure Trip* for February, and don't miss a trademark romantic suspense from Debra Webb, *Vows of Silence* in March.

Our collections in the first quarter of the year explore a variety of contemporary themes. Our Valentine's collection—*Write It Up!*— homes in on the trend to online dating in three stories by Elizabeth Bevarly, Tracy Kelleher and Mary Leo. February is awards season, and Barbara Bretton, Isabel Sharpe and Emilie Rose join the fun and glamour in *And the Envelope, Please...*. And in March, Leslie Kelly, Heather MacAllister and Cindi Myers have penned novellas about women desperate enough to go to *Bootcamp* to learn how not to scare men away!

Three original sagas also come your way in the first quarter of this year. Silhouette author Gina Wilkins spins off her popular FAMILY FOUND miniseries in *Wealth Beyond Riches*. Janice Kay Johnson has written a powerful story of a tortured shared past in *Dead Wrong*, which is connected to her PATTON'S DAUGHTERS Superromance miniseries, and Kathleen O'Brien gives a haunting story of mysterious murder in *Quiet as the Grave*.

And don't miss reissues of some of your favorite authors, including Georgette Heyer, Joan Hohl, Jayne Ann Krentz and Fayrene Preston. We are also featuring a number of two-in-one connected stories in volumes by Janice Kay Johnson and Kathleen O'Brien, as well as Roz Denny Fox and Janelle Denison. And don't forget there is original bonus material in every single Signature Select book to give you the inside scoop on the creative process of your favorite authors!

Enjoy!

Marsha Zinberg

Marsha Zinberg
Executive Editor
The Signature Select Program

SAGA

Janice Kay Johnson

Dead
Wrong

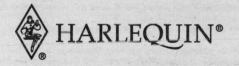

HARLEQUIN®

TORONTO • NEW YORK • LONDON
AMSTERDAM • PARIS • SYDNEY • HAMBURG
STOCKHOLM • ATHENS • TOKYO • MILAN • MADRID
PRAGUE • WARSAW • BUDAPEST • AUCKLAND

ISBN 0-373-83690-2

DEAD WRONG

This edition published by arrangement with Harlequin Books S.A.

® and TM are trademarks of the publisher. Trademarks indicated with ® are registered in the United States Patent and Trademark Office, the Canadian Trade Marks Office and in other countries.

www.eHarlequin.com

Printed in U.S.A.

Dear Reader,

When Harlequin asked me to do a Signature Select Saga story, possibly linked to one of my previous Superromance trilogies, of course it was PATTON'S DAUGHTERS that leaped to mind. I have other favorites among my books, but for some reason the characters in this trilogy and in *Jack Murray, Sheriff,* which followed, are more real to me than any others I've created. The sisters had such distinct voices, self-images and self-doubts. Writing those books, I sometimes felt as if I was channeling their stories, not making them up! In the back of my mind, I've always meant to revisit them. And what an opportunity...

Now if only I hadn't made Meg Patton's son, Will, such a well-adjusted young man. Note to self: plan ahead. However, even well-adjusted people get a little skewed when tragedy rends the fabric of their lives. Especially when they're left with a heavy load of guilt. Poor Will! Things have now gone very wrong since you last met him as a nice college student who was close to his mother and father.

I'd been contemplating a book about a serial killer for a while, too. So, here's hoping you enjoy meeting the Pattons again, or for the first time, and that this particular serial killer keeps you awake a little too late tonight!

Best,

Janice

CHAPTER ONE

GETTING THERE five minutes quicker wouldn't make any difference. They weren't racing to the rescue. They were going to view a corpse. Nonetheless, Meg Patton drove fast, with fierce concentration. If Detective Giallombardo said anything, Meg didn't hear.

This wouldn't turn out to be anything like the other murder, she kept assuring herself. The detail the kid who called 911 had blurted out would be an aside, something dropped at the scene, not a deliberate choice of murder weapon and staging. She'd feel like an idiot for tearing out here when she was supposed to supervise detectives, not respond to calls. She had already seen the way heads swiveled when she'd stood abruptly and said, "I'll take this one."

She'd garnered more surprise when she'd glanced around, choosing young Giallombardo almost randomly. *Eenie, meenie, minie, mo.* "Are you tied up? Then come with me." Everyone in the squad room had stared after them.

Butte Road ran yardstick straight for miles between rusting barbed wire fences holding back brown heaps of tumbleweed before terminating at a small volcanic cinder cone. The pavement turned to gravel not much beyond the Elk Springs city limits. Most of the year, their SUV would have raised a red cloud of cinder dust to trail them like a tail. Today, the hard-packed surface was frozen solid.

She drove this road every few weeks. Her sister Renee, the Elk Springs chief of police, lived out here on the Triple B Ranch with her husband, Daniel, and her two young children. Meg barely spared a glance for their gate when she tore by it. Renee would want to hear about the murder, even if it was outside her jurisdiction. Cops didn't like brutal murders happening in their own backyards. Even if, in this case, that backyard was a whole heck of a lot of empty country.

One of a half dozen in the immediate vicinity of Elk Springs, this lava cone, no more than a couple hundred feet high, wasn't even dignified with a name, as far as Meg knew. The county had once contemplated using its cinders for road construction, until Matt Barnard of the Triple B made a stink about having trucks roaring up and down his road all day long. After that, it was left in peace, except for Friday-night beer parties and fornicating teenagers.

A lone pickup truck sat in the turnaround at the end of the road. Two heads in it, real close together. Kids, cuddling against the horror they had suddenly understood walked their world.

Meg was careful to pull in right behind them, so as not to further damage any visible tire prints.

Uh-huh, her inner voice jeered. *On frozen cinders.*

She killed the engine and got out, slamming the door and then pausing for just a minute to take in the surroundings. The bitter cold stung her skin.

Funny how a dead body could give a familiar landscape a surreal look. The view out here was spectacular, with high country desert stretching to the horizon in one direction, brown and stark in winter. The jagged peaks of the Sisters sliced the sky to the west, while Juanita Butte seemed to float to the north like a perfect scoop of vanilla ice cream. A few thin patches of snow clung to the cinder cone and the red-brown soil between tumbleweeds. The sky was a cold, crystal blue, the stillness absolute.

Until Detective Giallombardo also slammed her door and crunched around the rear of the Explorer to join Meg.

In silence, the two women walked forward, both staring at the woman's naked body sprawled low on the slope of the cinder cone. Head uphill, resting on the pillow of a patch of snow.

In life, she had been long-legged and shapely. In death, she was bluish-white against the rust-red cinders, with the dark stain of bruises discoloring her flesh. Even before they closed the distance, Meg could see that her left breast had been mangled. Torn by an animal after death, maybe, although Meg thought that unlikely.

But the detail that riveted her was the jockstrap. The elastic of the waistband sliced into the victim's neck. The cup had been twisted to cover her face.

A message, or a gesture of contempt for the victim. Maybe for all women. Meg never had known. The man who had killed in exactly this way, who had left the body posed just as this one was posed, had insisted he was innocent. Was still protesting his innocence from the state penitentiary, where he was serving a life sentence.

Feeling sick, she said, "I'll talk to the kids. You call for a crime scene crew. We need pictures."

Giallombardo nodded and went back to the Explorer.

Meg knocked on the window of the pickup and then opened the driver side door.

"Chris Singer?"

The girl, a waif with a blotchy face and red, swollen eyes, nodded.

"And you are?" Meg asked the boy.

"Colin Glaser." He was trying to sound manly. The squeak at the end undermined his effort. He gazed through the windshield toward the ghastly sight. "That woman… She's, like, *dead.*"

"Yes, I'm afraid she is." Meg heard the grimness in her own voice.

He shuddered.

Meg looked at both of them. "Can you tell me when you arrived? Did you get out of the pickup? Touch anything?"

In unison, their heads shook violently. "We never got out," the boy said. "I wanted to get the hell—the heck out of here, but when I started to back up Chris said we should call 911. And wait until the cops got here. So we locked the doors and that's what we did."

"We were only here like a minute before we phoned," the girl said.

They'd been cutting school, Meg learned, because they had been having a relationship crisis. Despite the boy's comforting arm around the girl, Meg guessed the relationship was dead now. Chris had called her dad, who was on his way out here. He wasn't going to be a happy man.

She thanked them for being responsible, then left them to wait for the girl's father.

"Let's take a closer look," Meg said to Detective Giallombardo, who obediently followed her. Both slipped on the slope of red cinders as they scrambled the eight or ten feet up, then edged toward the body.

Unless bloodstains provided a trail—and they were going to be a bitch to spot on volcanic cinders this color—it was going to be impossible to tell where the UNSUB parked, whether he dragged or carried the body, etc. How much Luminol did it take to spot blood in a landscape this vast? Footprints and ruts didn't last in loose cinders, which tended to rattle downslope to fill any hole even when there was still a foot in it. Meg knew, because she'd climbed up to the crater several times as a teenager.

She crouched beside the victim, Giallombardo standing right above her.

Legs splayed in a grotesquely inviting gesture of sexual come-on. The savage bite marks on the breast were made by human teeth, if Meg was any judge. Maybe they'd get lucky and at least get a decent bite impression to match up with a suspect later. Arms spread to each side. The victim had been allowed no dignity in death.

And then there was the jockstrap. To appearances, it had been used to strangle the woman. It looked brand-new. Bought for the purpose.

This wasn't chance. The staging was identical to the murder six years ago that had cost Meg her son in every meaningful way, though he still dutifully arrived at her door for family holidays.

She didn't realize she'd spoken aloud until Giallombardo said, "Identical to what?"

Meg froze, her instinct to keep family history private until such time as there was no option. But when it came down to it, she'd been a cop too long to hide evidence.

"The crew's coming," she said, glad of an excuse to put off the moment of truth.

"And Dad," the young female cop observed.

A red SUV was gaining fast on the official convoy. It fishtailed once but didn't even slow. As a parent, Meg understood.

She and Giallombardo scrambled and slid their way back down to the foot of the lava cone. Crime scene techs bundled up as they climbed out of vehicles—as afternoon fell, the air became icier. Meg estimated the day hadn't reached ten degrees Fahrenheit when the sun was at its height, and the temp had probably already dropped to six or eight degrees with sub-zero to come tonight. Her cheeks and nose were numb.

She directed the crew to get them started, some spreading out to search for evidence, the photographer beginning to snap pictures, the coroner waiting to get to the body. The girl's dad erupted from his SUV almost before it skidded to a stop, and she flung herself right over her boyfriend into Daddy's arms.

Meg introduced herself, explained the situation and asked if he'd drive both kids back to town. "We've got his pickup boxed in." To the boy, she said, "Colin, can you get someone to bring you out here tomorrow after school to get your pickup?"

He nodded.

To his credit, the father squeezed the boy's shoulder and said, "Come on, son. Your mom home from work yet?" He led the two away and was soon backing out.

Meg leaned against the fender of her black Explorer. The young cop who'd been promoted to detective all of a month ago waited with a patience Meg admired.

Trina Giallombardo had risen fast in the ranks. She was only twenty-six, twenty-seven. A local girl who had gone to Oregon State to college, then come home. As a cop, she was smart, steady, mature beyond her years and dedicated. When Meg had interviewed her for the promotion, she'd claimed to have always wanted to be a detective.

She wore her thick, shiny dark hair drawn tightly

into a bun. Big brown eyes dominated an olive-complected face that gave an impression of stubbornness and intelligence rather than beauty.

Meg would have given anything to have Ben Shea, her longtime partner and brother-in-law, here instead. But Ben had broken his idiot leg—thank God not his neck—trying to keep up with Abby on the ski hill. His leg was still in traction.

But why did I have to bring a novice? Meg asked herself. Instinct? She didn't have a clue.

Gaze on the crew, spread out like giant ants below their hill, she finally answered Giallombardo's question. "Six years ago, we had a murder that looked just like this one."

"Six years..." Giallombardo frowned. "I was away at college. Wait. Not Will's girlfriend?"

"You know my son?"

"Only by sight." Did red tinge her cheeks? Hard to tell, with both their faces damn near frostbitten. "I was two years behind him in school. But I saw him play basketball. And since he was president of the student body..."

Meg nodded. "His girlfriend was raped and murdered when she came home with him for spring break from college. She was strangled with a jockstrap, and the cup was pulled over her face. She was posed just like that."

"Oh." The young cop exhaled the single, soft word.

They stood in silence while she processed the implications. "Isn't that your brother-in-law's ranch up the road?"

The fact that this body had been dumped so close to her sister's home was already bothering Meg. Their family had been targeted once before. Surely not again.

Surely this had nothing to do with the Pattons. It was happenstance that the previous victim had been Will's girlfriend. She'd gone to a bar on her own and left with the killer. She'd probably never even mentioned her boyfriend or the fight they'd just had.

Giallombardo interrupted her thoughts. "Did you catch the killer?"

Meg nodded. "He's supposed to be serving life."

They both glanced involuntarily toward the body.

"Paroled?"

"We'll find out."

The photographer signaled the coroner, and the two women joined him. Sanchez, an elected official, had run unopposed for as long as Meg had been with the Butte County Sheriff's Department. Unlike some elected coroners or medical examiners, he was good.

"Don't see any surprises," he said after a minute. "Looks like strangulation. See how deep the elastic has cut into her throat?"

They saw.

"Time of death?"

He hemmed and hawed. This cold made it harder to tell. It was like putting a body in deep freeze. "You find any ID?"

"So far, we haven't even found her panties."

He nodded. "I'm thinking last night," he finally concluded. "Maybe twelve hours ago. You might look for a young woman who waited bar, say, and didn't make it home."

"Okay." Meg was trying to take notes. She hoped they were readable. Either she wore gloves, or her fingers went numb. She alternated.

"Let's take a look at the face," the coroner suggested. "Then roll her."

Meg struggled to pull a latex glove onto her right hand, then reached out and tugged the jockstrap to one side.

The victim's mouth was frozen open as if in a scream, the grotesquely swollen tongue protruding.

"Was he hiding her face?" Giallombardo whispered. "If anything would shock you..." Before Meg could comment, the young detective was already shaking her head. "No. He posed her. He didn't kill her out here. She would have been scraped by cinders when she struggled. And if he, uh, penetrated her, he'd have had to expose his penis."

The coroner actually hunched, as if the very idea of baring himself to the sub-freezing air was so hideous he couldn't prevent a physical reaction.

"Plus he'd have had to kneel on the cinders... No."

Meg agreed. "She was already dead when he carried her here. A man horrified by his crime flees. He doesn't lay out the victim so carefully."

"He has to be a local. To know to come out here."

"That thought has occurred to me." Meg nodded at the victim. *"You're* local. Do you recognize her?"

Giallombardo swallowed. Meg watched as she focused on the face, made herself look past the distended tongue. To study glazed eyes that might have been hazel, the tiny mole on one high cheekbone...

"Oh, God," she whispered.

"You do know her."

Her breath rattled in her chest and she nodded dumbly.

"Who is she?"

Giallombardo swallowed again. Against nausea, Meg guessed. "Amy Owen. She might not be anymore. I mean, she might have gotten married. But in high school, that was her name."

Disquiet struck again. "That sounds familiar."

"I think…" The detective was taking quick, shallow breaths. "I think Will dated her."

Air hissed from between Meg's teeth.

"He brought girls out here. Sometimes."

With quick alarm, she thought, *Not Trina Giallombardo. Boy, would that complicate things.* "How do you know?" she asked, aware she sounded harsh.

Her deputy didn't want to meet her eyes. "Not because…" She closed her eyes, obviously struggling to regain her composure. When she spoke again, her voice was devoid of emotion. "I heard girls talk. That's all."

Meg's eyes narrowed. Was there some history here of which she was unaware? Damn it, had the young Trina Giallombardo had a crush on Will? If so, should she be jettisoned from the case?

But they didn't know that this had anything to do with Will.

Please God.

"I came out here when I was a teenager," she heard herself say. She was distantly aware that the other two were gaping. "With Will's father."

After what she realized was an appalled silence, Giallombardo said, "Um…I suppose almost everyone in Elk Springs has."

The coroner looked up at Meg with shrewd eyes. "You sure Mendoza is still locked up?"

"We should have been informed if he came up for parole." Meg stared down at the body. "Let's roll her."

Between rigor mortis and freezing, the job wasn't easy. Despite the cold, Giallombardo looked green by the time they were done.

The backside revealed lividity and more bruising, nothing else.

Meg raised her voice. "Let's bag her. People, has anyone found anything?"

General shakes of the head. No tracks, no discarded clothing, no convenient cigarette butts that didn't look as if they'd been left last summer. Truthfully, Meg hadn't expected anything different. The unknown subject—or UNSUB, to cops—had driven out here with the dead woman likely in his trunk. Maybe at night, maybe this morning. He'd carried her a few feet up the slope of the lava cone, splayed her limbs, adjusted the jockstrap like a man adding a flourish to his signature and left.

How in hell had he known every detail? Had he *seen* the body? Could there have been two murderers? Had he stumbled on the body before the cops found it? Or, she thought with a jolt, *was* this killer a cop?

And, whoever he was, why had he waited six years to imitate the previous rape and murder?

"Lieutenant?"

She knew on one level that Sanchez was talking to her, but still she stared down at the body and asked herself the one question she'd been avoiding.

What if Ricky Mendoza's protestations of innocence were real? What if he didn't do it?

And what if the real killer *had* been shocked by what he'd done? What if he'd been able to suppress his sexual perversion for six years—until something triggered his rage?

Something, say, like the fact that Will Patton had just moved back to Elk Springs?

Common sense revolted. *No!* Damn it, they had Mendoza cold. She'd been sorry, because she liked the kid, but he had to have been the killer. She was letting a mother's fear intrude, and if she couldn't think with the cool logic of a cop instead, she'd be the one who had to step back from this investigation.

"Sorry," she said, forcing herself to look up. "What's your question?"

"HEARD ANYTHING LAST NIGHT? Or early this morning?" As withered as the winter sagebrush, the old woman stared suspiciously through the six-inch gap between door and frame. Either she was worried about keeping the heat in, or this intruder out.

"Yes, ma'am," Trina said politely.

"We're to bed by nine o'clock."

Trina wouldn't have minded being invited inside. She was freezing on the doorstep with the sun sinking fast. This was the fourth house she'd stopped at, and at only one had she been asked in and offered coffee. The few swallows she'd managed were a distant, tantalizing memory.

She strove for a conversational tone. "You must not get much traffic out on Butte Road at night."

The old woman looked at her as if she were simple. "Saturday nights, it's like living next to Highway 20. All those young hands that work the ranches, they come hootin' and hollerin' by, two, three in the morning. Lean on their horns, stereos blasting to shake the windows. They even race sometimes." Her mouth thinned. "They turn onto our property, we get out the shotgun."

Trina considered mentioning that the law did not entitle a property owner to shoot someone for turning into his driveway.

Instead, she surreptitiously wriggled her fingers inside her gloves to see if they still functioned and said, "Last night wasn't Saturday."

"Some of them get drunk other nights, too."

Heaven send her patience.

"I'm sure they do." She shook her head as if scandalized. The old biddy. "Was last night one of those nights? You hear anybody heading home late?"

"Might have."

"Can you recall what time that was?"

Mrs. Bailey's lips folded near out of sight, as if it pained her to give a straight answer. Finally she sniffed. "Two-thirty-five. On a Thursday night. Then the fool turned around and went back to town. Bars shouldn't be open that late."

Despite her surge of excitement, Trina pointed out, "Someone might have been giving a friend a ride home."

Silence, followed by a grudging, "Might have been."

"Are you certain you heard the same vehicle coming and going?"

"Course I am! Wouldn't have said it if I hadn't meant it."

Maybe it was perversity that had her suggesting, "One pickup truck sounds an awful lot like another."

The woman didn't like explaining herself. After crimping her lips and thinking about it, she said, "This one sounded like my Rufus out there. Don't bark often, but when he does, you best jump."

"A deep, powerful engine."

"Isn't that what I said?"

Her own lips were going numb. "Did you notice when the truck came back?"

"Didn't look at the clock." She chewed it over. "Twenty minutes. Half hour."

The timing was just right.

"Mrs. Bailey, do you think you've heard this particular engine before?"

"Can't say."

"Would you recognize it again?"

"Might."

Trina gave her most winning smile, which considering she couldn't feel most of her face might look more like a death mask. "You've been a great help, Mrs. Bailey. We may need to speak to you again. In the meantime, I appreciate your cooperation."

With no "You're welcome," or even a "Mind you don't slip on the steps," the old lady slammed the door shut in Trina's face. A dead bolt lock thudded home.

If she wasn't so darn cold, Trina would have laughed. She hurried to the Explorer she was driving, started it and cranked up the heat. Intermittent shivers wracked her. But at least she'd learned something that might be useful, she thought with a small glow of triumph. Useful enough, maybe, that Lieutenant Patton would let her keep working the case.

She couldn't believe her luck to have been singled out today, and by Lieutenant Patton, of all people. Trina had become a cop because she wanted to be just like Meg Patton and her two sisters, the one Elk Springs police chief, the other an arson investigator. From the time she was eleven or twelve she'd read about their exploits in the newspaper, and since Will went to the high school people had talked, too. Lieutenant Patton had been the county Youth Officer back when Trina was in high school, so she'd talked at assemblies or in Trina's classes a couple of times a year. Trina thought she was amazing—beautiful and brave and smart. Everything Trina wanted to be.

In her interview for the promotion to detective Trina had almost blurted out something about how much she'd always admired the lieutenant. Thank goodness she'd been able to stop herself. Even if it was true, it would have sounded like the worst brown-nosing.

Now here she was, hardly a month later, partnered with her. Despite her shivers, Trina still marveled. Junior partner, of course. The lieutenant had gone back to the station to find out whether the killer from six years ago had somehow gotten out of prison and also to try to discover whether other jurisdictions had had murders with this same M.O. Lucky Trina had been assigned one patrol officer to help her canvass the houses along Butte Road.

But it had to be done, and she was pretty excited to have actually learned something. Maybe. Unless the deep-throated pickup or SUV *had* just been dropping some drunk ranch hand back at the Triple B or the Running Y. Except she'd stopped at the Triple B herself and no ranch hands had admitted to being out late last night. She'd find out from Officer Buttram whether the same was true at the Running Y. Those were the only two working ranches past the Bailey's place.

An hour and a half later, she hadn't learned a thing. Buttram and she agreed to meet back at the station.

There, he shook his head. His ruddy face glowed. "Bitch of a night."

"I would have traded my right arm for a thermos of coffee."

"With a dash of whiskey." He took off his sheepskin-lined gloves. "Nobody heard nothing."

"I found somebody who did. A Mrs. Bailey."

Her sense of triumph dimmed at the sight of his face.

"There's a nasty one."

"She calls in complaints?"

"Once a month or so." He shook his head. "Hates the

neighbors, hates teenagers, doesn't much like cows. You believe her, somebody is always being noisy or trespassing."

Noisy? "I don't remember a house near hers."

"She has damn fine hearing."

Trina quizzed him about who he'd talked to at the Running Y, then went to Lieutenant Patton's office.

Through the glass inset, she saw the lieutenant lift her head at the sound of the knock. She waved Trina in.

"You look cold."

"Yes, ma'am."

Her superior scowled. "Quit ma'aming me."

"Sir…"

"That isn't any better. You make me feel old."

"Lieutenant."

"A slight improvement." She sighed. "I suppose that was an exercise in futility?"

"Actually, I did get one report of unusual traffic."

Brows rose. "Really?"

Trina repeated what Mrs. Bailey said. "I understand she's something of a crank…."

"She?"

"Mrs. Bailey?"

"Not Luella Bailey! She's a thorn in the side of anyone who has dealings with her. Daniel—my brother-in-law—counts his blessings daily that his place isn't beside hers. Pete Hardesty of the Running Y gets hell every time a steer finds a fence break."

Crushed and trying to hide it, Trina asked, "Does that mean she's not reliable?"

"Hmm." Meg Patton rubbed her chin as she thought. "Well, she's not delusional. When she says a steer is eating her dahlias, by God there it is. Kids do drag race out on Butte Road. So…no. She might actually be a good witness. Most folks out there wouldn't pay any mind to a passing vehicle. Luella, though, lives to find grievances." Her gaze sharpened. "Tell me again what she said."

Trina did.

"Twenty minutes to half an hour. That would be about right."

Trina nodded at the phone. "Did you learn anything?"

"Ricky Mendoza is right where he should be. That lets him out. No sign of Amy's Kia. I sent someone to check her apartment complex and the lots outside the brewhouses and restaurants that seem like the most obvious choices. Otherwise, I've put out calls. Any kind of match through VICAP will take time." The federal database was a godsend to local law enforcement. Unfortunately, it had limitations; many small jurisdictions didn't input crimes.

Trina nodded.

"I've already talked to Amy Owen's parents. They still live here, only a few blocks from where I grew up in the old town."

"She hadn't married, then?"

"Married and divorced. The ex is next on my list."

"He's around?"

The lieutenant consulted her notes. "Doug Jennings. He's a ski bum, according to the parents. Amy wanted to think about buying a house, starting a family. He wasn't interested."

"So the divorce wasn't ugly?" From what she'd read, Trina was willing to bet this killer and Amy had been strangers, anyway, but you had to consider all possibilities.

"Not according to them. They say he'll be broken up to hear about her murder. I went by his place and he wasn't home." Meg Patton rose. "What say we go talk to him now, then take a look at her apartment."

"Am I going to stay on the case, then?" Trina asked, rising, too.

The lieutenant looked surprised. "I tagged you, didn't I?"

This didn't seem the moment to ask why. "Thank you, ma…um, Lieutenant."

Exhilaration wiped out her weariness. Her mind buzzed. She'd want to read the file on the six-year-old murder. Look for details that were the same—and ones that were different. Talk to whoever found that body. The cops who worked the murder. If this one was as similar as Lieutenant Patton claimed, this killer had to be close in some way to the previous crime. Copycats had a motive. What was this one's?

Wow, she thought, feeling giddy. *I'm a detective. A real detective.*

Not even missing the cup of coffee she hadn't yet poured, she followed Lieutenant Patton out.

CHAPTER TWO

WILL'S RESOLVE to move home to Elk Springs wavered from time to time. Pretty well daily, in fact. Tonight was a definite plunge in the Mood-O-Meter.

He was staying at his father's while he looked for a place to live. Their relationship was pleasant but cool, thanks to Will's long-held belief that his parents in their professional capacities were responsible for the scum who'd killed Gillian being out on the street and therefore free to rape and mutilate. If they'd done their jobs...

But they hadn't, for reasons he understood intellectually if not emotionally. Now, six years later, he also understood that his anger had mostly been misplaced. But things once said couldn't be taken back, and much as he regretted the fact, Will knew he couldn't have back what he'd lost that night.

This week, his father was away at a conference for sheriffs and police chiefs. With him gone, Will was able to relax a little. He got along well with Beth, his dad's wife, and with her kids.

Stephanie was a senior in high school this year, a really smart girl who had applied to private colleges like Whitman and even Vassar back east. Pretty, with her mother's dark hair and blue eyes, she was the same serious kid she'd been when her mother married Jack Murray, Sheriff of Butte County.

Redheaded Lauren, fourteen, was in contrast currently grounded because she'd been caught cutting classes. She was a cheerleader and, according to her mother, a social butterfly who was a teenager with a capital *T.* Will could see what she meant. Lauren was all giggles and glow one minute, sulky the next. He sympathized, since he remembered his own teenage angst when his mom and he moved to Elk Springs so he could finally get to know his father. One minute, he'd believed he could clear Juanita Butte in a single bound, and the next he'd been sure his mother was trying to ruin his life.

So far, both girls seemed pleased to have their stepbrother around.

He'd been okay earlier, watching a TV movie with Steph and explaining to her why the whole trial scene was crap. Lauren had wandered in once, curled her lip, said, "That looks boring," and gone off to instant message with the friends she was banned from seeing out of school until next Wednesday. "An eternity," she'd moaned at dinner, after Beth had declined to release her from purgatory.

But after the movie, when Steph disappeared to her room and Beth went to the den to work on orders for her stationery business, Will sat in the empty living room and thought, *What am I doing? I must be nuts.*

The room, the house, got to him. He'd helped his dad strip these floors and the woodwork and then stain and refinish them. They'd both learned as they went, repairing plaster walls, painting, plumbing, even rewiring. Maybe because he'd been without a father for the first fourteen years of his life, Will had been more eager to spend time with his than most of his buddies were. Now this big old Queen Anne style house made him edgy. Aware of times past, of lost trust and easy affection.

The house was part of his history with Gillian, too. She'd spent weekends and school breaks here with him. They'd had incredible talks right here in the living room, made passionate love upstairs in his bedroom. They'd had that last fight in his bedroom, too, one that had been quiet but intense until she'd walked out on him. He'd run after her and, not caring who heard, stood on the porch and yelled, "Go! I don't give a shit!"

But he'd given a shit when the cops were on his dad's doorstep the next morning to inform him that his girlfriend had been found raped and strangled in Deschutes Park. He'd given a shit when they politely and inexorably questioned his whereabouts during the night even as his gut roiled with disbelief and horror and guilt, because he'd let Gilly stalk out without trying to stop her.

From where he sat right now, in a leather club chair, he could see the entry. Empty, but for ghosts. A rangy, carefree version of himself with Dad, scraping thick layers of varnish from the stair banister. He and Gilly, tiptoeing in after going out with some of his high school friends, stifling giggles, pausing to make out just inside the front door, two or three times on the staircase, barely getting the bedroom door shut before shedding their clothes. A slightly older Gillian screaming, "We're done! Over!" before she flung open the front door to leave. Two officers wearing the familiar Butte County Sheriff's Department green, saying, "I'm sorry to inform you…"

He groaned and laid his head back, his eyes closed. He didn't even know *why* he felt compelled to leave cosmopolitan Portland for this small town that held so many complex memories. He loved Elk Springs, but he hated it, too.

Even for himself, the best explanation he could come up with for accepting the job in the Butte County prosecutor's office was that he needed answers. Closure. Understanding.

He had an uneasy relationship with both his parents, although Gilly and his accusations had gone unmentioned on all sides for five years or more. Mad because he'd hurt his mom, his aunt Abby hardly spoke to him, he didn't know his own half-brother and -sister the way he should, and the stories about his grandfather Patton had begun to seem apocryphal. Had he been anywhere near as bad as they said? Even if he was, did that justify both Meg Patton and Jack Murray being so soft on a troubled young kid that they let him slide out of taking responsibility for one crime after another?

And Gilly... Why hadn't she just driven back to Salem? Why did she have to go to a bar? Was she getting in her car with the intention of returning here, maybe to say, "I'm sorry," when a hand closed over her mouth from behind? Had she thought Will might still come after her? Somehow save her?

Still caught in that hazy nexus of past and present, he wondered with a dull ache why he *hadn't* gone after her. Her parents grieved to this day. They claimed not to blame him, but they must.

He blamed himself.

The doorbell rang, and he jerked, his eyes opening. Who in hell at this time of night?

Eyes wide with instinctive alarm, Beth emerged from the home office at the back of the house, but Will, who had reached the front hall before her, said, "Let me find out who it is."

Through the peephole he saw the dark green of sheriff's department uniforms. His sense of disorientation returned. Gillian?

But when he opened the door, it was his mother he found on the porch, along with another officer. A young woman who appeared vaguely familiar.

"Mom?"

Her face looked drawn, her eyes tired. "Will, I need to talk to you."

He backed up. Cold air rushed in with them. Or maybe the chill was inside him.

"Hi, Beth." Mom tried to smile.

"Meg." Beth pressed a hand to her breast. "Is everything all right? It's not Jack?"

"No, no. I'm sorry. I didn't mean to scare you. No, everybody in the family is fine."

But somebody, Will diagnosed, wasn't fine. Somebody Will knew, or she wouldn't be here.

The wife of a cop, Beth knew, too. She looked Will's mother over with an experienced eye. "Can I get you coffee? Better yet, a bite to eat? I'll bet you haven't stopped, have you?"

"I'm fine…" Meg stopped. She gave a faint laugh. "Actually, I'm starved. A snack would be great, if it isn't too much trouble."

"Don't be silly." Beth shooed them towards the living room. "Coming right up."

His mother pulled off her gloves, then began to shrug out of her coat. He took it and the other cop's, too, and hung them on the tree near the front door.

He took a few steps into the living room, then stopped. "What's up?"

"Detective Giallombardo, this is my son Will. Will, Trina Giallombardo. You may remember her from school."

"You look familiar," he admitted.

"I was a couple of years behind you."

That would explain it. By his junior and senior years, he and his friends hadn't been interested in lower classmen. Maybe a really hot girl. This Trina hadn't been that. So he'd probably passed her in the hall without ever really focusing on her face.

"Detective Giallombardo," he acknowledged, then faced his mother. "Tell me."

"A girl you dated in high school was found murdered today."

A sound escaped him. A profanity, maybe. He reached out and gripped the back of the leather chair.

"Who?"

"Amy Owen."

He'd expected… He didn't know who he'd expected. But not Amy.

"We only went out three or four times."

"That's what Detective Giallombardo thought."

This woman he didn't know, who had been two years behind him in school, was suddenly an expert on his life?

"You're well-informed."

Her returning gaze was expressionless. "You were the big guy in school. People talked."

His irritation vanished as quickly as it had appeared. "Amy. My God."

"Sit," his mother ordered.

"Here's coffee," Beth said behind him.

He sank into the chair, soul-sick. On the job, he dealt in murder often, but not the murder of people he knew.

Only with Gillian had he experienced firsthand the horror and grief family and friends felt.

Amy Owen, pretty, not smart but *sweet*.

"I saw her last week," he said.

"What?" Hand outstretched for a cup of coffee she hadn't yet picked up from the tray, his mother turned.

"I saw her." Jeez, he wished he hadn't. He wished Amy Owen was no more than a hazy memory. "She was at J.R.'s when I went there with Gavin and Travis." No surprise—the sports bar was a favorite hangout for locals. "She was with Jody Cox. Remember her? And a friend of hers, a newcomer."

"Another woman?"

He saw what she was getting at. "Yeah, a woman. Karin. Don't remember the last name. I have her phone number if you want it."

Will saw a fleeting expression of…*something* cross Trina Giallombardo's face. Another time he might have wondered at it. Right now, he was too wrapped up in the image of Amy jumping from the bar stool to wave at him.

"Will! Will! Over here. Wow! Hi!"

He guessed he'd flirted with her a little bit, because she'd been flirting with him, but it was her friend's phone number he'd quietly asked for before the women announced they were calling it a night.

His mother sat on the couch facing him. "Did she tell you she's divorced?"

"Yeah. Actually, her ex came in, too. Didn't look real happy to see her with a bunch of guys."

"Did he say anything?"

Will shook his head. "That's just my impression. He came over and she introduced him. He was polite."

"Was he with anyone?"

"Not that I saw." His mother was interrogating him,

he realized. She'd even flipped her notebook open. The coffee and toasted sandwiches Beth had made sat untouched on the table.

Her gaze was sharp on him. He could see her brain humming. "Did he stay around?"

"Uh…I don't really know." He frowned. "Wait. I did see him a little later. Maybe half an hour." Appalled, he said, "You don't think…"

"We don't think anything yet. No, he's unlikely. This didn't look like a crime of passion. Someone who'd loved her, however angry he was, would have felt remorse, regret. Treated her body with more respect."

"Was it a bad one?" Will asked quietly.

His mother looked older than she had since—damn, since he'd aged her with his accusations and wild rage.

"Yeah. Will…"

He wasn't going to like what was coming. Aware of both women watching him, he braced himself and waited.

"We have a copycat. Will, this looked like Gillian's murder."

He lurched to his feet. "What do you mean?"

She rose, too. "I mean it could have been the same killer. The body was left in the same condition."

An image of Gilly's body flashed before his eyes. Through gritted teeth, he asked, "Was she raped?"

His mother's expression was compassionate. "Yes."

In some part of his mind, he noted that Trina Giallombardo's dark eyes were only watchful. If she felt pity, suspicion, dislike, sympathy, she didn't show it.

"Strangled with a jockstrap?"

"Yes."

He wheeled away to stand with his back to the women. He was panting as if he'd sprinted the last half

mile of his daily run. Sweating. Sick. *Gilly, oh Gilly.*
The women's faces overlay like a double exposure,
both blond and fine-boned. *Not Gilly,* he thought. *Not
this time.* Instead, some sick son of a bitch had raped
and tortured pretty, sweet Amy Owen, then left her
body as if she were a whore. Garbage.

"Who?" he asked, voice guttural.

His mother sounded grim. "We'll find out."

"Was she in the same place?"

"No." Gillian's body had been left right in town,
among the willow trees in the town park on the bank of
the Deschutes River. "Amy was left at the lava cone past
the Triple B. A couple of kids found her."

He turned to face them all of them, Beth in the background. "Why are you here?"

His mother's expression changed. "What?"

"Is my name going to come up?"

She gaped. "Don't be ridiculous!"

"Yeah? Why not? I'd be a logical suspect, wouldn't I?"

Her mouth opened and closed like a fish's. He was
glad to have disconcerted her for once, put her on the
defensive.

Detective Giallombardo said, "Your mother didn't
want you to read about it in the morning paper. She
thought the news would be better coming from her."

Shame flooded him, as she'd intended. Will swore
and scraped a hand over his face.

"I'm sorry, Mom. God. I'm sorry."

His mother gave a twisted smile. "It's okay. Of
course you're upset."

He saw in her eyes that he'd hurt her. As, he realized, he'd intended. And he didn't even know why
he'd lashed out.

"Mendoza…" He hated the taste of the bastard's name in his mouth.

"Is still at Salem." The Oregon State Penitentiary was in Salem, Oregon's capital.

"A friend of his…"

"That's a possibility we'll pursue."

"But not a very good one."

She didn't have to answer. Of course, it was unlikely one of Ricardo Mendoza's friends would commit a crime this savage, and why? What was the motive?

For the first time, Will was thinking like the attorney and prosecutor he was.

"What's the point? What's this scum trying to say?"

"I have no idea," his mother admitted. "Maybe nothing. Maybe this guy just liked the idea. Thought wiping out her identity, metaphorically, by replacing it with a crude symbol of masculinity was funny."

"Like he's saying, 'In your face'?" Will asked.

She spread her hands. "Maybe he thought a jockstrap sounded like a handy murder weapon. Hard to trace, wouldn't hold fingerprints well, and, hey, you could carry it around in your pocket without exciting suspicion. You're on your way to the gym. What's the big deal?"

"Have you ever before or since read or heard of a woman strangled with a jockstrap?" he asked.

"No," she conceded.

"Here we are. Small town. Not all that many murders, and ninety-nine percent of those are your garden-variety shoot-the-abusive-husband type. Biker brawls. Not the work of serial killers."

They'd speculated back then that Gillian's murder was too "sophisticated" to be a killer's first. The savagery coupled with the care taken displaying the body, had seemed to be the work of someone who'd done this before. On the other hand, Mendoza had also done un-believably stupid things: he was seen leaving the bar with Gilly, his skin was beneath her fingernails and his semen was found in her body. Evidence of grandiosity and dis-organized thinking, everyone said. He'd felt invincible, never thought he'd be suspected. So what if he'd talked to Gillian in the bar? She'd talked to other men, too. Maybe he hadn't realized anyone at the bar could name him. It didn't matter—he'd been convicted on DNA.

"So what are the odds that, just coincidentally, we have a second killer with the same idea?"

She didn't have to answer.

"Are you going to talk to Mendoza?"

"Maybe. We'll concentrate on her movements yes-terday first."

"She told me where she worked." But, damn, he couldn't remember.

"She was a hairstylist. She had a chair at Mountain High Salon."

Beth made a sound. They all turned.

"Was she tall and blond? With a mole on her cheek?" She looked from one of them to another. Pressed her hands to her cheeks. "Oh, no! She cut my hair the last time. And Steph's been going to her. I should have recog-nized the name! I hate to tell Steph. Oh, that poor girl."

"I'm sorry," his mother said, uselessly.

"Does Jack know yet?"

"No. He hasn't called, and I figured there's nothing he could do, not tonight. I'll page him in the morning."

Will's mother and Detective Giallombardo ate then, both gobbling as if they couldn't remember their last meal. He knew from experience that his mother would be lucky to snatch a few hours of sleep tonight. She'd spend tomorrow talking to everyone who'd know anything about Amy's last day. Meg Patton was dedicated. Just…sometimes soft, in his opinion. Wanting to do the opposite of whatever her bastard of a father would have done. She and Aunt Renee both had seemed to spend their careers trying to bury their father's legacy as Elk Springs police chief.

The two women left, Will's mom promising to keep him informed. Then, he and Beth rehashed what they knew, Beth clearly upset.

"That poor, poor girl," she kept saying. "She was your age?"

"A year younger."

"Twenty-eight, then. Only twenty-eight."

He finally persuaded her to go to bed, in part by heading for his own. With the house quiet and dark, only his bedside lamp on, Will sat up against a heap of pillows and tried to read, but kept finishing the same page without remembering a word.

He was tired, but at the same time wide awake. Antsy. Feeling as if he should do something. Fight or flight. Will recognized that he was in shock, reliving the hours after Gilly's body was found, when a thousand, *if onlys* and *I should haves* had run crazily through his mind as if he were on crack. *Replay, replay. Change the ending.* He'd kept trying, over and over, until he *was* crazy and slammed his fist into the wall. He hadn't even noticed he'd broken bones for a while, the pain nothing, nothing, compared to the agony in his chest.

His book fell to the bedcovers, forgotten. He couldn't shut out the memories, the horror.

Amy, face alight when she saw him, waving in delight. "Will! Over here!" Gilly laughing up at him, staring at him with hate that in his imaginings became terror. Her face, Amy's face, one and the same.

Pulling himself back from the abyss, Will tried to remember how well Gilly and Amy knew each other. They hadn't become friends—nothing like that, but Amy was certainly part of the crowd he'd introduced Gilly to. They had looked a little bit alike. Both five-eight or -nine, leggy, boyishly slim, naturally blond. Neither blue-eyed. Gillian had had pale, almost sea-green eyes, Amy… He couldn't quite picture them. Brown? He flashed on Trina Giallombardo's brown eyes, assessing, accusing, judging, because he'd lost it with his mother. Angry at her intrusion, he shook his head and returned doggedly to his struggle to see Amy Owen. No. Not brown. Flecks of yellow and green.

Dead. Because, like Gillian, she was tall and blond and willowy? But their killers weren't the same man. Couldn't be the same man. Mendoza was guilty, guilty, guilty. Scum who had no business hitting on Will's girl-friend in the bar, becoming enraged because she'd re-jected him, raping, murdering, taunting.

Had Amy been chosen precisely because she looked like Gillian? A copycat crime required a copycat victim. But who in hell would imitate something like this? Could Elk Springs really have spawned two monsters? Copycat monsters?

It made no sense. None of it made sense. Gilly's murder by a man who'd hot-wired cars and fenced stolen goods but never committed a violent crime. This one now, six years later. Why six years? Why now?

Why two women Will had known? A stranger, killed exactly like Gillian, would have been bad enough, but Amy! Less than a week after they met again, talked about old times, flirted a little.

He went cold. Was *that* why she'd been chosen? Because he knew her? Because he'd flirted with her? Because, like Gilly, she'd once meant something to him?

But that made no sense either. He'd dated her a few times. Kissed her. Had sex with her once—after they'd both had too much to drink at a party. So what? He'd dated and kissed a dozen girls or more in high school. Slept with several. Had a couple of girlfriends who lasted months. One nearly a year. He knew Nita and Christine both were still around. Why not one of them? Why Amy? Opportunity? Just because in a small town there were only so many look-alike blondes?

Why? God, why? he begged, even as he knew he'd get no answer.

CHAPTER THREE

LIEUTENANT PATTON HAD somehow kept word of the murder out of the morning papers, but they all knew it would be on the five o'clock local news.

The downside was that Trina had to be the one to tell many of Amy Owen's friends and co-workers about her death. The task was made worse by the fact that Amy was apparently liked by everyone. No secret delight, no affected shock.

This particular friend, a plump, freckled redhead, turned milk-pale. "Dead?"

Seeing her sway, Trina said, "Please. Sit down."

"Murdered?"

Gently taking her upper arm, Trina backed her up to the couch and pushed. Marcie Whittaker never took her stunned gaze from Trina's face.

"How can she be?"

How did you answer that kind of question? It implied that there was a rational order, a why for every action, a series of logical consequences. It suggested that if you took to heart all of your parents' warnings, you'd be safe, loved, prosperous. Trina had been a cop long enough to know that things didn't work that way.

She and Lieutenant Patton had divided up names. Amy had had dozens of friends. After talking with the crew at the beauty salon, they'd each taken a list and started contacting anyone who might have spoken with Amy in the days leading up to her death, or who might have been with her yesterday. Since her vehicle had not yet been located, finding out where she might have gone that night was critical.

Trina remembered Marcie from high school. She and Amy had been part of a pack of popular girls—cheerleaders, homecoming princesses, stars of the spring musicals. As remote from Trina's world as Will Patton had been. They'd walked down the hall in groups of three or four, laughing and tossing their long, shining hair, their clothes always perfect, their complexions glowing from a weekend on the ski hill. Money was never a problem for any of the popular kids, Trina had believed then.

In the intervening years, Marcie had put on weight. She'd gotten married right out of high school and had two school-age children as well as a toddler. Trina had expected a fancy house and found her instead in a modest rambler on a street of mostly rentals. Marcie had invited her in with surprise and said, "My youngest is down for a nap. You want to talk about Amy? Why?"

Now, in answer to the unanswerable, Trina said, "Amy may just have been in the wrong place at the wrong time. That's what we're trying to determine."

"Was she..."

"Raped?"

Marcie bit her lip and nodded.

"Yes, I'm afraid so." They'd decided to admit that much.

"Oh God, oh God."

"Did you speak to Amy in the last couple of weeks?"

Tears oozed from Marcie's eyes. She nodded. "Excuse me. I need to—" She leapt to her feet and bolted from the room.

Trina used the time to study the framed photos on the mantel. Most were presumably of Marcie's children, redheads all like their mother. Trina recognized the man who appeared in many only because Marcie had taken the last name Whittaker. In high school, Dirk Whittaker had been one of the swaggering jocks, a state All-Star tackle. Like a lot of brawny guys, he'd put on serious weight in the ten years since he'd graduated.

What interested her most was that, displayed with the family photos, there were three framed snapshots, probably taken at several year intervals, of Marcie with her old crowd, including Amy Owen. In the first, all were recognizably the same people they'd been in high school—still slim, stylish, confident. By the next photo chronologically, although all were posing jauntily and laughing, some of the crowd had changed: begun to put on weight, quit expending so much effort on their appearances. Perhaps half were still sleek and beautiful. By the most recent photograph, the distinction was obvious. Some, like Amy, still looked beautiful, privileged and entitled, while others in the crowd showed the toll taken by jobs that didn't allow for hours at the gym, by scrimping financially, by the exhaustion of raising children.

Will Patton was in the middle photo. A young woman Trina didn't recognize stood within the circle of his arm. She bore a superficial resemblance to Amy: she was also tall, although dwarfed by his height, and her hair was the silvery shade of ash blond that had to be natural. Amy was prettier in a conventional way; the woman with him had a distinct bump on the bridge of her nose, ears that poked out a little, and a catlike slant to her eyes that gave her the look of an elf. Maybe not beautiful, hers was still the kind of face you didn't forget.

Trina suspected that the fine-boned, moonlight-pale

girl gazing up at Will Patton rather than at the camera was Gillian Pappas, the victim of the original murder. Her gaze lingering on the couple, Trina felt an odd squeezing in her chest she wanted to believe was pity but she knew was more complex.

"Those are my kids," Marcie said dully from behind her.

"What a cute little girl," Trina felt obligated to say.

Marcie came to stand beside her. "Amy is in some of these." She picked up the most recent, framed in silver. "Right there."

No Will in this photo. Trina wondered if he'd quit coming home, quit hanging out with his old friends. No, not entirely, because he'd been at J.R.'s with a couple of them.

"You stayed close friends, then."

Although Marcie had given no indication of recognizing Trina, she seemed to assume that everyone knew she and Marcie were best friends. "Well, naturally. We didn't spend as much time together, of course. I mean, I'm married and have kids. But we talked a couple of times a week and had lunch every week or two. She didn't mind if I brought Vicki. Amy wanted kids." Hit by the knowledge that Amy would never have a baby, Marcie began to cry again. Silently, with bewilderment.

Trina opened her notebook. "Had she mentioned anyone following her, some guy making her nervous? Anything like that?"

"No, I'm sure she didn't."

"Was she seeing a man?"

"She went out. But not with anyone special. She got divorced just last spring, you know."

"Are you aware of her dating in the past few weeks?"

Marcie named a couple of men. "Plus she was hoping this guy we knew in high school would call her. Will Patton."

Trina's fingers tightened on her pencil. "Had he called, to your knowledge?"

Marcie shook her head, eyes wet. "Amy would have been on the phone instantly if he had. She had this huge crush on him. I mean, she always did. She said she saw him last week, that he's moved back to Elk Springs."

"Was there anyone who might have felt jealous if he could tell how she felt about Mr. Patton?"

"Felt jealous? Oh. Like, did she blow some guy off so she could concentrate on Will?" Marcie shook her head again. "Like I said, she'd see men, but it was casual. The only one who might be jealous was her ex, but he had his chance."

Interested in her spiteful tone, Trina asked about the victim's relationship with her ex-husband.

"I think he wanted her back. But he still didn't intend to really settle down. You know? He's this big outdoors guy. He wants to ski all winter and mountain climb all summer. He works up at Juanita Butte in the winter, but he never even looked for a job in the summer. He got mad when she had to work. Plus, she didn't like to climb."

"Her parents described the breakup as amiable."

"It was." Marcie shrugged. "But he kept coming around. She slipped a couple of times and had sex with him, which was dumb."

"Did she have other sexual relationships?"

"You mean, did she screw guys? Sure." Marcie sounded surprised, as if a single woman being sexually active was a given.

No, there was more to her tone, Trina suspected; she was just a little envious. Married almost ten years, with three kids, she probably lived vicariously through Amy's tales.

"Anyone in particular?"

"Um…" Marcie thought. "Adrian Benson. She told me the other day he wasn't that good in bed, even though he's hot."

Benson was one of the men she'd said earlier that Marcie might have dated in the previous week or two. Trina starred his name. He wasn't anyone she recalled from high school.

"If she met a man over drinks and liked him, would she be likely to leave with him?"

"Yeah, why not?" The moment the words were out, Marcie's mouth formed an O. Amy Owen had very likely paid an extreme penalty for trusting a dangerous man.

Trina steered her gently back to the final day. Yes, she'd talked briefly to Amy midafternoon. "I told her I'd try to get a babysitter Saturday night so Dirk and I could go out."

Trina already knew that Amy had worked yesterday, leaving the salon about four. "Did she mention plans for yesterday evening?"

"She said she was bored and might go get a drink. She didn't say where or if she was going with a friend."

Trina wrote down Amy's favorite hangouts and then thanked Marcie. Handing her a card, she said, "Please call if you think of anything at all that you think we should know."

The next friend of Amy's on Trina's list actually recognized her.

Bronwen Fessler had started a clothing boutique in town that Trina had heard was very successful. Daddy Fessler was a banker and had had plenty of money to bankroll her.

The clothes in the window were bold and bright-colored. Stuff that shouldn't have gone together somehow did, like a hot-pink cashmere turtleneck and lime-green wool slacks. Maybe, Trina decided, studying the display carefully, the skinny loomed scarf worn as a belt accomplished the magic. Personally, she might have bought all three pieces and never in a million years considered putting them together.

Which, she guessed, was why she was a cop and not a fashion designer or owner of a boutique. And why everything she wore was boring.

She pushed open the door, making the bell that hung above it tinkle. Bronwen Fessler hadn't changed much, just become more stylish. A petite brunette with short, artfully tousled hair, she sat on a high stool behind a glass case that held jewelry and on top of which was the cash register. She appeared to be attaching labels to chunky bracelets laid out on the glass top in front of her. Through the window Trina hadn't noticed the two women browsing sweaters displayed in cubes on the back wall.

Bronwen glanced up with a practiced smile that she aborted. "Officer…" she began in surprise, then, "Wait. I know you, don't I? From school. No, don't tell me. Something like Teresa."

"Trina. Trina Giallombardo."

"Right." She seemed pleased by her memory rather than by Trina's appearance. "You're a police officer, huh?"

"A detective." Being able to say that still gave Trina a thrill. "I'm here to speak to you about a friend of yours."

"A friend of mine?"

"Um, excuse me," one of the women interrupted. "I'd like to try this on."

"Certainly," Bronwen told her. To Trina, she asked, "Can you wait a minute?"

"No problem."

Out of the corner of her eye, she watched as Bronwen Fessler charmed and flattered the two customers, who looked about forty but were probably older. There was nothing like being loaded to help a woman keep her looks. These two had perfectly dyed and coiffed hair, suspiciously smooth faces, skillfully applied makeup and carefully tended figures. In the end, one bought two sweaters and the other a necklace, all for prices that made Trina gape.

Staring after them, she exclaimed, "Did she just pay almost seven hundred dollars for two *sweaters?*"

"And they were on sale. Sweetie, people do, you know."

Not people in Trina's circles.

"Wow," she said, then flushed.

"I take it you dress from J.C. Penney?" Bronwen said with amused disdain.

"More like Eddie Bauer."

"Jeans and flannel shirts?" Her practiced eye swept from Trina's well-polished but sturdy black shoes to her unpierced ears. "Come in sometime when you're off-duty and I may convert you. For old times' sake, I'll allow you an employee discount. The first time you come."

Old times' sake? Trina doubted they'd ever exchanged a word. She thought they might have been in a class or two together; she'd been advanced enough in math to often be in classes with students a year or two ahead of her.

Glancing at a mannequin dressed in a beaded bustier and a pouffy black skirt, she was tempted, though.

Maybe the right clothes *could* accomplish magic. She could probably afford them if she wanted them….

Yeah. Sure they would. *And why do you want to be transformed?* she mocked herself. *So that you catch Will Patton's eyes?*

Uh-huh. That was going to happen. Like he ever dated a woman who wore bigger than a size four and wasn't blond.

"Thank you for the offer," she said formally. "But I'm here in my official capacity today."

"Right. I forgot. You wanted to ask me about a friend." Her tone became flip. "Do I know someone who's held up the bank?"

"I understand you've remained friends with Amy Owen."

"Well, sure." She laughed. "Amy's not the bank robber type."

"I regret to tell you that she's dead. She was murdered last night."

Bronwen stared at her with a complete lack of comprehension. "She can't be dead. I saw her last night. We had a drink." She reached for the telephone. "I'll call her. There must be a mistake."

Trina shook her head. "Her parents have identified her."

"If they were upset…"

Voice gentle, she said, "I saw her body. I recognized her."

"But…" She seemed to deflate, her vivacity gone, her face five years older. "Did somebody break in, or…"

"We don't know yet. We haven't found her car. That's why we're talking to her friends." Trina opened her notebook, hoping if she kept Bronwen talking to avert tears. "Had you made plans in advance to get together?"

Bronwen took a deep breath and straightened. "She called at about...oh, I don't know, six o'clock? I had some bookkeeping to do, but Amy said she was bored and pleaded with me. I met her at the Timberline. She wasn't hungry, but I had chicken wings and we both had a drink."

"Did she have something she urgently wanted to tell you?"

Bronwen shook her head. "We just chatted. She seemed restless. She was bummed because this guy hasn't called her."

"Will Patton?"

"How did you know? Oh. I get it. You've already talked to other people. Yeah, Will. Otherwise, I talked about what I'm buying for spring for the store and she bitched about her ex because he won't leave her alone. She thinks..." Bronwen's voice stumbled. "She *thought* her parents were sympathetic to him, which annoyed her."

"What was he doing to annoy her?"

"Not what you're thinking! Doug is an okay guy. He's just been regretting the divorce. He wouldn't get violent." She said it as if the idea was absurd, unthinkable.

"But somebody did."

Bronwen's fingers twisted together. "God. How was she killed?"

"We'll know more after the autopsy. It appears she was strangled."

"Was she raped?"

"Yes."

"Doug wouldn't have raped her," she said with certainty. "She admitted to me that she let him spend the night not that long ago. He didn't have to rape her."

"Rape is only peripherally about sex. It has more to do with control and power."

She kept shaking her head. "Not Doug."

Trina didn't really believe that the ex-husband would prove to be a serious suspect. This murder didn't have the hallmarks of domestic violence. But it was also possible that they were dealing with a killer who had strangled Amy in a fit of rage, then remembered the murder from six years ago and decided to imitate it to throw the police off. An impulse killer who was also able to keep his cool. Not common, but conceivable.

"Is Doug a friend of yours, too?" Trina asked.

"Mine? Heavens, no! Like I said, he's a nice guy. But honestly, he's not that bright. Just kind of big and dumb and fun-loving. Not my type."

No, Doug sounded like a lousy prospect to have kept his cool and used his head.

Trina determined that Bronwen and Amy had parted in the parking lot at just after eight.

"Do you think she might have gone back in?"

"No, we were parked next to each other and she pulled out of the lot right behind me. I had to get some work done, and I assumed she was going home even though she still seemed…I don't know." She visibly groped for a word and settled for the same one she'd used earlier. "Restless. Maybe a little unhappy. Not in the mood to go home and watch reruns and sip cocoa."

She suggested other brewhouses and pubs where they might show Amy's picture, other friends Amy might have called.

"Guys? Wow. Adrian Benson. Maybe. She was getting bored with him. I mean, they didn't have that much of a thing, and she was losing interest, but just for something to do… Um, Travis Booth. They were sorta friends, sorta something more."

"Travis." Wasn't he one of the friends Will Patton had mentioned being with the evening he ran into Amy at J.R.'s? "I remember him. He was a friend of Will Patton's."

"Right. Only he didn't do high school sports because he ski-raced. He actually made the U.S. ski team, but then he was hurt really badly training for the downhill."

"Yeah, yeah, I remember." Like most guys that age, Will had run in a pack. His buddies were jocks, but the smart ones. Most had gone on to college after they graduated. "I didn't realize he was still in Elk Springs."

"He's head of the ski school at Juanita Butte. But he's getting some success as an artist, too. Don't you read your newspaper? They did a feature on him—I don't know—a month or so ago." Her voice changed, relaxed fractionally as she reminisced. "He used to draw really wicked caricatures. He did this fantastic one of Mr. Jones, only one of the teachers snagged it when it was being passed around, and he ended up in detention for a week."

Mr. Jones, then high school principal and not a popular one, had been ripe for caricature with his double chins and beady eyes.

Trina forced herself back to more relevant subjects. Travis Booth, for one. He'd seen Amy fall anew for Will Patton, maybe resented it. Trina starred his name, too.

She flipped back through her notes. "Do you know a Gavin, who seems to be a friend of Travis's?"

Bronwen pursed her lips. "Gavin. You mean Huseby? He kind of hung around Will. I never paid any attention to him. I know he's around again."

Bronwen supplied a few new names of people in

Amy's circle. At the end, she asked, "Do you think this guy killed Amy in particular? Or was she just…"

"Convenient?"

"That sounds awful, but…" She fidgeted. "Yeah. I mean, should single women be scared?"

"At this point, we simply don't know the motive. It wouldn't hurt to use extra caution."

"Okay." Bronwen gave a wry smile. "Thanks, Trina. Wow. Business is slow, anyway. Maybe I'll close. Or maybe not." She shivered. "I don't want to go home alone. I could call around. Some of us could get together and have a kind of wake."

"That might help all of you." Trina nodded. "I appreciate your assistance."

She was at the door when Bronwen called, "Trina? That employee discount? I meant it, you know. Come back someday."

"I just might." Trina nodded and left, the bell tinkling as she let the door shut behind her.

She started her Explorer to get the heat cranking, but didn't pull away from the curb immediately. Instead, she thought about Amy Owen as her friends described her.

On the surface, a party girl. An easy victim, because she'd bar-hopped, lowered her guard by drinking and been sexually promiscuous enough to end her evening with any man who appealed. Yet, it was clear from what her parents, Marcie and Bronwen had said that Amy wanted something different. That she was filling time until she found the white-picket-fence ending she craved. As much as she liked to party, she also possessed a quality of sweetness that drew people. She had a huge circle of friends. Trina had two best friends, a couple more casual ones and a few other people who might invite her to Christmas gatherings. She thought she was more the norm than Amy Owen.

An amazing number of those friendships dated from high school. In fact, it seemed every conversation today had twisted back to the halls of Elk Springs High School. Maybe that was natural in a small town. But given that they'd all graduated ten years ago, wouldn't you think the group would include more newcomers, and that more of the high school crowd would have left town? The jocks were still the only desirable guys for the popular girls, who still clustered to flip their shiny hair and giggle at jokes no one else would get.

Not fair. Trina grimaced. They had lives. *She* was the one directing the conversations, asking them to dredge up memories.

Anyway, who was she to talk? She could have gone anywhere, but had chosen to come home to Elk Springs even though her childhood wasn't what you'd call happy. And didn't she still nurse a little bit of a crush on Will Patton, Homecoming King?

Besides—chances were none of this had anything whatsoever to do with Amy Owen's murder. She'd likely been chosen at random, because she was available: sitting alone at a table in a pub or walking out to her car in a dark parking lot by herself. The odds, Trina thought, finally switching on her turn signal, were against Amy having been raped and murdered by a friend or even acquaintance.

BETH HAD GONE TO WORK, the girls to school. Will had intended to hunt for an apartment today. He wanted to buy, but was finding little for sale at this time of year. Absentee owners could rent by the week at astronomical rates. Spring, when the out-of-towners melted away with the snow, was when houses appeared on the market, according to the real estate agent who was helping him look.

The guy had called that morning. His income was probably zip at this time of year, and he was trying like hell to find something Will would buy.

When Will had walked into the real estate office last week, he'd been startled to recognize Jimmy McCartin from high school. The guy had been a hanger-on to Will's group, too little and scrawny to play sports, but around all the time because he was manager for the football and baseball teams. Will hadn't liked to crush the guy, but he never seemed to notice when he wasn't welcome.

Heck, maybe that made him the salesman of the century. Successful real estate agents had to be damn pushy.

Jimmy was still scrawny and still able to make Will uncomfortable by doing things like slinging an arm around his shoulder when he introduced him to people and implying that they'd been best friends in high school.

"Hey," he said. "Did you hear about Amy? I saw Travis this morning. He told me."

Will had been hoping the caller was his mother with news.

After he and Jimmy hashed over the news for a couple of minutes, with Will pretending he didn't know any more than anyone else did, McCartin asked, "Did you think any more about that house at Crescent Ridge? If you buy now, you could pick your own tile, paint colors, maybe upgrade some fixtures."

The new development he was talking about was maybe half a mile from Will's mother's place, just off the mountain loop highway on the way up to Juanita

Butte. The handful of houses that had been framed in so far were going to be beauties. Different builders were working there, which avoided the cookie-cutter effect, too. There was a shingled one at the top of the ridge that Will had liked.

"It's just too big," he said. "What was it, thirty-five hundred square feet? I don't have any use for a place that size."

"You could think about buying a lot and getting one custom built," McCartin suggested.

"Yeah, but then I'd be looking at next fall before I had a place to live." He got cream out of the refrigerator and poured some into his coffee, cell phone to his ear. "I don't know. I'll keep the house in mind, Jimmy, but I'm thinking I'll wait a couple of months before I commit."

"You know I'll call you the minute I see any new listings," McCartin assured him. "Hey, you planning to go to J.R.'s this weekend?"

"Yeah, maybe," Will said, because he didn't want to be rude.

"Great! I'll see you there, then."

Will shook his head as he hit End.

He hadn't slept much last night, so at noon he was on his third cup of coffee and still trying to summon some motivation to get going. When the phone rang, he snatched it up.

"Pattons' residence."

"Will?" His father's deep voice was unmistakable. "I just talked to Meg."

"Are you coming home early?"

"I'm giving the keynote address at the banquet tomorrow night. I can't. Besides, what can I do that your mother can't?" Still, the growl in his voice betrayed his frustration. This was his county, his command. He wanted to be there, not exchanging tips of the trade with other law enforcement personnel in Seattle.

He wasn't coming home early. Then what was this phone call about? Will waited.

"You know we're going to have to consider the possibility that Mendoza was wrongly convicted."

"Bullshit!" Will exploded. "You had DNA! How much more solid can you get?"

"We had proof he'd had intercourse with Gillian," Jack Murray corrected. "In the absence of semen or hairs from another man, it was enough. But he's been saying since the day we picked him up that he had sex with her, and that was all."

"Bullshit!" Will said again. Intensely agitated, he paced the kitchen, wheeling each time he reached a wall. "Gilly wouldn't have gone out and screwed some stranger! You knew her better than that."

"What I know is that she was mad as hell. People do stupid things when they're drunk, and her blood alcohol level was sky-high." His voice softened. "She might have done it to punish you."

The raging pain tore into Will's gut, as it so often did. He stopped in his pacing and bent over as if he'd struck across the belly with a two-by-four.

Whatever Gilly had or hadn't intended, he had been punished a thousand times over. But he couldn't, wouldn't, believe that Gilly would have been that careless with herself. That cruel to him.

"No," he said. "No. He did it. He raped her and killed her."

"Will…"

"Copycat crimes happen. We both know they do. What if he talked some buddy into it so he could walk?"

"Goddamn it, Will, you know we'll consider every possibility. One of those possibilities is that we convicted the wrong man."

"You're back to defending him, aren't you? Still can't believe you could have been wrong about him? That he was using you?"

"That's low."

"Is it?" The phone creaked, he gripped it so hard. "Funny how fast you came to the conclusion that this murder clears Mendoza."

"I didn't say that—"

"The hell you didn't." He pushed End and slammed the phone onto the counter. Planting both hands there, he bent his head, teeth gritted. Fury and shame and renewed grief swelled in his chest until it hurt.

After a minute, breathing hard, he straightened. He'd been looking for motivation. Guess what. He'd just found it.

He grabbed his parka from the coat tree, checked to be sure he had his car keys, and left the house. If he had to rent a place that stank of cat urine, he'd do it.

Anything, to be out of here by the time his father got home on Sunday.

CHAPTER FOUR

TRINA AND Meg Patton, having failed to catch Doug Jennings at home, drove up to the Juanita Butte ski area on Saturday.

The lieutenant parked in the employee lot, taking a spot right by the slope of packed snow leading up to the lodge. Since her husband was the ski area general manager, she had reason to feel at home here.

Unlike Trina, who stepped out of the Explorer gingerly.

Despite frostbite-inducing cold, the lift lines were long, the slopes busy enough that skiers and boarders must be having to dodge each other. Never having learned to ski, Trina felt out of place here, which made her sulky and reminded her of her teenage resentment of the popular kids. But how could she help it? In contrast to all the tanned, long-legged, bleached-blond athletes heading for the lifts, she was pasty-skinned, dark-haired and compact.

She trailed ten feet behind Lieutenant Patton by the time they reached the A-frame that was, according to the lieutenant, the nerve center of the ski area. Ducking to save her skull from a snowboard carelessly swung by a teenage boy calling to friends above in the lift line, she slipped, knocked into a passing skier who yelled at her and finally righted herself at the foot of the snow-packed stairs leading up into the hut.

Naturally, the information center was staffed by a tanned, Nordic blond beauty.

"Oh, yeah! Doug's wife! That was such a bummer. I mean, he's going around with this tragic face." She sounded awed at his suffering. More practically, she added, "His shift should be ending in a minute, anyway. I can call him down here."

She got on the radio and his crackling voice agreed that he would rendezvous with the police officers at the ski school hut.

Stamping her feet and shivering, Trina thought about what Lieutenant Patton's husband had said about Doug Jennings. Enthusiastic, great with the public, no apparent ambitions beyond the next ski season.

"Of course, Scott doesn't know him well," she'd added. "Unless the guy had been a major problem, a lift operator is a pretty small cog in Scott's operation."

Now, Lieutenant Patton also had the Nordic goddess call the ski school and ask for Travis Booth, Will's friend who now headed the ski school. "If he could come down in, say, half an hour?"

Yet another crackling voice agreed.

Recognizable from photos in her apartment, Amy Owen's ex-husband slid to a stop right by the door, as beautiful and Nordic as the goddess inside. Tapping the bindings with the tip of one of his poles, he stepped off the skis and set them inside.

His eyes were actually brown, despite the sun-bleached blond hair. Brown and puppy-dog-like and mournful. "You're here about Amy?"

"Yes." Lieutenant Patton nodded toward the lodge. "Can we go inside and talk?"

"Oh. Sure. I guess you're cold?"

Despite heavy parkas and gloves, the lieutenant and

Trina weren't dressed for sub-zero weather. In just minutes, Trina had lost awareness of her face as a part of her body. When any of them talked, their breath froze in plumes that hung in the air. Trina wanted to say, *Gee, you think?*

Inside the busy lodge, they stamped snow from their boots. Meg Patton led the way upstairs to what appeared to be offices. A secretary smiled and said, "Scott said to give you the small conference room. Can I bring you coffee?"

"Please," the lieutenant said.

If she'd turned it down, Trina would have whimpered. She was shivering and trying to hide it. Damn, she thought. Why hadn't she taken a job somewhere warmer? She didn't even like snow. The LAPD must have openings on a regular basis. Or maybe San Diego.

In the conference room, Doug Jennings dropped his gloves on the table, stripped off his snow-white hat with the cute pompom and peeled off his form-fitting parka. Very reluctantly, Trina divested herself of her outer layers. Gratefully seizing a mug of the coffee the secretary brought, she sat next to the lieutenant and opened her notebook.

Lieutenant Patton asked, "Mr. Jennings, when did you last see your ex-wife?"

His face crumpled, as if he were about to cry. "Wow. I can't believe she's dead. Amy was…" He swallowed. "Um. When did I see her the last time. Maybe Monday?" He pondered. "Yeah. Monday. I ran into her at Safeway. Kind of on purpose. See, I know she shops there, and she usually goes after work. So that's when I shop."

"But you are divorced."

"Yeah, but…" He took a huge breath and let it out in a rush, his beseeching gaze moving from Lieutenant

Patton's to Trina's and back. "I didn't want to be! I love Amy! I shouldn't have let her go."

"And how did Ms. Owen feel about your pursuit?"

Expression ingenuous, he said, "I think she was coming around." As if reading doubt on their faces, he added, "Really! We've actually kind of gotten together a couple of times lately. You know."

They knew.

"Had you asked her to marry you again?"

"She said no, but not like she was mad or wanted me to leave her alone. More like…" He frowned. "Like she was teasing. I figured it was just a matter of time."

"And the issues that led to the divorce in the first place?"

"I told her we could have a baby if she wanted. Kids are okay."

Trina barely refrained from rolling her eyes at his magnanimity.

Lieutenant Patton's voice changed. "Mr. Jennings, I have to ask where you were from Wednesday evening until Thursday morning."

"Where I was?" He gaped at her, and Trina realized he really was naive enough not to have realized why he was being questioned in the first place. Bronwen was right; he was dumb. "You don't think *I*…" Wildly searching their faces, he saw that they did indeed think the possibility existed that he had murdered his ex-wife. "I loved Amy!"

"Mr. Jennings, we're obligated to rule out an ex-husband. If we can verify your whereabouts…"

He relaxed. "Oh, sure. Um…" More deep thinking. "I was here. I worked late shift on Wednesday evening. After the lifts shut down at ten, some of us stopped at the Timberline for drinks."

The same place Amy had been earlier in the evening.

"You didn't see Amy there?" Trina asked.

Both the lieutenant and Doug looked startled to hear her speak.

"No. It must have been close to eleven by the time we got there. She gets up early for work. She wouldn't have still been out…" His Adam's apple bobbed.

Hastily, before the moistness in his eyes could develop into a deluge, the lieutenant asked, "How late did you stay?"

He seemed to focus with an effort. "I don't know. Until about one? Then Steve and I went back to our place and crashed."

"Steve?"

"My roommate? Steve Bacon? He works lifts, too." "I see."

Trina could read her mind. Why the hell hadn't anybody mentioned that Doug Jennings had a roommate?

"Is Mr. Bacon here at the ski area today?"

"Sure!" He started to surge to his feet, then checked himself and sank back in the chair. "I think he's working Outback today."

The lieutenant abruptly stood. "Just one moment."

She slipped out, returning quickly. "All right, Mr. Jennings. A couple more questions. Was Ms. Owen dating other men?"

"Flirting sometimes. Maybe just to make me jealous." Even he didn't believe himself.

"Did she mention anyone making her nervous? Following her, bugging her for a date?"

"Nothing like that." He shook his head and pleaded, "Why Amy? Everybody liked Amy."

Voice gentle, Meg Patton said, "The chances are that she was chosen randomly, simply because she happened to be alone at the wrong moment."

His face worked. He cleared his throat. "Are you, uh, done with me?"

"Yes. Thank you for your cooperation, Mr. Jennings."

Face still contorted, he nodded, shoved the chair back and blundered from the room.

The two officers sat in silence for a moment. "What did you think?" the lieutenant asked.

"My impression is, he's sincere. Also not the sharpest knife in the drawer."

"No kidding." Lieutenant Patton let out a gusty sigh. "I'm liking the feel of this less and less."

Trina knew what she meant. A murder committed by a spurned ex-husband was one thing; a brutal, sexually motivated murder by a stranger choosing a victim only because she was available and fit a vague "type" was another altogether.

After a moment, Trina asked, "Did you send for the roommate?"

Still brooding, the lieutenant nodded. "Let's squeeze him in before we talk to Travis. We might as well accomplish as much as we can while we're here."

Steve Bacon arrived a minute later, dark-haired, at least, but otherwise fitting the mold: blue eyes sapphire-bright against that glowing tan skiers all seemed to have. Cold air and an aura of energy entered the conference room with him. His glance took in Trina, dismissed her in an all-too-familiar way and turned to Lieutenant Patton.

Irritated, Trina said too loudly, "We understand the area was open for night skiing on Wednesday."

She felt the flick of the lieutenant's gaze. Nonetheless, Meg Patton stayed quiet.

As if she were an idiot, Steve Bacon said, "Yeah, sure. It always is."

"And did you work?"

"Yeah. I ran the Gold Coast lift."

"Did you carpool up here that day?"

She must have sounded too bellicose.

He balked. "Is this about Amy's murder? Why are you asking *me* questions?"

"Can you just answer the question, please."

"I rode with Doug. Doug Jennings. We take turns when we're working the same shift."

"And you did that night."

"Yeah. That's right."

"What did you do after the lifts shut down?"

He told the same story Doug had. He was more certain about the time, because he'd glanced at the clock when they walked in their apartment. "We got home at 1:45. Then we sat around and bull-shitted for a while. I don't know. Maybe an hour. Neither of us had to be at work until one."

After letting him go, the lieutenant said, "So much for the ex-husband."

"It didn't look like a murder committed by an ex-husband."

Meg rubbed the back of her neck. "No," she said, voice weary. "No, it didn't." Her eyes were sharp when she looked at Trina. "You didn't like him."

Trina hunched her shoulders, a bad habit when she felt defensive, one she was trying to overcome. "No. I guess I didn't."

"Why?"

"He just seemed like a jerk."

"In a way relevant to this case?"

"Uh…no."

"Was coming on that strong justified, then?"

Trina looked back at her, face as expressionless as she could make it. "No, ma'am."

Voice milder than Trina expected, the lieutenant said, "On the job, keep your personal feelings to yourself."

"Yes, ma'am," Trina repeated woodenly.

"I didn't like him, either. Ah." Lieutenant Patton tilted her head. "Possibly Travis?"

Sure enough, Trish escorted in yet another handsome man with that unmistakable air of vitality and athleticism. He had changed from high school as much as Will Patton had. Adolescent cockiness had become masculine confidence. But something on his lean face hinted at pain and regret.

Both were obliterated by his grin. "Hey, Will's mom."

Smiling, the lieutenant stood. "Travis. It's good to see you. Congratulations on the Frye Museum showing."

"Thanks. It felt good. I guess I'm not just a local boy anymore."

Frye Museum?

"We'd like to ask you some questions having to do with Amy Owen's murder," the lieutenant continued. "I understand you'd stayed closer friends with her than Will had."

"Sure, no problem. Hey, Trish," he called over his shoulder. "Can I get a cup of that coffee?"

He dragged out a chair and turned it so that he was straddling it, arms crossed on the back. He studied Trina. "I know you, don't I?"

"I was two years behind you in school. Trina Giallombardo."

He nodded. "Nice to meet you, Trina Giallombardo. Again, if we ever actually met before."

"I don't think so."

"Okay, then." He smiled thanks at Trish when she

brought his coffee. Turning back to the police officers, he said, "As for Amy... I don't know about friends. She was more part of the group. We didn't have much in common."

Trina asked, "Did you ever go out with her?"

"Yeah, a couple of times. After she and Doug said bye-bye. But we didn't have much to talk about, and it didn't go anywhere. I doubt she was hurt when I didn't call again."

"Then the decision not to continue dating was yours rather than hers?"

"I really do think it was mutual. Amy was a sweetheart, but not much of a reader, no interest in art, didn't like to ski because she got cold..." He shrugged. "In turn, I have no interest in the latest movie opening at the cineplex, fashion, what everybody we knew back to grade school is doing nowadays... We ran out of things to talk about. She looked as restless as I felt."

"Surely you knew this when you asked her out."

"You'd think, wouldn't you? But when conversation is general in big groups you don't always remember who contributes what. She was fun, pretty, had a nice laugh. So on impulse I asked if she wanted to have dinner. This was...I don't know. Maybe six weeks ago. The next weekend we had drinks and she came to a gallery opening with me. Afterward she wanted us to join Marcie and Dirk Whittaker at Sister's, that new brewhouse. I made an excuse and left her there. End of romance."

The lieutenant asked, "Did you sleep with her, Travis?"

His eyebrows rose. "Does it matter?"

"We're gaining the impression that she tended to end her evenings in someone or other's beds. I guess I'm asking if that was true."

Expression conflicted, he appeared to be thinking furiously. "Okay," he said at last. "After our first date, she came home with me. Are you asking me to rate her performance?"

Lieutenant Patton gave a crooked smile. "No. What I'm trying to determine is whether she would readily have agreed to leave a bar with someone Wednesday night."

He was quiet for a moment. "Yeah. I think maybe she would. My take is, Amy liked sex. Or maybe what she liked was having a guy. She always seemed to be looking."

The lieutenant nodded. "Thank you for your honesty."

Forehead still creased, he asked, "Why would anyone want to kill Amy? She liked sex, sure. But to the best of my knowledge, she never hurt anyone."

"Knowingly."

He shrugged in concession. "Let me put it like this. I think she went out of her way *not* to hurt anyone."

Face drawn, Lieutenant Patton said, "Travis, I want you to think back. Way back. Do you know of anyone who has harbored a grudge against Will? Anyone who is still around town?"

He straightened, gripped the back of his chair. His gaze locked with Meg Patton's. "Will? What does…" He uttered a guttural obscenity. "Amy wasn't murdered like Gilly, was she?"

"There were…similarities."

He swore again. "You told Will?"

She nodded.

"How's he taking it?"

"I don't know," the lieutenant said in a voice Trina had never heard from her. "As I'm sure you're aware, he doesn't open up to me much."

"Why didn't that idiot call me?" He shoved himself

to his feet, hesitated, then sat back down. "No. God. I can't think of anyone who hated Will like that. Everybody liked him." He shook his head as if he were trying to clear it. "Mendoza was convicted. I called damn near every night during the trial! Will told me about the evidence!"

"Ricky always said there was another explanation. That he left her alive." The pencil in the lieutenant's hand snapped. She didn't seem to notice. Her voice had become raw. "What if he did?"

"God." Travis scrubbed his hand over his face. "Is Will still at his dad's? He hasn't found a place?"

"I don't know."

"I'll talk to him tonight." He stood then, and squeezed Lieutenant Patton's shoulder. "Hey, Will's mom. You're super cop. You'll find out who did this."

Her smile hurt to look at. "Thanks, Travis. You're a good kid."

His laugh wasn't any more real than her smile. "When I want to shed a few years, I just come see you."

She watched as he left the room, then met Trina's eyes. "I've known him since he was fourteen."

"Wasn't he around during the trial?"

"No, he was in Europe training for the World Cup tour. He had an exciting life in those days. Val d'Isere, Innsbruck, St. Moritz… Will would get postcards. Travis won the opening downhill of the season that year, at Chamonix. I remember how excited Will was." She fell silent for a moment. "Gillian was killed that spring. Travis was in Japan that week. By the time the trial started, he was back in Europe training for the next winter."

That's why she'd felt comfortable telling him as much as she had, Trina realized. He might be the only friend of Will's his mother could trust.

The lieutenant's gaze sharpened. "Trina, I'm going

to have you go see Mendoza in Salem. You have a fresh eye."

Trina kept her mixed excitement and trepidation out of her voice. "Do I tell him about this murder?"

"Why not? But first, learn what you can about his friends, cousins, nephews. Anyone who might care enough to think of a sick way to get him off."

"Or who wants to be just like Ricky," Trina said slowly.

"You got it. But beyond that, I want you to get him to tell his story about what happened the night Gillian Pappas was murdered. Just…listen."

Trina nodded. "Is there anything you want to tell me about him?"

There was a history here she didn't know.

But Lieutenant Patton shook her head. "Meet him, hear his story. I don't want to predispose you in any way."

"I have been reading police reports and the transcript of the trial."

"But talking to him in person, that's different." She got to her feet. "I'll call over to Salem, we'll set it up for tomorrow."

"If he'll agree to talk to me."

She snorted. "Oh, he'll agree. Ricky Mendoza never misses a chance to tell someone he's innocent."

THE APARTMENT WAS DECENT, the rent exorbitant. That was the price you paid for being in a hurry.

Will unpacked his suitcases and made the bed. After signing the lease that afternoon, he'd visited the storage unit where most of his worldly possessions were stowed and managed to find boxes labeled Bedding and Kitchen. He hoped like hell his coffeemaker was in one of them.

When the doorbell rang, he abandoned the box of

towels on the floor in front of the incredibly tiny linen closet and went to let Travis in. His friend glanced around the blandly furnished living room, wincing at the watercolor print of Juanita Butte that hung above the distressed leather couch and peeled pine end tables.

"You know, you could have stayed with me."

"It's looking like I won't be able to buy until spring. You don't need a roommate for months."

"If I'm not on the ski hill, I'm in the studio. You'd have hardly seen me."

"This will do." Will nodded toward the kitchen. "Beer?"

"Sure." Travis waited until he was popping the top of the dark German brew to say, "I talked to your mother today. She told me Amy's murder had similarities to Gillian's."

"Similarities?" Will made a sharp sound. "More than that. It was damn near a carbon copy. Too close for coincidence."

"Why didn't you call me? This must have stirred up some hellish memories."

Will deliberately took a swallow, feeling the cold, bitter beer slide down his throat. The pause enabled him to say almost steadily, "You could say that."

"Do you need to talk about it?"

Will looked at his hand gripping the bottle and realized it was shaking. The tremor was fine enough he hoped his friend hadn't noticed.

"That's all I've been doing! Even Jimmy McCartin called to talk about it!"

"My fault. I ran into him when I stopped for an espresso on the way up to the hill. I tried to back out the door, but he spotted me before I could make a getaway."

His gaze rested on Will's hand. So much for not noticing. "Come on, buddy. Tell me what you're thinking."

Will turned his back, staring out the small window
above the sink. "What is there to say? Some sick son
of a bitch thought it would be fun to copy another murder. Maybe it was chance he chose another woman I
know. Maybe it wasn't. Maybe he picked her because
that's another parallel. Either way... Do you know what
he *did* to her?" Will asked in anguish.

Travis clasped his upper arm, just briefly, a gesture
of support not so different from the reassuring slap on
the back when one of them struck out on the ballfield,
from the squeeze Will had given his arm when he visited
him in the hospital after his career-ending pinwheel
down the mountain at Kitzbühel. It meant something.

"Yeah," Travis said. "I know what he did to her."

Will felt his friend's scrutiny. He lifted his beer and
swallowed.

"Your mother asked me if I could think of anyone
who hated you."

Beer went down the wrong way. Still choking, he
gasped, *"What?"*

"She looked scared, Will."

Voice thick with fear of a different kind, fear that she
was right and he was wrong, Will said, "She's jumping
to conclusions."

"She's looking at all the options. She was up at the
Butte talking to Doug."

"And?"

"He worked Wednesday night. He told me after he
talked to her that he had been with other people until
two in the morning or so. And his roommate swears he
never left the condo."

Will set down the bottle on the counter so hard it clunked. "This has to do with Mendoza."

"But what?"

"Somebody is trying to get him off. To make everyone think Gilly's killer is still out there."

Travis would have made a hell of a lawyer. Mild enough to catch you off guard, he could still corner you. "Not many people are sick enough to kill like that. A man would have to enjoy it. You and I are good friends. I'd do a hell of a lot for you. But rape and murder? Nah."

Savagely, not wanting to hear the logic, Will said, "You've been talking to my father."

"You know better than that."

Will closed his eyes. Travis had stuck with him through the worst. And now he was being a jackass.

"Yeah. I know better. I'm sorry."

Travis just shook his head. "No need. Are you going to be able to start work with this hanging over you?"

"Yeah." Tension arced through him as if live wires were sparking. "I need to be busy. What am I supposed to do? Sit here and watch soap operas while I wonder if some other woman is being stalked?"

Relentless in his own way, Travis said, "If this guy stalked Amy, then that means he chose her. It had to be her. Why?"

"I don't know!" Will all but shouted. He paced a couple of steps, turned back, bounced his fist on the counter. "I don't know. I was using a figure of speech. Probably nobody is being stalked. Chances are the killer just grabbed Amy because she was available…"

"Has your mom figured out where she was snatched from?"

"Not as far as I know."

"Then maybe she wasn't all that available." Travis still leaned against the edge of the counter, seemingly relaxed, but his eyes were both watchful and compassionate. "You know, maybe the guy picked *her.* Maybe he had to plan how to lure her to him."

"Which brings us back to me." Will swore under his breath. "What did you tell her?"

"Her?"

"My mother."

"That I couldn't think of anyone who hates your guts."

"That's the kind of thing I'd know."

Travis gestured with the beer bottle. "I'm not so sure. If somebody is targeting women because you loved them, he hates you bad. It's not like this guy is telling the world what an asshole Will Patton is. This is something that eats at him. Takes the stomach lining, then his soul."

"I've put people away…"

"But you hadn't, back when Gilly was killed."

"Mendoza…"

"We're just supposing."

"That he didn't kill her."

"Or that somebody, somehow, put him up to it. Maybe it took that somebody six years to work up the nerve to do the dirty work himself."

Will wanted to reject a suggestion so unlikely, but he'd spent enough years in the D.A.'s office to know anything was possible.

"Do you remember that guy who set the fires because he blamed my grandfather for his mom's death?"

Travis accepted the seeming non sequitor. "I remember."

The first fire had been set inside a pickup truck

chosen because it looked exactly like Police Chief Ed Patton's. The worst was Aunt Abby's townhouse. She'd barely escaped with her life. Even Will, just sixteen, had been targeted. His bike, parked outside the grocery store, had been squirted with gasoline and set afire.

He remembered how he'd felt, knowing someone had been watching him, following him, hating him. For a while, until they caught the guy, Will had lived with the heightened perceptions of a soldier in a war zone. He'd searched the faces of people in line at the store or sitting in the bleachers at basketball games, been painfully conscious of anyone walking behind him, of every driver behind the wheel of an approaching car. It was like looking through a magnifying glass, so that his vision was both abnormally sharp and a little skewed. He hadn't trusted that anything was as it seemed.

If he bought into this theory, he would once again feel like an infantryman walking down the street in Fallujah and realizing he'd forgotten to put on his body armor. The smiles of old friends would look like the veiled faces of Iraqi women whose dark eyes were unreadable to that soldier.

Even with friends, he'd have to wonder what he wasn't seeing, what he might have done to provoke hatred so virulent.

He didn't want to revisit that kind of paranoia. Every cell in his body rejected the idea that someone he knew, maybe even someone he'd gone to school with, could do something so hideous.

He unclenched his jaw. "You're reaching. All of you are reaching. This doesn't have anything to do with me. It has to do with that sick bastard who murdered Gilly, may he rot in prison until the gates of hell open for him."

"You may be right." Travis opened the refrigerator

and handed Will another beer as if it were an olive branch. "Let's just hope we find out before another woman gets murdered."

"Amen to that," Will agreed, and popped the lid from the bottle. Goddamn it, but his hand was still shaking.

CHAPTER FIVE

THE ONLY MAXIMUM SECURITY prison in Oregon, the penitentiary complex in Salem was sprawling and impressive. Trina had never had reason to visit it before. Even at the county jail, she didn't like hearing metal doors closing behind her. The idea of being shut in forever gave her the willies. Today, she felt uneasy from the moment she drove in the gates.

She showed her credentials and surrendered her weapon, then allowed herself to be escorted to a glassed-in visitor room, furnished only with a single wood table in the middle and two chairs. Grateful she'd been allowed a "contact" visit and wouldn't have to attempt to interview Ricardo Mendoza through a telephone and thick glass, she set the tape recorder and her notebook on the table. Then, while waiting for him to be brought, she prowled the room. Trina prayed that Lieutenant Patton was right and he'd be eager to talk to her. She'd feel like a failure if she had to go back and admit she couldn't get him to open up.

A guard escorted a handcuffed inmate past the windows looking into the hall. The inmate shuffled with head bent, lank blond hair shielding his face. A moment later, a man and woman passed, both carrying briefcases and wearing dark suits. Attorneys.

Trina wondered if Will Patton had come here to see

inmates when he was an assistant D.A. in Portland. She'd heard that he was a hotshot there, quickly advancing from prosecuting misdemeanors and doing prelims to Domestic Violence and then Major Crimes. Supposedly he hadn't lost a trial.

So why on earth would he quit and take a job in Butte County, where half a dozen assistant D.A.s handled the entire caseload? Did he think he could make it to District Attorney faster on his own home turf? Most D.A.s seemed to end up being appointed to the bench. Maybe he wanted to be a judge so bad, he'd grabbed for the fastest route.

Or maybe something had gone wrong and his standing had sunk. Will Patton, she suspected, wasn't the man to hang his head and accept a demotion to some unit like Consumer Protection or Juvenile Crime. He might have to handle those cases in Butte County—all the D.A.s did—but he'd also get a shot at the big cases. The headliners. The ones that would put his face on the nightly news.

More footsteps in the hall. Why was she thinking about Will Patton? Trina turned to face the door.

She'd seen the photo taken of Ricardo Mendoza when he was booked. Not much more than a kid, he'd stared at the camera with a mix of defiance, fear and feigned indifference. The man who nodded at the guard and stepped into the room had changed in ways that had more to do with being an inmate than with the six years that had passed.

In the blue prison garb, he looked thin and tough. A scar, pale against swarthy skin, curled from his temple onto his cheek. No longer the cocky young man, he was still handsome despite the disfigurement, the complete lack of expression on his face and the lines carved by bitterness. She thought she saw a flicker of interest in his dark eyes as he studied her, but that might be because she was a woman, not because of her mission or her job.

"Mr. Mendoza," she said. "I'm Detective Giallombardo. Thank you for agreeing to see me."

"It's not like I have anything else to do." He went to the chair on the far side of the table, facing the glass wall and the guard who waited outside the room.

Trina sat across from him.

When she didn't immediately begin, he said, "You here to find out what makes me tick, so you'll be able to catch other guys like me?"

He was curious after all. She was interested, too, in the irony in his voice.

"I'm actually hoping you'll tell me about the night Gillian Pappas died."

His body jerked. Good, she'd surprised him.

"What's the point of that?"

"I've read your testimony. I'm hoping to hear what happened, as well as you can recollect it. Including anything you weren't able to say in the courtroom." She held up her hand when he started to speak. "I promise, I'll tell you why, but I'd like to hear your story first, uncolored by what I have to say."

She'd thought his face expressionless. Now, for a moment, emotions she could only guess at boiled to the surface. Finally, he gave a jerky nod.

"Like I said, I got nothing better to do."

"Thank you. Do you mind if I tape the interview?"

He shrugged. "Why would I?"

Trina turned on the recorder and had him repeat his consent. Then she began. "When did you move to Elk Springs?"

He answered her questions, explaining that his father

was a migrant worker, but legal, and that he, Ricky, had been born in this country. His parents still followed the harvests: strawberries, peas, apples, even tulip bulbs in Skagit County in Washington State. He had managed to graduate from high school and learn some mechanics along the way. Two years before Gillian Pappas's murder, Ricardo Mendoza had gotten a job in Elk Springs, at an auto body repair shop.

"They had this bullshit reason for firing me." Remembered anger roughened his voice. "That's when I got drunk and stole a car from the shop. I wrecked it on purpose. Yeah, I know. I was a goddamn genius."

Yeah, he'd shoplifted, too, when he first got to Elk Springs. "I was hungry," he said with a shrug. And, sure, he'd beaten the crap out of this guy who'd insulted Ricardo's girlfriend in a bar one night. "I had a temper."

After plea bargaining, he'd done six months for the auto theft. "Detective Patton actually put in a word for me. She helped me get a job when I got out. Otherwise I probably wouldn't have stayed in Elk Springs." His laugh was harsh. "Big favor, huh? God, I wish she hadn't done me any favor."

No, his girlfriend hadn't stuck by him. He didn't have a girlfriend after he got out of the joint.

He'd worked the day Gillian Pappas was murdered. It wasn't as good a job as his last one, it didn't take any skill, all he was doing was changing oil in one of those quickie places where people sat in their cars while guys with oil embedded under their fingernails worked in the pit, but it was okay.

"I mean, I figured, six months, a year." He shrugged. "I could show what a good employee I was. Then maybe a car dealer would hire me. Detective Patton…" His face closed.

"Detective Patton?"

"She knew someone at the Subaru dealership. She said she'd talk to him."

No wonder the lieutenant had wanted Trina to come alone. She'd had more history with Mendoza than she'd admitted. It sounded as if he'd been some kind of project of hers. Cops sometimes got involved this way, when they thought someone had gotten a raw deal or maybe just believed they saw a spark in someone who'd made bad choices. They thought if they fanned a little, the spark would burst into a warm, crackling fire. Sometimes it even worked. People did get raw deals. Kids with crappy backgrounds could turn around because someone said, "I see promise in you. I know you can do better."

But Ricky Mendoza hadn't turned his life around, according to a jury of his peers. Instead, he'd brutally raped and murdered Gillian Pappas. Trina didn't like imagining what the lieutenant had felt, knowing that without her intervention Mendoza would probably still have been in prison.

"After you got off work that day, what did you do?" Trina asked.

"I went home and had dinner, then decided to go have a couple beers at this bar. Maybe shoot some pool." He was silent for a moment, looking at Trina but seeming no longer to see her. "I stayed a couple hours. I was about to go when I saw this girl come in."

"Did you approach her?"

"Not at first. I figured she was meeting someone. But I kept an eye on her. She ordered a drink, then another one real fast. A couple guys hit on her, but she handled them. I went to take a leak, and when I came back this guy was giving her a hard time. I gave him a shove and told him to back off. I guess she was grateful, because she asked my name."

"Did she tell you hers?"

"Yeah, Gilly. Gilly Pappas."

He described how they talked. She had another drink, and he persuaded her to eat some chicken wings because he could see she was getting plastered.

"All of a sudden she stood up and said, 'You wanna screw?'"

"Did anyone else hear her?"

"I don't think so. I guess people did see us leaving together. Nobody seemed to be paying any attention, but turns out I was wrong."

"What did you say?"

"I asked if she was getting back at someone. She grabbed my shirt and said, 'Do you care?'"

"Did you?"

For the first time, he looked angry. "Shit, yeah, I cared! She was…she was classy. Okay? I knew that, but we really talked, and I thought…" He jerked his shoulders. "Well, I quit thinking. I'd have rather it wasn't revenge sex. You know? But it had been a while, and she was real pretty. So I said, 'No.'"

"You lied."

"Yeah, I lied. So sue me." He guffawed. "No, convict me of murder. Worked even better, didn't it?"

"Please tell me what happened next."

Lightning-quick, he reverted to anger. "What do you think happened? She came out to my car, told me to drive back to the alley and park. Then she unzipped my pants, lifted her skirt and bit my neck. She didn't want to come back to my place, and she didn't want pretty. Afterward, I thought she'd wanted to get it over with as fast as possible. It was like something she had to do."

"Did you have a condom?"

"No, and she didn't ask me to put one on. I figured she was on the pill or something. Or maybe too drunk to care. I don't know. I wish I'd worn a condom."

Trina bet he did.

"Did you talk at all after?"

"No. She got real quiet. Scrambled into her panties and adjusted her clothes like she felt dirty. She started to get out and I told her I'd drive her back to her car. She shook her head and just took off. Walking so fast she was almost running. I drove around the block and saw her come around the side of the bar. She was crying. I felt like shit." He fell silent.

"Did you see her get into her car?"

He shook his head. "It was one-thirty, two o'clock. The place was still busy. The parking lot's not that well-lit. She kind of disappeared behind a pickup."

"What did you do then?"

"I drove home. Got up, went to work in the morning. We listened to the radio in the shop. Late afternoon, I hear about this woman's body that was found. I didn't think anything about it. That night, I see her face on TV. That's when I started to feel scared."

"Did you consider going to the police and telling them that you thought you were the last person to see her alive?"

"Sure," he jeered. "Yeah. I screwed this girl without a condom, she bit my neck and drew blood, her fingerprints are all over my car, and anybody is going to believe I didn't kill her? Well, here's a news flash." He looked around as if in exaggerated surprise at their surroundings. "Nobody did believe me."

She wanted to argue that it might have been different if he'd come forward on his own. But she wasn't so sure. It *had* looked bad. His semen, her fingerprints in his car, the wound on his neck and scratches on his shoulder. His skin under her fingernails. The cops had had Gillian Pappas's boyfriend saying, "She would never have had sex with a strange man she picked up in a bar." And then they'd had Ricky Mendoza, a seeming loser with a record that included violence because of his temper. How could they call it any different?

"Did you have friends, family, to give you character references?"

She saw a flash of pain on his face.

"My parents. They came a couple of times. But they don't speak such good English. They kept saying, 'You wouldn't kill no girl, would you? We raised you to respect girls.'"

"You must have other family."

"Because we're Catholic? You think I must have ten brothers and sisters? Well, I don't. Just a sister. She's ten years older than I am. Back then, she was already married and had kids. Her husband had cancer. I think he got it from using so many pesticides in the fields. You know? But he was an illegal, so who cares? He died, and she had enough to do, raising three kids."

"You never heard from her?"

"She called once and said, 'I'm sorry, what happened to you, Ricky. I know you wouldn't hurt some woman like that.'" He shrugged, as if it didn't matter. "She sends me a Christmas present. And she writes sometimes."

"How old are her children?" Trina asked softly.

"Her oldest is eleven, her youngest is six. Ricardo. They named him after me." He sounded both proud and defiant, as if to say, *Somebody thinks I'm worth naming a son after.*

"Do you have other family? Cousins?"

His mood shifted. His eyes narrowed. "Why do you care?"

"I'll explain, I promise."

In a hard voice, Ricky Mendoza said, "I have cousins back in Mexico. Not here."

"Friends?"

"Nobody who stuck around once I was arrested."

Mildly shocked, she asked, "So people who knew you thought you might have done it?"

"I don't know if they thought that, or just didn't want anything to do with the cops. They were, like, people I had drinks with. My best buddy, he got knifed in prison. He ran this chop shop, see. Three months inside, and he was dead." Another shrug, more feigned indifference.

"Let me ask you this, Mr. Mendoza." Trina leaned forward. "Can you think of anyone who cares enough about you to try to get you out of here?"

He was either a heck of an actor, or he was stunned. "Get me out of here? You mean, like someone's planning a break?"

"No," Trina said. "Not a break. Someone murdered another woman and displayed her body in exactly the same way Gillian Pappas's was displayed. The crime is almost a perfect copycat."

"You think…" He swallowed. "You think someone did that so it would look like I couldn't have murdered Gilly. So you'd get a pardon for me because I must not have done it."

"We think it's a possibility that's the motive. Yes."

"Nobody would do that for me." He actually shuddered. "You think somebody would do something like that just to help out a friend?"

"We do think it's a possibility," she repeated.

"Yeah, well, the only people who care about me are my family, and they're not murderers!" He flattened his hands on the table and half rose. "You're not going to be trying to haul them in, are you?"

She didn't move and kept her voice nonthreatening. "We might look into their whereabouts. That's all."

"They live in Union Gap. They wouldn't be down here. It's winter. There's nothing to pick."

"If we can verify that, they'll be out of the picture."

His angry stare clashed with her steady one. Finally he dipped his head abruptly and sank back into the chair. After a moment, he asked, "This girl. The one that was killed. Did she look like Gilly?"

"Yes. Quite a lot like her."

"What was her name?"

"Amy Owen. She grew up in Elk Springs." She paused a beat. "Did you know her?"

"Why would I know her? I told you. Girls like Gilly. They didn't pay attention to someone like me." His bitterness could have etched metal. "Not unless they wanted to piss someone off."

She wondered if that was true. Ricky Mendoza had been a handsome young man. Possibly a little wicked looking. But if his story was true, he was essentially decent. He'd made the effort to follow Gillian Pappas to her car, to ensure she was safe. He must have seemed a godsend to her, a nice enough guy she could imagine having sex with him, but also rough enough around the edges to make him different from Will Patton. Someone whose identity she could fling at Will, use to hurt him.

What she had never dreamed was that the one who would end up hurt was Ricky Mendoza.

Because she ended up dead.

"Did it ever occur to you," Ricky asked now, "that

maybe I *didn't* kill Gilly? That maybe the guy who did
is still out there? That this Amy's murder wasn't a copy?
It was the real thing?"

"You were convicted of Gillian Pappas's murder."
She hesitated, debated, then said very carefully, "How-
ever, that possibility is also one we have to consider."
She clicked off the recorder and rose to her feet. "Mr.
Mendoza, thank you for your cooperation."

Looking as though she'd elbowed him in the gut, he
sat gaping at her.

She nodded and walked out, passing the guard on
his way in.

A WEEK AGO, his mother had asked him to Sunday-
night dinner. Nice to have her seem disconcerted to
have him show up.

"Will!"

"Do I have the wrong night?"

"No! No, of course not. Come in. I've just been
crazy with this murder...." Her voice trailed off and she
let him in. "Sorry."

"At least you're having dinner at home tonight." He
knew from experience that she might eat fast food for
a week straight when she was pursuing a fresh case.

She laughed. "Scott's amazed. He's actually the one
cooking tonight."

"Come to a dead end?"

His mother hesitated. "Maybe. No one close to Amy
looks like a viable possibility."

Following her toward the kitchen, he said, "That's
because Amy is such an unlikely victim. I mean, I know
beautiful women who enjoy enraging men. Amy isn't—
wasn't—like that."

"So everyone keeps repeating. Why Amy? they ask."

She sounded frustrated. "I have to say, 'I don't know.' If we knew why she was chosen, we'd be halfway to making an arrest."

"You working with someone in the D.A.'s office?"

"I talked to Louis Fein. Since I don't even have a suspect, we didn't have much to say."

Her husband, Scott McNeil, was stirring something on the stove. A big, athletic man with auburn hair graying a little at the temples, he grinned. "Hey, Will."

"Scott." He glanced around. "Are Emily and Evan here?"

"Evan's playing Nintendo. Emily is on the phone. She's *always* on the phone. She's been on the phone or the computer since the day she turned twelve. She only goes to school because her friends are there."

"Hey, maybe I'll go whip Evan's ass."

Scott muttered, "I wouldn't count on it."

Meg laughed. "Do you hear the note of wounded ego? Dad got badly beaten last night."

"You know, it's not skill." Will shook his head. "You shouldn't feel bad. It's age. You can't help it. Those reflexes start to go…"

His stepfather punched his shoulder. Laughing, Will stepped back.

This felt good, as if he really belonged here. He hadn't felt as comfortable in a long while. Even his mother looked relaxed as she handed him a glass of wine.

"So, you start work tomorrow?"

"I get assigned a desk, anyway."

"You'll probably be in court by afternoon. They've really been hustling to get briefs filed on time. Hamilton left six weeks ago, you know."

He frowned. "I should have started last week. They

kept insisting I should find a place to live, get settled, no hurry. So they were bullshitting me, huh?"

"I suspect so."

"Damn it!"

She patted his arm. "Don't worry. They've managed." She cocked her head and he realized the doorbell had rung. His mother set down her wine. "I'll get it."

Will watched her go. She'd had a peculiar expression on her face. Not surprise. Guilt, maybe. Had she invited someone tonight she thought he wouldn't be happy to see?

Scott was peering in the oven and seemed oblivious.

"Someone else coming to dinner?" Will asked casually.

"Hmm?" Appearing satisfied, his stepfather closed the oven door. "Not that I know of. Maybe Abby or Renee dropped by."

If so, his mother wasn't bringing her into the kitchen. The sound of voices had moved away, toward the living room or den. Curious, Will took his glass of wine and followed.

His mother hadn't shut the door to the den. Over her shoulder he saw that the visitor was her partner, Trina Giallombardo. She was dressed as if she'd been working, in slacks, a white shirt and blazer, her badge anchored on her belt.

"It was snowing part of the way, but I had no problem," she was saying, as he approached unheard.

Meg murmured something.

"You were right. He wanted to talk."

He? Will stopped, tempted to eavesdrop. But he was an adult and a prosecutor, for God's sake, not a teenager who lurked outside doors to hear what his mother was up to. He cleared his throat and took another step into the doorway.

His mother gave him a swift look, alarm—no, damn it, guilt!—apparent to an experienced eye. He was willing to bet she'd forgotten he would be here this evening, or she wouldn't have asked her partner to stop by.

"Will! Um...you remember Detective Giallombardo."

"Trina."

She nodded, unsmiling. Did she not like him? He remembered what Travis had said about enemies, and for the first time in his life wondered if he'd carelessly created dozens of them back when he was young and sure the world would lay a red carpet for him. Maybe he should ask Trina Giallombardo: had he been a jackass back in high school?

"I assume this is work. I'll leave you two," he said, starting to step back.

As if she'd arrived at a decision, his mother said, "There's no reason you can't hear what Detective Giallombardo has to say." She fixed a stern gaze on him. "As long as you don't interrupt."

"If you'd rather..."

"No. I'd have to tell you what she learned later, anyway."

"All right." Apprehensive without knowing why, he leaned against the wall.

"Please, sit," his mother said to Trina. "You look tired."

She did, he saw, but not as if she was ready to wind down. She was twitchy from caffeine or adrenaline, he wasn't sure which.

"I'm fine," she said, sounding impatient, focusing on his mother. Nonetheless, she settled on the edge of one of the leather chairs in front of the desk.

Meg took the other, then looked at Will. "Trina talked to Ricky Mendoza today."

Will stiffened but kept his mouth shut. He'd known this was inevitable. The surprise was that she hadn't gone to see Mendoza herself, instead deputizing someone else. Did she have the sense to know that she was too soft where he was concerned?

When she realized he wasn't going to throw a temper tantrum, she turned back to the young detective. "You said he was cooperative?"

"He kept saying he didn't have anything better to do than talk to me."

"Which is true enough." His mother gave a brisk nod. "Tell me how you handled it."

"I promised I'd explain at the end, but I wanted to hear his side of the story first. He agreed."

"You taped the interview?"

She nodded and reached into a bag at her feet, producing a recorder. His mother plugged it into an outlet, then hit Play.

Trina Giallombardo's voice was startlingly clear. "I'm asking for your consent for me to tape this interview."

"Yeah, you can tape." The man sounded indifferent.

Rage gripped Will at the sound of that voice. He'd heard it only once, the day Ricardo Mendoza testified in court. Will wouldn't have sworn he would even recognize it. He was shocked at his visceral reaction. Oh, yeah, he knew the voice.

On the tape, Trina asked, "When did you move to Elk Springs?"

Mendoza talked about his family, migrant workers. He told of getting fired from the auto body shop in Elk Springs and his drunken decision to steal a car and wreck it on purpose. Then he backtracked, admitting to having beaten someone up for coming on to his woman and to having shoplifted.

"Detective Patton actually put in a word for me."

Will watched his mother's face.

"She helped me get a job when I got out. Otherwise I probably wouldn't have stayed in Elk Springs." He laughed. "Big favor, huh? God, I wish she hadn't done me any favor."

Meg bent her head.

"…I could show what a good employee I was. Then maybe a car dealer would hire me. Detective Patton…"

There was a pause.

"Detective Patton?" Trina's voice prompted.

"She knew someone at the Subaru dealership. She said she'd talk to him."

His mother's little protégé. Sick with anger, Will wanted to punch his fist into the wall. He wanted to force her to look at him. He wanted to see on her face that she knew what she'd done.

Right that moment, he hated his mother.

"After you got off work that day, what did you do?" Trina asked on the tape.

Will closed his eyes. God. Mendoza was going to talk about that day. About how Gilly…

No! Everything in him rebelled. She wouldn't have done that.

"I was about to go when I saw this girl come in."

Rigid, Will listened as Mendoza talked about guys hitting on her, and about his own noble intervention.

"She was really tossing 'em back, so I ordered some food. She slowed down a little and ate some chicken wings."

Abruptly, Trina reached out and hit Stop. She looked at him and said, "You don't want to hear the rest of this."

"You mean, him claiming Gilly agreed to a quick one with him?" he said, deliberately crude.

"He's...more explicit here than he was on the stand."

The deep core of rage imbued his voice. "You're worried about my tender feelings?"

"You don't want to hear this," she repeated.

The face his mother raised to him was stricken. "I didn't think. Trina's right. I'll tell you the gist of it. I promise."

"I have a right to hear what he says."

"No. You really don't."

"It's been six years."

His mother said, "Does it matter how long it's been? I sometimes think your grief is as raw as it was the day Gilly's body was found."

"I listened to him in court."

"This is..." Trina hesitated.

"What? What is it you don't want me to hear?"

God help him, he'd swear that was pity in her eyes.

"What really happened."

"Then you believed him?" his mother asked, sounding eager.

Trina Giallombardo was still watching Will when she gave a brief, almost reluctant nod. "If he wasn't telling the truth, he's the best liar I've ever met."

Will uttered an obscenity.

Her pity vanished, and her gaze became cool. "Fine. Listen. Just listen." She hit Play.

Into the silence came Ricky Mendoza's voice. "All of a sudden she stood up and said, 'You wanna screw?'"

CHAPTER SIX

"WILL. Good to see you." Louis Fein, the elected head of the Butte County prosecutor's office, looked up from the paperwork spread on his desk. Unlike in a larger office, here the D.A. took a caseload and did more than play politics. His office showed it—except for two chairs for visitors, nearly every square inch was piled with books and files, presumably overflow from a row of beige metal file cabinets. A television and VCR on a rolling cart were squeezed between his desk and an overflowing bookcase.

With the build of a runner and a head of close-cropped iron-gray curls, Louis Fein was a career prosecutor—fifty-two years old, he'd admitted, and had been in the D.A.'s office for all but three years when he'd quit in hopes of making better money, tried private practice and hated it. "I couldn't think like a defense attorney. I kept looking for ways to nail this bastard instead of getting him off. Finally, I begged for my old job back. Then I figured if I was going to be here, I might as well run the show."

Now Will clasped his hand. "Good to be here."

"Don't want to throw you in too quick, but can you take a look at this interview? Cop wants to file, I'm not so sure."

Will drew up a chair while Fein put the tape in the VCR and hit Play. A familiar scene flickered to life, the poor quality of the videotape reducing dramatic value. They watched in silence as a balding detective interviewed the father of a six-year-old who had somehow gotten shut out of his house late at night on an isolated ranch and frozen to death. The detective thought Dad had locked him out for punishment; Dad claimed the kid must have sneaked out. Mom was distraught and not talking.

Will thought the father was lying, too, but he said finally, "We need more than a suspicion. Keep pushing. I'd ask if he'd sit for a lie detector. Make him sweat. Give her a few days, then talk to her, too. Are there any other kids in the home?"

They talked about it some more before Louis Fein nodded. "I'm wondering if you'd take Hamilton's place on the countywide child-death review team. No one else in the office has any special experience in child homicide prosecution."

The team, he explained, was comprised of social service workers, doctors, someone from the child protective agency, cops from Elk Springs PD and the sheriff's department, and an assistant D.A. "It doesn't take that much time. You review any reports from hospitals relating to the death of a child. We have our share of child abuse, but most deaths are accidents."

"I wouldn't mind," Will said. He'd been the lead prosecutor in a trial that had gotten nationwide attention. A plastic surgeon had become angry with his sick, screaming eighteen-month-old son and thrown him, then tried to cover up with an elaborate scenario involving the kid climbing onto a dresser that fell on top of him. Will had had a hell of a time persuading the head of the child prosecution section to let him file. The surgeon served on half a dozen charity boards, dined with the mayor and had backed the district attorney in her last run for office. But Will's gut told him the guy had lost it. That was tragic, but what had aroused his determination to see the guy in jail was the coldblooded way he'd tried to cover up what he did.

That trial alone had gotten him tagged in Portland as the guy for high-profile child abuse cases. They were never easy to do; he hated looking at photos of dead or injured children, but winning those cases made him feel good. Prosecuting, you could end up focusing on winning, not justice. But when a child was the victim, you never forgot the human side.

"Good," Fein said. "Say, let's walk down to the courthouse. I'll introduce you around. Not that you're an unknown in these parts."

"My name is known. I'm not."

Will hoped he didn't sound too short, but he didn't like the implication that all Pattons came out of the same pod. He didn't want to trade on the Patton name, but he also knew it gave him an automatic edge with judges and cops. How could it not when his father was the sheriff and his aunt was the Elk Springs police chief?

His boss slapped him on the back. "That'll change fast now that you're onboard."

The courthouse was imposing, built in the fifties with the standard sweep of granite stairs—a bitch when they were icy, Louis Fein told him—and marble columns. The sheriff's department and prosecutors had moved a few years back to a modern complex only a block from the courthouse. As the two men walked, both wearing long wool coats and leather gloves, Fein said, "I assume your mother is keeping you apprised on the Owen murder."

Will's stomach lurched at the reminder. "Yes."

The older man said, "I prosecuted Ricardo Mendoza."

Surprised, Will turned his head. Funny how he could

have forgotten that. He'd been so focused on the defendant, he'd hardly noticed anything else.

"Right. I remember."

"This makes me think."

Everybody was so damn quick to *think,* considering the case had looked open and shut six years ago. Had everybody but him been at a different trial? Seen a different defendant?

"You know Detective Giallombardo went to talk to Mendoza yesterday."

Fein raised scant eyebrows. "No. No, I didn't."

"Mom's idea."

"I assumed she'd go herself."

"She wanted a fresh perspective, she said."

They started up the steps, rock salt crunching underfoot. "What did he say?"

"He repeated the story he told at trial."

Fein glanced at him, catching something in his tone. "Nothing new?"

Reluctantly, Will said, "Details."

The truth was, Giallombardo was right—Mendoza had been more forthcoming. Or else he'd used the last six years to embroider his story. Which it was depended on who you asked. Will believed in the embroidery theory. He wanted to believe in it.

The only part that shook him was Trina Giallombardo's doubt. His mother he could ignore. She'd never bought Mendoza's guilt. But Trina *had* gone over to Salem without prejudice, and what Mendoza told her had the ring of truth to her.

"Serial killers are the best liars," she'd admitted. "I know that. Maybe he was playing me like a fiddle. I can't swear he wasn't. But…"

The way her voice trailed off told its own story. She didn't think he was playing her. She'd believed him.

Will could even see why. Mendoza sounded sincere on the tape. Will had asked his mother for a copy of the transcript of the trial so he could read it again. Memory wasn't always reliable. He wanted to see in black and white what Mendoza had actually said then. He wanted to catch the scumbag in a lie.

"He's still claiming to be innocent," Will told Fein. "Nobody would be listening to him if it weren't for Amy's murder."

"Crap." Fein's voice echoed as they entered the marble-floored foyer. He shook his head. "That's an ugly one. Must hit close to home for you."

"You could say that."

Fein raised his voice, which bounced in the huge, high-ceilinged foyer. "Martha! Come meet my new boy!"

Martha was a court reporter. In rapid succession Will met bailiffs, judges, clerks and public defenders. Too many of them greeted him with some variation along the lines of, "The sheriff's boy, huh? You're smart to come home."

Did everyone in town think he'd come home to Elk Springs to trade on his parents' reputations? Maybe they assumed he couldn't make it out in the wide world. Will curbed his growing irritation. He grinned like a country bumpkin, shook hands and hoped the defense attorneys, at least, believed the current line. He'd get some easy convictions before they wised up.

A young blond public defender flirted outrageously and slipped him her phone number on the back of her card. Fein watched with amusement.

On the walk back, he said, "Now why is it that Ms. Harris has never given *me* her cell phone number?"

"Could be she was afraid you'd use it," Will said with a straight face.

Fein gave a hearty laugh. "Could be. Could be. What about you? Do you intend to?" His tone was one of idle curiosity, not judgment.

Nonetheless, Will shook his head. "I'd like to get my footing first. See how she handles herself in court. How often I'm likely to face her. Dating someone on the opposition…that can be awkward."

Fein nodded, and Will had the sense that he was pleased. Will was a little disconcerted to realize he hadn't felt any stir of interest in Caroline Harris, even though she presumably had brains and was of a physical type that usually attracted him. Maybe he just felt too unsettled right now to be interested even in a casual relationship. He'd dated Amy Owen's friend Karin twice that first week in Elk Springs and found her nice enough, but during the second evening he found his mind wandering. He'd have rather been sharing a pizza, beer and some good conversation with Travis.

Since Amy's murder, he found himself shying from the very idea of seeing a woman who reminded him of Gillian. A couple of the worst crime scene photos would shuttle before his mind's eye in the space of time it took him to blink. A private PowerPoint presentation, he thought now, wryly. A form of aversion training. The pretty blonde wouldn't look as pretty dead.

Back in the office, he was handed a pile of folders and videotapes. "Damn glad you're here," a couple of his fellow assistant D.A.s told him with fervency.

Only one seemed to regard him with wariness if not outright hostility. Mark Gage was a couple years older than Will and currently, he gathered, the star trial lawyer on the team.

"Got to say, Mark Gage is damn good at grabbing the jury's attention," Fein had said, when talking about the other assistant D.A.s. "He's more likely to go for emotional punch than he is to help the jury really understand the law, but you can't argue with success."

Although he wanted to, Will diagnosed.

Will guessed Gage saw him as a threat to his standing in the small D.A.'s office. Only time would decide whether they could be barely civil colleagues or friends.

During what would otherwise have been his lunch hour, Will left to attend the service for Amy. The church was crowded, and he caught a glimpse of damn near everyone he'd known in high school, some of whom he hadn't seen in years. But he sat in the back and avoided talking to anyone, including his mother who stood by the doors scanning the crowd.

Amy had been Catholic and the service was far more formal than Gillian's had been, but Will couldn't take his eyes from the altar dominated by a gleaming coffin that looked too much like the one in which Gilly had been buried. He was intensely grateful at the end to mumur his sympathies to her parents and flee to the office. Thank God he felt obligated to get back to work. If he'd gone home, he'd have lost himself in the grief and in his rage.

Still not hungry, he dumped his brown bag lunch in the trash can and tried to focus on the first of the cases he'd been handed. A bar brawl had left one guy dead, stabbed. An open switchblade had fallen from his hand when he went down, so the guy who stabbed him was claiming self-defense even though one witness said the victim had pulled the switchblade out as he staggered back with the knife in his chest. Will settled back to watch the video of the interview with the ranch hand who had been arrested on the old television set that had already been at home in his office. Unfortunately, the picture had a greenish tinge and peculiar flesh tones he found distracting. He was fiddling with the knobs when someone rapped on the glass inset in the office door.

Will swiveled in his chair and, as he groped for the remote control, called, "Come in."

Trina Giallombardo opened the door and entered. His stomach did a dip and roll even as he felt a cramp of… No, damn it, not sexual attraction! Just a strange kind of awareness. Maybe because of who she was, what she knew.

The dip and roll had to do with the gravity of her expression.

"Did you make an arrest?" His voice was hoarse.

She shook her head. "No, I'm sorry. I'm just here to bring you the transcript you asked for." She dropped a thick folder wrapped with a rubber band onto his desk. "Did you go to Amy's funeral?"

Grief punched through his rigid control.

She must have been able to tell that he didn't want to talk about it because she nodded at the television. "Carlton told me about that one. Are you going for a plea?"

"We may have to," he said in disgust, finally locating the remote under some papers and hitting Stop. "The one witness who insists the victim hadn't pulled the knife before the assault was drunk. The cops let most of the bar patrons go home without getting their names, so finding more witnesses would be a bitch. This Detective Carlton might as well be the guy's best bud, he's putting so little pressure on him."

"The thing is, we all knew and hated the victim." She caught his expression. "Yeah, yeah, just because he beat his wife every Saturday night and deliberately hit a guy walking out to his car with his pickup because the guy flirted with the wife doesn't mean anybody on earth had a license to stab him. Still…"

"You're saying in a cosmic sense he deserved it."

"Something like that."

He mulled that over. "Well, that explains this Carlton's incompetence. Maybe he does better when he's really going for the truth."

"Don't you put a little more heat into your summations when your heart and soul is in a case?"

"I don't go to trial if my heart and soul isn't in it."

"All cases being equal?"

Did he hear a note of irony?

"I agree to a plea if it's not. We can't take them all to trial. You know that."

"Well, Detective Carlton can't pick and choose."

With some impatience, Will said, "He can do his job."

She shook her head. "First day here, and you've already decided Butte County cops are inept. Just out of curiosity, why *did* you come back to Elk Springs?"

She'd stung him and surprised him both in a matter of seconds.

The surprise was what really caught his attention.

"You know, I think you're the first person who has asked me that." No, the second; Travis had.

She eyed him warily with those big brown eyes. "Really?"

A smile that felt more bitter than amused curled his mouth. "Seems everyone thinks I came home to trade on the Patton name."

She was good at hiding expressions, but not good enough.

"You did, too." He raised his brows. "Admit it."

"I wondered if you thought you'd get your judgeship quicker here." She shrugged.

"I'm not even thirty!" Will protested. "It's a little early to be thinking about a seat on the bench."

"Then why?"

"The truth?" He told it. "I don't know. I felt…disconnected. As if I'd left too much behind that was unresolved." And why in hell was he telling her this? He nodded toward the TV. "As for Detective Carlton, I'm not generalizing from his performance to the entire department yet."

She flushed a little, if he wasn't mistaken. "I shouldn't have said that. I was jumping to conclusions."

"No, you expected me to be a jackass." He paused a beat. "Care to tell me why?"

"I like your mother. Every time she mentions you, I see this flash of pain." Trina's voice became wooden. "But I don't know anything about what happened between you, and it's none of my business."

"No. It's not." He didn't like being reminded that he'd hurt his mother, who would have done anything for him. He stared down the woman who'd taken it upon herself to do just that. "Thank you for bringing this by, Detective Giallombardo."

"Anything for Lieutenant Patton." She nodded and left, quietly closing the door to his office behind her.

Will swore, his voice loud enough to jar him.

Then he grunted. What was he doing, getting worked up about the opinion of some young cop who had a bad case of hero-worship for his mother? He should be glad Mom had her acolytes, not peeved because some girl he hadn't noticed in high school was now predisposed to dislike him.

She wasn't his type anyway.

Will started to pull the rubber band off the fat file, then hesitated and at last stuffed the file into the briefcase he'd stowed under the desk. Work first, personal later.

He picked up the remote control and hit Play.

"Now then," the cop with the thick neck prompted,

speaking slowly as if to a child, "you pulled your own blade when you saw the knife in Mr. Amato's hand. Is that right?"

The cowboy looked like a bobble-head doll. "That's right. Yes, sir. I saw that knife, and I pulled mine."

SHERIFF JACK MURRAY STROLLED into Meg Patton's office and settled into a chair facing her desk. He waited patiently while she finished a phone call.

Hanging up, Meg said, "Nice suit."

He looked damn good in a charcoal suit that had cost more than anything that hung in her closet. Funny that after all these years she still felt a proprietary pride because Jack Murray turned women's heads.

Johnny Murray had been her boyfriend in high school and was the father of the baby she had found herself carrying at sixteen. She'd known he couldn't stand up to her father, though, so she'd fled without ever telling Johnny that she was pregnant.

He'd taken it better than she deserved when she came back to Elk Springs almost fifteen years later and introduced him to the teenage boy who was his son. What she still couldn't figure out was why the man who by then went by the name Jack no longer stirred her hormones. Will sure would have liked them to get together.

As always, thinking about Will gave her a pang. He'd been such a good kid. He and she had been closer than most mothers and sons. She'd have sworn they were.

But she had been wrong, or Will couldn't have turned on her the way he had.

Now Jack glanced down, as if forgetting what he was wearing. "Had a meeting with the county commissioner and then I spoke to the Rotary Club."

"Ah."

He slouched comfortably, but Meg wasn't fooled.

"Anything new?" he asked, as if mildly curious about the ski conditions for that weekend.

"A bartender at the Deschutes Inn and Tavern says Amy was there that night until one or so. Here's the weird part—after talking to him, the patrol officer spotted her Kia. It was a block away parked on the street between a couple of cars that belonged to homeowners. He knocked on doors, and everyone thought the car was some other neighbor's. There are two houses on that street that are apparently overloaded with cars. There's always a row of them at the curb."

"Was the lot at the tavern full that night?"

"Yeah, maybe. It's that tavern over on Metolius. Has maybe three slots. Anyway, I just got a call. The only prints in it are hers. If it was moved, the guy wore gloves."

"The bartender see her with anyone?"

"He thinks she shot a game of pool, maybe danced with a couple of guys. But he says she left alone."

Jack's tone sharpened. "He's sure?"

"Yeah." She flipped open the file to read Giallombardo's notes. "He had the weekend off. Has a girlfriend in Ashland. Which is why he missed the initial news reports. Last night was his first night back. He says he told Amy about his plans for the weekend. She told him to have fun and do something nice for his girlfriend."

"Nobody else left around the same time?"

"He doesn't think so. He says they weren't that busy, it being Wednesday night. He's having trouble remembering who else was there. She stuck in his mind because she was pretty and she didn't usually come in there."

"Damn."

Meg closed the file and sat back with a sigh. "Dead end."

"What's your gut feeling? Was this personal?"

"How could it be anything but?" she exclaimed in frustration. "Maybe Amy was chosen at random, but there's a message here for someone. Maybe for us. Maybe…"

"For Will?"

She didn't say anything.

"That's what you're afraid of, isn't it?"

"Am I paranoid?"

"I hope so." He sounded grimmer than she'd hoped he would. Reassurance, this was not.

"I don't know where to go with this," she said tiredly. "We have nothing to work with. This guy was careful. Too careful."

"You have a couple of pubic hairs."

"And nobody to match them to."

He nodded. He looked weary, too, with creases between his brows. "Will isn't returning my calls."

"He started work Monday."

"He blew up at me when I tried to prepare him for the possibility that this murder would mean our having to re-examine the Mendoza conviction."

"And you're surprised?"

Jack grimaced. "I just didn't expect his reaction to be so heated."

"Will always was passionate about the things that mattered to him."

"You mean, he never liked to hear the voice of reason once he made up his mind."

They shared a chuckle, too brief. She knew he'd been as wounded as she was by Will's bitter accusations six years ago. Will was his only biological child, as Beth hadn't been able to conceive after their marriage.

Another silence had grown. Jack broke it. "You know this guy is going to kill again."

"But maybe he's moved on. He might be in Medford or Portland or L.A. by now."

"The guy was here skiing and the pressure just built up in him until he had to murder a woman."

She knew what was coming.

"It was just chance he damn near exactly mimicked a rape and murder that happened here a few years back. That your theory?"

"More like my prayer," she muttered.

"Uh-huh." He shifted gears. "Why do you have a newly promoted detective working this one?"

"I don't know," Meg admitted. "But she's doing a good job."

That sharp gaze stayed trained on her face for a moment longer. Then he nodded and rose with seeming effortlessness. "Whatever you need…"

"Yeah. Thanks, Jack."

After the door closed behind him, she sipped tepid coffee, thought about refilling it and didn't bother. Maybe it would have been better if she hadn't grabbed this case herself. She couldn't bring her usual objectivity to it. For her, it was an emotional minefield. She should be supervising from a distance. As it was, she was depending too heavily on a rookie detective.

But she knew herself too well to believe for a second that she'd have been content to sit back and wait for reports. Complications just gave her all the more reason not to be passive.

The phone rang and she grabbed it. "Patton."

"Hey," her little sister said. "Saw Will in court today."

"He hasn't been on the job three days!"

"It was a prelim. Still, he's a shark. He gobbled up some hapless public defender."

"What were you doing there?"

"Cooling my heels waiting to give testimony in that feed store arson trial." Abby was an arson investigator. "Stuck my head into Bertrand's courtroom out of sheer boredom."

"Did Will see you?"

"No. I faded away before he came out."

"Still holding a grudge?"

"He pisses me off." Abby was unrepentant. "He owes you better."

"Kids don't *owe* their parents," Meg protested automatically. "What do I do, whine, 'I raised you, I made sacrifices, now you have to be nice'?"

"Sounds fair to me."

"Uh-huh. Wait'll Sara hits thirteen."

"Yeah, five is bad enough." Abby groaned. "She's been invited to two birthday parties this weekend! Chuck E. Cheese's and the roller rink. I hate birthday parties."

"Can't you drop her and run?"

"As many parents as possible have been politely asked to stay. For good reason. Would *you* want to try to supervise twenty kids running wild at Chuck E. Cheese's?"

Meg just laughed. Prickly Abby, who had been far from sure she wanted to have children at all, had turned out to be a fiercely protective mother. "There's a lot of ugliness out there," she'd said once. "It's not going to touch *my* kids."

"Will needs our support. Amy Owen's murder brought it all back."

"For all of you. Yeah. I figured. Plus, Ben keeps reminding me. Have I mentioned what a lousy invalid he is?" In her usual abrupt conversational style, she abandoned the subject of her husband and asked, "You okay?"

Touched, Meg said, "I'm fine. I'm not so sure about Will, though."

Abby didn't want to talk about Will. "You getting anywhere on the Owen girl's murder?"

"No. We've got zilch."

"Not even..." Her voice became muffled, then clear again. "*Now* they want me in court. Sorry, Meg. Later." And she was gone.

Meg was left to brood.

A week had passed, and the trail had grown cold. If there'd been one in the first place. She looked down at her own notes, where she was comparing Gillian Pappas's murder with Amy Owen's. She had three columns: 1) Same; 2) Different; and 3) Questions.

Under Same she'd listed the fact that both women were raped, the condition of the bodies including bite wounds, the jockstrap used both as murder weapon and to cover the face and the positioning of the bodies. The coloring and physical type of the two victims were too similar to be coincidence, too. Now she jotted the addition that both women had evidently been picked up late at night outside bars.

Different: Disposal site, the fact that the killer had apparently used a condom. No skin under Amy Owen's fingernails.

Questions: Did killer make contact in bar? Why a six-year gap between murders? And finally, did this murder have something to do with Mendoza? With Will? Or was it truly personal, in the sense that the UNSUB wanted to humiliate, torture and erase Amy Owen herself?

Meg sometimes found that lists offered clarity. This time, she was left with the same questions.

What scared her was that it might take another murder, another body, to provide any answers.

CHAPTER SEVEN

WILL SPOTTED his friends right away across the crowded room. Travis and a buddy of his, an artist who welded steel into huge sculptures, had already claimed a booth. Jody Cox of the cute pointy face and half-inch-long fingernails was squeezed in next to Bruce Restak, the artist friend.

J.R.'s Sports Bar was a popular hangout for Will's old crowd, he'd discovered during brief visits home. It was a nice place, packed tonight. Flames flickered in a massive stone fireplace on one side; a bar lined with swiveling stools stuck out into the room like a horseshoe. Huge flat-screen television screens hung above the bar, visible from every seat in the house. Tonight, a hockey game played soundlessly. A side room held pool tables and was as crowded. Voices, shrieks and laughs almost drowned out the music, a top ten favorite by the Dixie Chicks. Pretty waitresses in short skirts, Ugg boots and tight Ts edged through the crowd with trays held deftly overhead. J.R.'s appeared to be the hottest spot in Elk Springs on a Saturday night.

It took Will ten minutes to wend his way to the booth, because he knew so many people he had to greet on the way. Dirk Whittaker, who'd put on another twenty or thirty pounds since Will last saw him, was well on his way to being drunk, and Marcie seemed pissed, while the other couple with them appeared to be amused by their squabbling. Bronwen Fessler sat on a stool at the bar with a couple of guys, but he stopped when she waved him over. She gave him a kiss that was more enthusiastic than he expected, then said, "Do you know Doug Jennings? He was Amy's husband."

"We've met." But he hadn't recognized him. No wonder the guy was swaying, glassy-eyed, on his stool. Will held out his hand. "I'm really sorry about what you're going through. We all loved Amy."

Apparently not noticing Will's outstretched hand, Jennings mumbled, "Loved Amy," and retreated again to his drink.

Bronwen introduced the other guy, who was Jennings's roommate, but Will didn't catch the name. Amy's ex looked like crap. What was he doing out with friends only a week after her murder? Will couldn't remember the first time he'd even pretended to have fun after Gillian was killed, but he knew it had been months later. He sure as shit hadn't been playing for sympathy from pretty women within days.

Or was he being uncharitable?

He excused himself, only to immediately come face-to-face with Karin, the friend of Amy's he'd dated. Why couldn't he remember her last name?

"Karin," he said, before seeing the man sitting across from her. "Gavin! Hey, aren't you joining us?"

His buddy said, "Didn't know we were doing anything tonight."

Damn. Nobody had called him.

Will shrugged. "No big thing. Travis and I figured we'd run into everybody here. If you two want to join the party, come on over."

Karin smiled at Will. "That sounds like fun." Belatedly, she said, "If you want to, Gavin."

Uh-oh. Maybe she thought he hadn't called again just because he was busy finding a place to live and starting work. It was going to be awkward if Gavin thought they were starting something and she was flirting with Will instead.

Gavin and he had never been best friends, but they'd hung out since—jeez—maybe middle school. Gavin had been too short to play basketball, but he'd been a wide receiver on the high school football team and played outfield in baseball. He'd talked about going pro, but everyone knew he wasn't fast enough to play even minor league. He was a smart guy, but his grades were erratic mostly because of his attitude. He'd gone to the community college for a while, but Will didn't think he'd gotten a degree. He seemed to be doing okay for himself, though, selling cars.

Will was actually a little surprised to see Karin with him, then ashamed of himself for letting the thought cross his mind. Still…Gavin had been a weedy-looking guy in high school, and the years hadn't helped. His hairline was already receding, his eyes were a little too close together, and he had a way of being pushy to the point of abrasiveness that didn't usually appeal to beautiful women.

As the two followed him to the corner booth, where they all wedged in amid general greetings, it occurred to him that their group had gotten rather incestuous. Everyone had dated everyone at some time since they all started hanging out in seventh grade or so. Any new addition to the group was welcome. In the couple years since she'd arrived in Elk Springs, Karin had already worked her way through most of the unmarried guys, from what he heard. Since Will hadn't called her again, Gavin was probably next on her list. And look at the way Jody Cox was hanging on Travis's artist friend, another newcomer to their longtime crowd.

Will liked Restak, a hulking fellow with shaggy black hair, acne scars and a hearty laugh. New blood was always a good thing. He was ignoring Jody while he and Travis engaged in some intense discussion about an exhibit that the National Endowment for the Arts had just pulled funding from because of complaints that some of the pieces were obscene.

"If art doesn't shock us in one way or another, it's not art. It's decor," Restak declared, before draining his mug.

A waitress brought another pitcher and more chilled mugs. At the same time, another group of friends grabbed the next booth. Vince Baker, who'd been a hell of a shortstop, had married Maria Rodriguez, his cheerleader girlfriend from high school, over the protests of his parents who didn't like the fact that she was Mexican. That's not what they said, but everyone including Maria knew that's why they didn't think she was good enough for him. Will wondered how she got along with her in-laws now. This was the first time he'd seen them in a while. Maria had a glow that probably had to do with her bulging belly.

Nita Voss had been Will's girlfriend for part of his junior year. He'd dumped her, not all that gracefully, when Christine Nylander arrived as a new student at the high school. He hadn't seen Nita in years; she'd been married and divorced, he'd heard. She looked really good in a figure-molding black turtleneck and tight jeans, her curly blond hair tumbling over her shoulders.

"Hey," he said.

"Will! Someone said you're back in town." Her gaze wandered from him. "Travis, hi!"

Before Will got a chance to say anything else to her,

Justin Hill, who'd arrived right behind her, wrapped an arm around her and she smiled up at him. She scooted into the booth between him and Maria, still nestled in the curve of his arm. Will could only see the back of her head now.

Justin had ski-raced with Travis and ended up being a hotshot in freestyle skiing. Travis, who had flung himself down sheer faces polished to gleaming ice in the world's toughest downhill races, had once said with admiration, "You know what? Justin is goddamn crazy. He'll do anything."

Tonight he gesticulated wildly with his free hand as he described some kind of complicated flip and the way he'd gone down. He guzzled half a mug of beer. "What the hell," he boasted, laying his arm along the back of the booth and half turning so that he was speaking to Will's table as much as his own. "I'll kick butt at the world championships."

Travis's expression didn't change, but his stillness spoke of regrets he tended to shrug off.

"Why are you home?" Gavin asked, before Will could change the subject.

"We have a week break. I didn't make it for Christmas, and the parents like to see me once in a while." Justin lifted a mug in salute to Travis. "Damn shame I don't get to run into Booth over there. We used to find ourselves in the same hotels in places like Schladming or Bad Gastein every so often."

Travis didn't say anything.

"Where are you off to next?" Jody Cox asked.

"Italy. Pozza di Fassa. Then back to Quebec."

Gavin said, "Did you see Doug Jennings here? Short mourning."

Will glanced at him in surprise. He wouldn't have

said that Gavin was the sensitive type, but the attempt to change the subject was pretty obvious.

Maria Baker nodded. "He cried when I told him I was sorry about Amy. I think maybe Bronwen talked him into coming tonight. She probably thought it would be good for him."

"My generous wife." Vince's grin gently mocked her. "More likely she's making a move on him."

"Nah," Nita contributed. "Take a look."

They all did, some more surreptitiously than others. Bronwen was laughing and leaning, none too subtly, on Jennings's roommate. Jennings himself was slumped, apparently oblivious to everybody around him, staring morosely into his drink.

If Will hadn't been looking in that direction, he might not have noticed the two women just entering J.R.'s. Trina Giallombardo, gleaming mahogany hair still pulled back, but more loosely than during working hours, with a second woman Will didn't recognize.

"Well, well," Travis murmured, "if it isn't your mom's sidekick."

"A cop?" Gavin said with interest.

"Yeah, don't you recognize her?" Travis nodded toward the pair, heading toward an empty booth a safe distance away, thank God. "Trina something. Will?"

Reluctant to talk about her, he said only, "Giallombardo."

Gavin studied the two and shrugged. "Should I remember her?"

His disdain irritated Will, who nonetheless kept his mouth shut. He didn't much like Trina Giallombardo himself.

Just as she was sliding into the booth, she saw Will. Their gazes locked for a startled moment before hers touched with seeming alarm on Travis and then the others with Will.

"Isn't that the cop that was coming around to talk to all of us?" Jody asked. "What's she doing here?"

"Maybe getting a drink," Will suggested. "Or dinner."

She seemed to be concentrating awfully hard on the menu, as if conscious of the stares.

"Even cops eat," he added.

"You should know."

Will glanced at Gavin, who was smiling but whose tone had sounded edgy. Oh, hell, Will thought; he was probably imagining things. Gavin was just ribbing him. He'd hung out at Will's house plenty often. He'd never seemed uncomfortable with the fact that Will's mom was a police detective.

"Yeah, that's right," Justin said, too loudly. "You're on the in, aren't you? Are the cops gonna arrest anybody, or do they not have a clue?"

Will unclenched his jaw. "Sorry, no in. You know as much as I do."

"But you're in the D.A.'s office now, right?" Vince asked.

Before he could answer, Gavin complained, "Why hasn't this cop I should recognize talked to *me?* Don't I rate?"

Will was getting a headache. He rolled his shoulders slightly to ease tension and realized Trina was watching them. She turned her head quickly and pretended to be scanning the room when she saw him looking.

"Which one is the cop?" Gavin asked.

"The one facing us," Jody told him. "She talked to me the day after Amy's murder."

"Yeah? What did she want to know?"

"You know. Who Amy was dating. Whether she'd been afraid of anyone. Stuff like that."

"What did you say?" Karin asked. "Did she complain about anybody to you? She didn't to me."

Jody shook her head. "Me, either. I mean, everybody *liked* her."

In the moment of silence that followed, Will guessed they were all seeing, as he was, an image of Amy's battered body, naked in the freezing night, her limbs sprawled obscenely in a message of contempt from someone who hadn't liked her, or maybe just didn't give a damn who she was, only what she represented.

"Poor Amy," Nita whispered.

"You have no idea if they even have a suspect?" Gavin asked.

Will shook his head. "I really don't."

He didn't tell them about Trina Giallombardo's drive to Salem to talk to Ricky Mendoza or the tape of the interview that he'd listened to. He sure as hell didn't say, *Did you know Amy was murdered just like Gilly was?*

Lack of knowledge didn't stop anyone from speculating. Jimmy McCartin showed up about then and edged into the booth next to Jody, who pouted and squeezed closer, if that was possible, to Bruce Restak.

"Wow, you guys talking about the murder?" McCartin asked.

"What else?" Travis said fatalistically.

They all had theories, it developed, most having to do with a Ted Bundy type who'd come here to ski.

"Even murderers like powder snow," Justin said, with a flippancy that made Will realize he never had liked the guy.

Bruce Restak, Travis's artist friend, tried to change

the subject, maybe because as a relatively recent arrival in Elk Springs he hadn't known Amy well or maybe because an ugly murder didn't seem like his idea of fun conversation, but the topic of a new art gallery in town fizzled. Nobody except Travis cared.

Will's headache worsened. Justin Hill wanted to talk about European ski resorts and the beautiful women who thronged after the top competitors. Gavin and Jody kept on about Amy and the investigation. McCartin kept trying to reminisce about wild parties in high school that Will didn't even remember him being at. Travis seemed morose tonight.

Meantime, Will was painfully conscious of Trina Giallombardo's presence, not that far away. He found himself assessing her in a way he hadn't when she wore a stern, authoritarian persona along with the regulation navy blazer, sturdy shoes and badge and gun on her belt. Tonight, like most of the other women, she was in a turtleneck, jeans and sheepskin-lined boots. She might have on a little makeup. Maybe that was why her face seemed more vivid, more intriguing. Different.

Despite her Italian heritage, her skin was paler than that of most of the women here. Which probably meant she wasn't a skier. Her lips weren't plump and pouty, her hair blond, her legs long. Studying the classic oval of her face, he found himself thinking Renaissance Madonna. A face of simple prettiness rather than exaggerated beauty. She sat there quietly, observing, as he guessed she always did.

Not his type, of course, but tonight he found her more interesting than he did the women at his table. Which probably had to do with his pounding head and restless mood.

"I'm going to call it a night," he said into a pause in the chatter. "Headache."

"Yeah, I'm a little under the weather, too," Travis said. "I came with Bruce. Can you drop me at home?"

"Sure."

"You're leaving?" Jimmy McCartin said loudly. "The party is barely getting started! Hey," he added, "have you thought any more about that house?"

"House?" someone asked.

"Yeah, I'm with Century 21," he told everyone. "I've got cards if anyone is thinking about buying. I took Will up to that new development at Crescent Ridge to look at some houses. There's some real beauties there, right, Will? He's considering one."

Will ignored him.

"Hey, give me a call," Gavin said, standing to let Will out.

"I can stop by the dealership," Will said.

"Nah, I'm not there anymore. The guy who owns it was an asshole." He shrugged. "He needed me more than I needed him. This is a slow time of year for sales anyway. I don't need to work for a few months."

"You make enough to take months off?" Will asked in surprise.

"Hell, yeah! My best month ever, I made $30,000. This year wasn't that good, but I did fine. This guy at the Toyota dealership wants me to sell cars for him, but I'm not in any hurry."

Justin Hill was loudly telling everyone about some endorsement deal and the shit pot full of money he was getting just for lending his name when Will walked away.

"I've been known to hide out in my room in Schladming or Bad Gastein when I knew Hill was in town," Travis said in a low voice. "Who invited him tonight?"

"Not me." Will shook his head. "I was just thinking what a jackass he turned out to be."

"Always was. Who invited McCartin?"

"No one."

Will's route had, by design, taken him in front of Trina Giallombardo's table.

"Hey," he said, stopping. "You here undercover? Should I pretend I don't know you and keep going?"

"I go out once in a while." Trina looked at her friend. "Sandy, if you haven't met him, this is Will Patton. Will, Sandy Kilts."

He tore his gaze from Trina to nod at the friend. She immediately reminded him of a colleague in the D.A.'s office in Portland. Smart, intense, passionate and completely uninterested in wasting precious time on makeup, beauty salons or shopping. This Sandy's dishwater-brown hair was captured haphazardly atop her head with some wooden implement that looked like a two-pronged fork. She seemed oblivious to the fact that she'd dribbled barbecue sauce from the buffalo wings down the front of her sweater.

"Are you a cop, too?" he asked.

"Me?" the friend exclaimed. "Wow. No. I write for the *Sentinel*. I did an article not that long ago about you," she said, looking at Travis.

Travis had been hovering in the background, but now he took a step forward. "Right! I knew you looked familiar. Hey. I was flattered. Thank you."

"You're incredibly talented. You don't need flattery from me."

"Haven't you heard how insecure we artists are?"

She gave him a brisk glance. "You don't look insecure."

Will laughed out loud for the first time tonight. "Cockiest guy I've ever met," he told her.

Travis elbowed him. "We've been talking about you," he said to Trina. "Or, more accurately, about how the investigation is going."

Her journalist friend said, "The police line is, 'We're pursuing several leads.' That's all I can get out of her."

"Doug Jennings is here tonight," Will commented.

"Just left." Trina nodded toward the door.

"Really?" He turned to see that Bronwen Fessler was now in their booth on Bruce Restak's other side. She was talking, and everybody else seemed to be listening.

"You think the guy is as heartbroken as he looks?" Travis sounded thoughtful.

"What makes you ask that?" Voice changing indefinably, Trina set down her glass.

"Hmm?" Travis turned back. "Just surprised to see him here. And from what I can gather, he spends most of his time weeping on various women's shoulders."

"Wait. You don't work with him, do you?"

"I see the lift operators around. And I remember Will here after Gilly—" He stopped, rocking on his heels. "Sorry."

"People mourn in different ways," Will said. "Some get mad, some turn into hermits, some talk."

"Uh-huh," Trina agreed. "Last year, I had to go tell a guy that his wife had been killed in a car accident. He grabbed a shotgun and started shooting. We had to cuff him and take him in."

Sandy traced a finger around the rim of her glass. "This older woman I worked with lost her husband to cancer. After that, he was all she could talk about. It was as if she thought she was keeping him alive. The sad thing was, everyone took to avoiding her."

Trina nodded. "For some people, grief seems to be intense but brief. Others…"

"Never quit mourning?" Travis didn't look at Will, but they both knew who he was talking about.

Will couldn't help the harshness in his voice. "Natural death is easier to accept than murder."

"But Amy Owen was murdered, too," Sandy Kilts pointed out.

"Remember they were divorced," Travis said.

Did that matter? Will wondered. From all he'd heard, Doug Jennings had wanted Amy back. He'd claimed—hell, he was still claiming—to love her. Okay, she wasn't part of the pattern of his life the way she'd have been if they had still been married. But emotions and memories had a great deal to do with grief.

Will and Gillian had fought the night of her death, with bitterness they probably couldn't have retreated from. Their paths had been diverging. She'd wanted to go into the Peace Corps and, like a jerk, he'd been saying if she loved him she wouldn't go. He hadn't been mature enough to let her go with the faith that she'd come back to him. After that last fight, he doubted she would have. If she'd really had sex with Mendoza to hurt him, it probably meant that she still did love him even if she didn't want to. But he judged himself harshly enough to know that, if she hadn't died, he wouldn't have been able to forget the slap in the face. After the police came knocking on his door— After that he'd have forgiven anything, if only he could have had her back.

"He might love the idea of her more than her," he heard himself saying. "I don't know why they got divorced…"

"She wanted to settle down and start a family, he didn't," Trina said.

"He loved her, she loved him, but they got a divorce

because he didn't want two a.m. feedings?" Will shrugged. "Not one of the great passions of the century, even if he is weeping into his beer now."

"You do have a point."

"Anyway, he was working when Amy was murdered," Travis said.

"Hmm? I thought we were talking about grief, not murder."

Her friend laughed. "Oh, come on! You had that cop look. We all saw it. We might not have been talking about murder, but you were thinking about it."

"I wasn't…."

"Yeah, you were." Will grinned. "Let me tell you, I can recognize it from a thousand yards. I'd be talking to Mom at breakfast, her sitting there in her bathrobe with her hair sticking out every which way, and suddenly something I'd said would make her point like a setter that sees a duck. It would turn out she was investigating this guy's father, or I'd just blasted someone's alibi out of the water."

A waitress edged past them, drinks rocking as the tray grazed his arm.

"You know," Sandy scooted over and patted the seat of the booth, "you two could join us."

He was tempted, but he was afraid their friends would be insulted to have them make excuses and then settle down at a booth with someone else.

"Thanks," he said, backing away, "but I've been battling a killer headache."

"Nice to see you again." Travis nodded at both women and followed once Will had said his goodbyes. Both grabbed parkas from the rack near the entrance and zipped up before stepping out into the frigid night. "We could have stayed," he said mildly.

"It would have looked like we were just trying to get away from the friends we were supposed to be having fun with."

Both paused to pull on gloves as they let a car pass, the lights briefly blinding them. "We *were* just trying to get away from them."

Funny, Will's headache had eased. "Pretence allows for civilized relationships."

Travis sighed. "Yeah, yeah. You're right." He held out a hand. Sounding less than enthusiastic, he said, "It's snowing."

Scattered, seemingly weightless flakes floated from the dark sky.

"You should be rejoicing."

Travis grunted. "I've been thinking of giving up the ski school gig. I want more time to paint. I want to sleep in."

Will's SUV beeped and the lights flashed as he unlocked with the remote. "You love to ski."

"Fires burn down to ashes."

Will paused with his hand on the door handle. "Tell me you didn't feel a pang tonight when that idiot Hill was going on about how sad it was you were sidelined while *he* was going to kick butt in the world championships."

Surprisingly, Travis laughed. "Sure, I felt a pang. But that's all it was. A man can move on, my friend." He got into the passenger side of Will's Toyota 4Runner.

"Can he," Will said softly, before opening the door and following suit. It was Trina Giallombardo's face he saw, not with her cop look, but rather from when she first spotted him inside, her eyes startled, her cheeks flushed.

Was he ready to let Gillian go? he wondered, sticking the key in the ignition. Maybe.

Maybe not.

TRINA ATE BREAKFAST reading transcripts of Ricky Mendoza's trial. She combed police reports about the investigation into Gillian Pappas's murder at lunchtime while she ate her sandwich without tasting it. She was back to the transcript that evening while she absent-mindedly sipped soup.

When did doing your job cross over into obsession? Did she care?

What else did she have to do with her time? Her social life wasn't exactly hopping, her kickboxing class had been canceled this week, and beyond the bare necessities she wasn't especially interested in decorating an apartment with cheap kitchen cabinets, regulation beige carpet and ugly drapes. Why not obsess?

She rinsed the bowl, put it in the dishwasher that didn't get anything clean that wasn't already, and opened the cupboard in search of something sweet. Darn it, she'd finished the bag of gingersnaps last night. She was way overdue to grocery shop....

Her search of the freezer yielded half a pint of Rocky Road ice cream. Happy, she grabbed a spoon and sat eating the ice cream right out of the carton.

Ten bites into the Rocky Road, she hit pay dirt. Buried in the autopsy report was the startling fact that, when Gillian Pappas's pubic hair was combed by the pathologist, a number of hairs not hers were found. They might belong to three or more men, an analyst later concluded. Two matched Ricardo Mendoza's. So far as Trina could discover, nobody had pursued the origin of the others. Excitement surged in her. Surely the hairs, evidence in one of the worst crimes this county had seen, had been preserved. They could be compared to the ones found on Amy Owen's body.

Trina turned back to the transcript of the trial, astonished that the defense attorney hadn't made more of the presence of unidentified hair. Okay, some were probably from Will Patton. But had she had sex with a *third* man?

The spoon suspended halfway to her mouth, Trina brooded. If Ricky Mendoza had raped and murdered Gillian Pappas, wouldn't that suggest a second man had also raped her? Gang rape wasn't uncommon; savage, sexually motivated murder was more commonly committed by loners. But there were always exceptions. If Mendoza had had a partner, Amy Owen's murder made more sense.

All along, the core assumption was that whoever killed Amy had to have seen Gillian Pappas's body. Trina wondered if Lieutenant Patton had tagged her to work this case in part because she was a woman. It had to have crossed her mind that the body had mainly been seen by cops. Cops, medical examiner, morgue attendants and the pathologist.

No, she reminded herself. Attorneys, even jurors, had also seen some pretty graphic photos. But the idea of someone imitating a murder because some photograph inspired him didn't work for Trina.

She licked ice cream off the spoon. Actually, she concluded, she didn't buy the copycat theory at all. It was so…calculating. Coldblooded. The antithesis of a murder driven by rage and frustration and hatred, where the killer could find satisfaction and a sense of power only by destroying the object of his desire and the cause of his low self-esteem. If you weren't driven by such all-consuming, blind rage, *could* you bring yourself to rip at a woman's breast with your teeth?

Trina didn't think so.

Her appetite abruptly deserted her, and she put the lid back on the carton and returned it to the freezer, adding the spoon to the rack in the dishwasher.

No, what made sense to her were two possibilities: that Ricky Mendoza had had a partner, or that Mendoza hadn't killed Gillian Pappas at all. That he'd told the truth: he left her, alive and well, if distressed by what she'd done, in the parking lot in front of the tavern.

What if Mendoza and a friend *did* rape Gillian? Maybe they participated equally in her murder as well. Or maybe not. Maybe the friend was the one welling with violent rage. Mendoza might have watched, or maybe he'd left but knew who must have killed her. If he hadn't actually seen her murder, it would make it easier for him to protest his innocence. Maybe to reshape events in his own mind so that he *was* innocent.

She turned pages in the transcript of the trial until she found the place in his testimony where he'd described meeting Gillian in the tavern and then having sex with her. The story was certainly much briefer here than the one he'd told Trina last weekend. He said nothing about his realization that she was trying to hurt someone else, nothing about the way she'd recoiled from him afterward, nothing about his self-repugnance.

Why? Because his attorney had advised against it for some reason? Because he didn't think it had anything to do with proving his innocence? Because, maybe, he didn't want to admit aloud that she hadn't really wanted *him?*

Or was all of that mere revision to the fiction that had him innocent? He'd certainly had plenty of leisure to expand the story, to add some affecting touches of emotion.

She'd found him convincing. More convincing than

she'd expected. But people lied, and some did it very well. Another thing Ricky Mendoza had had was plenty of practice at telling his story. Six years of practice. A man could get good at it.

She eventually, reluctantly, closed both the transcript and the fat sheaf of copies she'd made of the original police reports. She no longer knew for certain whether she believed Ricky Mendoza.

What she did believe was that the same man had killed both women. If the pubic hairs combed from the two victims matched, maybe she could convince everybody else of that much.

The investigation of Gillian Pappas's murder would have to be reopened, of course. How far they'd get after six years, Trina didn't know. People moved, died, forgot what they'd once known or seen. They revised even their own memories.

She knew one thing: Will Patton would be enraged by Trina's belief that Ricky Mendoza either hadn't acted alone or was actually innocent.

And *that* made her wonder: why was Will so angry at even the suggestion that the wrong man might have been convicted? Had he known and detested Mendoza, even though that fact was never mentioned in either the reports or the trial? Or did he just want someone, anyone, declared guilty?

She felt faintly sick at where her logic was taking her, but made herself frame the last question anyway.

Had anyone seriously considered Gillian Pappas's boyfriend as a suspect in her murder? The boyfriend who had moved away from Elk Springs for six years and coincidentally come back just in time for another woman to be murdered in the same way?

The boyfriend whose mother headed this investigation, and whose father was the Butte County sheriff? Or did those relationships mean some gigantic assumptions had been made from the beginning?

Trina went to bed and turned out the light, but had the bad feeling she wouldn't be sleeping well tonight.

CHAPTER EIGHT

"THEY ACTUALLY FOUND a pubic hair that was never identified?" Lieutenant Patton almost lunged from the chair behind her desk to snatch the copy of the autopsy report in Trina's hand. "How could I miss something like that?"

"Maybe because it was never mentioned in the trial." Trina sat in one of the chairs facing her superior's desk. "That's the part I don't understand."

Already reading as she sat back down, the lieutenant bumped an open drawer and swore under her breath without once taking her gaze from the report. "Hair from three different men," she read aloud, incredulously.

"What I'm hoping is that they've been preserved."

Lieutenant Patton let out a puff of air. "After that fiasco a couple of years ago, we'd better pray instead of just hoping."

Trina knew the fiasco she was talking about. Family of a man convicted fifteen years before of murdering his wife had remained steadfastly convinced of his innocence. They'd pushed the sheriff's department to request DNA testing of blood found at the scene that wasn't the victim's but had matched the husband's blood type. The sample, which should have been safely frozen, was nowhere to be found. Embarrassment had been acute and the family distraught.

"I'll request a comparison." Her superior studied Trina. "You believe this substantiates Ricky Mendoza's story."

"Maybe. But not necessarily." Trina told her what she'd been thinking.

"A second rapist." The lieutenant rolled a pencil between her fingers as she mulled over the idea. "That's good. It gives us an opening for looking at old evidence."

"I guess it would be awkward if it got out that we were reopening a case that already resulted in a conviction." Boy, wouldn't Sandy Kilts jump on that one!

"To put it mildly. We'd better be damn sure before even a whisper floats out."

Trina nodded.

Lieutenant Patton asked, "How the heck would you find a partner for something like that? 'Say, how do you feel about willing versus unwilling women?'"

"Look how common gang rape is." She'd been first responding officer a couple of years back when a hysterical mother called after her nineteen-year-old daughter got home from a drunken party. Three guys had raped her, and nobody else at the party had bothered to protest or call the cops despite her cries for help. The memory still gave Trina the creeps. "Men must somehow get around to discussing their fantasies."

"God knows women do."

Trina didn't share hers with anyone. Never had. Never would. She was too embarrassed to have wasted years fantasizing about the same guy. The very idea that the lieutenant should somehow find out about her pitiful dreams about Will was enough to give Trina the shudders.

Speaking of Will—and as delicately as she could—Trina asked, "Were any of the hairs ever compared to Will's? Since they had a relationship?"

The lieutenant responded with virtually no inflection. "Yes. He...found the experience distressing. Some did match his, not surprisingly."

"Strange," Trina mused. "I didn't find any note to that effect in the file."

Sounding impatient, Lieutenant Patton said, "You know as well as I do that some things never make it into files."

Trina cleared her throat. She'd rehearsed the most tactful way she could think of to phrase what was really a question. "As upset as he was, he must have hated being considered a suspect, even briefly."

The lieutenant's brows rose, and her tone cooled further. "I don't think he was a suspect." She hesitated, then made a face. "That's a stupid thing to say. Of course the investigating officers would have had to consider him."

Trina crossed her fingers that she didn't get demoted for being so pushy, but she had to ask. "Then he was eliminated right away?"

"Yes. Thank God he didn't go storming out of the house that evening after Gillian took off! He was staying with his father, also a good thing as it turned out, because Stephanie had a couple of friends spending the night. With the house so busy, he had a more than adequate alibi. He apparently got quietly, disgustingly drunk while the girls watched movies, then snored away in his bedroom down the hall. It seems Steph's friends had a crush on her stepbrother and giggled like mad every time he staggered down the hall to use the bathroom. Jack said he finally got up to shut Will's bedroom door because his snoring was keeping him awake. No, Will couldn't have left the house without someone noticing."

Thank God for small favors. It was bad enough to

have nursed a huge crush on some guy who would never notice dark-haired, sallow-skinned Trina Giallombardo. But at least she wanted to believe he was worthy of her youthful adoration. She'd hated even having to consider the possibility that he could have murdered his girlfriend and then let some other poor schmuck go to prison for the crime.

Now Trina nodded. "I'll bet you were relieved."

"You know, it's funny. At the time, it didn't even cross my mind that anyone would think Will could have done it. Now I realize…" She stopped "Getting sloppy drunk is rarely the best treatment for heartache. This was an exception, as it turned out."

"You must have known her well." It belatedly occurred to Trina.

"Gilly? That's what Will called her, you know." Meg Patton's eyes lost focus. "She was a sweetheart. Always nice to the kids—Jack's two stepdaughters adored her. She was one of those people who seem to glow with some inner serenity. They were such a good pair, both determined to change the world. In those days, Will intended to defend the indigent, battle evil landlords and take on corporate America." Her voice was gentle, tinged with a parent's amusement and pride that blurred into grief. "Gilly wanted to go into the Peace Corps. She'd volunteered for a summer in Nigeria, and she wanted so much to go back." She fell silent for a moment. "Will's never really said what they fought about. Maybe because in retrospect it didn't matter, or maybe he felt he'd behaved badly. I don't know. Whatever they argued about, he kept believing in her. I suppose that's a large part of why he can't let himself consider the possibility Ricky didn't rape her and kill her."

"Because that would mean admitting that Mendoza's

story was true." Trina could understand how he felt. "That she'd do something like that."

"Exactly."

This silence quickly felt awkward to Trina. She cleared her throat and stood. "Um, would you like me to request a comparison of the hairs found on the two victims?"

"I'll take care of it. What do you intend to do next?"

"Well, I already put in a call to Union Gap, up in Washington, and talked to an officer who actually knows Mendoza's family. He confirms that they're all there and haven't made any quick trips. Which doesn't sound very practical. The dad drives some rattletrap pickup, and neither mom nor the sister drive at all." *You're rambling,* she told herself. "Anyway, I thought next I'd try to track down Mendoza's former bosses and landlord. Maybe neighbors, if they weren't too transient. Find out if he had any friends who hung out a lot." She heard herself sounding more and more tentative. "That is," she concluded, "if you think it's a good idea. I could keep interviewing people who knew Amy...."

"No. The two murders are linked, no question. We've got to figure out how. You've been using your head. I'm glad one of us is." The lieutenant nodded dismissal.

Trina left the office feeling ridiculously like a first-grader whose teacher had just told her she was the smartest girl in the class.

Half the desks in the detectives' unit were unoccupied. Phones rang, unanswered. Berkshire was interviewing a sullen teenager in the baggiest pants Trina had ever seen. Carlton was on the phone as she approached his desk, his face flushed red.

"You're suggesting I coached him?"

She slowed her steps, suspecting she knew who was on the other end of the line.

His voice rose to bellow. "You interviewed him without notifying me? What the hell was that about?"

The answer made his color deepen to plum. As he slammed down the phone, she wondered if he'd had an EKG lately.

"Who does he think he is?" Carlton asked the room at large. "Doesn't know shit about the victim or perp, and he's telling *me* what happened!"

None of them had heard the office door open. Lieutenant Patton asked, "Problem?"

He spun in his chair, mouth opening, but despite the swelling capillaries in his head, he still possessed some sense of self-preservation. "No. Nothing I can't handle."

"Good," she said coolly, before her gaze found Trina. "You're still here?"

Her pleasant little glow dimmed. "On my way," she said, snatching for notes and her parka and making a hasty escape.

LIKE MOST DAYS in any investigation, this one was unproductive.

Trina started with the Quik Lube where Ricky Mendoza had worked before he was arrested. The first guy in a dark coverall who asked if he could help her shook his head. "I've only worked here for three months. I don't think anybody's been here even a year. Try the boss."

The boss, when he emerged from a tiny inner office, frowned. "Yeah, sure, I remember that guy getting arrested. Mostly I remember hoping the papers wouldn't mention where he worked. And that he didn't follow that woman home after she got the oil in her car changed here."

Aware of the three young guys loitering in the garage in the absence of business, all undoubtedly eavesdropping, Trina asked, "Is there someplace we can talk?"

"We've got a waiting room." The boss, perhaps forty, with frown lines embedded in his forehead, a pen tucked behind his ear, and coveralls that were marginally cleaner than his employees', held open the door for her.

The waiting room was just big enough for four plastic chairs, a pop machine and a coffee table covered with tattered magazines.

"I got to tell you, I hardly remember the guy," he said. "I don't know what I can tell you."

When pressed, he produced a personnel record, which consisted entirely of a brief, scrawled application and a date of termination. Both application and the file folder were spotted with greasy fingerprints.

Asked if Ricky Mendoza had had friends who dropped by when he was working, the boss said, "Unless the friend is paying for an oil change, he's got no business here."

"Did he get along well with other employees?"

"You know, I don't remember a problem, but, like I said, he was just another kid until the news broke. He was here, what, three months?" He shrugged. "These guys, they come and go."

Trina noted Mendoza's then address and the names he'd given as references on his application, the most influential of which presumably was Detective Meg Patton.

The boss did look up the names of a couple of other employees who'd worked at Quik Lube at the same time as Mendoza and gave her their last known addresses and phone numbers. "Good luck finding 'em."

The building where Ricky Mendoza had lived was actually an old house broken up into six apartments, two in the basement. Nobody home in any of the apartments had ever even heard of him. Two spoke no English, and Trina's Spanish was rudimentary. Still, both the woman who came to the door at one of the upstairs apartments with toddlers clinging to her legs and the old man downstairs shook their heads at the name.

"No sé nadie con este nombre."

The owner of the auto body shop where he'd stolen the car remembered him without fondness.

"I don't know why he got off so goddamn easy. He didn't just steal the car, he wrecked it! He wasn't any prize anyway. Bad attitude." In response to her question, he said, "Friends? He didn't have any." His eyes narrowed. "What do you care about him, anyway? Isn't he in jail?"

"I'm actually looking for a man Mendoza hung out with back then," Trina lied. "Unfortunately, we don't know his name."

"Yeah?" He shrugged. "Good luck."

What she needed, Trina decided, was to send one of the department's two Latino officers out to talk to guys in Mendoza's age range. He had to have had friends. Everyone did.

She gave up for the day, deciding to stock up on groceries. The morning news had promised a snowstorm. Unpacking them at home, she listened to phone messages. The first was from her sister, drunk as always.

Voice slurred, she said, "I could use a little help. You know. Just enough to cover the rent this month. I got a job. I mean, I know he's going to call me. Once I start, I can pay you back." A moment of silence. "I always say that, don't I? But someday I will. I promise, Trina. So, what do you say?" Beep.

"Hey." This was Sandy Kilts. "Want to have dinner or something? I'm working on a story about why the state has dragged its feet about widening the highway between Elk Springs and Bend. Bo-ring. Save me."

Trina liked Sandy and was pretty sure the friendship was genuine. Nonetheless, she had noticed that Sandy was calling way more often since Amy Owen's murder. She guessed it was natural for Sandy to hope that being good friends with the investigating officer would earn her an exclusive. Since Trina didn't intend to give one anytime soon, she deleted that message and ignored the phone when it rang later in the evening.

She made herself watch TV for an hour while she ate a microwaved dinner. Normal people didn't look at autopsy photos while they dined. She occasionally appalled even herself when she did stuff like that.

But after she cleaned up her few dishes, she sat down at the table and spread out Gillian Pappas's autopsy report and the photos taken by the pathologist's assistant. After straining her eyes for too long, she admitted defeat—there really wasn't a clear impression of teeth. The killer had ripped her breast. Bruises around the perimeter were too diffuse.

In contrast, they did have one really good cast of a bite on Amy Owen's breast. If only they could have compared a bite impression from both victims. Or, better yet, had a suspect to match it to…

She sighed and replaced photos and report in her bag. She fell asleep that night with macabre images of rended flesh floating before her closed eyes.

SHE WOKE ABRUPTLY in the dark. Disoriented, she stared at the amber numbers on her clock, trying to make sense of them—5:54.

The phone rang, and she realized that's what had awakened her. Fumbling on the bedside stand, she found it by the fourth ring.

"Hello?"

"This Trina?"

The voice was male and familiar. Her head had begun to clear. Dave Berman and she had partnered on patrol for a year.

"Dave?"

"Yeah. Listen. You're on that Amy Owen murder, right?" He didn't wait for agreement. "I've got something here you'd better see."

Her stomach clenched. "A body?"

"Yeah. A blonde, strangled with a jockstrap."

She turned on her bedside lamp and put her feet on the floor. "Where?"

"You know those new houses being built on Crescent Ridge? One of them was torched. When firefighters got there, they found the body."

"Burned?" She was half-dressed, the phone held between ear and shoulder.

"Nope. Laid out in the driveway."

"He wanted to make sure she was found." Her toenail snagged as she tried to tug on a sock. "Okay. I'm on my way. Thanks for calling me, Dave."

"You're welcome."

She finished getting dressed, then looked up Lieutenant Patton's home phone number and dialed it.

The man who answered on the first ring sounded wide-awake and as if he expected a call. "McNeil."

"May I speak to Lieutenant Patton?" Trina asked.

"Meg? She's still asleep. Is it important?"

"Yes, this is Detective Giallombardo. We've been working a murder. There's been another one."

"Oh, God. Hold on."

Maybe a minute later, the lieutenant came on. "Another murder?"

Trina told her what Dave Berman had said.

"That was fast. No six-year intervals anymore." A muffled thump was followed by, "I'll see you there."

Bundled up and carrying an insulated mug of instant coffee, Trina stepped outside into a winter wonderland. Dawn had grudgingly lightened the sky. Snow must have fallen all night long. For once, the meteorologists were right. A good six inches blanketed cars, street, rooftops. An SUV passed on the street, chains clanking, making her realize how quiet it was out here otherwise.

The cold stung Trina's face. Thank God, covered parking for all tenants meant all she had to scrape from her windshield was ice. The driver's side door opened with the snap of an arctic floe splitting. Why, when she didn't want to ski, did she live somewhere with such a crappy climate? she wondered for the nine hundred and seventy-fifth time.

Backing out, she started carefully down the street, following the tracks of the few vehicles that had gone ahead of her.

She'd never had to handle a crime scene enveloped in new-fallen snow. Snow that still fell, if only in gentle, scattered flakes. They'd be able to get a good idea how long the body had been left out, she thought, but footprints, tireprints, almost any other trace evidence would have been obliterated.

It took her half an hour to make a drive that would have taken ten minutes on most days. As early as it was, she found herself in a line of other vehicles heading up the mountain loop highway toward Juanita Butte, most sporting racks of skis and snowboards. Between the falling snow and the splatter from the tires of the Subaru in front of her, visibility was darn near zero even with her wipers going full bore. She might have missed the new road altogether in the all-white landscape if it hadn't been for the column of smoke rising above treetops and the tracks leading into the new development. The sign announcing Crescent Ridge had been buried in snow.

Many of the lots were still empty. The houses that had been built were hulking big, expensive ones with steep-pitched roofs. From what she'd heard, none were completed yet, which meant no residents. What a place to dump a body.

The road climbed a quarter of a mile up a ridge she knew was formed by a spine of old lava before the first roof came in sight. She crawled around a bend to see two fire trucks in front of that first house. Over the top of the truck she glimpsed oily black smoke and an arc of water from a hose. Probably freezing by the time it hit the fire.

Beyond the trucks, parked on the side of the road, were a red Fire Marshal's four-by-four and two Butte County Sheriff's Department Explorers. Trina was chagrined to realize that one was Lieutenant Patton's.

She parked at the end of the line and stepped out into snow even deeper than they'd had at a lower elevation in town. It wasn't like slogging through wet snow, though; this was dry and virtually weightless, an airy dream for skiers. Unfortunately, powder snow fell only at bitterly cold temperatures. Part of her was focused with a cop's instinct on what lay ahead, but, already cold, she worried about how they'd stand out here for hours.

A cluster of Ponderosa pines and the row of vehicles briefly blocked her view of the driveway. All she could see was the house, a beauty built of logs with a metal roof and a huge stone chimney. But she forgot it the moment she cut in front of one of the Explorers.

The body lay spread-eagled in a bed of snow, perfectly lined up with the garage. As much as an inch more of snow had fallen since the victim had been left, dusting her with a pale film. Her flesh was bluish-white beneath the snow, but for crystallized blood on her chest and throat. The white jockstrap engulfing her face made Trina think of the faceless killers in horror movies.

Lieutenant Patton separated herself from the cluster of police officers and firefighters standing beside one of the fire trucks. Dave Berman lifted a hand and Trina nodded in return.

Joining Trina, the lieutenant greeted her. "I've sent for a crew. They're supposed to bring a canopy of some kind."

"I was trying to figure out how we'd keep her from getting buried." Unexpectedly, bile rose in her throat. She swallowed. "Buried too soon, anyway."

The lieutenant didn't seem to notice Trina's rookie moment. She was staring toward the body. "Have you ever met my adopted daughter, Emily? Her mother's body was found dumped near one of the trailheads a few miles up the road, just about this time of year. Worst kind of crime scene."

Trina had heard the story about the baby left in the

Juanita Butte ski area parking lot after everyone had gone for the night. Scott McNeil, the general manager, had almost decided to bed down at the lodge, as he sometimes did, but instead headed out into a frigid night and found her buckled in her car seat, set on the icy parking lot next to his SUV. She'd have been dead long before morning if he hadn't come out. Everybody's guess was that Emily's mother had persuaded her killer to leave the baby in hopes she at least would survive. Scott and Meg Patton, the lead on the case, had ended up getting married and adopting little Emily.

"Our guy left footprints all over," Trina observed. Her breath hung in a frosty cloud before her.

"Yeah, we might get lucky. We can do a cast of them, if somebody gets here quick enough."

With snow filling them, Trina couldn't imagine that the cast would be able to show much detail. A general shoe size, maybe. Powder snow wouldn't compress well enough to hold an impression, either, she suspected. But she could be wrong; she'd seen evidence techs accomplish miracles.

The footprints headed toward the front of the house. The bay window was shattered, and the interior a hell of roiling black smoke. Firefighters maneuvered hoses and trampled around the side of the house, trying to avoid destroying those original tracks. Their voices rang out as they called instructions to each other and the engine of one of the two trucks still rumbled.

"Gasoline," a voice behind Trina said.

Trina turned.

"Have you met my sister?" the lieutenant asked. "Abby Patton. She's Ben's wife."

Trina had seen her from a distance. She and Meg Patton looked startlingly alike, but Abby was the beautiful one, with vivid blue eyes and wheat-blond hair. The red cheeks and nose that made Trina suspect she looked like Rudolph instead added vivid color to Abby's face. The youngest of the Patton sisters, she was married to Ben Shea, the second in command in the Major Crimes unit and the sexiest man Trina had ever seen except for Will. She was also one of only two arson investigators in the county.

"Abby, Trina Giallombardo."

"Marshal…"

She shook her head. "Just Abby, please."

"He threw something through the front window," the lieutenant observed.

"Maybe an open can of gasoline. If so, we'll find it." Abby pushed out her lower lip while she thought. "Risky. The air would have been full of gas fumes by the time he tossed in a firebrand."

"It looks like he did run," Trina pointed out. Damn it, she was shivering. Her body didn't seem to want to stop. "His footsteps are way farther apart coming back than they were going."

Meg Patton looked more closely. "You're right. I hadn't noticed."

Abby made a humming sound in her throat. "I'm guessing he tossed something that didn't spark for a moment. Or the fire was enclosed, say inside a box. The fumes wouldn't hit it as quickly."

"But he must have stayed to be sure the fire took. He wouldn't have wanted it to fizzle."

"You know how quick it goes up when gasoline is involved."

"Which means, the minute he saw flames he'd want to skedaddle."

They all looked, as if in concert, toward the body.

Trina, for one, had been trying *not* to look since her first, appalled examination. Somehow it bothered her that they were standing around coolly discussing the mechanics of committing the crime without having even uncovered the victim's face first, found out who she was. She knew they couldn't until photographs were taken, permanently recording the positioning of the body and the footprints and drag marks made in the snow around it. Accepting the necessity didn't come easily.

What if she knew this victim, too?

"So he laid her out first." The lieutenant stomped her feet, presumably to restore feeling to toes going numb. "He must have come prepared to set a fire."

"He picked this place because he knew it was deserted," Abby agreed. "He could take his time with the body, then torch the house and bring the troops running."

"Otherwise, it could have been weeks before she was found, depending on when contractors got back up here to work on the houses." Trina drew her chin inside the collar of her coat and blinked when a snowflake clung to her lashes. "And he didn't want that."

Lieutenant Patton nodded. "So he killed her because he gets pleasure from it, maybe *needs* to kill. But there's more to this."

"He likes the publicity," Abby suggested.

"Maybe." But the lieutenant wasn't convinced by the theory any more than Trina was. "Hey!" she yelled suddenly. "Watch where you're going!"

A firefighter advancing toward the front window with an ax retreated.

It was true that most serial killers liked to read about their crime in the newspaper. But that didn't mean they went to elaborate lengths to be sure the body was found immediately. Thinking aloud, Trina said, "He wants us to know he's the one who killed Gillian Pappas. Not Mendoza."

Abby shot her a startled glance.

Meg Patton didn't seem to notice. "Then why wasn't he killing women while the trial went on? Or right afterward, so we'd look like fools?"

"He was in jail for something else." She could go by rote through the possibilities. "He was scared by what he'd done. Joined the army and was off in Afghanistan."

"Or he was satisfied," the lieutenant said. "The act was complete in and of itself. Then. But something has happened since to sting his pride. Or trigger his rage."

"Whoa!" Abby ordered, holding up a gloved hand. "Did I miss something? You two are seriously considering the possibility that the wrong man was convicted?"

"We have to." Meg Patton narrowed her eyes. "But it's one possibility we're keeping to ourselves for now. Understand?"

With the same hand, her sister snapped a salute. "Yes, ma'am. Lieutenant, ma'am."

"Behave yourself."

"Wouldn't know how to do otherwise," Abby said, only semiseriously.

"Damn it," her sister growled, "I'd like to get to that body."

Trina glanced toward the road, where a convoy of black sheriff's department vehicles crept up the steep curving street. "Here they are. Isn't that Ron behind the wheel?"

The lieutenant grunted. "Where's the coroner?"

"It'll take a while to get pictures." Unfortunately. Trina tried wriggling her toes and wasn't sure if they were still there. She kept flexing her fingers and tucking her face down inside the collar of her parka like a turtle retreating.

The department's star evidence techs, Ron Niemi and Sheila King, were wizards, according to about anyone Trina had asked who'd been on the job for long. They didn't just know their stuff, they were creative.

Both were in their thirties and were divorced. Rumor had it they had something going, even though Sheila at a skinny six feet tall towered inches above pudgy Ron. Watching them work, their concentration intense, Trina imagined them in bed together excitedly discussing immunoblot assays for blood or how best to draw out usable prints from textured surfaces. Not the kind of thing a normal spouse or lover would want to talk about.

They'd brought several canopies. Crew readied them to set up, easier said than done with clumsy gloved hands, while Sheila took dozens of photographs of the body, footprints, house and shattered window. Trina felt herself turning into a block of ice.

"No tire tracks," Sheila complained.

A fire captain turned. "Goddamn it, we were responding to a fire, not a murder! We didn't see the body until too late."

"Yeah, yeah." She flipped a hand at him. "Okay, let's get those canopies set up. Crap, I wish it would quit snowing."

If anything, the snow was coming down harder, spreading a white veil over the vehicles parked alongside the road and over the body. Trina thought of all the skiers heading up to the mountain, anticipating fresh powder, maybe idly noticing the smoke and wondering in passing whether someone had knocked over a space heater or whether a wire had shorted. Fresh-fallen snow had a purity that made more hideous the body it was trying to disguise.

The medical examiner's van joined the lineup and Sanchez hurried to them, looking unhappy, only his eyes and nose showing between a wool hat and the collar of a bulky parka. "Won't be able to tell you much under these conditions," he announced. "But let's get it over with."

He was right; he had nothing to say they hadn't already heard two weeks ago, when he gave Amy Owen's body a first, superficial examination.

"Can't have been out here much over an hour, hour and a half, given how much snow has fallen. She's been dead longer than that, but not by much. Look, there's still flexibility." He moved an arm.

Everyone present winced.

"With her damn near frozen, I can't give you a good estimate. Couple hours ago, tops." He shrugged. "Depends on whether the body has been outside the whole time. Damn it, I'm looking forward to summer."

They all stood in a circle around the victim, just under the edge of a bright blue canopy.

"Let's take a look and see who she is," Lieutenant Patton said. But neither she nor anyone else moved for a moment, as if they were all reluctant to know.

With long blond hair and her face covered, the victim could have been Meg or Abby Patton. Trina wondered if the two women were conscious of the resemblance.

The lieutenant finally crouched beside the body, pulling off her warm gloves to put on latex ones. Trina hovered behind her, while the coroner remained on the other side.

The cup of the jockstrap was frozen in place. It cracked as Lieutenant Patton tried to pull it to one side with fingers that were obviously stiff with cold. She muttered a few choice words and finally wrenched it to one side.

Trina wasn't the only one who sucked in a breath.

Tiny hemorrhages from the strangulation disfigured a face frozen in a rictus of terror and desperation.

"I've seen her," Trina said.

"Damn, damn, damn." The lieutenant lurched back. "I talked to her two days after the Owen murder. She's a friend of the other victim's. Karin Kristensen."

With a sick sense of inevitability, Trina said, "Isn't she the one whose phone number you got from Will?"

Meg Patton breathed an obscenity. "You mean, the one he dated."

"This is a small town. That doesn't have to mean anything."

They all stared at the ghastly, frozen face of a woman who had died in torment.

"Or," the lieutenant said, voice quiet, hollow, "it could mean everything."

CHAPTER NINE

"UH-HUH." Phone tucked between shoulder and ear, chair leaned back, Will listened to an attorney explaining why his client should get a deal that included no prison time.

"He suffers from the disease of alcoholism," the defense attorney said, voice rich with sympathy. "We all know that. What's important is that he get treatment. Sixty days in jail isn't going to have any impact on whether he'll reoffend. Thirty days in treatment might."

Rather mildly, Will remarked, "The thirty days of treatment court-ordered the last time he got arrested for a DUI didn't seem to work. Here he was, drunk driving only six weeks later."

The attorney had an explanation for that. A party his client had to attend, his struggle with all that alcohol around him, a designated driver who left early. Blah, blah, blah.

Listening with only half an ear, Will rummaged for a particular file, then flipped it open and started scanning a police report on a case of cattle rustling. Not something you saw in Portland.

Someone knocked on his door. He swiveled in his chair and waved Louis Fein in.

Not liking the expression on his boss's face, he said into the phone, "Listen, I'll have to get back to you. But my gut feeling is that your client needs to go to jail. We've been lenient twice. Third time's the charm." He hung up. "You don't look like you have good news."

Expression grim, Fein sat down. "I just got a call from your mother. There's been another murder like Amy Owen's."

Somehow he'd known it would happen. But he had failed to prepare himself. A sick feeling of dread spread from Will's chest to his stomach and upward to his throat. "Who? Have they identified her yet?"

Fein watched him with grave eyes. "A Karin Kristensen. Your mother said you knew her."

His first thought, absurdly, was, *Oh yeah, that's her last name.* He didn't know why he hadn't been able to remember it.

With the crushing impact of a rear-end collision, that first trivial thought was obliterated. Images flashed before his eyes, white elastic embedded in a slender neck, small breast ripped by teeth more savage than any wild animal's, eyes speckled with burst blood vessels and glazed in a stare of horror. *Gillian.* He didn't want to see these other bodies, but God how he wished he could put a different face on the hideous images he would never forget.

"God," he said hoarsely. "I dated her."

"Your mother asked me to tell you that she's going to need to talk to you. She said she'd stop by your apartment later. Maybe evening. Will, you need to go home?"

"She—Karin—wasn't…wasn't my girlfriend."

"She was a friend. Go."

"Yeah. Okay." With shaking hands, he shoved files in his briefcase. He had to do something today. Distract himself, or he'd go crazy.

He'd have walked out without his coat or gloves if

Fein hadn't thrust them at him. He blundered out the front door past another assistant D.A. escorting a big family group in. They turned to stare after him. His expression must have been terrible.

Somehow he got his 4Runner started and pulled into the snow-covered street without hitting anyone.

Karin. It was only four days ago that he'd sat in the same booth with her at J.R.'s. *God.* Were she and Gavin dating? Should he call Gavin? But what if Fein was wrong? Or his mother was wrong? What if it wasn't Karin?

He realized he was gasping for breath, his fingers flexing on the steering wheel. *Let it be somebody else,* he prayed. *Someone I don't know.*

As if that would be any better. As if this imaginary woman he didn't know wouldn't have parents, sisters, brothers, lovers, friends, whose lives would be shattered by the words, "I'm sorry to have to tell you..."

He surfaced to realize he wasn't on his way to his apartment. He was crossing the Deschutes River on a concrete bridge built by the WPA in the late thirties. The house where his mother had grown up was only a few blocks east. The house where her father, the Elk Springs police chief, had abused and terrorized his three daughters after their mother abandoned them. His mother and Aunt Renee spoke of him with revulsion and maybe still fear resonating in their voices. Everything they had become had to do with Ed Patton. All the choices they made. Most of all, because they were determined not to be like him, even though all had followed in his footsteps by going into law enforcement.

The irony of Gillian dying here, blocks from the house Ed Patton had ruled with cruelty, had seemed especially bitter. Will had believed—God, he'd believed—that she wouldn't have died if it weren't for that endless fight with a ghost. If his mother hadn't showed mercy where mercy wasn't deserved... But what if it had been? What if Ricky Mendoza had been working hard to deserve Meg Patton's trust when he pulled out of that dark parking lot, fully believing Gillian was safe, getting in her car, going home to throw what she'd done in the face of her boyfriend?

Will risked getting his 4Runner stuck in snow by pulling into the unplowed parking lot for the small city park that nestled here on the Deschutes, south of the bridge.

In summer, it was green, lawn kept irrigated and manicured by city workers so that it remained plush and rich, emerald-green even in the heat of August. Weeping willows, down close to the bank, long sighing branches creating shadowy caverns within, perfect places for children to dream or teenage boys to make out with their girlfriends. He could close his eyes and smell the new-mown grass, hear the murmur of the river, running low in late summer, the muffled voices of kids splashing in the shallows under mothers' watchful eyes, see the shifting shades of a thousand colors of green as a breeze stirred the veil of branches.

On a cool spring night, it was the perfect place to leave a body, deep in the shadows beneath a willow.

Today, shrubs and trees were bare of leaves, branches black or gray. Snow laid an untouched white carpet down to the ice that glazed all but the deepest channel. It mounded like whipping cream on rocks in the river, puffs here and there, white against gray and black. Even the houses on the other side of the river were colorless today, as if the cold and the snow still falling had changed the film to black and white.

Will sat behind the wheel, engine and heater running, and looked at the tree under which Gillian's naked body had been found, her face smothered in the goddamn cup of a jockstrap. The idea revolted him still. It was a last horrific insult, for the killer to metaphorically shove her face in his crotch.

Now Amy and Karin, too. Why? *Why?* Did their deaths have anything to do with his decision to come home to Elk Springs? If so—he gripped the steering wheel so hard it creaked and his knuckles burned—if so, he would leave. He'd never come back.

The tires spun as he put the 4Runner in gear and stepped too hard on the gas. Maybe he should go *now*. Throw his stuff in a suitcase and just drive. Never look back. Maybe in seeking peace, a return to a time before he was consumed with rage and grief, he had brought down vengeance from on high. Maybe he was *meant* to suffer.

More selfishness. No God would rain unspeakable torment onto two innocent women only to teach him a lesson.

Shaking, he took his foot from the gas. His breath rasped. A minute passed. Two. Three. Finally he was able to drive out of the deep snow onto the street and start back the way he'd come.

He made it home without incident, dropping his briefcase on the table, his wool coat over the back of a chair. Using his cell phone, he called Travis. Got his voice mail.

"There's been another murder. I'm home. Call me."

The phone rang not ten minutes later. He picked up his cell phone before realizing it was the one hanging on the wall that was ringing.

"Patton."

"Damn it, Will." Travis's voice was ragged. "Who?"

"Karin Kristensen. Mom left me a message at the office this morning. I don't know anything else yet, except that her murder was like Amy Owen's."

"And like Gillian's," his friend said softly.

He bowed his head, squeezed his eyes shut. "Yeah. Like Gillian's."

"Karin." Travis said her name with quiet disbelief. "We just saw her."

How could she be dead? Will shared that incredulity. He could hear the timbre of her voice, her laugh, see the sway of her hips as she walked ahead of him through the crowded room. Her face was vivid in his mind.

"She seemed like a really nice woman." Will slumped onto the couch and shoved his fingers into his hair. "Marcie can sometimes be irritating. Bronwen a bitch. Why not one of them?"

"Because they aren't blond. Karin looked one hell of a lot like Amy."

"And Gilly."

"He either likes the type, or he chose Karin and Amy because they looked like Gillian."

Will swore.

Travis cleared his throat. "Buddy, has it occurred to you that one of the few things all three had in common was you?"

Anguish welled in him, choked his voice. "I took Karin out twice. Goddamn it! Twice. Amy a few times ten years ago. How can that mean anything?"

"Maybe it doesn't," his friend said heavily. "But Elk Springs is filled with beautiful blondes, most of whom you've never met. Especially at this time of year."

"But out-of-towners don't come alone," he argued, because he didn't want Travis to be right, that the killer targeted these two women in particular. "They leave bars in couples, or with a pack of friends. They'd be harder to snatch."

"I'm not necessarily talking about out-of-towners. What about all the women who work the lifts at Juanita Butte? Teach skiing? Wait tables? Think about J.R.'s alone—half the waitresses are hot blondes. Why hasn't one of them been killed? Why only women you knew?"

"You knew all of them, too."

"Sure I did. I dated Amy and Karin both, too." He paused. "But not Gillian. That's why I keep thinking this has something to do with you."

"Maybe I killed them," Will said harshly. "Is that what you're suggesting?"

"You know it isn't."

"Then what?" Suddenly, he was yelling. "God-damn it, *what?*"

"I don't know!" Travis yelled back. "You think if I knew I wouldn't say?"

Will yanked on his hair hard enough to hurt. "No. God. I'm sorry, Travis."

"You want me to come over?"

"No. Were you painting when I called? No," he said again. "We might as well both get some work done."

"You'll let me know if you hear anything?"

He agreed and hung up. For the longest time, he just sat there, feeling exhausted, baffled and helpless. He couldn't *do* anything. And he hated that feeling.

Will had always known what he wanted out of life, and he wasn't given to waiting patiently for it to come to him. When he and his mom first moved back to Elk Springs, she kept chickening out of going to his father and saying, "Guess what? I never mentioned being pregnant, but, well, we have this kid together, and he wants to meet you." Not easy to say. As an adult, he could see that. As a fourteen-year-old kid, he'd decided to quit waiting for her to make the first move and made it himself.

He could still remember the expression on Jack Murray's face when without warning he came face-to-face with a teenage boy who could only be his son. Photos of the two of them taken at the same ages could have been of either.

But it turned out okay. Another week, two weeks, however long Will's mother would have dragged her feet, wouldn't have lessened the shock any for Will's dad.

Will had been a hard-driving basketball player, all-state in high school and a starting forward in college. In class, he led discussions, played the devil's advocate, challenged teachers. Since passing the bar, he'd been decisive and aggressive on the job. He didn't wait for opportunities; he seized them.

But this—this, he had no way of combating. He didn't even know that these murders had anything to do with him! Maybe speculating that they did was pure egoism. What could be more self-centered than to believe that, if there was an enemy, it had to be his?

Because no one else counted in this universe?

Eventually, as the day went on, he sat down at the table with his files spread out. He worked on an opening for a negligent homicide trial he'd inherited from his predecessor, looked over notes in preparation for a meeting with a victim's parents the next day, and even made a couple of calls. Maybe half an hour of work that took him all day. But his concentration was fragmented, shattered into glittering, razor-edged shards spread far and wide. Past gluing together. Easy to cut himself on.

Travis called in the late afternoon, but their conversation was brief.

"I haven't heard anything."

"Call me when you do."

Shortly afterward, other friends started calling. Jody Cox was the first.

"Have you heard?" Her voice was high, tremulous, on the verge of hysteria. "Amy's murder was awful! But now Karin, too? Will, I'm scared!"

He couldn't honestly tell her not to be. Jody was blond. "Dye your hair" didn't seem like comforting advice. And would it matter? Did the victim have to be blond when the murder happened, or did it only matter that the killer knew she was?

"We're all pretty shaken up," he said. "But Jody, if I were you I wouldn't go anywhere without a girlfriend. Or two or three."

"But wouldn't I be safer with a guy?" Her breath hitched. "You mean…"

"I mean, we don't know who's doing this. It may be coincidence that Amy and Karin were friends. But the guy who killed them may be someone they both knew."

"Someone *I* know," she whispered.

"Just…don't date. Don't trust anyone."

"The police will find him. Won't they?"

"Sure they will. But every woman in this town needs to be damn careful until this maniac is locked up."

Two minutes after he hung up from talking to her, the phone rang again. Gavin.

"Hey, you heard?"

"Yeah, I almost called you. But I was still hoping they might have been wrong when they IDed her."

"That girl we knew in high school came to talk to me. The one who's a cop now." He sounded upset.

"Trina Giallombardo?"

"Yeah, her. Why'd she come running to talk to me?

I wasn't that good a friends with Karin. Have they been pounding on *your* door? You dated her!"

"A couple of times," Will said. "I thought you and she had hooked up since then."

His voice rose. "Did you tell them that? Is that why they acted like I was some kind of suspect?"

"They haven't talked to me yet. And you shouldn't assume you're a suspect because they asked you questions. Any time there's a murder, the investigators interview everyone who's spent time with the victim in the recent past. You know that."

"Yeah, sure," Gavin muttered. "There was just something about the way she looked at me. It got to me. I mean, she tells me a friend has been murdered, and I'm not supposed to be upset? Instead I'm having to explain to her where I was last night?"

"Had you seen Karin since Saturday night?"

"No! She and I were both at J.R.'s early Saturday. We had a drink together. We were hitting it off, but I hadn't even gotten around to calling her to see if she wanted to take it any further. I though of calling her last night, but I'd rented a couple of DVDs, kicked back and never got around to it."

"Did they tell you any more about her murder?" Will asked. "I don't know anything. Just that they found her body."

"It was dumped in front of a house that was being built at some new development. A fire started in this unoccupied house, and when the fire truck arrived they saw the body. I guess she was frozen, so they think she was killed the night before."

"They haven't figured out where she was snatched, then?"

"What makes you think they'd tell me?" Gavin

asked, with that edge in his voice. "You're the one who'll get the goods. Tell me when you find out any more, will you?"

Will thought about denying once again that he had any in, but they both knew it wasn't the truth. His mother probably *would* tell him what she'd learned so far when she came by.

Knowing she rarely got a decent meal in the first days after a murder when she was the investigator, Will decided to put together dinner. It would give him something to do. He actually liked to cook. He'd taken over doing a lot of the cooking when he was in high school. Scott worked really long hours up at the ski area from first snowfall through April, and once Will's mother got promoted into Major Crimes, her hours got worse, too. Will had opened the first cookbook in self-defense, but he'd discovered he had a knack for making food taste good. He started tweaking recipes, even making up his own. These days, he cooked because he enjoyed it, because moving around in the kitchen, dicing, measuring, stirring, relaxed him.

Today he couldn't get too fancy since his kitchen was still minimally equipped. But he made a hell of a spaghetti sauce, if he did say so. Already opening the refrigerator, he decided to add meatballs.

He sauteed onions and garlic, lamented the lack of fresh tomatoes and chopped canned ones. He dumped burgundy in with a free hand, diced green pepper, spiced. By the time he'd defrosted ground pork in the microwave, his phone had rung three more times.

Bronwen Fessler contained her fear better than Jody did, but she felt it. "I'm afraid to even close the store by myself," she said. "If this wasn't my busy season, I'd take a vacation. A long one."

Like everyone else, Jimmy McCartin was sure Will

would know every gory detail and was disappointed that he didn't. "You know, that house may get away if you don't make up your mind," he said at the end.

"I've made up my mind," Will said from between clenched teeth, and hit End.

Vince Baker sounded as if he'd called at his wife's urging, under the belief that Will would know more than everyone else did.

"Carlos—her brother—is a firefighter. He called her this morning, and she's been on the phone all day. It's all anyone can think about."

Will shaped a meatball and set it on waxed paper. He kept on eye on the small TV on the kitchen counter, because the local news was coming after a commercial break. The sound was muted, but he was ready to turn it back up once the pair of newscasters started talking about the murder.

"The women are scared," he said.

"They should be." In Vince's voice Will heard an echo of his own sense of helplessness and shock. "You know, Karin was crocheting a baby blanket for us. I don't think she and Maria are even that close, but she said she loved to do handwork. It was…" he faltered "…it was yellow, because we don't know whether we're having a boy or a girl."

Will was momentarily taken aback by the image of the sleek beauty he knew sitting on a couch with her feet tucked under her, crocheting. Dreaming, maybe, about the booties and caps and crib blankets she would someday make for her own baby.

He looked down to see that he'd squeezed the meat mixture in his hand so hard, it was oozing between his fingers. He opened them and scraped the mess off on the side of the bowl.

"Hey," Vince said. "Turn on the news. They're talking about the murder."

With his elbow, Will hit the volume button on the remote.

"...the shocking discovery of another young woman, brutally raped and murdered." The broadcaster wasn't any older than Karin had been, a pretty blonde as well. Her tone was breathless, avid. "A source tells us she had apparently been strangled by the elastic waistband of a jockstrap. Police refuse to confirm whether Amy Owen, murdered just two weeks ago, was also strangled with a jockstrap."

Shit. His mother would be furious to find out that kind of detail had been leaked. One of the firefighters must have talked.

He said a hasty goodbye to Vince and hung up as the image onscreen shifted to yellow crime scene tape stretched across several sawhorses blocking the snowy expanse of what was probably a street, judging by the tire tracks. Will tried to figure out whether the development was one he'd seen, but the snow hid any identifying landmarks. A black Butte County Sheriff's Department Explorer was parked just on the other side of the blockade. The uniformed deputy standing in the falling snow said, "I can't comment until the investigator has released a statement."

They'd already dug up some backstory on Karin—she'd grown up in Boise, Idaho, where her grieving parents still lived. She worked in the assessor's office and had gone to Elk Springs, according to a brother who briefly appeared on the porch of a modest brick ranch style house, because she loved to ski.

Her family must be thinking, if she'd gone to Sun Valley, Idaho, or Vail, Colorado, she'd still be alive.

If she'd gone to Bend, Oregon, just up Highway 20, she'd be alive. She'd never have met Amy Owen or Will Patton.

Her bad luck.

He swore and turned the TV off when the newscasters started talking about a three-car accident with a fatality south toward Medford.

Thanks to somebody's big mouth, people would soon make the connection between Karin's murder and Gillian's. Not many women were strangled with a goddamn jockstrap.

Then, damn the consequences, the investigation would have to be widened to include the case long since closed. Ricardo Mendoza would be getting exactly what he wanted.

Will stared unseeing down at the half dozen meatballs he'd already formed and the bowl of spicy ground meat.

But how could a man who'd been in the state penitentiary for five and a half years possibly have arranged for a crime so brutal, so personal, to be committed?

The wrenching anguish in his chest was answer enough. Mendoza hadn't. Couldn't.

Which meant that everything Will had believed for six bleak years wasn't true. Gillian's murderer was still out there.

And Will knew himself to be a self-righteous son of a bitch who'd hurt people he loved without even the excuse of being right.

He couldn't imagine that saying "I'm sorry" would cut it. Too little, too late.

"THIS MUST BE IT." Meg Patton stared doubtfully up at the dark bulk of the apartment building, distinguished

only from the ones to each side by an artfully illuminated letter C on the facade.

"There's visitor parking." Trina pointed ahead.

The lieutenant nodded and pulled into the slot. She
turned off the engine, but for a moment didn't move.
Then she said wearily, "All right. Let's go talk to him."

She didn't sound at all like a mother relieved to be
able to see her son after a tough day. She sounded like
she might when she had to knock on a door to tell
someone a loved one was dead. The chore was neces-
sary but terrible.

Trina accompanied her to the second story, where
Lieutenant Patton rang the bell at 203C.

Will opened the door almost immediately. His lean,
rough-hewn face was haggard, his jaw shadowed with
stubble. His brown eyes were bloodshot. He wore dress
slacks and a white shirt but no tie. The collar of his shirt
was unbuttoned, and something red had splattered the
white fabric that even Trina's uneducated eye recognized was expensive.

Alarm quickened the lieutenant's voice. The mother
had reawakened. "Did you hurt yourself? Is that
blood?"

"What?" He stared at her without comprehension,
then glanced down at his shirtfront. "Oh. No. It's spaghetti sauce. I've been cooking."

"You'll never get it out of that fabric," his mother
scolded. "Tomato sauce stains."

He shrugged, and Trina could tell he didn't care.
"Come in. Are you done for the day? Can I get you a
glass of wine? Or would you like coffee?"

"The first sip of wine, and I'd topple over," Meg
Patton admitted. "Do you have some juice?"

His face softened. "You never did like having to live

on fast food and coffee when you were hot on a case, did you?"

"No." She smiled back at him, crookedly. "Good nutrition is important."

"Trina?" He lifted his brows. "Coffee? Juice?"

"Actually…the juice sounds good to me, too. I've had an awful lot of coffee today. In fact…" She hesitated. "May I use your restroom?"

"Second door on the left."

The first door was closed. The one on the other side of the hall was open, allowing her a glimpse of a bedroom that had obviously come furnished with a "rustic" bed and dresser that had probably been made in Bangladesh, so little resemblance did they have to local furniture handmade of peeled Ponderosa pine. Only the duvet, halfheartedly straightened that morning, and the sheets partially exposed looked as if they belonged to Will. The duvet cover was indigo flannel with a bold, scroll pattern in ivory, matched by ivory sheets. A couple of framed photos sat on the dresser top. As much as she itched to take a few steps into his bedroom to see whose photos he kept close, Trina knew it would be inexcusably nosy.

The bathroom was bland but spotlessly clean. An electric razor sat on the counter, but otherwise his toiletries were behind cupboard and medicine cabinet doors. Towels were thick, expensive jacquard in forest-green and cream.

After using the toilet, Trina washed her hands and dried them on one of those luxurious towels. She heard the murmur of voices as she came soundlessly down the hall.

Will's voice, leaden. "He's smarter than all of us, isn't he?"

"No. Careful, sure, but you know we'll get him. It

worries me, though, that there was only two weeks in between murders. That's quick. This guy must be very angry to feel the need to kill again so fast. Usually there's an interlude where the killer feels some satisfaction. But two weeks... He must have started looking for his next victim immediately."

"Or have already chosen her," Will said.

Meg, in an easy chair that faced the hall, saw Trina. "Hey. Come sit down."

Trina hesitated between a rocker that looked uncomfortable and the other end of the couch from where Will sat, finally choosing the couch. He picked up a glass of apple juice from the coffee table and extended it to her. Their fingers brushed as she took it. She sipped to hide her reaction.

Your idol touched you! an internal voice mocked. *Do you plan to swoon?*

Shut up, she told the voice, and absolutely refused to listen when it didn't.

"Detective, will you take notes?" the lieutenant asked, in a voice that had become formal. "Let's find out what Will knows about Karin and her friends before we call it a day."

Out of the corner of her eye, Trina saw him stiffen. She took a drink, then set down the glass and pulled out her spiral notebook and pen.

"I've been getting calls all day." A muscle jerked in his jaw and his tone verged on bellicose. "Everyone I know is scared. The women that they're next, the men that they're suspects."

"What are you saying?" his mother asked.

"Now I feel like a suspect."

"Don't be ridiculous." She frowned at him. "You know better than that."

"It hasn't occurred to you what a sublime coincidence it is that my girlfriend was the first to die, and that her look-alikes are being murdered only now that your prodigal son has returned to Elk Springs?"

"It's occurred to me," she said shortly.

"Do you want to know where I was last night?"

"Will, I know you didn't kill Gilly."

His face contorted briefly, then he scrubbed a hand over it. "I was home alone last night. Not what you wanted to hear, is it?"

"For God's sake!" his mother exploded. "What is this, pity Will day?"

He stared at his mother, who didn't back down. A flush darkened his cheeks. "Yeah," he said in a strange voice. "I guess it is. I've spent the whole goddamn day wondering what *I* did to visit something so horrible on two perfectly nice women. Maybe on three." After a brief internal battle, during which the tic reappeared along his jaw, Will cleared his throat. "Then I examined my monumental arrogance, to think that every tragedy relates somehow to me. The jury is still out on which it is: Will Patton, egoist, or Will Patton, angel of death."

With no apparent sympathy for her son, Lieutenant Patton said crisply, "Angel of death? That sounds like another dollop of arrogance. Will, whether these murders have some tie to you doesn't mean you have *any* responsibility for them!"

"Do you blame me for worrying that I do?"

Worry and weariness on her face, she said, "No. At least this time the body wasn't dumped in any place that has meaning to you. The fact that Amy's body was out by the Triple B was probably just chance."

Suddenly he leaned forward, voice harsh with ur-

gency. "Wait. I heard it was a new development. God.
Tell me it wasn't Crescent Ridge."

Trina and the lieutenant stared at him.

Seeing their faces, he breathed an obscenity.

Meg Patton made a ragged sound. "All right, Will.
What do you have to do with Crescent Ridge?"

CHAPTER TEN

"THANKS TO Jimmy McCartin, everyone I know heard that I'm considering buying a house at Crescent Ridge. I told Jimmy I'm not, the place is too damn big, but he can't find anyplace else to sell to me, so he won't let up about that house."

"Everyone you know," his mother repeated. "Who?"

He ran his hands through his hair, creating wild disorder. "Travis, his artist friend, Bruce Restak, Jody Cox, Gavin Husby, Justin Hill, um, Vince Baker and his wife. Let me think. Nita Voss. Remember her? She was there hanging on Justin. There were people at a couple of nearby tables, too." He reeled off a few more names, which Trina wrote down. "And, you know, any of them could have told anyone. Bronwen Fessler joined the group after Travis and I left."

"That was the night I saw you at J.R.'s," Trina realized.

He gave her a distracted glance. "Yeah. Remember how crowded the place was?"

"So what it amounts to," his mother said flatly, "is that pretty much anyone in Elk Springs could have heard that you were seriously considering buying a house at Crescent Ridge."

"That's about it."

"Was it *that* house?" Trina asked.

The other two looked at her.

"I don't know," Will said. "Which one was it?"

"The first one on the left. A big log house."

He shook his head. "I didn't even look at that one. It was even bigger—damn near five thousand square feet, I think. No, the one Jimmy showed me was at the top of the ridge."

"In other words," the lieutenant said, "our killer knew you were thinking of buying there, but not which house."

His forehead furrowed. "Jimmy didn't say, that night at J.R.'s. We didn't get into details. He just said something like, 'Have you thought any more about that house at Crescent Ridge?' No. Wait." He shook his head, as if trying to clear it. "I think he said something like, 'Have you thought any more about the house?' and someone said, 'What house?' or something like that."

"Who?"

He looked haggard. "I have no idea."

"This can't be chance," the lieutenant said.

He sat up straight and shoved the fingers of both hands into his hair, yanking at it. "I should leave town. This morning, I almost packed up and started driving. If this has something to do with me, it'll stop."

"It might not," Trina said. "He has your attention now. He's going to know you'll hear about every development, whether you're in town or not. How many women here in Elk Springs have you dated? He can keep killing and know that he's getting to you, whether you're here or not."

He muttered a profanity.

"He could follow you, too," his mother said. "Unless you want to change your name and disappear, he could let you get settled somewhere else, maybe start seeing a co-worker, and then kill her."

As if he could no longer contain his anguish, he shot to his feet and prowled the living room, movements jerky and shoulders rigid. "Then what in the hell am I supposed to do?"

"Help us catch him," the lieutenant said. "*Think*, Will. Who could hate you this much?"

He made an inarticulate sound and slammed one hand against the wall, fingers splayed. Both women jumped. "I don't know! Goddamn it, I don't know!"

His mother went to him, wrapping her arms around him. He stood stiffly within her embrace, and after a moment her arms fell away.

Voice soft, she said, "Will, you may not have done anything. This guy's sick. We all know that. But I also believe that, if you think long and hard enough, something he's done will mean something to you. The rape and the way he displays the bodies have to do with how he feels about women. That's unrelated to you. But why the jockstrap? Why is he choosing women that, in his view, you had? Did those three women in particular reject him? Or did you always get the girls and he didn't?"

Will stood silent for a long moment, his eyes closed. Finally, he scrubbed a hand over his face. Sounding lifeless, he said, "Okay." He walked like an automaton to the couch, sat down, braced his elbows on his knees and looked down at his hands. "You already had questions. Ask me what you have to."

It was a moment before his mother followed, looking ten years older than she had an hour ago.

Trina took notes as he answered her questions.

No, he hadn't seen Karin Kristensen since Saturday night, when she had joined his group at J.R.'s Sports Bar. He wasn't aware that she was dating anyone.

"She was with Gavin when I got there." He briefly lifted his head. "But he says they just happened to be the first two to arrive. He was thinking of asking her out. That's all. He's pretty upset."

"We spoke to him already. Somebody else mentioned that he was with her Saturday night."

Will nodded.

"Amy was apparently, ah, fairly relaxed about sex. Everybody agreed that she often went home with a man on a first date. Would Karin have done the same?"

"Is that a subtle way of asking whether I slept with her? The answer is no. I didn't ask. She didn't offer. So I can't tell you."

He didn't know anything they hadn't already heard from friends who had been closer to Karin Kristensen.

Once he looked up, his eyes red. "Vince Baker told me today that Karin was crocheting a blanket for the baby he and his wife are having. I had no idea she was the type to do something like that."

"Jody Cox says that Karin was a homebody. That all she was really looking for was a husband. She liked to ski and enjoyed living here, but always made clear that she was just having a little fun before she settled down." Lieutenant Patton looked down at her own notebook. "She wanted, I quote, kids more than anything."

"God," he said in a strangled voice.

"So, whether intentionally or inadvertently, our UNSUB has now chosen two women who were PTA moms-to-be. Ironic, if he thinks he's punishing loose women."

"Do you have any reason to think that's why he chose them?"

The lieutenant sighed and shut her notebook. "I have no reason to think anything except that he hates women."

"You saw the TV coverage?"

"I heard." Her eyes glittered. "Somebody's head will roll."

"Was she left in the house?"

Lieutenant Patton told him about the fire, the body laid out in the snow in the driveway, and their probably futile attempts to take casts of the footprints. "If the snow had just been wet!"

"Tell that to the skiers."

"Wouldn't you think people would be scared off by the news that a serial murderer is killing young women in Elk Springs? Scott says daily ticket sales are at an all time high." She shook her head. "Go figure."

When it was obvious she was done, he stirred. "I'll bet neither of you have had anything to eat all day, have you? I can have spaghetti on the table in about ten minutes."

Trina's mouth had been watering since they'd walked in the door. She'd assumed that he had already eaten before they came. But if there were leftovers, she could go for them.

The lieutenant's smile glowed. "That's nice of you, Will, but I talked to Scott a little while ago and he's expecting me. He's been cooking, too. But, Trina, you should take him up on it. My son would be a master chef if he hadn't gone to law school."

They were both looking at her. Panic set in. The invitation had included her only because his mother had brought her. Having to make conversation with her over dinner couldn't be what he'd had in mind, especially not in the state he was in. "Oh, I, um, I planned to get something at home."

He lifted a brow. "You mean, you were going to throw something in the microwave?"

"Well…"

His mother rose. "Will, can you run her home? We came together."

He stood, too. "Sure."

She nodded at Trina. "I'll see you in the morning. One of us will have to stand in at the autopsy."

Trina had been dreading her first autopsy, but she might as well get it over with. "I can do that."

The lieutenant smiled. "Bless you. I hate them."

Will shook his head. "What do you expect to learn?"

"Absolutely nothing," Lieutenant Patton admitted. "The tricky thing is time of death. She may have been alive until shortly before she was deposited there. Otherwise her body should have been too stiff to lay out. That's the one thing that's different this time around—he signaled us to come running. That took some planning on his part. It looks like he snatched her last night—we found her car in front of the Timberline. So why didn't he dump her until five o'clock this morning? Did he hold her captive to whet his anticipation? Or did he have to be somewhere else, so he saved her until he was free?"

The idea was creepy—too much like tucking away a goodie from the bakery for a later moment.

"Once Sanchez examines her body closely, we'll have a better idea. If we're really, really lucky, he'll find something to indicate where she was held."

A tiny nub from a carpet caught in her hair would give them something to go on. Right now they had zilch.

Lieutenant Patton said, "Enjoy dinner," and left.

The moment the door closed, Trina said to his back, "I'm sorry. I'm sure this wasn't what you had in mind. It was nice of you to offer, but…"

Turning, he rolled up a cuff. "I'm glad to have your company. Cooking gave me something to do. I wanted to…" He stopped abruptly, furrows forming on his brow. "Oh, hell. Do something for Mom, I guess. But, really, I'm glad you stayed. I've spent the day going crazy, wondering what you'd found, fielding calls from all my friends who assumed I'd know more than they did. Now, after finding out where Karin's body was found…" His shoulders hunched, and he fell silent for a moment. With a visible effort he relaxed and nodded toward the kitchen. "Come and talk to me while I start water to boil."

Following him, she asked, "Haven't you eaten?"

"No." In the small kitchen, he took a large stock pot from a cupboard and turned on the tap. "I wasn't hungry. Cooking relaxes me. And what the hell. I figured I'd have dinners for the next week."

"It smells fantastic."

"Thanks." He ran water into the pot and set it on the stove. "Can I pour you a glass of wine now?"

Was she still on duty? Even sort-of on duty? Trina gave an internal shrug. Maybe a few sips would help her be less nervous.

"Thanks." She sought desperately for a topic of conversation that would be neutral and have nothing to do with the murders. "So," she finally came up with, "do you still play basketball?"

His glance told her he knew what she was trying to do, but he went along with it. "Pickup games." Shrugging, he poured ruby-red wine into two glasses and handed one to her. "I hear there's a league made up of cops and judges and attorneys. Maybe I'll join that."

"Yeah, there's a women's league, too. I'm not much of a basketball player, but I play. It's the one place you can ram an elbow in a judge's stomach and not get slapped with contempt."

His laugh may have been forced, but she had to give him credit for effort. "Hey, I'm sold. Every time somebody pisses me off in court, I can hope they play on an opposing team."

"The league is in the fall, though, so you're too late for this year."

He was deftly chopping vegetables for a salad. Sitting on a stool at the breakfast bar, she watched his hands, large and capable, engaged in such a domestic chore. He had wonderful hands.

Trina felt slightly light-headed. How very strange to be sitting here, in Will Patton's apartment, sipping wine as she watched him put together dinner for the two of them. There was a time she'd have believed she could die happy if only she could have one date with him. And now, here she was.

Not exactly on a date, of course; he'd pretty much gotten stuck with her. Still...

"What's it like?" she heard herself ask. "Being back after so long away?"

For a moment his hands went still. "Weird." His voice was gruff. "Home isn't home anymore. Maybe someday it will be again, but right now I feel like a stranger in a strange land." He resumed chopping a green onion. "Did you leave for college?"

"Yeah, but I always meant to come back when I graduated. Lately I've been wondering why. Cowardice, I suppose." She took a hasty swallow of wine. For Pete's sake, why had she said that?

"Because the familiar seems safe?"

She nodded.

"The truth is, there's nothing more emotionally loaded than our relationships with families and old friends. 'Easy' is dinner with a casual friend who you didn't ditch for a year in middle school because you'd gotten too cool for him. Who in fact didn't know you in middle school. You have plenty to talk about, none of it charged with resentment or regret."

"Or the memory of the time you sneaked out in the middle of the night to go sledding in the dark, or the time your friend admitted to something he didn't do because you'd have been in more trouble than he was."

He gave her a wry smile. "There you go. The problem is, easy isn't always the most fulfilling." He took salad dressing from the refrigerator. "Have you been thinking about leaving Elk Springs behind?"

"Only when it's really cold. I hate cold weather. I don't ski, never learned how, and honestly it doesn't look that appealing to me. I could be a cop in Scottsdale, Arizona, or San Diego."

"In the midst of strangers." He put spaghetti into the boiling water.

"Maybe in the midst of people who look more like me." Oh, God—she really should have said no to the wine.

He studied her with obvious surprise and curiosity. "What do you mean?"

Flushing, she wished she'd kept her mouth shut. What was she doing, fishing for a compliment that wouldn't come? "Every woman around here seems to be a Nordic goddess," she muttered. "And the men are Nordic gods. They all have that ruddy glow skiers seem to get, and they're athletic, and they have gleaming, straight teeth."

"Your teeth aren't crooked."

"I didn't say they were. But you know what I mean. This has turned into a resort town for rich, beautiful people."

To her surprise, he said, "It's true, Elk Springs has

become a mini-Aspen. But spring will come and the beautiful people will disappear."

She sighed. "When? June? My father used to say Elk Springs has a nine-month-long winter and just time left over for summer."

Will gave the first genuine laugh she'd seen from him tonight. "I'm afraid that's about right. Portland had great springs. Lilacs in bloom…"

"And rain pitter-pattering."

"That's pretty much a year-round thing. At least it wasn't cold."

"So why *did* you come back?" Awed at her boldness, she held her breath waiting to see if he closed up the way he had the other time she asked.

He turned off the stove and poured spaghetti and water into a colander in the sink. "You know, I've asked myself that a hundred times. I guess the truth is, I was lonely. I'd made friends, but not the kind who'd lie and get themselves in trouble to save you from deep shit." He switched gears. "Why don't we just dish up in the kitchen?"

"Sure." Trina hopped off the stool and circled the end of the counter. He handed her a plate and, when she extended it, filled it with spaghetti.

"Sauce is on the stove."

When she lifted the lid and breathed in deep, her knees grew weak. For a moment she closed her eyes and just stood there savoring the smell. "Wow. I think I'm getting drunk just breathing in the scent. Your mom's right. Quit the D.A.'s office. Open a restaurant."

"You haven't tasted it yet."

"I don't have to." She swallowed saliva and opened her eyes. "Yes, I do."

He brought the salad and garlic bread she hadn't

even noticed him putting in the oven to the table, then dished up for himself once she'd carried her plate to the small eating nook.

The spaghetti tasted as good as it looked. The meatballs were tender and spicy, the perfect accompaniment. "Your mother was crazy not to stay," Trina declared after the first bite.

"My stepdad is a pretty good cook, too. And they still seem to be madly in love."

"That's nice."

"Yeah, it is. I was jealous as hell when she started dating Scott. I was fourteen and used to having my mother to myself. But I became reconciled. He's a great guy."

"You're lucky. You have the perfect family."

A flash of intense pain twisted his face. After an obvious pause, he said in a tight voice, "Yeah. Unfortunately, I don't seem to have noticed soon enough."

Trina cocked her head. She'd guessed from hints the lieutenant dropped that something was wrong between them. But she couldn't imagine what. "What do you mean?"

"I don't know how long you've worked with Mom, or whether she's told you our history."

Trina shook her head. "I was thrilled when she tagged me for this investigation. Before that, the only time I'd talked to her was when she interviewed me for the promotion."

He seemed to be looking into the past, not really even seeing her. "When she got pregnant with me, Mom left home. She was scared of her father. I guess he beat the crap out of her."

Trina was shocked but not altogether surprised, if that made sense. She'd heard rumors that Elk Springs police chief Ed Patton had been a violent, cold man.

Supposedly he'd dealt horrible deaths to a couple of suspects but had been lauded for keeping his town safe instead of questioned on his brutal methods. She didn't know how true the stories were, but they'd come from enough sources, she assumed they couldn't be completely fictional.

"She didn't want him to know she had a child. So she raised me entirely on her own. She joined the army and became an MP. I was fourteen when she ran into someone by chance and found out her father was dead. That's when she brought me home to Elk Springs."

Trina had tumbled head over heels in love with him right away. He'd been a ninth-grader, she was in seventh. In those days, the middle school had been attached to the high school, which gave an introverted twelve-year-old glimpses of the older kids. She had thought the new boy dark and mysterious. She could close her eyes and see him, a head taller than most kids his age with big hands and huge feet. A lock of dark hair had tended to fall over his forehead and he would shake his head to flip it back. Of course every girl in school had pursued him from the beginning. Trina would have been way too shy to join them even if he'd been a seventh-grader. As it was, she worshipped from afar.

"I remember when you moved here. New kids weren't that common."

He nodded. "Anyway, there I was, fourteen and suddenly I had a big, extended family. Aunts, uncles, cousins. And a father. I really wanted a father, and mine came through for me. He hadn't even known I existed, but he was great."

Hadn't known Will existed? Trina filed away that tidbit to wonder about later.

"Because it was all new to me, I didn't take family for granted the way most kids did. I never went through a stage of not wanting to be seen with my parents."

She wouldn't have been ashamed to be seen with his parents, either. They weren't regular mortals. Like the time his father had exchanged himself as a hostage for a teenage babysitter to save her life, then ended up dramatically killing the kidnapper, rescuing the other hostage and walking out alive.

Her father couldn't get up from his recliner to get himself another beer.

In an odd, faraway voice, Will said, "I guess I thought things would be the same forever. That they would forgive me for mistakes, but I didn't have to do the same. I don't know." He sat in silence for a minute, brooding, before giving himself a shake. "As you've probably gathered, I blew it."

In puzzlement, she said, "But…they obviously still love you. Your mother does, anyway."

"Love is one thing. Liking and trust are another." He lifted the bottle and refilled her wineglass, then added a splash to his. "What about your family? Are they still here in Elk Springs?"

"My father and one brother are. I don't see much of them. My mother died when I was a kid. I had another brother who killed himself driving drunk, and a sister who's in Portland. She and I were allies, the two girls, you know, but…" Trina shrugged. "She's an alcoholic. Mostly I hear from her when she needs money."

His eyes were warm. "That's rough."

"For her. Not me. I mean, I'm doing all right."

"Why did you come back to Elk Springs, then?"

"I guess, like you said, it seemed safest. Besides, believe it or not I grew up wanting to be like your mother and your aunts. Hiring on with the sheriff's department or the Elk Springs PD seemed logical. I remember the first time your mom came to talk at the middle school."

He grimaced. "She talked at the high school assembly the same day. Okay. That was one time I pretended I didn't know her."

"Really?" Amazed, Trina stared at him. She'd sat there on the bleachers, squeezed between classmates, transported from the smelly, restless, noisy crowd of middle-schoolers to imagining herself in a uniform with a badge on her pocket, a gun at her hip and a confident, cool way of staring down insolence and evil alike.

Will laughed again. "No, our last names were the same. I had to admit to a relationship. Fortunately, she didn't say anything embarrassing."

"She's amazing. I still want to be like her."

His expression changed and his voice became harsh. "Did you know I told her she'd as good as murdered Gillian herself? She and my father both? I was angry and cruel and I meant every goddamn word."

Trina gaped at him. "Murdered Gillian?"

"Both of them, but especially my mother, were so determined to see a possibility for redemption in everyone, they gave them chance after chance after chance. Ricky Mendoza had a chip on his shoulder. He walked around just waiting for an excuse to blow his top. Every time he got fired, it was because the boss was out to get him. It never occurred to him that he had such a piss-poor attitude, no one would want him around. He got arrested half a dozen times. He broke one poor son of a bitch's nose. Finally he stole a thirty-thousand-dollar SUV and wrecked it. But guess what? My mom went to bat for him. Got him a light sentence and then a job.

Because she was convinced he'd had a rough childhood and he only needed someone to believe in him. If she hadn't believed in him, he would have been in prison the night Gilly was murdered."

Shocked as much by his acid tone as by the story itself, she said, "You really believed your mother was responsible?"

"And I've kept believing it all these years. I wasn't about to forgive either of my parents." He drained his wineglass, then poured more. His hand shook. "So, are you going to tell me what a bastard I am?"

"I...I wouldn't presume...."

He laughed, not a pleasant sound. "Or maybe you should tell me how richly I deserve my comeuppance, which I'm about to get."

"What do you mean?" Trina asked carefully.

"Even I have a hell of a time imagining Ricky Mendoza conning someone into committing vile rape and murder just to sow enough doubt in the minds of public officials to earn him a pardon." His dark, angry eyes challenged her. "Do *you* think we have two different killers?"

Trina bit her lip, but shook her head.

"Me, either. Mendoza might have ended up committing a crime. Who knows? But if he didn't kill Gilly..."

"Then you hurt your parents without even having the justification of being right that they'd misjudged Ricky Mendoza's potential for violence."

"Exactly." His mouth twisted, the torment on his face painful to see. "Do you want to know why I really moved back to Elk Springs?"

She gave a small nod.

"Because I wanted to forgive them. I wanted them

to forgive me. I had some fantasy of going back to a time before everything went wrong."

She couldn't think of a single thing to say. "Oh."

"Funny, isn't it? I was going to forgive my parents." He gave a jeering laugh. "How goddamn noble of me. You know something else? Today I even briefly had the thought that God is punishing me. As my oh-so-wise mother observed, another piece of arrogance in the guise of remorse. Even I can't believe God visited unspeakable suffering on Amy and Karin just to humble me."

He sounded as if he loathed himself. Pity stirred in Trina, but it was mixed with a shocked awareness that she didn't actually like this man. How could he have said such awful things to his mother? Hadn't it occurred to him that she would be thinking them anyway? That she'd feel horrifying guilt without any help from him? Why, in his grief, had he been so angry he wanted to hurt other people?

When had the charming, confident boy Trina remembered from high school become capable of such rage?

"How could you?" she asked quietly.

CHAPTER ELEVEN

PERHAPS SHE DESERVED for Will to turn on her. Who was she to judge? She'd never lost anyone she loved deeply, and in such a dreadful way. Maybe you *would* be angry, at everyone and everything. Maybe that was natural.

She hoped not.

Eyes dark, mouth still bitter, he said, "So I'm a bastard after all."

"I shouldn't have said that."

He shrugged carelessly. "I asked. And do you want to know the truth? I *feel* like scum. You can't tell me anything I don't know."

None of her business, but... "Have you told your mother how you feel?"

"God, no!" He gave a harsh laugh. "It's a hell of a lot easier to ask for forgiveness after you've bestowed it. Now I find myself the only one in the wrong. Not the same thing at all."

"No," Trina agreed. "Now apologizing requires real humility."

This laugh was more amused. The skin beside his eyes crinkled. "You're right. Unfortunately, humility appears to be a virtue I'm lacking." The amusement vanished. "I'm...working myself up to it. God knows they deserve their pound of flesh."

"Do you think that's what they want?"

She sounded so priggish. And who was she to lecture? She, who despised her father and enabled her sister's alcoholism because the mere idea of cutting her off, too, left a gigantic chasm inside her. Face it, she knew next to nothing about how normal, loving families worked.

"I don't know what they want anymore." Will picked up the wine bottle, then set it back down. "I haven't gotten drunk since the night Gilly died. And here I am, thinking about it."

"From what your mother said, the fact that you were drunk saved you from being a suspect in your girlfriend's murder."

"My being drunk?" He seemed startled.

"You, ah, snored."

He blinked. "That bad?"

"So rumor has it."

"Jeez." He laughed without humor. "Okay. One more reason not to get plastered."

"You don't like feeling out of control?"

"Or like shit in the morning." Naked emotion flared in his eyes. "But most of all, I didn't like knowing that I couldn't have helped Gilly. If she'd somehow gotten away and called, I wouldn't have even heard the phone. I was too drunk, too busy wallowing in self-pity." He shrugged. "I suppose in the end, you're right. I just don't like feeling out of control."

"You're ashamed that you were getting drunk while she was being raped and murdered." His face stiffened; Trina hurried on. "If you can admit that to me, why can't you say 'I'm sorry' to your mother?" Then she realized. "No, silly question. It's not the same, not when you don't really care what I think about you. What was this, a trial run?"

"You're easy to talk to. You know enough to under-

stand the issues, but you're not emotionally invested."
He shook his head. "My apologies."

"No, it's okay," she began awkwardly, but he'd already risen to his feet and was gathering dirty dishes.
"Let me help…"

"No, have some coffee." His tone was cool, pleasant. That of a stranger. "This will only take me a minute."

He brought her a cup of coffee and she presumed was gulping some himself to counteract the wine. Trying to control her inner turmoil, she tried to enjoy coffee that had nothing in common with her usual instant or the crap they brewed at the station. Wouldn't it figure that Will Patton, amateur chef and assistant D.A., served an intense, rich brew, encompassing bitterness as well as subtler flavors?

When he returned from the kitchen, he said, "I'm sure you're wanting to get home."

She finished the coffee and stood. "I'm sorry I have to drag you out."

"I offered."

Her parka still lay on the back of the rocker in the living room. He put on a long wool coat from the closet and leather gloves. Pride kept her from asking to use his bathroom again.

Unlike her complex, his included a garage for each unit. Narrow spots, though. He backed out to let her in.

Like most cops, she hated being a passenger, but Will drove so capably even on the snowy streets that she was able to sit still without her foot wearing out the floorboards and without any impulse to grab the steering wheel.

Snow still fell in slow motion, the ghostly flakes visible mainly in pools of light cast by street lamps. Trina gave brief directions, then sat rigid as he followed them. She kept stealing glances at his profile, which gave away absolutely nothing.

A block from her apartment complex, she said, "That was a wonderful dinner, Will. Thank you."

"You're welcome." He put on the turn signal. "Is that your Explorer?"

"Your mother and I split up some early interviews, then she followed me here so we could double-team on some others."

"Ah." He gently braked behind her Explorer, then turned to look at her. "I'd appreciate it if you wouldn't say anything to my mother about what I told you."

She put her gloved hand on the door latch. "Of course not."

"When I saw you Saturday night at J.R.'s, do you know what I thought?"

Surprised by the change in topic, she shook her head.

"I thought you have a face like a Renaissance Madonna." His voice had a soft burr. "There's more than one kind of beauty, Detective Giallombardo."

"I…thank you," she squeaked.

He dipped his head. "Good night."

She scrambled out, managed a flustered, "Good night," and hurried to her door, aware of his 4Runner hovering until she'd unlocked and slipped inside.

The cynic in her thought, *He was buttering me up. Using that vaunted charm to make me forget what a jerk he really is.*

She took off her coat, hat and gloves, and hurried into the bathroom. She paused momentarily, caught by her image in the mirror. Her nose and cheeks were red, her dark eyes wide and spooked.

A Renaissance Madonna. *Uh-huh.*

Was flirting with women so automatic for him, he couldn't turn it off? Why else would he bother saying something like that to her?

The annoying part was, she couldn't help feeling a flutter under her breastbone. He hadn't *said* she was beautiful, but he'd implied…well, that she might be.

And he hadn't said it earlier, when she'd made that stupid comment about moving to where people were homelier, where she'd fit in. When she'd practically begged for him to deny that she was ugly. Then, she would have discounted his polite rejoinder—*don't be silly, you have a face like a Renaissance Madonna.*

But he hadn't said it then.

So why had he said it at all?

She got ready for bed, angry at herself for dwelling on something so meaningless. She should be thinking about why the killer had dumped Karin Kristensen's body where he had, why he'd wanted it found right away. Not about whether Will Patton was a jerk, or a decent man struggling with his pride.

"JACK, we need to make a public plea." Meg stood her ground despite the sheriff's scowl. Literally, since she'd chosen not to sit and was gripping the back of one of the chairs facing his desk. She'd gone to his office to make her case, knowing that he would resist.

He rose from behind his desk and tugged impatiently at his tie. "We're going to have a goddamn panic once people start thinking serial killer. Better yet, believing we don't have a clue!"

She reminded him of unpalatable reality. "We don't have a clue."

He scowled at her. "Talk to Mendoza again. Who else did he see in the bar that night?"

She snorted. "He's going to remember faces of people he didn't know six *years* later?"

Jack unbuttoned his cuffs and started rolling up his sleeves. He must be done with politicking for the day.

"It was the most memorable night of his life. You don't think he's rewound it in his mind a couple hundred times?"

"Maybe," she conceded.

"Anyway, who says we're looking for someone he didn't know?"

Meg blinked. "True."

"Isn't the autopsy this morning?"

"Giallombardo went."

He shot her a look. "Chicken."

"I went to Amy Owen's."

"This her first?"

Feeling a little ashamed of herself, Meg nodded. "She's going to get stuck watching one sooner or later."

"So you decided to make it sooner." Jack sounded amused.

With a snap in her voice, Meg said, "I decided it wasn't the most important thing that needed doing today. Damn it, Jack, if we don't get on the five o'clock news, we'll lose our chance! Some people who went up skiing today will be heading out of town in the morning."

She didn't remember from their long-ago romance, but Meg was willing to bet that Jack Murray didn't ask for directions when he got lost. It stood to reason that asking for the public's help went against his grain, too.

He paced a few steps each way, fighting the inevitable. Finally he growled, "All right! Do it. Just don't give anything in return you don't have to."

"Jack, I'm not a rookie."

He grunted. Maybe it was supposed to be a laugh. "Talk to the press yourself. Giallombardo might blow it."

"She's pretty closemouthed. You'd approve," Meg said. "Anyway, is there a single detail that hasn't already been aired?"

He settled back in his chair behind his massive desk. "I haven't heard Mendoza's name."

"Yet."

"I want answers before the press ask questions." He rotated his shoulders, letting her see his tension. "We're going to have every news organization in the country here any day. These were real colorful murders. We may put Elk Springs on the map by ending up on the cover of *People* magazine."

Meg shuddered.

"Go. Set it up." A tight smile crossed his face. "I see you had enough faith in your coercive abilities to dress for the occasion."

"I relied on your common sense," she said serenely.

A rough laugh rewarded her. "I assume you don't need me there?"

"No. It's going to be short and sweet."

Back in her own, much smaller, office, Meg started making calls. "I'm holding a press conference at noon to discuss the Amy Owen and Karin Kristensen murders."

Half an hour before showtime, Detective Giallombardo knocked and presented herself. Her eyes were glassy, her skin pasty.

"How'd it go?" Meg asked, interested to find out how honest this interesting young woman would be.

"I missed half of it puking."

"I did my first time, too." She hesitated. "Just between you and me, I can't get past the nausea. I know cops who hardly notice the smell anymore, but I'm not one of 'em."

"And the sounds." Giallombardo shuddered. "When Sanchez sawed her skull open..."

A shudder of her own worked its way down Meg's vertebrae. "Not my favorite part."

"Do you have a favorite part?" Giallombardo asked, with pardonable incredulity.

"Walking out at the end."

The detective laughed, healthier color returning to her cheeks.

"What did you learn?"

"Sanchez got a really clear bite impression. The killer is definitely the same as Amy Owen's." As if either of them had doubts. "He combed some pubic hairs, sent them for analysis."

"Anything else?"

"Her body was as clean as Amy's. As Sanchez put it, she had to have been raped on a floor you could eat off."

"Nice thought."

"She was more battered than Amy. He guessed she fought back. One wrist was cut and bruised from a handcuff. She'd wrenched at it repeatedly."

"That's how he held her so long. Didn't even need a locked room. God." Meg shook herself and glanced at the clock. "I've set up a press conference at noon. Join me."

"I don't have to talk, do I?" Giallombardo looked horrified.

"No, you can stand to the side and nod solemnly at every pearl of wisdom that falls from my lips."

"I can do that."

Meg had indeed dressed with care this morning, having formulated her plan during the night. She wore a royal-blue pantsuit, businesslike but elegant. No reason women cops had to be perceived as dowdy. Abby had lectured her on the subject enough times to have an impact.

"Why try to look like a man?" Abby had asked, curling her lip at some blazer Meg had pulled from the rack when they shopped together. They were women in a man's profession. So what? Her rule was, you don't hide the fact that you're a woman. You advertise it. You're feminine, classy and smart enough to have shown the men on the job a thing or two.

"Take a look at Jack's wardrobe," she'd advised. "In those million-dollar suits of his, he's sexy and powerful. You can be, too."

Meg strode through the halls of the public safety building, her heels clicking on the gleaming floors, conscious of turned heads and enjoying them.

The auditorium was half full. She stepped behind the podium, Giallombardo taking her place to one side a few steps back. A babble of voices shouted questions.

Conscious of the dozen or more camera lenses aimed at her, Meg lifted her hand. "I called this press conference to ask the help of the public in apprehending a murderer." Silence fell. "As you know," she began, "a young woman was murdered in the early hours yesterday morning, her body abandoned at an unfinished housing development that does not yet have any residents. The street is a dead-end. The killer drove into the housing development and departed the same way." She looked at each camera in turn, leaning forward slightly to emphasize her words. "His vehicle was the only one to turn into the Crescent Ridge development from the time it started to snow until firefighters, responding to a call, discovered the body at 5:15 a.m. We believe the fire was set by the killer to draw our attention, which means he likely left the scene between four-forty-five and five. We're asking for the assistance of anyone who traveled the Mountain Loop highway early yesterday and might have seen a vehicle entering or leaving the development. Certainly some employees at Juanita Butte would have been on the road by that hour, maybe some eager skiers. If a vehicle turned off the highway ahead of you onto a road covered with fresh snow just past mile marker eight or emerged from any road that appeared largely untraveled, please call." She gave the telephone number, then repeated it. "Thank you."

In response to questions, she confirmed that Karin's parents planned to have her body flown home to be buried in Boise and that there were similarities in the murders of Amy Owen and Karin Kristensen. Yes, investigators did believe it likely there was one killer.

"Was she raped?" a local television newscaster asked.

"I can't comment."

A reporter she recognized from the *Oregonian* in Portland called, "An eyewitness reported that Karin was strangled with a jockstrap. Was Amy also?"

"I'd also rather not comment on which aspects of the two crimes were similar and which different." She maintained a pleasant tone. "I'm sure you understand why."

"Do we have a serial killer in Elk Springs?" called a voice from the back.

"By definition, any murderer who kills more than once is a serial killer. In that sense, yes, it appears likely we do. Is this a Green River type killer who will continue to strike? At this point, I can't say. The two victims do have physical similarities. I urge all young women to take particular care until we apprehend the perpetrator. Thank you." She nodded and walked away, Giallombardo closing in on her heels, both women ignoring the storm of voices rising behind them.

When the door swung shut behind them, Detective Giallombardo said, "Wow!"

"They're a little scary, aren't they?"

"More than a little."

"The trick," Meg told her, "is to plan in advance what you want to say. Then don't deviate, no matter what they ask. Don't let yourself get thrown off balance. 'No comment' is an endlessly useful response. You stick to your message. Period."

Forehead puckered in concentration, Giallombardo nodded.

"All right. Let's go take a look at Karin's apartment."

During the drive, she asked, "How was dinner last night?"

The young woman started, but kept her gaze on the road. "Wonderful. You were right. Will's a great cook. I almost begged him for leftovers, but I clutched at my pride."

"I hope I didn't put you on the spot."

"No, it was fine."

Did that sound just a little forced?

"This is a rough time for Will." Meg thought. She wished she knew better what he was feeling.

"We didn't talk much about it." Giallombardo's voice was noticeably restrained.

"Ah? Well, I wish he'd talk to somebody." She was grateful at least that he had Travis, but she also knew from experience that men didn't always open up to each other. Even when they did, it might consist of a few words and a rough pat on the back. A man needed a woman to drag every tormented word out of him, to make him articulate his grief or imagined guilt. Will, she suspected, was shutting most of his in.

Karin's apartment offered few clues. She'd lived in

Elk Springs for barely a year and a half, and perhaps because of that hadn't accumulated the possessions Amy Owen had. The apartment was decorated on the cheap, with posters and throw pillows from the local Pier 1 store. She'd brought mementos from home—framed photos shared space on a bureau with a tattered stuffed bunny, for example. Meg studied the photos. They looked much like Amy's, some of family, some of friends. But the people in them were all strangers. She wasn't invested in the group of friends she'd made here.

Unfortunately, she'd died because of them, whether they'd meant much to her or not.

Karin had liked James Dean—a large poster hung over her bed and her wall calendar for the year featured photos from his movies. An occasional note on the calendar suggested a doctor or dentist appointment or a date.

7:00 Will!!! noted one entry. Interested, Meg saw Trina's eyes linger on that entry before she abruptly turned away and went to study the multiple photos and lists attached to the refrigerator with magnets.

"No appointment that night. Certainly nothing exciting. She did like her exclamation points."

"So I see." Trina pointed to a grocery list, where items were apparently given priority by the number of exclamation points following them. Pepsi had four, contact lens solution two, cereal one, paper towels none.

Karin appeared not to have been a reader. She owned a couple of dozen movies on DVD, all fairly recent hits, had a cheap stereo system and CDs of country-western music, and kept a basket of maga-zines in the living room. Meg watched as Trina went through them. *People, Entertainment Weekly, Premiere, Cosmopolitan.*

Probably not surprising she and Will hadn't kept dating.

A giant tote bag held an unfinished crochet project. On her knees, Trina gently touched the downy soft yellow blanket. It made Meg think of chicks and Easter morning. She hoped Maria Baker or someone she knew would finish the blanket. She felt sure Karin would want them to.

In the bathroom medicine cabinet they found birth control pills, generic ibuprofen, toothbrush, toothpaste, cold cream and makeup. No prescriptions. Nothing unusual.

Her undergarments were surprisingly chaste for a woman as beautiful as she'd been. She favored boy-cut cotton panties with cute sayings on the butt.

Meg closed the last dresser drawer. "This was a waste of time."

Trina turned from the closet. "We had to do it."

On a surge of grief, Meg said, "She was a nice, normal young woman with her whole life ahead of her. Goddamn it."

That was what got her most with kids and young adults: the life they *hadn't* had. Not so much the untapped potential, the possibility that this woman would have dreamed up a cure for cancer or become a teacher and influenced a generation of children, but rather the loss of the simple, satisfying experience of getting married, raising children, buying a first house, planting a tree in the yard and watching it grow to a stately size that could hold a tire swing for grandchildren. She'd been denied so much.

Meg felt profoundly depressed when she and Giallombardo closed the door to Karin Kristensen's apartment.

In the Explorer, she said, "Let's stop for lunch. I want to think, and I know my voice mail will be full. I don't feel like dealing with it yet."

She suggested a sandwich shop near an antique mall housed in the old Elk Springs police station, a grim, gray building that looked like an old Carnegie library and was much improved, in her opinion, by the gaudy banners hung on its basalt block facade. She liked it even better in the spring and summer, when pots of flowers decorated the outside steps and windsocks twirled from the porch pediment. It gave her great pleasure to imagine what her father, whose old office was now a space dedicated to the sale of vintage clothes, old quilts and lace and doilies and table linens, would think if he could know. She ate here often, just so she could contemplate how pissed he'd be.

Giallombardo gave her a sidelong, startled glance and Meg realized she was smiling. She wiped it from her face.

"I've never been here," the young detective said, after they were seated at a round oak table in the reception area of the old station that now held a restaurant. Faded cabbage rose wallpaper, mismatched antique chairs and a carved fireplace mantel lined with old glass bottles gave the place atmosphere.

"I come often." Meg picked up the menu. "You know that used to be the police station." She nodded out the window.

Giallombardo followed her gaze. "Sure. I remember."

"These are my old stomping grounds," Meg said, choosing not to explain further. "I like the food here, and I like the fact that the diners are mainly tourists. I don't have to sit here thinking, Damn, why is that man glaring at me? He looks familiar. Did I arrest him?"

Trina Giallombardo smothered a laugh. "I've already had that happen. It gets worse, huh?"

"Oh, yeah." Meg smiled at the waitress who arrived at their table. "I'll have the soup and half sandwich."

Since the lunch hour was past, they shared the room with only one other group, three women laden with bags and engrossed in their own conversation.

Giallombardo had obviously checked them out, too, because she said in a low voice, "Some of the bags are from Bronwen Fessler's shop. She has beautiful clothes."

"I bought a couple of Christmas presents there this year."

"Really? Her stuff is so expensive, but…" For a moment, naked longing turned the detective into a young woman who coveted pretty things, just like all young women did.

"A couple of spectacular sweaters can transform your wardrobe," Meg said, then felt absurdly like a surrogate mother.

"Maybe," Trina murmured, primarily to herself, Meg suspected. "Oh, thanks," she told the waitress, who brought their drinks.

Meg sighed, hating to drag them both back to thinking about a serial killer but knowing they had no choice. He might already be stalking another woman. Probably was, at the very least, casting around for possibilities. Savoring the last kill, yet feeling rage and hunger swell again.

"Back to business," she said. "What do we have so far?"

Giallombardo barely blinked. "We have bite impressions when we have a suspect to match them to."

"But nothing so distinctive about it, we could spot the guy because one front tooth overlaps the other. We should be so lucky. No response yet on the pubic hair from the Pappas murder."

"Olmos left me a message yesterday." Rafael Olmos was the young Hispanic officer who was cruising for former acquaintances of Mendoza. "He found a guy who says they were friends. But not good ones. He said no one was. He insists Mendoza was a loner. This guy says Mendoza didn't party much when he got out of the joint. He said, quote, 'Man, I want to get a good job and be able to send money to my sister.'"

"That jibes with the Ricky I remember. Smart, volatile, but…" Meg hesitated, trying to wrap words around her impression of the defiant young man she'd had such a gut feeling about. "Ready to grow up," she finished, dissatisfied but thinking that was good enough.

Their lunches arrived, and after smiling at the waitress, Giallombardo picked up her spoon. "Was he a special case for you?"

"Yes and no. Obviously, I stuck my neck out and talked Louis into offering a good plea."

"And you got him a job."

"I put in a word." She shrugged. "I've done the same for maybe a dozen kids I arrested. Ones I thought would go bad if they were in prison too long. They needed a scare, not to learn the culture."

Giallombardo nodded between bites. "There was this girl last year. She got caught shoplifting with a bunch of friends. They were all seventeen. She'd just had her eighteenth birthday. She was scared to death. She was just a kid, you know? It hadn't occurred to her that she was any different from her friends just because one more birthday had passed. I put in a word for her."

"Good for you." Meg looked down at her sandwich. "Will's gotten so hard," she said unhappily. "He doesn't want to see the possibility for redemption in anyone."

Rather awkwardly, and avoiding Meg's gaze, Giallombardo said, "Give him time."

Meg regarded her. Maybe they'd talked more than Trina had wanted to admit. Meg would give a great deal to know why Will had decided to come home to Elk Springs, but she could be patient.

"Well," Meg said, as if dusting off her hands. "Ideas?"

"We could talk to Mendoza again," Giallombardo suggested. "And the bartender who remembers seeing Amy that last night. So far, they're the closest thing to witnesses we have. How did this guy pick the women if he didn't see them in the bar?"

"Saw them arrive. Followed them there because he'd been stalking them."

"Possible with Amy. Not likely with Gillian Pappas, whose decision to go to the bar was impulsive and who hadn't been in town that long anyway. Would a killer spot her driving and follow her? Chances are any woman driving by is heading home, to the grocery store, someplace where an abduction isn't going to happen. No, I believe this guy was in the bar. Maybe even tried to talk to her."

"Maybe," Meg said, straightening in her chair, "was rejected by her."

They stared at each other.

Giallombardo said slowly, "If the killer is the guy Mendoza chased away, think how nicely the evening played out from his point of view. He not only vented his rage on the woman, the guy who humiliated him took the fall for the murder."

It sounded plausible. As did a dozen theories. Meg pointed out, "Even if the guy was in the bar, he might have approached her earlier. Didn't Ricky say a couple different guys hit on her? Or maybe the killer tried to hold her gaze across the room and she deliberately averted her eyes. Heck, maybe he just couldn't work up the guts to make a move at all, and he got mad because she was such an intimidating bitch. Somebody like this tends to suffer from such a feeling of inadequacy, he can magnify anything into a rejection."

Giallombardo leaned forward, her voice quickening. "We're back to the connection between victims. If he perceived that all three women rejected him, he'd had contact with them before."

Hating to be the wet blanket, Meg said, "Unfortunately, it's equally possible that none of them rejected him. They may look like someone who did, once upon a time. It could be a mother, a teacher, his first crush, a wife who left him…"

"Or he picked them just because they'd dated Will."

Meg hated the idea. "We could still be jumping to conclusions. Maybe he's part of that social circle and chose them because of their looks."

"Or maybe," Giallombardo had started to lift her spoon to her mouth, but now she set it back in the soup, "he *wishes* he was in that circle. We should talk to Will. Back before Gillian Pappas's murder, did someone try to join the group?"

"Will and Gillian were over in Salem at Willamette," Meg reminded her.

"Did she come home with him often for breaks?"

"She spent part of most breaks here. He'd spend the

other part with her in Beaverton." Meg shook her head, remembering. "The miles he put on his car. The two of them were virtually inseparable."

"Then she must have gotten to know his friends here in Elk Springs. How long had she been here that spring break before she was killed?"

Meg thought back. "Most of the week, I think. They stayed with Jack that time—you knew that. I don't know how much socializing they did. Jack said they spent most of the time taking walks or sitting outside having intense conversations. Something was obviously up between them. The fight the night of her murder wasn't out of the blue."

"It's tempting to see Will as the tie," Giallombardo said, "but you're right. Whatever we said to him last night, we'd be jumping the gun to make that assumption."

Tempting? Meg held her temper only by reminding herself that her subordinate hadn't meant that the way it sounded.

"Then what triggered the first murder? Why the six-year gap, then two murders with victims who were friends and in the same social circle as the first one?" Tasting acrid frustration, she shook her head. "We're going in circles. Why, why, why? What we need to do is focus. Which theory seems likeliest? Then let's bring in some more officers and pursue it hard."

Without hesitation, Giallombardo said, "It's somebody in their circle who feels slighted—or someone who wants to be in their circle and feels rejected."

Meg nodded. "I agree. Let's interview every single friend or acquaintance again. But this time, we want to find out what everybody thinks about everybody else."

Giallombardo finally took a bite. "Who shall I start with?"

"Will. I can't interview him without bias. At least you can be up-front with him. Get his impressions on everyone. Get him thinking."

"He may be busy this afternoon."

Meg shook her head as she picked up her own spoon. "Unless he's in court, he'll make time for you. Count on it."

CHAPTER TWELVE

"THANKS FOR TAKING the time for this." Trina Giallombardo sat in one of the two chairs that faced Will's overflowing desk, setting down a bag beside her.

He closed his office door and retreated behind his desk. "If I can do anything to help, you know I will."

She looked as thrilled to see him as he was to see her. He was coming to think he didn't much like himself, but he hadn't planned to announce his more distasteful motives to anyone, far less her. Will suspected she'd been ordered to interview him. Who else would do it? This was one time when his relationship to the senior investigating officer was awkward as hell.

Well, they had to do this. *Keep it businesslike,* he told himself.

"What do you want to know?"

She had opened her ubiquitous notebook on her lap, but she didn't look at it. "We're hoping you've had time to think."

It was as if she'd touched a raw wound without warning. He all but snarled, "You're asking me to imagine that one of my friends is not just a killer, but a madman who rips women's flesh with his teeth."

Her big brown eyes gazed warily back. "Not necessarily a friend. You've seen profiles of this kind of serial killer. Typically, they're…"

"Yeah, yeah! Caucasian, between the ages of twenty and forty, have low self-esteem and tend to fail at pretty much everything they try. The profiles all sound alike."

"That's for a good reason. Most of us have had enough successes, enough pats on the back, to balance the failures and the sneaking feeling we're inadequate. A killer like this doesn't have that balance. The only way he can feel good about himself is by dominating and destroying the symbol of his failure."

He'd heard all this before and knew profiles, even a generalized one like this, had their basis in fact. He also knew these guys could be tough to pick out of a crowd. Some were married, although their marriages tended to fail eventually. Some held jobs, although they also tended to lose those on a regular basis. They mowed their lawns. Neighbors were surprised when the guy was arrested.

Friends were surprised.

Shocked.

He rocked back in his chair. Had he done any thinking? Was she kidding? That's all he'd done. His eyes burned from lack of sleep and his gut churned from staring into the darkness thinking, *Dirk. He got seriously pissed when Amy went to a Homecoming Dance with me after lying to him and saying she already had a date.* Or, God, *Gavin. He didn't get the dates. He bad-mouthed girls all the time. Vince. Jeez, didn't Vince and Amy go out for a while, maybe sophomore year? She broke up with him. How mad was he?*

Oh, yeah, it had been a fun night.

"The killer may not be a friend of yours," she continued, in the absence of comment from him, "or of the victims." She sounded like someone tentatively offering a favor. "He may be someone who wanted to be. Someone on the fringes. Maybe he came to big parties but never got invited to the smaller ones. The pretty girls in your crowd ignored him."

"You seriously think we're looking for someone from as far back as high school."

Now her eyes held compassion. "Not necessarily. Think about the Christmas break and the week right before Gillian was killed. But the fact is, most of your friends here in town are from longer ago than that. Yes, I know Karin and Gillian weren't part of your group in high school, but they may have been chosen because they were representative, not because either of them rejected our guy. Maybe the pretty girls *always* rejected him."

He felt as if he were standing next to the road looking at the twisted remains of a car accident he didn't remember being in. Those days seemed so long ago. He'd been a kid. A goddamn, cocky *kid.*

"We were the popular kids, the jocks. Jody, Marcie, Amy…they were the cheerleaders. Amy was Homecoming Queen. Marcie was one of the princesses. Damn near every guy in school would have liked to date any of them."

Why did saying, *We were the popular kids,* make him so uncomfortable? Because Trina Giallombardo wasn't one of them, as far as he knew? Or because he'd begun to wonder when he'd started to be so goddamn sure of himself, he knew everyone else would genuflect?

"I remember all of you. Like ninety percent of the kids in the school, I wished I was one of your crowd." She gave a funny little laugh. "See, I know where our killer is coming from."

His jaw flexed. "Are you angry because Travis or I

or one of the other guys didn't ask you out? So angry you've spent the last ten years seething?"

"No. Of course not. But I do think envy is the first step down the road toward hating everyone who didn't somehow magically make you someone you aren't."

Will didn't get it. She was pretty. Maybe not beautiful—she wouldn't make a Hollywood starlet—but her face had character. In fact, she was a more interesting woman than Karin Kristensen, who'd been nice and rather ordinary aside from her looks. So why did Trina Giallombardo have such an inferiority complex?

"Who did you want to be?"

Her gaze shied from his and color ran up her cheeks. "We aren't talking about me."

"I thought we were."

"You were wrong." She bent and lifted a book from the bag at her feet.

The moment she held it out, he recognized the burgundy cover imprinted in gold with the seal of Elk Springs High School. The yearbook from his senior year.

"Mine's in storage." He took it from her, turned it around and opened the cover. "My God, we were young," Will murmured.

For the front page photo, the student body officers had posed in a tree. He was standing on a high branch, clutching the trunk in mock terror. Vince Baker hung upside-down by his knees. Christine sat on a broad branch in a yoga pose. Dirk—dumb-as-a-box-of-rocks Dirk—appeared to be in the act of swinging up. Travis lounged at the base of the trunk, ankles crossed, as suave as the rest of them were juvenile.

They were all gawky, fresh-faced and skinny. Christine was a pretty girl, interchangeable with a thousand pretty girls. Back then, every guy in the high school had thought she was smokin'. He shook his head in amazement.

Even then, Dirk's neck had dwarfed his head. Will had uncomfortable memories of the ways they'd kidded him about how dumb he was. He'd been an anomaly in their group, a barely more than failing student in a group of guys who talked about applying to Stanford, popular because of his athletic prowess and brawny muscles rather than personality. Gavin had been an anomaly, too, but Gavin had had the smarts, they'd all believed, if he'd just done the work and shut his mouth.

Vince Baker had been a math whiz-kid and was now a CPA. Justin Hill may have turned out to be an ass, but, man, he'd talked them all through AP English. Travis was a good student, but his gift had been in his ability to draw. Most of the teachers didn't mind that he sketched constantly. Anyone else doodling in the middle of a lecture or class discussion, they'd have come down on. With Travis, they'd wander by to see what he'd drawn and often find a caricature of themselves. More than once, teachers had asked if they could keep what he'd drawn.

Will realized that Trina had been saying something. Wrenching his gaze from the photo, he said, "What?"

"I'm hoping we can go through the yearbook. Student by student, with you telling me a little about everyone you remember."

"There must have been nine hundred students!"

"We can probably skip the freshmen. Maybe the sophomores."

"That's what you were."

Her gaze flicked to the yearbook as if it were a snake. She didn't, he diagnosed, want him to look at her class photo. "Uh…yeah."

"If you were jealous, maybe someone else was."

"Different kind of jealousy. We were younger. We didn't expect to be part of your crowd. We wanted to be *like* you when we were the upperclassmen. That's different."

"Maybe," he conceded. "Okay. If I shove some of this crap aside, you can bring your chair around here and sit next to me."

He moved the television and VCR on their wheeled stand and cleared the top of his desk by piling books and manila folders on the floor. Trina pulled her chair around to his side, hesitated, then sat. They were so close their shoulders touched when he sat again, too. He glanced sidelong, his gaze caught by the tiny gold studs in her ear lobes. A delicate whorl decorated so simply, her ears had something of the purity of her face, that Madonna quality. He wondered about her sexual experience, then stamped down on the speculation.

Concentrate, he told himself, irritated.

"Let's start with the juniors," she said. "We can back up later if…"

"Whoa." He lifted her hand off the yearbook. "I want to see your picture."

"It's horrible!"

"So what? We're talking ten years ago." He flipped to the sophomores. First spread was A through F. He turned the page and there she was. Wearing braces that made her look self-conscious and even more absurdly young than he and his friends did. Her dark hair was loose and glossy smooth, her eyes panicky-aware that how she looked *today,* this minute, was going to be printed for immortality. Only the most beautiful girls, he saw, scanning the page, looked smug. The others had un-doubtedly been brushing their hair and wiping lip gloss on and examining zits in the mirror and moaning, "I hate picture day!" until the moment they heard their name.

Trina made a choked sound. "I hated those braces."

"Most kids get it out of the way earlier."

Still staring at herself, she wrinkled her nose. "My dad wasn't working and we couldn't afford it. That year he finally had a job that offered some orthodontic coverage. I couldn't decide which was worse: having crooked teeth, or braces."

"So what's the verdict?"

She actually did laugh. "I'm glad my two front teeth don't overlap. Okay? And, yes, plenty of other kids had braces, too. I still felt like mine glowed in the dark or something."

"Ah, adolescence."

He flipped quickly through the sophomore pages and found faces that looked vaguely familiar, as hers had done, but not much more. He knew the guys who'd played on sports teams with him and a few girls who'd dated friends, but that was all. None stood out in his memory.

Trina asked him to comment on the girls, too, when he turned to the junior class. "Maybe one of them will trigger something."

He talked his way through the juniors, surprised by how readily the past welled from some storehouse in his mind. There were so many people he'd known well but hadn't given a thought to in years, but a mere glance at a tiny black-and-white photo would send him tumbling back.

"Damn," he murmured. "Sean Kavanagh. What an arm! But he was stoned all the time. We all knew it. Remember when the administration brought dogs in to sniff the lockers? The dog went crazy at Sean's. He got expelled. I wonder what happened to him?"

Trina made notes, but Will had already moved on. "Michelle King. She and Justin Hill went out for a while. He dropped her for…someone. Nita, maybe, after she and I broke up? Michelle went around telling anyone who'd listen that Justin was a daredevil on the ski hill to make up for his lack of sexual expertise."

"I suspect she was a little cruder than that."

He grinned. "Oh, yeah." He looked at the next picture. "Billy Landon. Now, there's a guy who tried way too hard. He was kind of like Jimmy McCartin. Only Billy at least made the team. But he was always second-string. That didn't stop him from swaggering and talking like he kicked ass."

"Girlfriends?"

"Uh…" He drew a blank. "He must have had them. But nobody I knew well."

"Is Billy still in Elk Springs?"

"Hm." Someone had just mentioned Billy. But who? Frowning, he said, "I just heard someone say he was back. I haven't seen him."

"What about six years ago?"

"I think he went to Oregon State. I don't know if he did graduate school or what. I don't remember him being around, but, honestly, I'm not sure I would."

"Who was Jimmy McCartin? I don't remember him."

"Who does? Oh, shit." He shook his head. "That's the eighteen-year-old me talking. What the hell difference does it make if the guy was short and scrawny? But in those days, that left him below the radar, as far as I was concerned."

Trina had turned her head to look at him. "I take it he wanted to be a blip on it."

He talked about Jimmy, but was suddenly very conscious of how close she was. If he turned his head, too, their mouths would damn near brush. Will felt an uncomfortable stirring at the idea.

"Ronald Lee," he said, a little too loudly. "He had a thing for Amy. He trailed her around like a puppy with its tail going nonstop. I think she kinda liked having an admirer who worshipped her whether she had a boyfriend or not."

"He might have become enraged when he realized one day she was never going to turn to him."

"But what about Gillian?"

"She reminded him of Amy?" She was testing a new theory. "He was angry, but not angry enough yet to hurt her?"

"I haven't seen Ronnie since high school. He's probably married and has kids. Young love does die."

Amy's picture hit Will hard. She'd been one of those people you wanted to hate but couldn't. Amy was always in a good mood, always able to see the best in everyone and every situation. She seemed to have been born with a sunny, optimistic outlook on life. You always knew Amy was sincere. Of all the girls he'd grown up with, Amy should have been the last to inspire hatred so vicious.

A couple of hours passed with him talking until his voice got scratchy. Finally, he groaned and leaned back.

"I need a break." He saw the clock. "It's after six. I need dinner."

Sounding equally tired, Trina closed her notebook. "We can start again tomorrow."

He saw her move her shoulders surreptitiously and realized she'd hunched over the damn desk for hours, scarcely moving. His own ached, and tension squeezed his neck.

"No, let's get it over with," he said. "Unless you have plans this evening?"

"No."

"I can whip up a stir-fry. Then we can sit down at the kitchen table where it's more comfortable and finish." He rolled his chair back and stretched. "What do you say?"

"You're offering me dinner?"

"Yeah, why not?"

"You don't *have* to feed me."

"You're not hungry?" He started throwing files in his briefcase, although he doubted he'd open it tonight. He watched her out of the corner of his eye, intrigued by her obvious skittishness.

"Um…I could get something at home."

"Your choice." He paused. "But my ginger beef stir-fry is Mom's favorite dinner."

"Over your spaghetti?"

He grinned at her.

She made a soft sound in her throat to indicate surrender. Did she make the same one when a man suckled on her breast? Will had an image of her arching, her skin golden, her nipple dusky.

Damn. There he went again. He snapped the briefcase shut. "Well?"

Despite his testiness—or because of it—she nodded. "Thank you. That would be very nice."

His mood swung 180 degrees again. He *wanted* her to come home with him, to kick off her shoes and tuck a foot under her, to loosen her hair and unbutton the prim neck of her shirt.

This wasn't a date. What in hell was he thinking?

He let her precede him from the office. "You can find my place again?"

"Sure. See you in a bit." As he locked up, she walked away, her heels clicking on the glossy vinyl floor, not once looking back.

She didn't show up at his apartment for almost an hour, and when she did she'd changed clothes. Her cheeks and nose were bright from the cold, her hair was in a ponytail instead of a bun, and when she struggled out of her parka and gloves, beneath she wore jeans and a green turtleneck.

"I'm sorry to be so slow." She let him take the parka. "I just had to change. And then I made the mistake of checking my voice mail, and that took a while."

"Mistake? Did you get bad news?"

He hung up her parka, noticing as he did that it carried a faint spicy fragrance. He resisted the urge to bend closer to inhale it more deeply.

"No-o." Her tone was doubtful. "Just my sister. I sent her a check to get her through a week or two, but then she didn't get the job she thought she would, so now she's in trouble again. Story of her life."

"You said she's an alcoholic?"

"Unfortunately." She followed him to the kitchen. "For that matter, so is my dad. I suppose my brother is, too. I don't see him that often, but he always seems to have a beer can in hand."

He turned on the wok. "You've never been tempted?"

"Not for a second." Steel underlay every word. "I grew up knowing I didn't want to be like my father. I think I sort of…cast around for a role model, until your mother came to speak that day. I really wasn't kidding when I said I'd always wanted to be like her."

"Have you told her that?" He took oil out of the cupboard.

"Are you kidding? She's my boss!"

"Yeah, I guess it could come across as ass-kissing."

"You think?" She wrinkled her nose at him, then nodded toward the food he'd set out in bowls. "What can I do?"

He gave her an easy grin. "Absolutely nothing. I'd just finished cutting everything up when the doorbell rang."

Trina narrowed her eyes. "You could have waited."

"I was hungry."

"Uh-huh. I have a suspicion you *never* let anyone help in your kitchen. I wouldn't slice or dice to your specs. You'd be so filled with anxiety watching me mangle the green onions, you wouldn't be able to bear it."

Will threw back his head and laughed. "You've got me. I do, uh, have my standards."

"Well, then," Trina retreated from the entrance to the kitchen and reappeared on the other side of the breakfast bar, "I'll just sit and watch the master at work."

"I wish I could oblige with a show, but stirring things around in hot oil isn't that exciting." Boiling water sizzled on the stove top behind him and he swung around. "Damn! I forgot I'd put on water for the rice!"

"I distracted the master." A smile quivered on her mouth. "So sorry!"

He let his gaze travel to the swell of breasts beneath her turtleneck. "Yeah, you did," he said, voice deepening. Satisfied by her blush, he turned down the heat and added the rice.

The oil in the wok sizzled, and he dumped the strips of beef in, deftly stirring. He'd changed, too, when he got home. His mother had been right; the tomato stains were permanent on one of his favorite white shirts. He didn't need to ruin another one with grease spots. He now wore jeans and an old blue sweatshirt.

"Actually," he said, "if you'd grab silverware and napkins, that would be great. Oh, and wine if you want it."

She slid off the stool with such alacrity, he knew she was relieved to have something to do. "I think maybe tonight I'd better keep my head clear."

"Then why don't you pour us both some milk. Or there's juice or pop if you'd rather."

This time he brought the rice and stir-fry to the table in big bowls so they could dish up there. While they ate he tried to set her at ease. He was an idiot to have introduced even the idea that he was sexually attracted to her! Life was way too complicated right now, for him if not for her.

She told him about her mom, who'd died when she was eight, and about having her dad, brother and sister over for Thanksgiving dinner this year. "It was actually kind of nice. My sister was obviously stoned and my dad and brother watched football all day, but hey! It still felt…" Her brow creased as she considered what she had felt. "Like family," she said with a shrug. "What about you? Did you come home for Thanksgiving?"

"I do every year." He almost stopped there. Should have stopped, in the interests of keeping conversation light, but heard himself go on, "I sat there this year and realized I felt like a stranger who'd been kindly invited. No. Worse than that. An acquaintance nobody much liked but who'd been invited out of a sense of obligation."

He saw exactly what he'd feared in her eyes: pity.

"Surely you're imagining things."

"My aunt Abby makes a point of avoiding me. I enter a room, she leaves. She gave me hell six years ago and told me no amount of grief excuses the things I said.

Until I apologize to her satisfaction, she makes it plain she doesn't have anything else to say to me. Mom bustles around trying to act as if everything is fine. Aunt Renee makes forced conversation, which is almost worse than Aunt Abby's route. Most years, I wish I could go sit at the kids' table."

Trina contemplated him for a moment with an expression that made him want to squirm. "You know, I wonder if you *aren't* imagining most of this. Maybe Thanksgiving is just like it always was, and you're the one who feels like you don't belong. Other people probably don't waste as much time thinking about you as you seem to believe they do."

After delivering this bit of devastating insight, she continued eating without apparently noticing its effect on him.

He sat frozen, staring at his plate. It seemed everybody was all too happy these days to point out how self-centered he'd become. Or, hell, had always been. Once he would have brushed them off. Now...

Now he felt his inner core of certainty crumbling like a clay bluff battered by rainstorms. Because she was absolutely right. At Thanksgiving, like at every other holiday where he'd felt like the odd man out, probably everyone else had laughed and talked and celebrated and given him no more than a passing thought. Even hard words lost their power as the years passed. He had pictured every one of them conscious at all times of Will's loss, Will's anger, Will, Will, Will. And the truth was, their lives had gone on. Aunt Abby had had two children since Gillian's murder, Mom and Aunt Renee were busy raising his younger half siblings and his cousins. They'd gotten promotions at work, tough cases, dealt with emotional blows.

They'd probably all been less than delighted to hear that Will, still carrying his hurt and rage, was rejoining the family circle. Boy, they'd done enough tolerating him at the occasional holiday. Now they were going to have to see him all the time? Yee-haw.

Crap, he thought, dazed. There he went again. Feeling sorry for himself. His specialty.

"Will?"

He yanked himself back to the present. "Yeah?"

"You seemed, um, absent for a minute."

"Sorry." He forced a smile. "Just wool-gathering. Nothing like thoughts of home and family to set me off."

She helped him clear the table and loaded the dishwasher while he poured coffee. With his mood pisspoor, he was grateful to have her here, even if he wasn't looking forward to the rest of the evening.

Trina got out the damn yearbook again, opening it to where they'd left off. He took a chair beside her instead of across the table, again feeling a tug of awareness just because she was close.

Ignoring it, he concentrated on the photos of the senior class, these in color and slightly larger than the ones for the other classes. As if he'd never left off, the muscles across his shoulders tightened.

"Vince Baker," Will began. "He was at J.R.'s the other night. He dated Amy. I can't remember if it was the sophomore or junior year. She ditched him, although—Amy being Amy—I think she did it really nicely. He never seemed to have a problem with staying friends. Anyway, he started to go with Maria Rodriguez not that much later, and they got married once he graduated from college. She was there the other night, too. She's pregnant."

Softly, Trina said, "It was their baby that Karin was making the blanket for."

"Right. Uh. I don't know what there is to say. Vince was a good guy. He's a CPA here in town."

She nodded.

He kept talking. Ted Bettinger, wide receiver, vegetarian, political activist. Katie Rose Bickham, teacher's pet and determined to keep her virginity until her wedding night.

Trina actually touched the photo of Katie Rose, with her red hair curled like a Southern belle. "I wonder if she succeeded."

"My guess is…yeah." He grinned wickedly. "We all did our damnedest to change her mind, and to the best of my knowledge, nobody got below the waistband."

"Will!" Laughing, but also looking shocked, Trina shook her head. "You guys all tried to get in her pants just because she said you couldn't?"

"Hey, a challenge is a challenge." Laughing himself, he evaded her punch. "Come on. We were teenage boys. I *have* grown up."

"Sure you have," she muttered.

Ignoring that, he said, "Travis. You know him."

"Right. Your mother says he was definitely away when Gillian was murdered."

"Half a world away. He's not your kind of guy anyway."

To his surprise, she agreed. "No. His self-confidence is too ingrained."

Will felt a flicker of jealousy. Because Travis *was* so together and he wasn't? Or because Trina sounded as if she admired him. Maybe more. Damn it, Will thought, had Travis appeared interested in her?

He kept going. Teammates, friends, distant acquaintances. He dredged for memories of who dated whom, who had one-nights with whom, who'd been spurned by whom. The mini-dramas of high school seemed too long ago and silly to matter, but Trina kept urging him on. He knew she was right. Gillian had been murdered during their first year of graduate school—not that many years after these photos had been taken for the high school yearbook.

Bronwen Fessler, always sharp-tongued. He liked her better now than he had then.

"You know," Trina commented, when he fell silent. "It occurs to me that your male friends turned out to be more successful than the girls did. Look how many of them still live here in Elk Springs. A lot of them didn't even go to college. I mean, Amy was a hairstylist, Judy Cox is a dental technician, Marcie Whittaker a stay-at-home mother."

"Christine Nylander went to Lewis & Clark and is a teacher." He sought for another example and couldn't think of one. "Bronwen is doing okay…"

"But I hear her father set her up in business."

"I heard that, too." He scratched his jaw. "You know, you're right. I hadn't thought about it. I don't even know why that is."

Tone tart, Trina gave him a look that he couldn't entirely read. "Gee, could it be because the girls made the cut because of looks, not brains?" She tapped another photo with her forefinger. "Amber Greer, for example. Didn't I hear she went to Sarah Lawrence and is now a New York editor?"

They both gazed at the picture of an earnest, freckle-faced girl with too high a forehead and too big a nose.

Embarrassed, Will said, "She was in most of my classes. She was really funny." Another person he hadn't thought of in ten years. He hadn't heard that she was an editor.

"But not one of your friends," Trina pointed out, with an edge he couldn't mistake.

"You're right." It galled him to admit it, but hadn't he come home to Elk Springs to remember who he'd been and figure out who he wanted to be? "I really liked Amber, but it never occurred to me to ask her out. She was homely." Anger gathered in his voice. "But what's your point? What in hell does this have to do with anything?"

"Let's find the guys who were like Amber but maybe didn't find success after high school," Trina said simply.

So they returned to the search.

Justin Hill. Eliminated, Trina told him, because he'd been in Europe when Amy was murdered.

He didn't fit the profile anyway.

Gavin Husby. What to say about Gavin? Will was ashamed to have had that moment of surprise when he saw him with Karin.

Trina caught his hesitation, because she turned her head. "Will?"

"Oh, crap." He leaned his head back and squeezed his eyes shut, shoving both hands in his hair. "Gavin Husby. You talked to him, didn't you?"

"Yes."

Some restraint in her voice told him that she hadn't liked Gavin. The truth was, *he* didn't much like Gavin. But they had a history. That counted for something.

He began reluctantly. "Like I said before, he didn't quite fit in our group. I wouldn't have said he *was* in our group, except he always hung out with us. He had a hell of a temper. His real dad was out of the picture—just took off. His mother remarried, and the stepfather beat Gavin. He sometimes had a black eye, or missed a couple of days of school and came back hurt. You could see it. He'd make excuses. I don't think he wanted us to know how bad it was." Disquieted, Will found it all coming back to him. "Maybe that's why we let him stick with us. That, and he was gutsy on the field. Not a real talented athlete, and he tended to tangle with coaches, but I think his best came out when he played sports."

"Smart?"

Oh, he had her attention, Will could tell. Suddenly he hated this whole thing. Hated himself. These were friends, and here he was, trying to remember the worst about them to deliver them up to be suspects in a ghastly crime.

"This sucks."

If he expected sympathy, he didn't get it.

"Remember the dead women. You didn't see their bodies. I did."

"I saw pictures of Gillian's." His throat closed. After a minute, he swore under his breath. "Okay. Yeah. Gavin's smart. His grades were all over the place, because he didn't want to do the work, and because he also tangled with teachers. He could be pretty abrasive."

"What about girls? Did he have girlfriends?"

He sighed. "Yeah. Off and on. But never the really hot girls. I don't think it was looks. I mean, Dirk Whittaker had muscles but not much else going for him. And look at him. Marcie married him." The fact still surprised him. She wasn't any genius, either, but she could think circles around Dirk.

"Then what was it?"

"Personality. He could be really crude, angry, just plain unlikable."

"Nice friends you had," Trina commented.

"He could be funny." Excuses, excuses. "Gavin liked

pranks. Putting wet paint on coach's bullhorn, so he had a black circle around his mouth and didn't know it. Dumb things, but…creative."

She all but rolled her eyes. "His one virtue."

Angry now, Will said, "What do you want me to say? I didn't like him? Well, I didn't. I didn't like the way he talked about girls, I didn't like the way he'd throw everything he could get his hands on in the locker room just because Coach pulled him from the game. I didn't care that his father was beating the shit out of him. Okay? I was filled with compassion. Can you tell?"

Flatly, she said, "You're describing someone who fits the profile."

Voice savage, he said, "You know what? I knew a bunch of other losers, too. Bigger losers than Gavin Husby. Did you make sure you got notes about all of them? Is every guy at the high school who couldn't get a date with Nita Voss suspect?"

Trina seemed not to have heard. "Will, did Gavin know you didn't like him?"

As if a fist had slammed into his gut, the air in his lungs rushed out.

"You mean," he said, low and harsh, "does he have a good reason to hate me?"

CHAPTER THIRTEEN

GAVIN?

Instinctively, Will shook his head. At the same time, he said, "Yeah. I stepped in a few times when he threw temper tantrums. And I told him to stuff it when he went off on what sluts some of the girls we knew were. Sure. He knew how I felt about him." His mouth twisted. "But we all made fun of Dirk Whittaker for being stupid, too. Jimmy McCartin knew I could hardly be bothered to remember his name. The truth is, I thought I was a good guy, but I know damn well I thought of myself as superior, and I doubt I hid it."

"Did you know," Trina said reflectively, "the crowd in the hall would literally part when you walked down it?"

He stared at her.

"You didn't?" She shook her head. "It doesn't matter. The point is, of course you had a big head! I mean, you were the quarterback, the student body president, the Homecoming King! Some students probably were jealous. But hate…that's a lot stronger."

"Doesn't arrogance automatically predispose you to being insensitive to other people's feelings?"

"Maybe." She waggled her hands. "But high school kids are not famous for thinking about other people."

A reluctant smile pulled at his mouth. "You've got

me there." He sighed and leaned back. "So, what are we looking for here?"

"Someone you really humiliated or bested in some way. The trouble is, you might not even have noticed."

He looked at the open yearbook with its rows of pictures. "It's hopeless."

"No. Gavin bears a closer look. You *are* describing someone with the kind of problems and personality that fit the profile."

Grasping for an out, Will said, "It sounds like he's been really successful as a car salesman."

"But how does telling people he's a car salesman sound compared to attorney and assistant D.A.? It doesn't help that two classmates were members of the U.S. ski team and Travis is becoming a widely known artist."

"Gavin probably makes more money than I do!"

"Does he know that?"

Will was silent.

"Some of these others sound like possibilities, too." She glanced at her notes. "Billy Landon, Jimmy McCartin." She named a couple of others. "Another thing for you to consider—frequently serial killers were bed wetters, set fires when they were young or tortured animals."

Repulsed, he said, "I wouldn't know about the bedwetting. I didn't move here until I was fourteen."

"Okay."

"Fires… Yeah, there was a string of small ones at the high school. In teachers' wastepaper baskets. That kind of thing. Ended with one in shop that did some major damage." He swore at a memory. "My bicycle was set on fire when I was sixteen. This guy was after any Patton, and he did a bunch of stuff. Staged a couple of scenes to let us know he knew everything about us. We assumed he was the one to torch my bike, but I don't remember if he ever admitted specifically to it."

"Interesting."

"I don't know of tortured animals. Aren't there always some cases?"

"Yes, but if we could connect any to one of these guys when they were younger..." She made more notes, then lifted her head. "We've still got a ways to go in the yearbook. Let's finish."

He ran a hand over his face. "Yeah. Sure."

He talked until they'd turned the last page and he was hoarse. Closing the yearbook and pushing it toward Trina, Will wondered if he could ever stand to look at it again.

"Now what?" he asked. "Are you going to talk to them?"

"I'm going to try to do some fact checking first. I mean, obviously we have to find out whether they were in Elk Springs when Gillian was murdered. And, of course, whether they're here now. I might be able to look at their work history. Police record, of course. People with explosive tempers are likely to pop up with a few domestic disturbance calls, maybe a restraining order." She shook her head. "You know all this. Why am I telling you?"

"Because I asked. I'm finding that it's different, being on this side of the fence. Now I know why the victims' families and friends ask for so much reassurance."

She didn't, thank God, mouth the kind of platitudes he'd opened himself to. *Maybe you'll be better at your job. More compassionate.* Maybe.

"We'll try to narrow down where some of these guys were on the nights in question. Some aren't people we considered before. Like I said, I don't remember Jimmy McCartin or Billy Landon or several of these others. We had no reason to question them regarding either murder."

"And if you find they were all in Elk Springs at the right times, you won't be any further ahead than you were."

"Not unless something interesting pops up on their records."

Gavin. Yeah, Will could picture him beating his girlfriend or becoming enraged after a few too many drinks some night. Jimmy. Heck, he couldn't even picture Jimmy without that big grin on his face. Which didn't mean he wasn't brewing a real sick cocktail of anger behind that smile.

Wanting to think about anything else, Will asked, "Do you want more coffee? Wine?"

She made getting-up moves. "I should probably go."

He didn't think, just said, "Don't."

Her lips parted. "What?"

"I'd rather not be alone right now." He hunched his shoulders uneasily. "If you'd stay for a while, just to talk, I'd be grateful."

She looked spooked, but after a momentary hesitation nodded. "I…sure. For a bit. Um. In that case, I'd love some more coffee."

He pushed back from the table. "Let's go in the living room. It's more comfortable."

Trina chose the easy chair, kicking off her shoes and tucking one foot under her as she sat. She accepted the fresh cup of coffee from him and smiled uncertainly. He sat on the couch and they looked at each other.

Sick of thinking about himself—*Well, isn't that a change!* an inner voice mocked—and intensely curious about a woman who'd chosen a path so different from her family's, Will nodded at her. "Tell me about you in high school. Were you a good student? Did you do sports? Have a boyfriend?"

"There's about two minutes of conversation. The crowds did *not* part when I walked down the hall."

"Can we·forget about me?" he asked, more harshly than he'd intended.

Her eyebrows rose. After a moment, Trina bit her lip. "I sound pathetically jealous, don't I? And honestly, I'm not. I wasn't," she corrected herself. "I never particularly cared if I was popular. I had a couple of good friends, I had a date to the prom—"

"Who?" he interrupted.

Her eyes widened, then shied from his. "A guy named Mark. Mark Dwyer. He and I went together for a while my senior year."

"What happened to him?"

"He went to Portland State and then off to some school in the midwest to become a chiropractor. I have no idea after that."

Will nodded.

"I played soccer in high school, but I wasn't good enough to play in college, except intramural. I did debate and Knowledge Bowl."

"Hey!" A pleased smile spread on his face. "So did I. Neufelt was one of my favorite teachers."

"Mine, too. I loved going to tournaments."

Sipping coffee, they talked about good times and mutual acquaintances. Teachers, grades, college, first job interviews, living alone. He liked listening to her and watching her face, far more expressive than he'd realized. He'd been irritated by what he thought of as her cop mode—the poker-faced stare, the tiniest curl of her lips that masterfully expressed disdain. What he hadn't realized was that he had to look closely to catch

the amusement that narrowed her eyes, the quick dila-
tion of pupils when she was startled, the faint wash of
color in her cheeks when she was embarrassed. When
she laughed, a dimple quivered in one cheek, giving her
a puckish look. And her laugh—he really, really enjoyed inciting it, because it was so unexpected. She
giggled rather than guffawed. The merry ripple of
amusement lightened his mood every time he heard it.

She was the one to glance at her watch and start.
"Oh, no! It's one o'clock! How did that happen?"

He checked his own, equally surprised. "Wow. I'm
sorry. I didn't mean to keep you out all night."

Feeling for her shoes, Trina said, "No, it's okay. I'm
one of those people who does fine on six hours of
sleep."

"You'll be lucky to get that now." He fetched her
parka from the closet and said, "I'll walk you down."

A crinkle between her dark arch of brows made her
look vaguely puzzled. Apparently she wasn't used to
being treated like a girl. "You don't have to do that."

"I want to."

The whites of her eyes showed. "Oh."

Will didn't bother with his coat; he wouldn't be
outside that long. She fetched the yearbook and her
spiral notebook from the table and dug keys from her
pocket. He followed her out onto the cold landing and
down the stairs, where each footstep thudded hollowly.
A blue Subaru was in a slot marked for visitors not far
from his garage. She hit the remote control and the
lights flashed. After opening the door, she hesitated
and then turned to face him, waiting with his hands
shoved in the pockets of his jeans.

"Thank you for dinner, Will. I think I'll still vote for
the spaghetti as number one, but the ginger beef was
great, too."

She was six or eight inches shorter than he was, which meant she had to tip her head back to look up at him.

"Any time," he heard himself say. "I really appreciate you staying tonight. The walls were closing in."

"I know the feeling."

"I guessed you did. Maybe that's why I like you." Without giving himself time for a second thought, he bent and brushed her cheek with his lips. It was silky-smooth and cushiony, her startled breath warm, her scent surprisingly exotic for a hometown girl. To avoid temptation, he stepped back. "Good-night."

She gaped, then blushed. "Um. Sure. I'll, uh, let you know if we turn anything up." She leaped into her car and slammed the door. It was a second before the engine roared to life and the headlights came on, making him wonder if she'd had to fumble with the keys.

He lifted a hand and went back to the foot of the stairwell, watching as she backed out and drove away.

What, he wondered, seeing her brake lights flicker, would she have done if he'd turned his head just a little and transferred that kiss to her mouth?

He was moving to go up the stairs when he heard a second engine roar to life in the next row over and saw red taillights before this vehicle turned the same direction Trina had. He caught only a glimpse when it reached the street—he thought it was black, a big pickup with a canopy, maybe, or a huge SUV.

Funny, he thought, frowning after it, that he hadn't heard anyone come out of an apartment or the slam of the driver's side door when someone got in. It was as if the driver had been sitting there, waiting for her to leave.

Hair on the back of his neck stirred. Had someone been watching when he kissed Trina good-night?

"BETH." Will accepted a hug from his stepmother, then went down the hall of his father's house to poke his head in the media room to say hi to Lauren and Steph. Lauren was playing a computer game, Steph reading *The Invisible Man.*

"AP English?" he guessed.

She groaned.

Laughing, he went to the kitchen. His dad was making dinner tonight, as he often did. Jack Murray had been a bachelor until he was thirty-seven, plenty long to have become accustomed to doing the cooking.

Will paused a few steps into the kitchen, feeling something at the sight of his father that he hadn't in a long time. His heart seemed to lighten and then swell. He'd wanted a father so bad, and then he'd gotten a prize one.

Jack had never once argued that Will couldn't be his son—how could he, when they looked so much alike? After his immediate shock, he'd taken his role seriously. Will had gotten to know his grandparents and the rest of the family on his father's side. Jack had introduced him to camping and fishing. He'd become Will's biggest fan, rarely missing a game.

Will could still feel the shadow of terror from that time his father had violated every rule and offered himself up as a hostage in place of a sixteen-year-old girl. Ben Shea had called Will over at Willamette to let him know what was happening. He'd been able to turn on the television and watch his father walk across the street, no hesitation, face so serious and disappear inside the garage of the house belonging to a deputy he'd just fired for drinking on the job. The door had rolled shut behind him, swallowing him. A few minutes later, the front door opened and the girl fell outside onto the porch, then picked herself up and ran, face wet with tears. SWAT team members swept her up and carried her back behind the police line to reunite with her parents. Will had been able to do nothing but wait, sick with fear, thinking, *I haven't had him long enough. Please God don't take him. Please God.* Newscasters kept chattering away and Will sat frozen on the old battered couch in his fraternity living room, staring at the TV, waiting, waiting, desperate to know what was happening behind the closed blinds of the ordinary house on which the cameras were trained. And then the distant crack of gunshots and consternation among watching police officers, the excited leap of the newscaster's voice. First the deputy's wife, also held hostage, had walked out the front door, splattered with so much blood Will felt sick. Cops wrapped her in blankets and led her away while the camera focused on the open front door and the newscaster kept saying, "It's not clear yet what has happened inside the house. All we know is that gunshots were fired." And then his dad walked out, bloody, too, looking like he hurt, but lifting a hand toward the cameras to say, *I'm fine.*

Having parents in law enforcement, Will had always known they sometimes risked their lives, but seeing it play out on television was different.

Standing here now, Will thought, *I came closer to losing him when I told him he'd as good as murdered Gilly as I did that day, when he offered himself up to die in someone else's place.*

"Will?" His father turned from the stove. He wore jeans as old as Will's, a sweater and a white apron.

Shutting out the dark reflections that were his constant companion these days, Will nodded at the apron. "Cute."

"Didn't want to ruin the sweater Beth bought me for

Christmas." The craggy, near-homely face Will saw in the mirror every morning gained character with the years, it appeared. His dad had acquired ruts and grooves that deepened with anger or worry or laughter. He was smiling now, but with a reserve that gave Will an ache under his breastbone.

He deserved that reserve.

"What are we having?" he asked, straddling a stool.

"Nothing fancy. London broil and new potatoes."

"Sounds good. Thanks for inviting me."

His father checked the potatoes and turned on the burner under another pan. "How are you settling in at work?"

They talked like that for a while, nothing special. They could have been two people getting to know each other. Or else it was the natural way of catching up. Will hardly knew anymore. He always felt this barrier now, a wall of reserve that had bothered him even when he was nursing anger. It had been childish, he realized now. Parents were supposed to take any amount of acrimony from their offspring and remain open to more, apparently.

Well, that might be true when offspring was a thwarted five-year-old or a resentful sixteen-year-old, but he'd been a man when he said what he did, not a child even if he'd acted like one.

Jack called the family for dinner. Three or four conversations were going on before they even sat down. Stephanie moaned about having to wait until April to hear which colleges had accepted her. Lauren admitted to a new boyfriend, which from the narrowing of Jack's eyes didn't seem to delight him. Will was amused but found himself bristling as well at the idea of some punk pressing his little sister for sex.

"How old is he?" Jack asked.

"Noah is a junior," she said blithely. "He has his own car. How cool is that? You know how much I hate the school bus…"

"You're not getting in the car with a kid who just got his license," her stepfather said. "Especially not with the roads still icy."

"He's a good driver!"

"For a sixteen-year-old? Don't care," Jack said.

"Mo om!" she wailed.

"Nope," her mother said placidly. "You're not going anywhere with *any* new drivers. You know the rules."

"Maybe I should stop by the high school and check this guy out," Will said.

"You wouldn't!" Seeing the laughter in his eyes, she kicked him under the table. "Noah is nice! You guys all just think I shouldn't date until I'm thirty!"

Pushing his plate back, Jack said easily, "Works for me."

She huffed in indignation, but had too much to say to let the conversation move on without her. "Coffee?" Beth suggested when their plates were clean and no-body was reaching for thirds.

Stephanie excused herself to go back to her home-work and Lauren said, with a pointed sniff, "I have phone calls to make," and left the table, too.

Will thanked Beth when she put a mug in front of him, then, scarcely aware when she left the room, looked at his father. "You knew my grandfather. Was he as bad as Mom says he was?"

Jack raised his brows at the question, but answered. "Oh, yeah. He was a son of a bitch."

"But you worked for him."

"I knew he was a hard-ass. He beat the crap out of

me when he caught me with your mother. He was angry, but also icy cold. Seriously scary." Jack shook his head. "But I didn't know how malevolent he could be until years later. You remember that poor bastard Jim Cronin?"

Cronin was the one who'd stalked the Pattons, determined to have revenge for what he claimed Chief Ed Patton had done to his family.

"Sure. Just a day or two ago I was telling…someone about my bike being set on fire."

His father didn't miss the hesitation, but he didn't comment, either. "We had to figure out who could have reason to hate any of the Pattons. Thanks to your grandfather, we found plenty of folks.

"For example. A woman told us about this idiot of a boyfriend of hers who came up with a scheme to get her back after she'd booted him. He wanted to heroically rescue her, so he decided to torch her place, then 'happen' to be passing and dash in. She heard him outside and called 911. She knows Ed Patton got there in plenty of time to see the boyfriend pouring gasoline all over the back porch of her place. She saw Patton sneak around the side of her house. Long pause. He apparently didn't do a damn thing to stop the fool from lighting a match. Burned himself to a crisp, of course. She came out and ol' Ed nodded at the guy and said, 'Can you identify him?' She's puking because the guy is just melting on her lawn—you can imagine what that smelled like—and Ed laughs and says, 'Guess you can't recognize him now, can you?' That story pretty well summed him up."

"My God."

Jack's face hardened. "What I didn't know, back before your mom took off, was that Ed would start to hanker to see someone hurt, and, damn, he had three girls he'd terrified into silence. Meg always made excuses for a broken arm or the bruises or the painful way she'd hold herself for days on end. Me, I bought it hook, line and sinker."

"They never told anyone."

"Nope. That's not uncommon. Their mother had taken off, and they didn't have anyone else. Besides… Ed Patton was a hero! Nowadays, he'd be kicked off the force for any one of the things he did, but then people just thought he was tough on crime. Only pansies had sympathy for the criminals. With their dad the police chief, who was going to believe three girls?"

Will knew some of this history, but it had never been presented so bluntly to him before. He imagined his mother sixteen years old and pregnant, knowing if she told her father he wouldn't just be angry and disappointed, he would beat her bloody. Even that, she'd always said, wasn't why she ran; she ran because what scared her most was the idea of him doing to her child what he'd done to her and her sisters. Worse yet, influencing him to grow up to become the same kind of man her father was.

It hadn't been herself she was protecting. It was him.

Slowly, he said, "Mom raised me knowing that I was the most important thing in the world to her, that she'd do anything for me."

Brown eyes somber, his father let the silence ride.

"I got here to Elk Springs, and suddenly I had you, too, trying hard to make up for all those years when I didn't have a father. And there were your parents, Aunt Abby, Aunt Renee, Uncle Daniel teaching me to ride his cutting horses. Except for the little hitch when Mom ignored me long enough to fall in love with Scott, I felt like a prince. Everybody was so set on enfolding me in

the family, giving me every experience I'd never had."
He shook his head.

"Are you saying we spoiled you?"

He met his father's eyes. "I'm saying somewhere along the way I got arrogant. I started thinking the world revolved around me."

The ruts he'd noticed earlier in his father's face deepened. "You were a good kid."

"Sure I was. Because everything went my way."

His father mulled that over, sizing Will up. "Is this by way of being an apology?"

Will shifted in his seat. "I was working up to it."

"Have you said any of this to your mother?"

"That's a little harder."

"She's the one who needs to hear it most." Jack took a long swallow of coffee, then shifted gears. "I hear you dated Karin Kristensen, too. Will, I'm sorry."

Will felt his face stiffen. "Dating me was apparently the biggest mistake those women ever made."

"It may have nothing to do with you."

He lifted his cup and swallowed in turn, needing the moment to collect himself. "What are the odds of that?"

"Meg has tied the three murders together."

"I know she's been talking…"

"Detective Giallombardo noticed in the report from Gillian's autopsy that pubic hair identified as being from three men were found on her body. Somehow we all got distracted from that at the time."

"Three?" he repeated, dazed.

"I suppose nobody wanted to say anything to you. Ricky Mendoza's attorney should have jumped on those extra hairs."

Acceptance of the probability that Mendoza in fact hadn't killed Gilly had been seeping into Will's mind.

He hadn't let himself dwell on it yet, because that would take him places he didn't want to go. He'd have to believe things about Gilly that came hard. But this…

"What if there were two rapists?"

Pity softened Jack Murray's craggy face. "Do you believe that?"

Will bent his head and looked at his hands, loosely clasped around the mug. No. God help him, he didn't believe Ricky Mendoza had had a confederate. The savage assault and the staging of the body were too personal.

"No."

"They've been talking to you?"

"Mostly Trina. Detective Giallombardo," he amended.

"She must be about your age," his father said thoughtfully.

"A couple of years younger. I remember her from high school."

"Is she sharp?"

Will gave a rueful laugh. "You know, she reminds me of Mom. With a little of Aunt Abby thrown in. She sees right through me and doesn't hesitate to offer her considered opinion, even if it punctures my ego."

He felt a small jolt, thinking that. Without actually articulating it, he'd spent a lifetime looking for a woman as gutsy as his mother, a woman who would sacrifice everything for someone she loved. Until now, he'd never been able to say those words: *She reminds me of my mother.*

Unaware of what was going through Will's head, his father laughed. "Abby still not speaking to you?"

"Not a word in damn near six years."

"Ben Shea is a braver man than I am."

"No shit," Will agreed.

The two men laughed together.

Jack rolled his shoulders and stretched. "Tell you what, son. Where it comes to Abby, 'I'm sorry' are the magic words."

All amusement fled. Will heard the gravel in his voice. "What about Mom? I said things that strike me now as unforgivable. After everything she did for me…" His throat closed. It was a minute before he could go on. "I can't take those words back."

"No, you can't." For the first time in longer than Will could remember, his father's eyes were kind. "But wishing you could, that's a start."

A start, Will thought with a pang. That's all he asked. The easing of that reserve he saw on both his parents' faces when he was around. The pain in his mother's eyes muted.

A start would be good enough.

CHAPTER FOURTEEN

LED BY LIEUTENANT PATTON, half the major case squad spent the next two days conducting interviews of Will Patton's classmates. They asked many of the same questions Trina had put to Will and came up with more names.

Meantime, Trina hunched by the hour over her computer keyboard, courting eyestrain as she searched DMV, criminal and bankruptcy records, voter registration, firearm licenses and credit reports, laying bare the lives of every male who fell within their circle of interest.

She also had the job of picking up the phone and leaving messages for Will, saying, "Do you remember a Miles Smith?" Or Terry Gammel, or Alan King, or Bob Linn?

Four or five times a day, she heard his voice, either when he answered or on message. He had a distinct voice, deep, resonant, yet just a little gritty. She could imagine how compelling it would be during summations in court.

And damn it, every time she heard it, she had flashbacks.

I really appreciate you staying tonight. The walls were closing in. Then, invariably, her heart gave an uncomfortable lurch when she heard him say, *Maybe that's why I like you,* just before he bent his head to kiss her cheek.

Why had he done that? Because he thought they were getting to be friends? Or—worse yet—he saw her as sister material?

But then she'd remember the way she would occasionally catch his gaze lowering to her breasts or lingering on her mouth. Had she been imagining things?

She was getting really, really tired of reliving the most exciting kiss of her life. Because it was also the most boring. He'd kissed her on the *cheek,* for Pete's sake! She'd have scared him to death if she'd turned her head and their lips had brushed.

Forget it, she'd order herself, and almost succeed.

Until she had to call him again.

He had pulled his own yearbooks out of storage and she knew he was looking up the schoolmates that she asked him about, hoping pictures would stir memories. When he called her back, he would admit that he had found the guy's face in a football team photo, but couldn't remember him.

"Wasn't Bob Linn a couple of years behind me?"

"One."

He muttered something she took as a profanity. Pages fluttered. "I don't know," he said doubtfully, as he evidently studied the class photo. Then, "How can someone I don't even remember hate me?"

"Because you never noticed him?" She closed tired eyes. "We're reaching, I know."

Why did you kiss me? she begged silently.

"Sorry to keep bothering you," she said, and made herself focus on her computer monitor instead of a stupidly juvenile crush that should have died a natural death years ago.

Because she was careful, she started her computer search with friends of Will's who she knew were in town, whether they were likely candidates or not.

Vince Baker had been in graduate school at the University of Washington when Gillian Pappas was murdered. The spring break did not coincide with Willamette College's. After all these years, Trina had no way of verifying his actual attendance that week, but considered the possibility that he'd happened to be cutting a week's class unlikely. Once he'd earned his CPA, he and Maria had come home to Elk Springs where he'd gone to work for Juanita Butte Ski Area. Five years ago, he went into business for himself and did taxes and books for local businesses. It appeared he was prospering. He and Maria had bought a house three years ago on the outskirts of town in a development Trina knew to be upscale. He and Maria owned a red Subaru Legacy and a silver Honda Civic. He just didn't fit the profile.

She was able quickly to verify that Justin Hill had in fact competed in a freestyle World Cup skiing event in Bad Gastein, Austria, the day after Amy Owen was murdered. She crossed off his name.

Ditto Travis Booth, who had not only competed but won a downhill race the week of Gillian's murder. A favorite of the European press corps, he'd been photographed repeatedly that week at Val d'Isere, seemingly romancing a different woman every night.

She discovered that Billy Landon had been arrested at a Gay Pride parade in Portland for assaulting a protester representing the Christian right. Voter rolls showed him resident in Portland for the past seven years. She called his parents without identifying herself and said, "Hi, I heard Billy is home," only to be told,

"I'm sorry, he doesn't get over here much. We went over to see him for Christmas. Can I tell him who called?" Trina crossed him off her list.

Dirk Whittaker had lived here in Elk Springs since graduating from high school. His work record was spotty, and he and Marcie had been in credit counseling. He drove a Ford Explorer SUV, dark green. Worth talking to again, Trina noted.

Jimmy McCartin proved to be more interesting. To begin with, he had a permit for a concealed weapon. He'd changed real estate firms three times—she made a note to ask him why. Most intriguingly, he'd worked in Beaverton outside of Portland and in Astoria, apparently returning home to Elk Springs only the previous summer. She believed they'd find the killer had left Elk Springs during the six years since Gillian Pappas's murder and recently returned, so finding that McCartin had done just that was the equivalent of waving a red flag. She couldn't verify whether he'd been in Elk Springs when Gillian was murdered, but she knew he hadn't gotten his real estate license until that summer. Living at home while he studied for it—that made sense. Vehicle: a brand-new black Dodge Durango SLT 4X4. Made for the treacherous winter conditions—and conveniently sized for hauling bodies. At the time of Gillian's murder, he'd owned a ten-year-old Ford Escort, but interestingly enough his parents lived less than a quarter mile from the park where her body was found. No criminal record surfaced, but that didn't stop Trina from starring his name.

She'd interviewed Gavin Husby after Karin's murder, and found him helpful but…odd. Antsy. She found a divorce record first, in September of the previous year, from a Jennifer Ann Husby who asked for and was granted the right to have her maiden name of Ryan restored. Two domestic disturbance calls were recorded in the month preceding the divorce filing. In both cases he'd knocked the wife around. He served thirty days in the county jail for the second offense. It was while he was in jail that she filed for divorce and apparently packed up and left Elk Springs. Trina wondered how long he'd been married.

Gavin had apparently never bothered to register to vote. DMV records showed him possessing a valid Oregon state driver's license with an Elk Springs address at the time of Gillian Pappas's murder, but shortly thereafter it expired without being renewed. Three years ago, he acquired a new Oregon license, showing an address in Portland. A year later he was in Linn County. A year after that, in Salem. He'd returned to Elk Springs sometime last spring or summer. About the same time as Jimmy McCartin, Trina mused.

She dug deeper and found he'd lived in Washington State during the years immediately following Gillian's murder. Bellingham, up near the Canadian border, then Seattle for perhaps a year, and finally Vancouver across the Columbia River from Portland, where he moved next.

He changed jobs at least once a year, sometimes twice, it appeared. Apparently car dealerships were always happy to snap up an experienced salesman. He always drove brand-new vehicles, traded in almost as often as he changed jobs. However, he had filed for bankruptcy when he was in Linn County. Either no one was buying cars, or he wasn't doing a very good job selling them.

Current vehicle: a Chevrolet Duramax Diesel 4X4 crew cab. She rocked back in her chair, wondering what the payments were on it. She bet it had cost darn near $40,000. And diesel—it might have the deep-throated engine Luella Bailey had described hearing the night of Amy's murder.

Oh, yeah, Gavin Husby deserved further investigation.

While she was still mulling over Gavin's history, Jerry Dixon strode into the squad room, shedding outer clothing as he came. One of the detectives the lieutenant had reassigned to work on the Kristensen and Owen murders, Jerry was nearing retirement. Thick through the middle, he had skinny legs, short salt-and-pepper hair surrounding a bald pate, and ears that stuck out enough to earn him the nickname "Dumbo" Dixon.

"Made a woman cry," he announced.

"Who?" Trina asked.

"Marcie Whittaker." He rolled his chair over to Trina's desk. "Turns out she doesn't actually know where her husband was the night of either murder. Works at a tire place. According to her, he claims he was helping someone rebuild an engine. She's afraid he's having an affair."

"Did you talk to him?"

"No, I figured I'd nail him right after work. The garage doors are open. He's definitely there."

"Good." Trina nodded. "My gut feeling is, Dirk Whittaker isn't smart enough to have committed these murders. Our guy understands fingerprints and trace evidence."

"Well, Dirk obviously doesn't understand women." Jerry cackled at his own wit. "But maybe he watches *CSI* and *Law and Order.*"

"Possible," she conceded. "In the meantime, do you want to come with me to talk to Gavin Husby?"

"To offer a second opinion, or because you want back up?"

"Both." She went off-line. "If there's time, we can talk to Jimmy McCartin, too. They're my two current favorites."

She braced herself for him to ask whether Lieutenant Patton had okayed her decision to go talk to Gavin. To her faint surprise, he didn't. He only grinned at her, face crinkling and giving him the look of a gnome. "I'm your man."

The one good thing about this investigation was that she felt herself growing more confident by the day. When she and Lieutenant Patton closed themselves in the lieutenant's office to talk about what they'd found and where to go with it, Trina had quit hesitating before expressing her opinion or even contradicting her superior. She was starting to think she was good at this. That she didn't have to ask permission to run with an idea.

Gavin Husby's apartment complex was a poor twin to hers: stucco and brick instead of clapboard siding and brick, but also boasting covered parking and, according to the For Rent sign, a laundry room. His huge, gleaming pickup truck with a sleek black canopy didn't belong here. The few other vehicles here midday were ten years old or more. She saw an old white Dodge Caravan with clear tape covering a broken taillight, a rusting Chevy half-ton with no tailgate and a Mercury Cougar with a cracked windshield and one flat tire.

An unpleasant odor and the shriek of an unhappy toddler came from behind the door of the apartment below his. A woman's voice screamed at the kid, who only cried harder. Trina saw Jerry shaking his head.

Trina would have sworn the same kid was crying and the same mother yelling as the last time she was here. Some of her enthusiasm for Gavin as serial killer evaporated. What would he do, bring victims home, then carry their bodies back out to his truck? These walls were obviously thin. The back of his pickup? Maybe. She'd noted the tinted windows. But the killer had been so careful not to leave trace evidence, would he really commit his crimes in his own vehicle, where the thrashing victim was bound to leave hair, blood and fingerprints? And even then, where would he park to be sure he wouldn't be interrupted?

She rang the bell, and Gavin came to the door after a minute. Barefoot, he wore low-slung, baggy jeans and a thin gray ribbed tank top that bared stringy muscles. "Hey. Detective Giallombardo is back."

Trina didn't like the way he said her name, each syllable enunciated. It felt mocking. She was trying real hard not to dislike Gavin Husby because he had a weasly face and poor impulse control where his ex-wife had been concerned.

"This is Detective Dixon. May we come in?" she asked. "We'd like to talk to you again."

"Yeah. Sure." He stood back. "I wasn't expecting anyone."

Despite what she took as an apology, the place was neat to the point of being sterile, just as it had been the first time she saw it. It could have been a vacant furnished apartment.

"You're pretty tidy for a bachelor," she commented.

"I've got nothing better to do while I'm not working." He turned off the television, which had been tuned to some shoot 'em up movie or show she didn't recognize in the one glance. "Go ahead. Sit down. There hasn't been another murder, has there?"

Why was she so sure he knew there hadn't been? She chose one end of the couch, Jerry at the other.

Gavin sat down in the recliner facing the TV. An open beer can and the remote control were the only indication he actually lived here. He shook his head. "Karin. Boy, that hit hard. She and I really had some chemistry. You know?"

"You did say that you'd intended to ask her out."

He rocked a couple of times, quickly, pushing off hard with his bare feet. The recliner creaked. "Yeah, yeah. Jeez. Have you found out anything?" His gaze flicked between them.

"We're pursuing several leads." Trina opened her notebook. "Mr. Husby, did you know Gillian Pappas?"

Muscles tightened around his eyes. "Sure, I did. Will's girlfriend. Why are you asking me about her?"

"I'm sure you've seen television and newspaper accounts suggesting similarities between the two recent murders and Ms. Pappas's."

"Yeah, but that guy is in jail for killing her." He leaned forward, expression avid. "You don't think...?"

She deliberately made her tone wooden. "We're exploring the possibility that this killer saw Ms. Pappas's body or attended the trial. He's gotten some details wrong, but similarities certainly exist."

So quickly she might have imagined it, anger flashed on his face. Or maybe she *did* imagine it. Certainly when she studied him, his expression was ingenuous.

"I didn't go to the trial. I can't tell you who did."

"You did live in Elk Springs at the time?"

"Yeah, I went to the community college and then I started working out at Rick Haydon Chevrolet. That's why I never went. I was working."

"I see," she said. "Perhaps you can tell us if you recall anyone seeming especially interested in talking about the crime and the trial. Perhaps reading obsessively about it."

"You mean, friends?" He shook his head. "Well, of course you do. You figure the killer has to be someone who knew Karin and Amy. Somebody who hung out with Will and me."

Noting the casual way he paired himself and Will, she wondered whether he particularly wanted the investigators to think he and Will were best friends. Or was it *he* who wanted to believe they were?

"It's certainly a possibility," she agreed.

"I don't want to rat on friends."

"Mr. Husby, this was a terrible crime. Surely you want to help us catch this monster before he kills again."

His face twitched, expressions crossing it too quickly for the naked eye to read. "Okay. I mean, you're right. Uh…Travis. Travis Booth. You know him? The skier whose career bombed? He wasn't here then, but he called constantly. He had me send him newspaper clippings. He might have kept an album or something."

"I understand he and Will Patton are close friends."

"They were in high school. I don't know so much anymore."

She pretended to scribble a note. "Anyone else?"

"It's hard to think. I mean, that's all *anyone* talked about. You know?" He looked from one to the other detective. "We all knew Gilly. We figured she and Will would end up married. He was *destroyed* afterward."

"Let me suggest some names. Perhaps you recall whether they were here in Elk Springs at the time." She flipped back a couple of pages in her notebook, as if needing to check a list. "Billy Landon."

"The faggot?"

She didn't quite hide her surprise. "He'd come out in high school?"

He sneered. "No, but you could tell. There was no way *he* raped anyone."

"Jimmy McCartin."

"Wannabe McCartin? We couldn't shake him in high school. He sells real estate now, you know." He frowned. "Yeah, he was around then. I'm almost sure he was. Probably sniffing after all our girlfriends."

"Sniffing?"

"Yeah, you know. Haven't you ever had a dog follow you when you were having that time of the month? Maybe try to hump your leg?"

Startled and offended by his crudeness, Trina was careful not to let her expression change.

"That's what Jimmy was like. At dances he'd just kind of ooze up to girls like Nita Voss and Amy. The hot ones who didn't even know he was alive. He'd cut in on dances. That kind of shit." He shook his head. "Pathetic."

"And you, Mr. Husby?" She allowed doubt to creep into her tone. "Did you date the 'hot' girls?"

He didn't hide the anger as well this time. She wondered why he bothered.

"You kidding? They liked jocks. I even screwed around with the great Will's girlfriend, Christine Nylander, at a party once. He never knew." His eyes widened. "Unless you tell him. But you wouldn't do that, would you, Detective Giallombardo?"

She stared back at him, face impassive. After a moment, she said, "I understand that you moved back to Elk Springs just recently?"

"Yeah, last summer." He shrugged. "Seemed like the thing to do."

"At the time you were married."

His face contorted. "Yeah, shit, you know that bitch

got me sent to jail. Nothing was ever *her* fault." Facial muscles relaxed. "Good riddance."

Something in the way he said the last rang an alarm for Trina. It wouldn't hurt to follow up on the where-abouts of the former Mrs. Husby and be sure she was all right.

"Where were you living before last summer?"

"Me? Oh, I'm the regular rolling stone. You know, gathering no moss." He chortled. "I get bored and move on. I've lived all over the Northwest. Portland, Seattle, you name it."

"I gather you have no trouble finding work."

"I'm too good to have trouble." He sprawled back in his chair, all but preening. "Any dealer is lucky to have me, and they know it."

"But you're currently out of work."

"This is a slow time of year. Why hustle in shitty weather when you can afford to stay home?"

"Then it's not true that you tend to leave jobs be-cause of quarrels with your bosses? Because of an un-cooperative attitude?"

He shot forward, his voice rigid with fury. "Who the hell told you that? I've got a right to know!"

"I'm afraid I can't tell you," she said blandly, satis-fied to have gotten an unambiguous response. "Can you answer the question, Mr. Husby?"

"Whether I get along with my bosses? Some of them are pricks. Okay? They undercut me doing my job, I tell them. That makes me uncooperative? They're idiots! I'll forget more about selling cars than they'll ever learn!"

"And yet they keep hiring you."

His eyes narrowed to glittering slits. "I average twenty-two cars sold a month. Year in, year out. Bad

months, good months, no matter what dealer I'm working for. My top month, I sold fifty-one cars. That makes
me the goddamn Van Gogh of car salesmen. See?"

Hadn't Van Gogh first cut off his ear in a fit of mad-
ness and finally killed himself? Why not Rembrandt?
Michelangelo? Did Gavin Husby imagine himself to be
both brilliant and insane?

She closed her notebook. "Thank you for your cooperation, Mr. Husby. We'd appreciate you staying
available should we need to speak to you again."

"Don't leave town?" He stood. "Why would I?"

Trina didn't like the sensation of having him standing over her. She got up, too, not allowing herself to step
back to open distance between them.

"I'm sure there's no reason at all that you'd want to
leave Elk Springs," she said, holding his gaze with a
cool one of her own.

"You bet your sweet titties there isn't," he said in a
low voice she sensed was meant for her ears alone.

Jerry Dixon heard him. "You're speaking to an officer of the law, Mr. Husby." His voice was steely.
"Please remember that."

Gavin held Trina's gaze for a moment more, as if he
wanted to be sure she saw that he couldn't be pushed.
Then he turned with exaggerated surprise.

"I didn't mean anything by that. Sorry, Detective
Giallombardo. It was a figure of speech."

"Uh-huh," Jerry muttered.

Trina nodded at Will's not-quite-friend. "Good day."

Not until the door was closed behind she and Jerry
did she realize that goose bumps prickled over her skin.

The two detectives walked in silence to the Explorer.
Inside it, both doors closed, he said, "That's our guy."

She wanted to agree, couldn't remember when she'd

despised someone more. "He's scum, that's for sure. That doesn't mean he's a serial killer."

Jerry's face was unusually serious. "He forgot I was even there. You're a woman, and that guy has plenty of trouble dealing with women. You pushed pretty hard. He hates your guts, Giallombardo. You need to be careful there."

"I'll be careful," she said, with bravado she didn't feel. "It'll be interesting to see what Gavin Husby does now."

"I like him for our killer," Jerry said stubbornly.

"Maybe." Trina started the engine. "What say we go talk to Jimmy McCartin?"

"Today, you're the boss."

The Century 21 office was in a storefront on Main Street, sandwiched between a jeweler and a café/bookstore. Photos of properties for sale were artfully arranged on boards set on easels of varying heights in the window. Trina noted a cluster of homes available in Crescent Ridge.

Inside, a pretty young receptionist said, "Mr. McCartin? Let me check to see if he's available."

He came out a moment later, beaming, hand extended. Trina doubted she'd have recognized him from his high school yearbook photo. Then, he'd been scrawny and geeky looking. Now, she guessed his wiry body was that of a runner. He wasn't a handsome man, but he radiated pleasure at the chance to meet them.

"Did you see a listing with my name on it?" He shook Jerry's hand vigorously, then Trina's. "You look familiar."

"I went to high school here," she admitted. "A couple of years behind you."

"Ah! That'd be it." He looked from one to the other. "What can I do for you folks?"

She introduced herself and Jerry and asked if they could speak to him privately.

His smile scarcely dimmed. "Why, of course you can! Awful thing up there at Crescent Ridge! Not so good for the developer, either. He's pretty nervous right now, thinking it's going to affect sales. I've already had one good prospect shy away."

Will? she wondered.

McCartin led them to a conference room with upholstered chairs around a veneered oak table. A binder with more photos of houses lay open. He closed it as they sat around one end of the table.

"Now, what can I tell you?"

Shot in the dark. "I understand you dated the victim at one point."

His face reminded her of Jim Carrey's, with that malleable quality that allowed him to effortlessly change expressions. Now it spoke of grief and solemnity.

"Karin. Yes, last fall we dated a few times. Nothing earthshaking. But you understand how shocked I was to hear it was her."

With a few nudges, she got him to talk about how they'd met, how long they'd seen each other, why the relationship fizzled. She couldn't read any resentment into his admission that Karin was the one who moved on, but then Jimmy McCartin's expressions were an awful lot harder to interpret than Gavin Husby's, despite their exaggerated quality.

"Did you know Amy Owen as well?"

"Yes, in high school."

"Did you date her as well?"

He laughed. "Lord, no! I was the equipment manager, not the star quarterback. In those days, I'd have been lucky if she remembered my name." His features reassembled to express sadness. "Terrible thing."

"Did it bother you that she couldn't be bothered to remember your name?" Trina asked.

"Not a bit. She was a star to be admired from afar to someone like me." He bobbed his head, shrugged a couple of times in a twitchy way. "Okay, that's not totally true. I mean, what kid *likes* knowing he's invisible? Me, I pretended a lot. Hey, as equipment manager, I was part of the team, right? More important than the bench sitters, that was for sure! So I hung out with those guys, told myself they were my friends even though I knew better."

Trina felt a painful twinge of sympathy, even identification. *What kid* likes *knowing he's invisible?* But she couldn't allow that sympathy to affect this interview. Not if there was the slightest chance Jimmy McCartin had let his sense of alienation blossom into an anger so violent, all he wanted was to destroy the girls who'd ignored him—and the man who had been one of the acknowledged leaders of the guys who hadn't really been Jimmy's friends.

"Like Will Patton?" she asked softly. "Was he one of those guys?"

"Funny you should mention Will. He's the client I was telling you about…" He broke off. "Wait. Will's girlfriend was the one who was murdered back— what?—six, eight years ago."

"That's right."

"He and Amy had a thing in high school." His forehead crinkled earnestly. "But Karin…"

He wasn't likely to forget that a woman he'd dated had been seen shortly thereafter with Will Patton.

"The two of them recently dated a couple times."

His eyes opened wide. "You're thinking…"

"Tell me, Mr. McCartin. Did you dislike Will Patton? Resent the fact that you were invisible to him, too?"

"No, no!" Finally he registered alarm. "Will was a good guy! Always decent to me, even if we both knew I wasn't in his league."

"Were you in Elk Springs when his girlfriend was murdered?"

He blinked quickly, several times. "Yes…well, let me think…yes. Uh-huh. Sure. I remember reading the paper, hearing people talking. I didn't know her, of course. It wasn't as if Will and I had stayed friends once we graduated." He gave an unconvincing laugh. "Once I wasn't the equipment manager any more!"

"And during the trial?"

"Sure, I was living at home that year. I remember now. That's when I was studying for my real estate exams."

"Did you follow the trial closely, Mr. McCartin?"

"Jimmy. Jimmy, please!" He gave her a big, meaningless grin. "After all, we went to high school together. As for the trial. No. No, not really. Just casually."

"And you're aware of the similarities between these two recent murders and the murder of Will's girlfriend back then?"

He was squirming now, but managed still to sound expansive, amiable, a salesman to the core. "Sure, sure. I've been following the news. Strangest damn thing. And tragic, of course."

"Do you remember where you were on the night of either murder, Mr. McCartin?"

"I was home both nights. I'm not seeing anyone right now, not seriously, and I do live alone. Nice place out in Metolius Heights."

Her gaze dropped to his hand, drumming the padded

arm of his chair, the soft sound reminding her of chattering teeth. Jimmy McCartin was a nervous man.

Because he was a normal citizen who didn't like the implication behind her questions? Or because he'd never expected the eye of the law to turn his way at all?

Perhaps he'd said it best himself. Wasn't Jimmy McCartin invisible? Consumed by rage, did he gain some pleasure from taking advantage of the fact that no one ever remembered whether he was there or not?

"Thank you for your cooperation, Mr. McCartin." Trina closed her notebook and stood, conscious of Jerry doing the same. "We'd appreciate it if you'd stay available."

He all but bounded to his feet. "Naturally! Anything I can do. Anything at all!" He hustled around the table, grin in place. "Let me walk you folks out."

Have you ever had a dog follow you when you were having that time of the month? Maybe try to hump your leg?

Okay, Trina thought, Jimmy was as creepy in his own way as Gavin was. *Nobody* could be this good-humored, this eager to please, not after being asked for their whereabouts on the night of a brutal murder. Jimmy was just better at suppressing his anger.

But anger had to come out somehow, didn't it?

CHAPTER FIFTEEN

WILL WAS working up a search warrant when Trina marched into his office.

"Well, you have some real scum for friends," she declared, flinging herself into a chair.

"What?" He wrenched his attention from the monitor on his laptop.

"You heard me. I just spent a fun afternoon talking to Jimmy and Gavin. Good guys. They both made my skin crawl."

Feeling pulled two ways, he shook his head. "Hold the thought." He read over his embroideries on the boilerplate warrant and hit Print. On impulse, he said, "Want to walk with me? I've got to find a judge." He put on his wool coat and grabbed the pages feeding out of the printer.

She looked over his shoulder. "A warrant. Sure. You have a preference? I saw Shuh turn around and go back into the courthouse with someone."

Will hadn't met His Honor Duane M. Shuh yet, but he shrugged. This one was a gimme. "Let's hustle."

She had to trot to keep up with his long strides. "Who wants it?"

"Aunt Abby." He glanced back at Trina as she tore around a corner in the hall after him. "She's not a patient woman."

"I met her."

"You did?" He held open the outer door for her, his nose catching that faintly exotic scent even as the cold air hit them. Floral, but not your average roses or lilac. An interesting contrast to her pedestrian clothes and a face bare of makeup. With an effort he recovered his train of thought. Aunt Abby. Trina. How did they connect? "Oh, yeah. Crescent Ridge."

"Speaking of which, ol' Jimmy couldn't decide whether to be more upset by the tragedy of a woman's grisly death or the fact that property values up there may be affected."

Will shook his head. "Why doesn't that surprise me?"

She looked cute with her cheeks turning pink. He wished she'd lose the navy blazer and slacks. Plainclothes, that was not. She might as well be wearing a uniform. That *was* her uniform. She must have a closet full of identical slacks and white Oxford cloth shirts.

He had to slow down, with the sidewalk still icy. A thin blanket of white still cloaked lawns and weighted the branches of trees and the gray framework of shrubs. He'd forgotten how damn cold winters were here. The snow *wanted* to melt, he'd swear it did. Daytime highs of nineteen degrees Fahrenheit made sure it didn't happen.

The snow had been plowed from major roads, leaving a sheet of black ice that kept traffic slow. Will grabbed Trina's arm when they crossed the street in front of the courthouse. In dress shoes, his own traction wasn't good.

Rock salt crunched underfoot as they climbed the granite steps to the imposing old building.

"You really think Jimmy is a possibility?" he asked, incredulous even though he knew better than most that the average criminal wasn't a hulking creature with a perpetual sneer. In law school, he'd attended a family court hearing just to see what a father who sexually abused his daughter looked like. The guy was maybe five-four, soft and meek. Will remembered feeling the same incredulity. *Him? How could he be a monster?*

"Don't know." She slipped through when he held open the ornate entry door. "Shuh's office is upstairs." She led the way.

His Honor looked irked at being interrupted until he heard this new young D.A. was Sheriff Murray's son and the investigating officer was Abby Patton, after which he listened to the circumstances and signed with a flourish. "Give Abby my best."

"Glad to."

"See you in court," the judge said with a nod, returning to his phone call while Will retreated. The moment the etched office door closed behind him, he pulled out his cell phone and called his aunt.

"Will?" She didn't sound entirely pleased to hear his voice. Given that she'd been snubbing him for six years, she probably wasn't any more pleased than he was to find out they'd be working together on a case that looked likely to end up at trial. "I'll be by your office in five minutes," she said. "Who signed it?"

"Duane Shuh."

"Hmph." Dead air told him she'd hung up.

"Nice," he muttered.

"Who's nice?" Trina asked.

He ignored the question. "You done for the day?"

Matching her footsteps to his as they returned around the rotunda, she said distractedly, "Huh? Oh. Yeah, I suppose." She heaved a sigh. "I thought I'd drive by McCartin's place on my way home. Just to see what it looks like."

Just like his mother, she couldn't let a case go once she started worrying at it. "You mean," he said, "to check out whether a neighbor would be likely to hear a woman scream if he was holding her in his garage."

"Something like that," she admitted.

Out in the cold, they started down the broad steps again. "At his own house." Will shook his head. "That seems risky. Our perp has been so careful."

"Yeah, but where, then?"

"I don't know." He grabbed her arm again when she slithered on the sidewalk just as a Saab, loaded with skis, drove by too fast. This time, Will didn't let go, and Trina didn't object.

"Dinner?" he asked. "Sweet and sour prawns?"

"Bribery, just so you can pick my brain." She paused, as if to give him a chance to deny it. "Okay, but let me go home and change first. *And* drive by McCartin's house."

"See you," he said, turning into the first entrance to the Public Safety building while she continued down the sidewalk to her Explorer.

While she got in, he looked up and down the street, real casually. He didn't see a big pickup truck with a canopy or any black SUV but hers. Didn't see anyone just sitting in a parked vehicle of any kind, and no other vehicles started up to follow her when she set off down the street and turned the corner.

Will didn't consider himself a paranoid guy, but he couldn't shake his sense of unease when he returned to his office. It had undoubtedly just been chance the other night. Some guy had been waiting for his girlfriend to come home and gave up when she didn't. Or Will had been thinking about Trina and just didn't notice the sound of another resident at the apartment complex coming out.

But he still thought, *I shouldn't have asked her over. I should stay away from her until she and Mom catch this guy.*

Then he pictured calling and trying to think of a good explanation for canceling, one that wouldn't hurt her feelings. He was scowling when he walked into his office.

"Happy to see you, too," his aunt snapped, turning from the bulletin board where he'd posted comic strips that amused him. She held out her hand.

He put a signed copy of the warrant in it. "The frown wasn't for you."

"No?" Looking uncannily like his mother, she gazed stonily back at him. "Just your natural expression these days?"

He went around his desk and sank into his chair, feeling the same bone-deep exhaustion he had in college when he got mono. Actually having a conversation with his aunt after all these years was proving to be a real pick-me-up. "I've been a son of a bitch. Tell me something I don't know."

Looking intrigued, she planted a fist on her hip and considered him. "Well, well. Is the Will I once knew and loved stirring inside?"

"I think I went a little crazy when they told me about Gilly." Uh-huh. What an excuse for leveling his rage at the people he loved most.

Unimpressed, voice unyielding, Aunt Abby said, "I think you'd turned into a jackass sometime before that."

"You noticed?" He gave a tired laugh. "Why didn't you take me down a few pegs?"

"I tried. You were too busy feeling godlike."

He muttered an imprecation. "I'm sorry, Aunt Abby. Sorrier than I can ever tell you."

Just like his father, she said, "You're telling the wrong person."

"I'm getting warmed up," he admitted.

"You know she'll forgive you in a heartbeat."

"I know she'll say she does," he corrected. "Maybe she'll even believe it herself. But we both know she's never going to feel the same about me."

Amazingly, Abby Patton's blue eyes softened. "Will, here's a tip. Your mother never has felt any different about you. Sure you hurt her feelings. But she doesn't love you any less. No more than she loved you any less after you were such a shit about Scott. She almost lost him, thanks to you, but did you ever, for a moment, think your mother didn't still love you?"

There seemed to be a great stillness inside him. Made mute, he shook his head.

"Well, then?" She smiled, catlike, held up the warrant and said, "Good to work with you, Will Patton." The next second, she was gone, leaving him to gape after her.

WHILE HE COOKED and they ate, Will kept conversation easygoing and off the one subject that undoubtedly preoccupied them both.

Trina kept thinking, *He wants to know what's happening real bad, to give up his evenings like this.* What other explanation was there?

It was idiotic of her to wish they could keep talking like this forever, about nothing and everything, with no ulterior motive on either side.

Only when he poured the coffee did Will say, "So, you didn't like Gavin either."

"I wasn't kidding about my skin crawling." She reached for the cream. "Jeez, Will! He's really a *friend* of yours?"

"What did he say to you?"

"Not so much that was overt. But he mocked, he sneered, he seethed." A shudder traveled up her spine. "He tried to shock me. I don't think he liked the fact that a woman was interviewing him."

Worry lines aged his lean face. "I thought maybe he'd changed. He was married, you know."

"And arrested twice for beating his wife. And that was only in the three or four months they lived here in Elk Springs before the divorce."

He swore.

"Yeah, you know how to pick 'em."

His voice became dangerous. "Don't keep saying that."

Startled and intrigued, she tilted her head back to study him, standing on the other side of the table with the coffeepot still in his hand. "That I don't like your friend?"

"I told you I never liked him."

"But you hang out with him."

He slammed the coffeepot down on the table "Do you want to know why? Goddamn it, I'll tell you why! Guilt!"

"Guilt?" she whispered.

Will sank into his chair as if his legs didn't want to hold him. "I treated him like shit in high school. Somewhere along the line, I grew a conscience. I've been trying to make up for it ever since."

Finally, she got it. His arrogant persona was a cover. Beneath the expensive clothes, the commanding figure, the sexy voice, the intelligence that reputedly made him a brilliant trial attorney, was a man who knew he had more going for him than most people did, and felt guilty about it.

Trina was appalled to realize that her teenage crush had just metamorphosed into something a lot deeper and scarier.

"Um." She had to clear her throat. "You know that's ridiculous, don't you?"

He glowered at her. "What's that supposed to mean?"

"From what you've told me, Gavin Husby was a creep in high school, too. Instead of laughing off his nastiness toward women, you called him on it. Why do you now see that as treating him like shit?"

"It was more than that." He rubbed his hand over his jaw, making a rasping sound. "I knew he had trouble at home. Maybe I could have made a difference. Instead, I just didn't see him as measuring up. He wasn't a good enough athlete, he wasn't good-looking enough, he wasn't popular enough." Will's tone was filled with self-loathing. "My friends were the best. We knew we were. Man, he was like an ugly blot on a beautiful picture."

"And yet, you and your friends did tolerate him, at least some of the time."

He made a vague gesture. "Some of the others put up with him better than I did."

"Travis?"

"No, he hated Gavin's guts." He shook his head. "I don't know. Justin. He thought Gavin was funny. Egged him on, sometimes. Dirk. Even Vince. Vince is so easygoing, he always wants to see the best in everyone."

"Okay. So you've been including this guy ever since you graduated from high school because you feel guilty you didn't treat him better when you were no better than a teenager yourself."

His mouth twisted. "You think that's a good enough excuse?"

"I think you're wasting your self-pity on a scumbag." She shrugged. "Just my opinion."

His eyes sharpened and he gave a soft laugh. "I can just hear you when you have kids, bucking 'em up, sending them back out into the fray armed with common sense."

The sting surprised her. "So I sound like an old-fashioned schoolmarm?"

"No." His voice caressed her. "You sound like a mother."

She tried to make her shrug careless. "No chance of that happening for a while."

His eyes narrowed, just for an instant. He swallowed coffee, watching her over the brim of the cup, finally setting it down. "You know too much about me, Trina Giallombardo. Time for you to confess something."

She felt herself stiffen. "Confess?"

"Why this massive inferiority complex?"

She blinked in genuine surprise. "What are you talking about? I like myself just fine!"

"Then why are you always implying that you don't see yourself as attractive?"

"I know what I am and what I'm not," she said with dignity. "I'm okay looking. I'm not a…a Nita Voss or Christine Nylander."

"You mean, you're short, dark-haired and curvy instead of tall, long-legged and blond. So what?"

"So nothing," she floundered. "They're beautiful. I'm pretty on a good day."

"Why did you pick them as examples?" he asked softly.

Uh-oh. She shrugged as if the whole conversation was absurd. "What am I supposed to say? I'm not beautiful like Amy Owen and Karin Kristensen? After seeing their bodies, I can't feel all that envious of them!"

He contemplated her, and she had a feeling he was looking a lot deeper than she wanted him to. "Were there girls in your own high school class you were jealous of?"

"Um…" Her mind was a gigantic blank. She couldn't think of a single name. Not one! Compared to her own classmates, she'd felt smart and been as popular as she wanted to be. The last two years of high school, after Will was gone, she'd been content, living in her own little bubble. A few friends, a boyfriend briefly, a date to the prom and a determined vision of her future. She wouldn't be just a cop, she'd be a detective. As good as Meg Patton.

Always Pattons, she thought in shock. On a squeeze of misery, she realized that she'd been entirely shaped by the Pattons all unknown to them, by her hopeless desire to measure up. If that wasn't pathetic, she didn't know what was.

"Nobody you'd know," she finally said, voice gruff. "I was using your classmates as a for-example."

"Uh-huh."

"I was!"

"You know what I think, Trina Giallombardo?" A half smile played with the corners of his mouth. "I think you had a crush on one of my friends. Now, which one was it?"

Humiliation burned her cheeks. Just to get it over with, she blurted, "You. Who else?"

His smile died. They stared at each other.

Struggling to find air in a room that seemed to have become a vacuum, she said in a small, desperate voice, "It was a long time ago. I knew you'd never notice me."

Sounding strange, he said, "You were wrong."

Now she really couldn't breathe. "What?"

"I've noticed you."

His pretence infuriated her for reasons she couldn't

have defined. "Oh, come on! I was invisible to you. One of the masses who parted to let you pass."

"Then why did I recognize you when you came with Mom to tell me about Amy's murder?"

Her mouth opened and closed.

"But that isn't what I was talking about anyway." He got to his feet, as fluid and athletic now as he'd been on the court when she watched from the bleachers, all those years ago. He circled the table and held out a hand. "Come here."

She stared at his hand as if it were a bomb she had no idea how to defuse.

"This is the third time I've had you to dinner," he said, in a tone of reason. "Why did you think I kept inviting you?"

Licking dry lips, she stole a glance up at his face. "Because we were working together?"

"I haven't had anybody from the D.A.'s office over for dinner yet. In fact," he looked thoughtful, "except for Travis, you're the only person who has sat at that table."

"Really?" She despised herself for the way that single word squeaked out.

"Really." He waggled his fingers. "Come on. Don't be a coward."

If there was one thing she wasn't, it was cowardly. Trina took a deep breath, grateful that air did seem to rush into her lungs, and pushed her chair back. She stood to find herself alarmingly close to the man she'd been in love with forever.

"So?" she said, tilting her chin up in pretend brazenness.

He smiled. "So this." He reached out and cupped her face with his big, warm hands. One thumb brushed her lower lip, sending a burst of sweet feeling that was almost painful shooting to her toes and fingers.

She exhaled with a soft sound that darkened his eyes. When he bent his head, her lids seemed to flutter down of their own volition.

The touch of his mouth was as gentle and undemanding as the pad of his thumb. He brushed her lips, tugged gently on them, grazed them with his teeth. Paralyzed by her reaction, she just stood there, hands at her side, neck becoming weak so that her head fell back.

He half laughed, half groaned. "Do you plan to kiss me back, sweetheart?"

Sweetheart? Had he said that, or was she home, deep asleep and dreaming?

"I'm stunned," she whispered.

He nuzzled her ear, his voice a soft rumble. "Does that mean you don't want to kiss me?"

"No!" Her eyes popped open in alarm. "No. I want to kiss you."

"Good," he murmured, his mouth curved in a smile when it met hers this time.

This time, when he sucked on her lower lip, she sucked on his, too. She lifted her hands to his shoulders and felt muscles bunch under her touch. They toyed with each others' mouths for a sweet eternity, until he muttered something under his breath, tilted his head sideways and abruptly deepened the kiss, his tongue in her mouth, one hand sliding lower to wrap her neck. Hunger buckled her knees, leaving her hanging on for dear life. Everything seemed to come down to the hot urgent contact of their mouths, their tongues, the rough scrape of his jaw, the flare in his eyes when she drew back briefly to look at him.

Then somehow he was gripping her hips, pulling her tight against him, groaning against her mouth. His fingers squeezed her buttock. "I think," he said against her cheek, his voice as scratchy as his unshaven jaw, "if you're going to leave, you'd better go now."

This was the nicest dream she'd ever had. *Don't let me ever wake up.*

"Are you asking me to stay?" she whispered.

He laughed and nipped her lower lip. "Do you want me to beg?" he asked, in a voice that sounded shaken despite the amused undercurrent.

"Um…" Giddy with amazement, she pretended to think. "Since you're giving me the chance to live out a high school fantasy…sure."

This laugh was rough. "What I'd really like," he said, "is if this didn't have anything to do with high school."

She couldn't say she blamed him, the way his old friendships had been playing out lately. Trina kissed his throat, loving the way his Adam's apple jumped. "That's okay, too," she murmured. "Just so I get my begging."

"Trina Giallombardo," he obliged, "please will you stay tonight? I could go down on bended knee…"

Except that he was pretty much holding her up, since her legs were feeling about as reliably sturdy as a couple of lengths of licorice.

"Please is good enough," she decided. Common sense did kick in. "Assuming you're, um, prepared."

"I haven't used them in one hell of a long time, but yeah. A man lives in hope."

She almost wished he'd had to go out and buy some, nuisance though that would be. The fact that he had condoms on hand just like he kept garlic in the kitchen cupboard for the next time he needed it made her feel commonplace.

Implying that she was the first woman he'd wanted in a long time was nice, though. She appreciated kindness.

Despite everything, she still felt that extraordinary, bubbles-in-champagne giddiness. Maybe she was one of many, but…he did want her. That was more than she'd ever imagined would actually happen.

Trina smiled at him. "Well, then, what are we waiting for?"

He made an exultant sound and crushed her to him, his mouth descending on hers with a ferocity that stole her breath and her last ability to think. Instead, she just *felt*. Kissing him back with helpless pleasure, she hardly knew when he maneuvered them a step at a time down the hall. The big bed she'd peeked at the once was just there, behind her.

Will undressed her slowly, his gaze caressing every inch of her as he bared it. First her pale belly and breasts that were large enough to occasionally be a nuisance but seemed to please him. While he was unzipping her jeans, she struggled to kick off boots. He slid the jeans and panties over her hips and down her legs until she stepped out of them.

"Pretty," he murmured in a thick voice.

She wanted to see him, too. When she tugged his shirt upward, he obliged by lifting his arms. His chest was wonderful: lean, muscled, the hair dark and soft. When she froze at the idea of touching the bulge beneath his jeans, he took her hands and set them there. Head bent, he watched as she undid the metal buttons that made up the fly, one at a time, pop, pop, pop. Her mouth was dry as she peeled plain gray boxers off to slide down to the floor.

"Ohh," she breathed.

"That's it, sweetheart." Eyelids heavy, he weighed her breasts in his hands and then stroked down her waist to her too-well-rounded hips, squeezing. "Touch me."

She touched, if clumsily, knowing her relative inexperience showed. With a choked, private laugh, she thought, it wouldn't have mattered if she'd had a dozen lovers! This was Will Patton, naked and groaning and calling her sweetheart. Dreams did come true.

He bore her back onto the bed and proceeded to kiss her and touch her until she was dizzy and whimpering, pleasure singing in her blood, pooling in her belly.

They had one moment of desperation when he groped in the drawer beside the bed and failed to find anything but a packet of tissues. Swearing, he went to the bathroom, where she heard the frustrated bang of a cupboard door and then drawers.

Her body seemed to be quivering like a tuning fork and she sent a brief wish/prayer into the ether. *I didn't mean it when I was sorry he had condoms here. It's okay that he does.* If he did.

"Really," she whispered.

It must have worked, because the medicine cabinet slammed and he reappeared with a handful of packets that he dropped on the bedside table. Trina was glad to see his hands shaking as he ripped one open.

The urgency rose again with no more than a kiss, a few murmurs, his hand between her thighs.

He entered her with a long thrust, his eyes fierce on hers, his shoulders slick with sweat. He made love to her with control so unrelenting, she'd come twice before his teeth bared and he pounded into her, a groan seeming to be wrenched from his chest.

Tears burned in her eyes when he jerked and finally collapsed onto her, heart slamming against hers. She reveled in his weight on her, in his scent, pure male, in the silky brush of his hair against her cheek.

Holding on to him tight, she closed her eyes and felt a few tears leak out. She hadn't known it was possible to feel happiness so intense, it hurt.

I can die happy now, she thought, and in the next breath shuddered with the remembrance of the bodies of women who'd also had Will Patton, and then died.

CHAPTER SIXTEEN

TRINA REALLY DIDN'T look forward to seeing Lieutenant Patton the next morning. She cringed to imagine what her superior would think to know her son had spent the night romping in bed with a rookie detective who should be concentrating on her career. A career she owed almost entirely to Lieutenant Meg Patton, who had promoted Trina and then tagged her for this case.

Her phone rang while she was pretending absorption in a criminal database.

"Major Crimes, Giallombardo," she said warily.

Will said, "Hey, Detective Giallombardo."

Her heart took a big thump. She was proud of her casual tone. "Hey yourself." She sneaked a glance around to be sure no one heard her.

"Dinner again tonight?"

"At your place?"

"I was thinking *pasta e fagiole.*"

Whatever that was. "You don't have to cook every night. I could make dinner."

He laughed. "Why does that offer sound so luke-warm?"

"Gee, maybe because it would be like a teenager who plays violin in the high school orchestra performing in front of Isaac Stern. So okay. We could go out."

"You object to *pasta e fagiole?* How about penne pasta

with artichokes and shrimp? Of if you don't like Italian…"

Don't be dense, she told herself. He either really wanted to cook, or he didn't want to dine out. At least, not with her. She didn't have enough pride to ask why.

"Pasta whatever sounded good. The first one."

"Good." His voice was low and intimate. "Got to go. I'll see you when you can get there."

She hung up the phone feeling buzzed—and bothered. This would be her fourth dinner at his apartment. Wouldn't it be normal at this point, since they had something going, for him to suggest they eat out or go to a movie or something?

But combating her niggling fear that he was ashamed to be seen with her was her delight that they *weren't* going out. Fantastic food, lovemaking, pillow talk and more lovemaking… Who needed a movie?

Behind her, the lieutenant announced, "Everyone working the Kristensen and Owen murders, let's gather in the conference room and compare notes."

In a group, Trina thought. She could handle that.

Most detectives stopped to fill coffee cups, then spread themselves around one end of the long table. Trina opened her notebook.

Sitting at the head of the table, Meg Patton said, "Jerry?"

"We need to put more pressure on Dirk Whittaker. He won't give me the name of the guy he's supposed to have been rebuilding that engine with. Can't meet my eyes, either."

"What's your feeling about him?" Lieutenant Patton asked.

"That he and his wife are having troubles and he's either having an affair or has just fallen to temptation a couple of times," he said without hesitation. "I can't be sure, because he's hiding something, no question, but murder…" He shook his head. "I can't see it. There's no anger bubbling under there. You know? Just…despair."

After a moment of silence, the lieutenant nodded. "Keep on him."

Somebody had interviewed Adrian Benson, who'd apparently had something going with Amy Owen before her death. Several of Amy's friends had suggested that she was tired of him, which gave him a motive. But he'd flown to Mazatlan with a group of friends a week later, and still been there when Karin was killed.

"You talked to friends?" Lieutenant Patton peered above reading glasses.

"Yep. Never left."

"Good." She looked toward Trina. "McCartin?"

"Makes me uneasy." Trina tapped her pencil on the table. "He has no alibi for either night, and he seems weirdly undisturbed by the murders even though he knew Amy in high school, if distantly, and actually dated Karin."

"Capacity for violence?" a detective down the table asked.

"Can't tell. He's got this surreal grin that doesn't touch his eyes. You know? Projects this likable persona that feels skin-deep to me. What's below that? From things other people have said about what he was like in high school, there's got to be resentment."

Other names came and went. They'd spread their net wide. Most were eliminated, having accounted for at least one of the two times in question.

They ended with Gavin Husby. Trina told the half

dozen detectives about his record, his seeming contempt for women and how uncomfortable he'd made her feel.

"But a jerk isn't necessarily a killer," she concluded.

"Where do we go from here?" Lieutenant Patton asked finally.

"I'm assuming nothing obvious eliminates any of our best prospects as the source of the pubic hair?" Jerry asked. "As in, one of these guys is a redhead and the hair was…"

"Brown," Trina supplied.

"No," Lieutenant Patton said, "they all have coloring that ranges from light to medium brown hair. Since body hair tends to be darker…"

Nods all around.

"Could we ask each suspect to give a pubic hair for comparison?" Randy Wheeler suggested.

"At some point, we could try." The lieutenant looked dubious. "Right now, we don't have enough evidence against any one individual to call him a suspect. Gut feelings don't count. They'd be well within their rights to refuse, and to be insulted that we'd asked. These were horrific crimes. Saying 'You knew all three women' ain't enough."

"What if we show Ricky Mendoza photos of these possibles? If the guy was in the bar the night Gilly was killed…" Trina suggested.

They threw the idea around, but agreed that his motivation for fingering someone else was so powerful, his testimony might be unreliable. He'd *want* to recognize one of these men.

Trina nodded and sat back in discouragement.

Into the resulting silence, Jerry said, "I think we should back up and ask ourselves again, why a six-year gap between killings? Where were all these people? Why kill once, then take a big break? Once guys like this start, they don't usually stop until somebody makes them."

"The jockstrap just hasn't popped up anywhere." The lieutenant looked as if she'd lost weight, her cheekbones more prominent than Trina remembered them.

Randy Wheeler said no more than they were all thinking. "A serial killer doesn't change his signature."

"That's true," Trina said, "but he might change his M.O."

They all stared at her.

The distinction was a fine one that the FBI Behavioral Sciences Unit at Quantico tried to drum into local law enforcement investigators. And it so happened that it was one everyone here in Butte County had lost sight of, Trina realized.

"What is his signature? The rape for sure. Tearing the victim's breast with his teeth—always the left breast. Probably strangling her."

"But not necessarily using a jockstrap," the lieutenant said slowly.

Jerry leaned forward. "But covering her face. That must mean something to him."

"Maybe." Trina warmed to her theory. "But maybe not. Maybe that part isn't for him."

"It's for Will," Meg Patton murmured.

"It could be. What if the jockstrap isn't part of his signature? It's a message." Her skin was prickling with the belief that she was on to something they'd missed. Something important. "Maybe the message is for Will, maybe for someone else. But it's supposed to mean something to him."

"Good God," Randy Wheeler said.

Jerry objected, "Then why doesn't it?"

Trina just shook her head.

Lieutenant Patton said in a dry, precise voice, "Because whatever incident the jockstrap refers to meant a whole lot to our killer and not much to Will." She glanced at Trina. "Or to whoever the message is meant for. Isn't that the whole trouble? The killer feels slighted, angry precisely *because* he was left out, ignored, made to feel insignificant. And in a sense, he was right. Whatever that jockstrap symbolizes *didn't* mean much to Will and has been forgotten. Think how frustrated the killer must be."

Trina stirred in her seat. "He's going to kill again soon."

"I agree. If we don't stop him." Lieutenant Patton looked around the table. "Let's ask media contacts to remind women to be very, very careful. Don't go out alone at night, don't—for the moment—start dating anyone new. Let's step up patrols through the parking lots of every tavern, brewpub and bar in this county. I'll talk to Renee and ask the Elk Springs units to join us.

"In the meantime, Detective Giallombardo, I'm putting you in charge of contacting police departments wherever our likeliest suspects have lived in the past six years. Start afresh. Forget the jockstrap. What unsolved rapes/murders do they have on their books? What can they tell us about them?

"Jerry." She turned to the short, grizzled detective. "What about right here at home? Was Gillian Pappas the first victim, or had our killer gotten some practice first? That was a pretty sophisticated crime. He was real careful, real organized. He had someplace planned to take her so that he didn't have to hurry. Despite the bloodlust roaring through his head, he used a condom and probably wore gloves, and he apparently wrapped the body in plastic to transport it so that it didn't pick up any trace evidence from his vehicle. He was good."

"Too good for a beginner," Jerry agreed slowly. Nodding, he pushed back his chair. "I'm on it."

"I'll talk to Will," the lieutenant said, standing, too. "Something about a jockstrap has got to be there in his head. A joke, maybe. Who knows? But the killer expects him to remember, which means he was there when whatever it was happened."

Energized, they all went back to work.

Trina was at her computer station when the lieutenant paused beside her. "That was good thinking, Trina."

"I...thank you."

Lieutenant Patton nodded again, her blue eyes friendly, and continued toward her office.

Feeling a buzz again, but for a different reason this time, Trina opened the book for Karin Kristensen's murder. A binder was used to compile reports, notes, pictures, actions taken and not taken, on every murder. This one was swelling.

Which of their suspects had lived where?

Jimmy McCartin—Beaverton and Astoria. Maybe other places, but she'd start with those. Gavin Husby was the restless one who'd moved frequently. Bellingham, Seattle and Vancouver in Washington State, then Albany, Portland and Salem here in Oregon.

She decided to start with Beaverton and Astoria. She especially liked Astoria, which was a really small town. An unsolved murder as grisly as these current ones would be memorable in a place like that.

She got a gruff sergeant who said, "I'll do some checking, Detective, but I got to tell you I don't remember anything like that. I'll check with folks at the

county, if you'd like. Could be Seaside would be worth
a call, too. Things are slow right now, it not being our
tourist season. Give me your number, I'll get back to
you in a day or two."

"Bless you." She gave him her number and called
Beaverton PD next.

They were more distracted and less interested, but
promised, too, to check their files of unsolved crimes
in the relevant two years.

She worked her way down the list, finding cooperation and delays everywhere. Homicide/Robbery detectives had enough to do without hunting old records.
On the other hand, all were interested in the idea of
solving a cold case.

It took her all day, making calls, sitting on hold,
getting transferred, leaving messages and waiting for
return calls. At the end, she felt as if she'd put notes in
bottles and let the tide take them out, not knowing if any
would ever float back in and be found.

Waiting never had been her strong suit.

THAT NIGHT WAS AS GOOD as the one before. Trina had
had only a couple of lovers before. Neither had been as
skilled as Will. Neither had touched her and claimed her
with the kind of urgency and pure *need* that he did.

Of course, it helped that she hadn't been in love with
either of the two men, although she'd tried to kid herself
both times that she was.

As she got dressed to leave, Will said to her back, "I
have to drive over to Salem tomorrow to talk to a defendant and since I'm there, I've set up a meeting with
a victim's family. I'm expecting to be late home."

She pulled on a sock. "I should concentrate on the
case anyway. I just keep thinking, any day…"

When she didn't finish, Will did. "He'll kill another woman? It's been two weeks, hasn't it?"

"And counting. Maybe he's having a harder time isolating his next victim. He might have had to give up on a first choice and select someone else. Since, if we're right, she has to have something to do with you, his options are limited. We've tried to impress on every woman we've talked to that she's got to be careful. More than careful."

"Jody Cox called yesterday. She was talking about taking a few weeks and visiting a college roommate who lives in Dallas. I told her I thought it was a good idea."

"I'd like to see Nita Voss do the same." She pulled her turtleneck over her head and then her hair out of the snug neck. "Maybe. He could follow one of them. If they felt too safe because they'd left Elk Springs behind, they'd be vulnerable."

"Do you think he'd do that?"

"No," she admitted, "but how can we be sure? Especially if he gets desperate for a victim. I mean, how many women are there in town who meet his requirements?"

"Which are?"

There was something funny in his voice, but she didn't tune into it. "Dated you, obviously. Slim, blond, pretty. Unless that's chance, because it's been your preference."

Watching her, not seeming to pay attention to what he was doing, he pulled on a pair of sweatpants and reached for a T-shirt. "I've dated women who weren't blond."

She thrilled to the sight of his long, lean body and was sorry when he yanked the shirt over his head.

"Bronwen Fessler?"

He shrugged. "A few times a couple of years ago, when I was in town for the holidays."

Her voice got prickly. She couldn't help it. "Who in town *haven't* you slept with?"

Mouth grim, he said, "I didn't say I'd slept with her. I didn't."

"Amy?"

"Yeah. Amy I did."

She tried to sound brisk and professional, ignoring the wrench because she'd seen him with Amy back in high school, when her own crush on him hurt it was so intense. "So that's not necessarily a criteria. Or maybe he assumed you'd had sex with Karin." She faced him. "Did the subject ever come up with anybody? Did anybody *ask?*"

"Gavin made a couple of crude remarks. I ignored them."

"McCartin?"

"He saw me out with Karin." Will sounded reluctant, as if he wished he didn't remember. "He asked if I had something going with her. Not those words, but something like that. I think I admitted I was going to have dinner with her that night."

Damn. She kept thinking she could eliminate one of the two men. Focus. If only it were so easy.

At the door, as she put on her parka, Trina said, "Will, it might be a good idea if you'd list every woman in town you've dated. Slept with. Heck, flirted with! If the list isn't too long, maybe we can try to keep an eye on them. Get *them* to be proactive, notice who suggests a drink, who drives by their apartment."

He abruptly turned her to face him and kissed her. Hard, with what felt like anger or maybe just frustration. When he lifted his head, he said, "You make me feel like a bastard. The goddamn Don Juan of Elk Springs!"

She stepped back, a chill inside. "The list is going to be that long, huh? Just don't put me on it, okay?"

Without checking to see how he reacted, she opened the door. "Drive carefully tomorrow."

"I'm walking you out." He crowded her on the landing.

She started down the stairs, footsteps echoing in the well. "I'm a cop, Will. See?" She pulled her sidearm from her parka pocket to show him, then shoved it in her waistband at the small of her back. "Let some bastard try to mug me."

"Or rape you," he said, in a rough voice. He was following her down the damn stairs, still in his shirtsleeves and wearing only slippers.

Old pain squeezed her chest. "Don't worry," she said carelessly over her shoulder. "I don't look like Gillian. Besides, who's to know?"

At the bottom of the steps, he stopped her with a hand on her arm. "Let's keep it that way, okay? For now?"

"No problem." She jerked away. "See you."

He just watched as she got in her Explorer and backed out. He didn't wave, and she didn't, either.

Some jackass in a big mother of a pickup truck came up behind her immediately and crowded her on the way home, his headlights enough higher than hers as to blind her in her rearview mirror, which pissed her off enough to keep her from crying. He made a couple of turns right behind her, but kept going without slowing when she turned into her complex. Not interested in her, she decided, surprised by the release of tension to realize how much had gnawed at her. Nope, he was just your garden-variety jackass. She should have let him pass and then hit the roof lights and ticketed him.

Safe in her apartment, door locked and double-locked, she forgot about the pickup truck and thought instead about Will's last words.

Let's keep it that way, okay?

She guessed he wouldn't be suggesting they join his friends at J.R.'s or the Timberline some night soon. She wanted to think he was reluctant to be seen with her because of what was happening to every other woman he'd dated around here, but why wouldn't he have said that to her? No. That was just wishful thinking. Trying not to care, she checked phone messages and found one from Sandy Kilts, her journalist friend.

"I've called every night this week. Have you quit answering your phone? Or are you never there anymore?"

Hitting Delete, Trina realized she'd have to think up some lie or other. Gee, this must be how it felt to have an affair with a married man. Sneaking around, lying to everyone you knew.

The sad thing was, for the first time, she understood why a woman would do something that went so utterly against her deepest values.

She'd never understood before because she'd never really been in love. Not like this, with the desperate, hungry knowledge she'd do anything at all to have another night with him, to have him kiss her with that light in his eyes one more time, to hold him one more time.

Standing stock-still in the middle of her living room, she closed her eyes and felt tears leak out.

And she'd thought she was pathetic before.

WILL HAD BEEN sleeping badly anyway, but now his dreams swirled around the crux. He'd be playing basketball, and realize he and everyone on both teams running down the court wore nothing but jockstraps. Standing on the free throw line, the ball in his hands, he would turn in shock to scan the bleachers, only to discover that the guys in the audience were naked but for jockstraps, too.

Or someone would call out a question and he would turn to answer and see that the other person's face was covered with a jockstrap. Pretty soon *everyone* was faceless in his dreams. He woke up sweating after he looked at himself in the mirror and saw that he, too, wore a goddamn jockstrap wrapped around his head and covering his face like a hockey mask.

Even awake, he hardly recognized himself in the mirror these days. He looked like hell.

"Think," his mother had said, during a brief phone call.

That's all he did. All he *had* been doing when he was alone and sometimes when he should have been concentrating on a judicial decision he was studying or a police report. It was a good thing he wasn't trying a major case right now. He couldn't possibly have given it his best.

What his mother had done was give him one more thing to think about. One more gem on top of bedwetting, arson and the torture of small animals.

Hadn't there been talk back in high school about a bunch of guys tying a dog to the bumper of a car and dragging it down a gravel road, laughing as it tried to run fast enough and fell and writhed and finally became dead weight? He couldn't remember who, only feeling sickened. Fires? There'd been a streak of them during his junior year, he thought, culminating in the one that gutted the shop building. Again, everyone talked. Didn't they always? Gavin had been the one who liked bonfires and threw on logs until flames leapt high into the night, sparks scattering to rival the stars. But they'd all stood and stared, mesmerized by the power.

But jockstraps… Who thought about them? It wasn't like women's panties that came in a variety of styles and colors, lacy, racy, staid. Jockstraps were pretty well all alike, white and utilitarian. Wearing them, guys looked somehow defenseless, butts hanging out.

He could recall a thousand scenes in locker rooms with guys strutting around wearing nothing else. Razzing someone because his jockstrap was size small instead of large. Hooting down any suggestion that the sizes represented waist measurements rather than how impressive your equipment was. Occasionally they'd been used as slingshots or even shot like giant rubber bands in a free-for-all.

He'd never seen anyone pretend to strangle someone else with one, or pull it over his face for God knew what reason. The truth was, he had no meaningful memories that involved a white elastic jockstrap.

He even called Travis and asked if he did.

After a long silence, Travis said, "They're thinking the jockstrap has to do with you, huh. Like a message? Damn. No, nothing comes to me. If it does I'll let you know."

"Thanks."

"Haven't heard from you much."

"I'm…seeing someone."

With more heat than Will had expected, Travis said, "Are you crazy? Some maniac is raping and murdering women you've dated, and you decide to red flag one more woman?"

The bitch of it was, he was right. Will tormented himself daily with fear that Trina might be the next victim.

He was arguing as much with himself as with Travis when he said, "You're the only person who knows. We're keeping it quiet. We haven't gone out. The killer doesn't know. He can't know."

Unless, God, he'd been following her and had seen Will kiss her cheek.

"Don't tell me who it is," Travis said. "Don't say her name out loud to anyone."

"You think he's tapped my phone?"

"Who the hell knows? Just keep her safe, okay?"

"Yeah." He rubbed his breastbone to ease the burning beneath. "Okay."

"You talked to your mother yet? Groveled?"

Trust his buddy to prod another ache.

"No," he admitted. "When I see her, we talk about the murders. The words make it to the tip of my tongue, and I keep letting myself off the hook. We're easier with each other than we've been in years, and I'm coward enough not to want to stir up the bottom of the pot."

"You make a better soup if you do stir," was all Travis said, before changing the subject.

Trina was all that kept Will sane. He made it through dark, sleepless nights by thinking, *I'll see her again tomorrow.* She listened like nobody he'd ever known, and he loved to hear her talk in turn. She was a fascinating mix of innocence and toughness. Blunt one minute, shy the next, Trina had the same strength he'd always seen in his mother, the same dogged determination, the same intelligence and single-mindedness. There was a reason they were both cops, both detectives. He wondered why he'd wasted so many years dating women who were never going to measure up to the expectation his mother and then his aunts had instilled in him.

Gillian…well, she'd been different. He had loved her, and he thought he would have kept loving her if she'd lived and he had matured fast enough to be ready for a strong woman.

Oddly, since he'd been thinking about Gilly, Trina asked about her the night after he made the run over to Salem. He'd cooked dinner again, and they sat lazily talking after they ate, still sipping wine.

"You never mention Gillian," she said out of the blue. "Do you not like to talk about her?"

A month ago, he might have said no. But he didn't want to keep secrets from Trina. Not that he had many left, he thought ruefully.

"No, it's okay. What do you want to know?"

She shrugged. "Tell me about her."

So he did, and realized it felt good. He'd met Gillian his freshman year at Willamette. They were in an intro to psych class together. He already knew he wanted to go to law school and thought the more he knew about how people's minds worked, the better attorney he'd be. She was interested in child therapy. Once she saw the world, she said, in the grand way college freshmen did. Once she made a difference. She'd had an inner serenity that drew him from the beginning. She could be beautiful one minute, plain the next, and she didn't care either way. She rarely bothered with makeup, ran 10K races for fun and was passionately involved in half a dozen campus organizations that raised awareness of women's issues and money to build schools in African or Honduran villages. One summer, she went to Africa and volunteered for Save the Children, coming back more committed than ever.

"You'd have liked her," he said, gazing at the past but very conscious of Trina's warm brown eyes. "She was smart, kind, nosy." He lifted his glass in salute. "Like someone else I know."

She let that pass. "Then what went wrong?"

Count on her to go right for the jugular. But he'd known this was where they were going. He'd never told a soul what he and Gillian had fought about that night.

"Me. That's what went wrong." He shook his head. "Gilly matured into the woman she'd promised to become. She wanted to go into the Peace Corps. I talked her into putting it off and getting her masters degree first. The Peace Corps sounded great back when we were sophomores and juniors. I had some sort of hazy image of me flying over during summer break from law school to see her in Kenya or wherever she went. But at some point I started thinking I could distract her and eventually she wouldn't want to go. I was going to be a big important attorney." Shame clawed at him. "Doing my bit crusading, of course, but also making a shit pot full of money. I was starting to think about going into politics down the road, once I'd made partner in some important firm. It was okay if she became a child psychologist. I wanted a smart wife, one who'd impress the people *I* wanted to impress." He gave a harsh laugh. "What I didn't want was her to up and leave for two years. Just disappear. See, our ambitions were supposed to circulate around me. Not her. Oh, I didn't say that. I'm not sure I even realized that's what I thought. But she knew."

When he fell silent, brooding, Trina nudged. "What happened?"

"She let me know right before that spring break that

she'd applied to the Peace Corps and been accepted. She didn't know yet where she was going, but once she finished her degree in May, she'd be leaving for language training. She wanted me to be excited for her. I said, 'Don't go.' We fought about it all week. She tried to reason with me, and I wouldn't listen. In retrospect, I realize I was afraid she was ditching me."

"You didn't think she'd come back to you."

"Yep." His mouth twisted into a mockery of a smile, the best he could do. "So I issued an ultimatum. Her dream, or me."

"And she chose the dream," Trina said softly.

He swore. Realized his cheeks were wet. "She told me what an idiot I was, grabbed her stuff and tore out the door. I thought she was driving back to Portland. Instead, she went to a bar."

Not just a bar. It was a crummy place, a world away from the upscale tavern or brewpub she might normally have chosen if what she'd really wanted was a drink and a few minutes to think. No, just as Ricky Mendoza had said, she'd gone there to find a quickie with someone who would shock Will.

Trina touched his hand. "And she was dead a few hours later."

It still hurt, but the pain was duller. Was it his fault she'd died? He'd been a jackass, but he wanted to believe he'd have woken up one day after she left and had the sense to write her, to say, *I'm sorry. I was a fool.* Any choices, any possibilities, had been taken out of his hands, out of hers. With wonder, he discovered that somewhere along the way he'd learned that no, he wasn't to blame. For losing her, yes. For her death, no.

"I loved her." He refilled his wineglass again even though he knew he shouldn't. Time muted pain and memories; alcohol just muddled them. "But, you know, sometimes I have to pull out a picture to remember what she really looked like."

"You didn't have to put them away because of me."

Startled, he said, "How did you know?"

She smiled. "You don't dust."

He found himself grinning back. "Right. You're a detective. I guess I forgot."

Laughing, she said, "Sure you did."

They made love, and afterward, with her sprawled atop him, he thought with pleasure about how different her body felt than any other woman's he'd ever held. She wasn't delicate, coltish. Instead, she was lush in the right places, taut and strong in others. He liked that contrast, along with all her others.

Stroking a hand down her spine, Will spared a glance for the dresser, where a couple of framed photos were missing.

He didn't think he'd be putting them back.

CHAPTER SEVENTEEN

NOTHING LIKE HAVING a split identity. By day, Trina was a composed, prosaic detective hot on the trail of a serial killer. At night, she was Will Patton's lover, dazzled and feeling so unbelievably lucky, she refused to think beyond the moment.

Tomorrow was as far as she'd let herself look. Of course she'd hurt eventually, but wasn't this week worth any pain? Yes, it was, she told herself.

Over and over again.

The hardest part was maintaining her cool in front of Lieutenant Patton.

Trina hated this kind of secret. But she also knew it would be a heck of a lot easier to keep her head high around here if nobody ever knew she'd had a brief affair with Meg Patton's son.

Lord, she thought, with the Butte County Sheriff's son.

Oh, yeah. She didn't want anyone to know.

It still stung when Will mentioned a Sunday dinner at his aunt Renee's house without, of course, inviting her. "The clan gathers," he said carelessly. "Unless you want to have a late-night tryst, I won't be able to see you until Monday."

Trina didn't have much pride where he was concerned, but she did still have some. "Nah, I've got plans Sunday, too."

"Plans?"

"Some friends talked me into going sledding," she improvised. "We'll have dinner, and then see."

"Ah." Lines deepened between his brows. "I wish…" He stopped, shook his head. "Never mind." The frown deepened before he said explosively, "Why can't you catch this bastard?"

"He doesn't know it, but we're closing in."

She hadn't told him that Dirk Whittaker had been eliminated as a suspect after Jerry had confirmed his admission that he'd had a brief affair, one he now regretted. Or so he claimed. Trina had felt sad, thinking of Marcie, who'd lost her best friend and her closest connection to her days of glory as one of the sought-after girls. Remembering the mantel display of photos of their kids, smiles bright, she shook her head.

She'd learned that Astoria and vicinity had only one unsolved rape from the relevant time period, and it had key differences from the ones here in Elk Springs, even aside from the fact that these had culminated in the strangulation death of the victims. The woman there had been in her early fifties. She'd gone out to the car from her hotel room to get something and been dragged behind a Dumpster, where the perp held a knife at her throat and made her perform oral sex on him, after which he'd told her he'd be back if she went for help before morning. She'd believed him.

"By that time, half the folks in the hotel and all the nearby ones had checked out," the gruff sergeant said in disgust. "She claimed not to remember his face. Of course, she was sure he was six foot three or four minimum."

"Which means he was five foot nine. Maybe." Trina

thanked him profusely for his help and crossed Astoria off her list.

Vancouver and Portland, right across the Columbia River from each other, not surprisingly came up with a long list of unsolved rapes and murders from the two-year span Gavin Husby had lived in the area. The detective who'd compiled it and faxed it to her had starred three rape/murders, all of young, attractive women snatched from the parking lots of bars, all found displayed in obscene poses, bite marks in savage evidence.

Trina called and asked for photos. He scanned and e-mailed them. Just today she'd looked at them, bothered that none of the victims had any resemblance to Gillian Pappas, Amy Owen or Karin Kristensen. Two of the three were Caucasian, one short, plump and brunette, the other model-thin, freckled and redhead. The third was Hawaiian, a racial mix that defied categorization but resulted in an exotic, dark-eyed beauty. The brunette was a prostitute, the Hawaiian woman a bartender, the redhead just out for the evening. One had a broken neck while two were strangled manually, leaving livid marks of the murderer's fingers. Other elements of the crimes were highly suggestive, but Trina was uncomfortable jumping to a conclusion. Killers tended to pick victims with a lot in common. Starting with looks, of course, but in other ways as well. If they went for prostitutes, they usually stuck to prostitutes. They weren't likely to target a hooker one time, a nice girl the next. And the way they killed usually stayed consistent. Maybe the broken neck was an accident; maybe he'd been pissed because he didn't get the chance to strangle her. But maybe not. Maybe that one was killed by somebody different from the other two. Or maybe the Portland/ Vancouver area murderer didn't care so much *how* he killed the women.

She shared what she'd learned with Lieutenant Patton and the other detectives, getting mixed opinions resulting in a great big *maybe*. She e-mailed a request for details—had any fingerprints or hairs been recovered?

Lieutenant Patton mentioned the family get-together on Sunday, too, telling people where to reach her if they needed her. Trina talked Sandy and another friend into going sledding halfway to Juanita Butte and then out to a fondue restaurant, where they got tipsy and bitched about men.

Monday she decided to push Jimmy McCartin a little harder and stopped by the Century 21 office. But when she went in, the perky receptionist said, "I'm afraid Mr. McCartin no longer works here. But someone else will be happy to show you property or discuss your listing with you."

Trina showed her badge. "Who's the boss?"

The owner of the office, a no-nonsense middle-aged woman, told her that Jimmy had tendered his resignation on Friday. "He offered to give notice, but honestly this time of year is slow enough, we're all twiddling our thumbs anyway."

"Did he say why he was leaving?"

"Only that he had some personal issues. I know he plans to leave central Oregon."

Jimmy wasn't home, which alarmed her. A For Sale sign on a folding sandwich board sat by the street. She seemed to remember that serial killers often looked for an excuse to leave the area once an investigation made it too hot for comfort.

She parked at the curb several houses down and waited for half an hour, but he didn't reappear. Where was he? She got out and walked back to the front door, ringing the doorbell again, hearing only silence. She glanced around the neighborhood and saw no one. The development had a deserted look, residents all at work, kids in day care. No stay-at-home moms here. She also didn't see any curtains twitch as a neighborhood busybody watched her, so she strolled around the side of Jimmy's house and peered in a small window at an obscenely tidy garage, sans Dodge Durango. So he wasn't really at home, ignoring the doorbell. The fence, gate closed, discouraged her from circling around back to look in other windows.

Back in the station, she told Lieutenant Patton, "I'll check on my way home. Could we send a unit by to see if he's home this evening? We don't want him to skip on us."

"Not likely when he owns the house. But, yeah, this is suggestive." She sighed. "Nothing yet from other jurisdictions?"

Trina had just checked her e-mail. "Portland has a couple of pubic hairs combed from one victim. They're faxing the analysis. The other two victims were clean. Too clean, to quote them."

"Doesn't that sound familiar. I'm getting a bad feeling about this."

"Portland is a busy place. Lots of bad guys. If we get something similar from Albany, say…"

Their eyes met. The lieutenant nodded.

"Don't go talk to McCartin by yourself. See if he's home. If he is, wait until tomorrow."

Remembering how grateful she'd been not to be alone at Gavin Husby's, Trina didn't argue.

She was about to leave for the day when Will called, voice hurried.

"Caught you. Good. I've been in court all day. Learned anything?"

"Jimmy McCartin quit his job and is selling his house."

"Really."

"Wasn't home, so I couldn't ask why."

"Jimmy's an odd duck, but I'd have sworn he was a decent guy."

"Yeah?" she challenged. "Doesn't he make you a little uncomfortable? Isn't there something about him that just doesn't feel quite right?"

He was silent.

"That's what people say later, you know. 'He was a good neighbor,' the cops will hear. 'Always polite.' 'Shoveled old Mrs. Douglas's driveway for her.' But invariably there are always a few people who admit they avoided him because, in some way they could never pin down, he made them uneasy. When I read about this stuff, it seems like a few people always notice this guy's expressions never reach his eyes, or sometimes his responses are just plain inappropriate. He's not normal, and if only on a subconscious level they knew it."

"God."

"The thing is," she said, thinking about the Portland murders, "Jimmy may *be* nothing more than an odd duck. I'm just asking."

"I don't know! Damn it, if I did do you think I wouldn't tell you?"

"I'm sorry." Boy, she sure knew how to make sparkling conversation with a man. No wonder dates had become few and far between.

"I'm not mad at you. Just frustrated." He paused. "Is it too late to invite you to dinner tonight?"

She hesitated, pride timidly raising a hand to suggest she not be *too* willing. "You sound tired."

"I'm beat," he admitted. "I'd still enjoy your company."

Trina slapped down pride and suggested, "How about if I bring over a pizza? Forget fine cuisine. Beer and pizza with everything on it works for me."

"Me, too." He apparently covered the phone, because she heard muffled voices for a moment. Then Will came back. "Seven?"

"Pizza in hand," she promised.

Jimmy McCartin's house, way too big and ostentatious for a young single guy, was still dark when she drove by. Had he hired movers to bring his stuff and already left town himself? That was damn quick. More likely, he'd just gone out for the day. Or maybe taken a couple-day-long trip to hunt for a rental wherever he intended to go.

Still, the dark house left her feeling unsettled when she went home, called in a pizza order and changed clothes.

She stopped at a corner grocery store for a six-pack of beer and then picked up the pizza, setting it on the passenger seat beside her. To hell with pride, Trina thought. It would have condemned her to an evening alone in her apartment pretending she cared what was on TV when she could be with Will. Her mood had done a turnaround when he called. Yearning for his company, his kisses, his touch, had her feeling warm despite the cold night, already a little aroused even. Girly, instead of her usual tough self.

She parked in her regular spot at his complex, opening her door, then grabbing the plastic grocery bag with the six-pack and the large pizza, which she had to maneuver over the top of the steering wheel. Trina was thinking how good it smelled and backing awkwardly out so she could shut the door of her Subaru when a hand whipped around her and pressed a sharp blade against her throat.

"Pizza," Gavin Husby said. "I was getting a little hungry. Nice of you to bring the food."

Trapped between the open door and the Subaru, her throat burning where the blade cut, both hands on the damn pizza box, she threatened, "I'll scream."

"And I'll slit your throat."

The blade bit deeper. She felt the warmth of blood trickling and gagged.

A hand groped her underarms, her breasts, her waist, finally reaching her weapon, tucked in the waistband of her jeans. He pulled it out, tossed it on the seat of her wagon, and murmured, "We won't be needing that." Then he prodded her to turn toward the parking lot, his breath hot on her neck, his mouth close to her ear. "Come on, Will's bitch. We have lots to do tonight."

WILL RACED HOME at 6:45, yanking off his tie as he went in the door. Quick shower, change to cords and sweatshirt. He emerged from the bedroom at seven on the nose, looking forward to Trina's arrival and to pizza. He'd forgotten to have lunch today and his stomach was now belatedly grumbling.

She tended to be prompt, but at 7:10 he figured she was having to wait for the pizza. At 7:15, growing antsy, he called her place, got the answering machine. 7:16, her cell phone. Ditto.

She had it on and wasn't answering it?

Maybe she'd left it on the seat while she went in to get the pizza or the beer. The explanation was logical, but foreboding had knotted in his belly anyway. He picked up the phone again and called the closest pizza joint. No order for a Trina or Giallombardo. Okay, maybe she'd gone farther to get one from Mario's, acknowledged by locals to have the best pizza in town.

"Sure," an absurdly young voice told him, "a Trina picked up her pizza, uh, like, maybe twenty, twenty-five minutes ago?"

He swore, slammed down the phone and, without even thinking about it, put on a parka and grabbed keys, wallet and cell phone.

Foreboding had spasmed into pure dread, even though he knew he was jumping the gun. She was a cop. She could have gotten a call.

Why hadn't *she* called him?

He'd drive her route. Maybe she'd broken down. Maybe…

Halfway down the steps, he saw her bright blue Subaru in the visitor's parking slot. A ragged sound of relief escaped him. He hit the parking lot and saw that her door was open. She'd just been running late. He could carry the pizza up for her.

But he didn't see anyone inside. The lot was completely quiet, the sodium lighting murky. Moving slowly, tension building again, terror nudging it, he walked up to the open door and saw the empty interior of her car.

And the handgun lying carelessly on the seat.

MEG WAS JUST FINISHING a late dinner and looking forward to the Ben & Jerry's she'd picked up on the way home when the phone rang.

"Ignore it," her husband said hopefully.

She rolled her eyes. "Too late."

"I'm getting it!" one of the kids yelled, followed by a body slam and a wailed, "I was first!"

Scott half laughed, half sighed. "How is it we've failed to teach our children normal civility?"

She shook her head.

"Mom." Evan reappeared in the dining room. "It's Will. He sounds…" The boy's eyes were wide, frightened.

She snatched the phone from him. "Will?"

"Mom." His voice was hardly recognizable. "He's got Trina."

"He?" Understanding and horror flooded her. "Oh, my God. How do you know?"

He explained, voice thick, raw. She was bringing pizza to his place. Her car now sat abandoned in the complex parking lot right outside his apartment, door open. Her handgun lay abandoned on the seat. No Trina.

"Don't touch anything," she said unnecessarily. He was the son of two cops. "I'm on my way."

She made phone calls, Scott listening in silence. All he said was, "Shall I come?"

She hesitated. Will would need someone, and the kids would be okay… But she didn't like the idea of leaving them alone. Not when, once again, someone was targeting a Patton. "No. I'll suggest he come over here."

Scott walked her to the front door, said, "I love you," and gave her a hard, purposeful kiss.

Filled with a roiling mix of fear, anguish and fury, she drove to her son's apartment building.

Other units had already arrived, as she'd intended. They'd unwounded yellow crime scene tape. Sheila was just pulling in with the van that held all her paraphernalia.

Meg ignored everyone else and went straight to Will, who stood near the foot of the stairs, gaze riveted on the Subaru Forester.

When she wrapped her arms around him, he almost

crumpled. She felt the moment when his knees buckled, heard the beginning of a sob.

"I did this," he said harshly. "If I'd just stayed away from her…"

"He would have picked another woman. You know he would have." Ignoring her own sickening fear as she saw in her mind's eye Trina's face, so damn young, she made her voice brisk. "Trina's better equipped to fight back."

He shuddered in her arms. With what she knew took enormous effort, he stepped back, face haggard, eyes wet. And he said the words that were a stab to her heart. "I love her."

Gillian's murder had almost destroyed him. If he'd finally allowed himself to love a woman again, and she too was brutally killed, he'd never recover. She knew that, deep in her soul. What if she had to tell her oldest son, for whom she would have done anything in the world, that Trina's naked, obscenely posed body had been found?

She gave a brief nod of acknowledgement, her lips pressed together. "He can't have her," she said, then more strongly, "People, we've got to find her. This son of a bitch isn't going to rape and kill a police officer."

Her pronouncement was met with murmurs of agreement and outrage.

"Have we started knocking on doors?"

"Just got here." Jerry signaled to others. "Come on, let's hit it."

Behind her, Will said, "Nobody will have seen anything. Heard anything. They never have."

"Every serial killer makes a mistake eventually. To snatch her right here, fifty feet from your door." She shook her head.

"But that was the point." Will's stare from sunken

eyes was awful. "He wanted me to come down here, just like I did. See the open door. Feel relief. Then be gutted with fear."

She turned to him, voice fierce. "The only way we're going to find her is to figure out who this bastard is. Have you remembered anything?"

Gaze fastened to hers, as if only her presence kept him upright, he shook his head.

"Then go get your address book if you need it. You're coming with me. What you're going to do is call friends. Ones you trust. Ask them. Does anybody remember an incident with a jockstrap?"

"Yeah." He nodded, but slowly, and she recognized that he was in shock. "Okay."

"I'm going to the station. I'm going to rouse somebody in Albany and Beaverton and wherever the hell else I have to so that I get some answers. Meantime," she said, turning to other people, "I want a unit out to Jimmy McCartin's and one to Gavin Husby's. Find them."

"What if it isn't one of them?" Will asked.

Then Trina is dead, Meg thought.

"No 'what ifs.' Not yet."

Her heart ached as she watched him stagger upstairs to get his address book as if he were drunk. When he came back, he looked her age. Older. Gaunt, cheeks sunken, bones prominent.

During the short drive in the dark, he sat silent. Street lamps and headlights flickered past. Once she had to slow on the main drag to let a large, laughing group cross the street to a restaurant that spilled warm light and voices onto the sidewalk. She glanced sideways to see Will staring straight ahead as if he didn't see them.

A moment later, she was speeding into the parking lot when he said, "I never told you I was sorry."

"What?"

"The things I said. After Gilly…"

"We were all wrong about Mendoza."

"No. You *weren't* wrong. Your gut feelings were right on. You never quite believed he'd done it, did you?"

She hesitated. "That's not true. I did believe it. There was too much evidence. The things you said to me… They shook me, because you were right. If not for me, he'd have been in jail that night."

She pulled into a parking slot.

Will didn't move, even after she pulled out the key. "But whether you were right or wrong, you were behaving with…humanity. Isn't it better to try to do good and make mistakes than be rigid and without heart?" He made a sound, a soft, keening sound. "I became what I wanted you to be, and it's not better."

"Will Patton, you've never been without heart. Look at me."

He did, eyes blind.

"You are a good man. Trauma affects us all in different ways. You were angry. I understood that. The distance between us all these years hasn't been because of what you said. It's been because *you* couldn't forget what you'd said, what you felt for me when you said it." She leaned over, hugged his rigid body, and whispered, "I love you." Then, more briskly, "Let's get to work."

"Oh, God." He leaped out, beat her to the back entrance.

Her cell phone rang. "McCartin still isn't home," Randy Wheeler said. "Neighbors don't know where he is."

"You looked in windows?"

"Place is empty. I'd like to go in, but…I really think it's empty."

She heard his police radio crackle. "Husby isn't home, either," he said a moment later. "Or isn't answering the door."

"We need warrants. We need reasons for our suspicions that a judge will buy."

She shook her head when Will looked at her with desperate hope. He hunched his shoulders and hit Send on his cell phone.

She logged onto Trina's e-mail account. Maybe something had arrived late. Nothing.

Albany. She'd try Albany first. And Bellingham. Two relatively small cities, where there wouldn't be so many unsolved rapes and murders as to cloud the issue.

She struck pay dirt in Albany. Her call was forwarded a couple of times, until finally a detective came on.

"This isn't Detective Giallombardo?"

"I'm her lieutenant. Meg Patton."

"Lieutenant Patton. I was going to call earlier, but I got sidetracked. A ten-year-old kid shot and killed his best friend. It's been one of those days."

She was too driven by urgency even to feel pity or to exchange sympathetic chitchat. "What do you have for us?"

"Two women, raped and murdered in a way that sounds one hell of a lot like yours. Six months apart, in the time frame your detective gave me. Left breasts damn near ripped off. Both were strangled, both posed. Guy wore a condom, gloves, was damn careful. Even so, we've got a nice sample of DNA. One of the two victims got him good with her fingernails. She had blood *and* skin under her nails. With the second victim, we were able to photograph a really dandy bite impression. You find us a suspect, we'll nail him."

"Gavin Husby," she said. "His name is Gavin Husby. And he just snatched another woman. This one is a police officer. Detective Trina Giallombardo."

He said something, an obscenity probably. She hung up just as Will ended a call and turned.

"Gavin," he said. "Goddamn it. Gavin."

"What?"

"I just woke up Justin Hill in…I don't know. Somewhere in Switzerland. Vince Baker told me to call him, that Justin had said something." He shook his head. "Justin remembered this time in the locker room. Gavin had asked out Amy and she'd said no. He was calling her obscene names and I told him to shut up. Hill says Gavin walked over in front of me, pulled off his jockstrap, stretched it out and said, 'I'd like to shove her sweet face right there.' He says I took a swing at him and someone grabbed me." He wiped a shaking hand over his face. "Crap. I still don't remember."

Meg looked at the clock—8:15. He'd had Trina for at least an hour. Maybe as much as an hour and a half.

Will's gaze followed hers. "She might already be dead."

"He kept Karin alive for half the night or more. Quick isn't his style. We'll find him." She sounded optimistic but didn't feel it. Where did he take his victims? Goddamn it, *where?*

And would they get there in time?

CHAPTER EIGHTEEN

TRINA CROUCHED, like a cornered animal, one wrist shackled with police handcuffs to a pipe that ran from open metal roof to rough concrete floor in—she didn't know what the building was. Some kind of loafing shed or barn, long unused, she guessed, from the lack of animal smell. Open-air from head high to eaves. Floor ran down to metal drains. Cold despite the space heater thoughtfully provided by a serial killer. Lit by bulbs along the center rafter. So—someone was still paying the utility bill.

A large rubber mat, maybe designed for a stall, had been cut so that the pipe rose from the middle of it. A nice, clean rubber mat, kept spotless for killing, she guessed.

He'd taken her by surprise when he walked her to his huge black pickup. She had decided to scream, to fight, even if he cut her bad. She'd die either way, and she didn't want to be raped first. But just as they reached the tailgate, without warning he slammed her forward, headfirst into the frame. Shattering pain and…nothing. She had come to with the cold snap of the handcuffs closing on her wrist as he fastened her to this pipe, but had had the sense to stay limp until she heard his footsteps recede.

Her head pounded, wave upon crashing wave of pain. Her vision didn't seem quite right. Nonetheless, she assessed her surroundings, realized with shock that she was naked and covered with goose bumps. Examined the sense of vulnerability that knowledge brought and dealt with it. To hell with modesty. She had bigger things to worry about.

Trying not to rattle the handcuffs against the metal pipe, she tested it. There was no give. It was solidly embedded in concrete beneath the mat.

Maybe she should lie back down, pretend to still be out. How long would he wait? Or would he start hurting her to hasten consciousness?

Too late. He appeared in her peripheral vision, circling her like another animal. A starving predator. Skinny, sweating, eyes insane. He would kill eventually, but what he wanted was to hurt her.

"Are we having fun yet, Will's bitch?" he crooned. "You're mine now. My bitch." He savored the idea as if he could taste it. As he would taste her blood when he ripped her flesh with his teeth.

She scrambled, crablike, to stay facing him. God, her head throbbed and he wavered before her eyes. But adrenaline, terror and rage fueled her.

"I'm not yours. I'll never be yours. Did you know I've been in love with Will since I was about twelve years old? Yup," she taunted. "All my life. And I plan to stay in love with him until I die."

Husby's face darkened, engorged with blood. She was making him angry, and she didn't know if that was good or bad. All she knew was that she wouldn't beg. Not even for her life.

He called her names she'd never heard before, foul, degrading, obscene, hate-filled names. She laughed, teeth showing.

"That the best you can do?"

He lunged and she kicked, high and hard, just as she'd planned, slamming him in his chest. Taking kick-boxing was the smartest thing she'd ever done.

"Bitch!" he screamed and came back for more. She kicked again, savagely, right for his balls, and he went down, kneeling just out of her reach, screaming his fury. Her foot hurt like hell and she wondered if she'd broken some bones in it. One more small problem.

And no one was near, she realized with an icy cramp in her chest. He didn't care how much noise they made. There was no one to hear.

No one to save her.

Trina steeled herself. Maybe no one would. But she'd make Gavin Husby very, very sorry he'd chosen her.

8:20.

Half a dozen detectives gathered around the confer-ence table, faces drawn, voices tight, rising to quick anger. Will couldn't sit, even if his prowling was a dis-traction. He'd never known he could feel so violent. He wanted to smash in Gavin Husby's face. Rip out his rotting excuse for a heart.

"I've put out a bulletin," Meg Patton said. "Every cop in Elk Springs and the county is looking for Husby's truck. But he had a long enough lead time to get it under cover. We need to figure out where."

"His dad," Will said. "No, wait. He's a stepdad. Dif-ferent name. Oh, crap. What's his name?" He pounded his fist into his other palm. "What's his name?"

"It'd be on school records." Jerry Dixon half rose. "We can get someone out there to turn on a computer."

And how long would that take? Will thought with a savage lack of detachment. Forty-five minutes? An hour? Too long.

Oh, for God's sake! He wasn't using his head. "Let's not waste time. I know where he lives."

"Go with Jerry." Her gaze swept the table. "Fisher. You, too."

The three men ran out to the sheriff's department SUV.

"Old part of town," Will told Dixon as he tore out of the parking lot. Faster than was safe without flashers. Not fast enough.

"Elm. No." He swore, dragged a hand through his hair. "A block over."

"Maple?"

"Yeah, yeah."

Five minutes, Jerry slowed. Darkness made the houses look one hell of a lot alike. The wrong side of the river, these were smaller than those in the neighborhood where Will's mother had grown up. Bungalow style, shabby, lawns frozen and lumpy, cars lining the curb, a few set up on blocks. Will looked from porch light to porch light, wracking his memory. He'd only been here a few times to pick up Gavin, who hadn't liked anyone coming to his house.

"That one," Will said suddenly, with assurance. Yeah, yeah, he remembered the tree, an enormous lone pine Gavin's stepdad wanted to cut down before a storm dropped it on the house. But it was still standing.

"House is dark." Jerry cut the headlights and drifted to the curb. Sharply, he said, "Will, you stay here. Okay, let's go."

The two men slipped out, closed doors quietly, unholstered weapons. They ran into the darkness around the house, separating to each side.

Waiting didn't sit well with Will. What if Trina was in there? If that crazy son of a bitch had her in the basement? But he knew better than to screw things up, maybe get himself shot.

A porch light came on at the neighbor's. The front door opened and light streamed out, casting in silhouette the stooped figure of an old man.

Will got out and walked up to the porch. "I'm with the sheriff's department, sir. We're looking for Gavin Husby. I believe his stepfather still lives here."

"The Gaines have gone to Arizona for the winter. That boy," the old man spit into the darkness to the side of the porch, "he weren't welcome here last I knew. That Gavin, he's never been right. I ain't surprised you're looking for him."

"What do you mean, not right?"

The old man peered at him. "Rochelle Gaines, his mom, why she likes cats. Don't care for 'em, myself. Always crapping in the flower beds. But that's nature," he said philosophically.

Will braced himself. He knew what was coming.

"Her cats kept disappearing. Found pieces of one of 'em." He shook his head. "Then Wayne caught the boy, fourteen, fifteen years old, hurting the kitten she'd brought home. He had to kill it. Then he beat the crap out of the boy, for what good that does."

Will swallowed. That long ago, it had already been too late. Gavin Husby, for whatever reason, had been programmed to become a monster.

"Have you seen him around? Does he use the house when his parents are away?"

"Wayne changed the locks a few years back. I've got a key so I can water Rochelle's houseplants. You want to take a look in there?"

"Please," Will said.

The two detectives reappeared, walking across the

frozen grass toward the Explorer. Before they could realize he wasn't in it, Will called, "I'm over here, talking to the neighbor."

The old man unlocked the house, and they separated to search the house from basement workshop to the single car attached garage that faced the alley.

"Nothing," Jerry said, when they met again in the living room. Seeing Will's face, he added, "Your mom'll have a warrant by now and be in his apartment."

Will was shaking his head before Jerry finished. "He won't have taken her there." Fear thickened his voice. He'd just looked at his watch.

9:00. Gavin had had Trina for two hours and counting.

Splayed limbs, torn breast, blood-splattered belly, white cup covering the face. Horrific images, frozen in black-and-white photos, flipped before his eyes.

He wished he didn't know what she would look like.

TRINA FOUGHT VICIOUSLY, noisily, screaming like a wildcat.

He flung himself atop her, slammed his fist against the side of her head, which bounced off the mat. Darkness rolled in like a bank of fog. She stayed ahead of it. He flattened her, splayed so that one hand was immobilized by the handcuff, the other by his cruel grip.

"Crawl, bitch. Beg!" He sank his teeth into her breast.

She screamed and freed one leg enough to knee him.

Obscenities streaming from him like the sick smell of his sweat, he rolled off her and she pulled herself into a crouch again.

"Can't get it up, can you?" she jeered. "Only way you can is if you make a woman snivel. What a way to cure impotence. Guess what? You ain't gonna get it up tonight."

Snarling, he launched himself again. He was frighteningly strong; and her own strength was failing. Shock and cold and wounds that smeared her with blood were taking a toll. They rolled on the floor with him squeezing her breast until she screamed, her kicking and bucking and telling him what a loser he was.

As he circled her again, her scrabbling to be prepared for the next assault, he sneered. "Ask your boyfriend what a loser I am. I've managed to have all his women and then make them beg. They quit thinking about him."

"You killed Gillian."

"Took 'em long enough to figure that out."

"And you just let Ricky Mendoza go to prison for six years. Couldn't even take credit for your own work."

"Didn't matter."

But it did, she saw, from the way his face tightened, his lips drew back from his teeth.

"Having fun yet?" She laughed at him. "There's no way you'll clean me up, you know. I've got your blood under my fingernails, your saliva all over me. We were moving in to arrest you. See, we knew you were the killer. They're hunting you right now." She shook her head. "Too bad we don't live in Texas. You could fry for this. But fifty years in a cell, that sounds good, too."

She braced herself as he came at her again like a rabid dog.

"WE'LL NEVER FIND THEM." Will swayed on his feet in the middle of the Gaines' living room. "Trina. Oh God."

Jerry gripped his arm. "Keep it together. We can

figure this out. He's got to have a place he feels safe. Someplace that would be deserted at night."

"A storage unit," the other detective suggested.

"Yeah, yeah. Call it in. Have 'em start searching."

"Does anybody rent out garages? What about a cabin?"

Help, Goddamn it! Don't mourn yet.

Will shook his head. "He doesn't own any real estate. Trina searched county records." Her name caught in his throat; he forced it out anyway.

"All right." Jerry's face was haggard, his eyes kind. "Let's go back to the station. He's not here."

On a burst of fear and rage, Will whirled and slammed his fist against the wall. "Why isn't he? Goddamn it, why *not?*"

Jerry looked at him as if he'd gone crazy. "There's no *why*."

"There is. Goddamn it, there is!" He nursed his hand, his thoughts suddenly sharp, crystalline. "He knows his parents are gone all winter. The house is deserted. Totally available. There's a basement. He could put his truck in the garage."

"Neighbors would notice."

"And they might hear screams," the other detective said.

"Fine. So this house is out. He needs someplace that's isolated. But does he rent it year around? Does he know someone else who's gone?" He was shaking his head even before he finished. "He doesn't have that many friends. He just moved back here last summer. Nobody I know has a cabin on the river. A few friends own houses, but they live in them."

"Somebody's parents who also winter south?"

"Nobody that I can think of." Will walked in a circle,

yanking at his hair as he walked. "And six years ago. Did he use a *different* place? Or does he know of some-place that's been deserted all this time?"

"Or is closed at night?" Wheeler said.

"Wait. Isn't he a car salesman?" Jerry pulled out his cell phone and hit buttons.

Will was still pacing, still thinking even as Jerry told someone to send units by every goddamn car dealer in town.

Yeah, a service bay might work. But why hadn't any of the victims picked up oil or grease? The showroom? Too open. Didn't they always have a wall of glass? Too hard to clean. Offices too cluttered. Couldn't let her crash into a desk or file cabinet.

"He has to be able to really scrub. Or know that no-body will see the place and a little blood doesn't mat-ter." His pacing brought him to the door to a small, crowded den. His gaze swept it without interest. He'd been in here once. He was already turning away when he stopped dead. Swung back.

Tacked to a bulletin board were several ribbons. Gaudy ones with rosettes. The biggest one said Butte County—The Cattleman's Fair.

Will stepped closer. A few photos were tacked up, too, all of huge muscular bulls or beefy steers or calves, groomed and polished and being displayed at the fair. He barely recognized Wayne Gaines. The sullen boy holding the calf's lead had to be Gavin.

"He was new at the high school the same year I was." Will studied the photos. "They were ranchers. I remember him complaining about the life. Only they were going broke, so his stepfather took a job selling insurance and they bought the house in town." He shook his head as if to rattle memories, make them float to the surface like snowflakes in one of those globes. "I think his dad kept running some cattle. Do you suppose they never sold the ranch?"

"Depending on where it was, there hasn't been much market for grazing land."

Land was gold toward Juanita Butte, but to the east, where it stretched barren but for sage and tumbleweed and scant grass, cattle-ranching days were all but over and the land too bleak to hold much appeal for anyone else.

"They were out toward Newton," he said, surprised he remembered.

"Don't they bus their kids to Elk Springs High School?"

"They didn't in those days." Will sat down at the desk and yanked open the first drawer. "There have to be records here somewhere."

Jerry went for a tall metal filing cabinet.

The minutes ticked.

"Here we go," the bandy-legged detective said suddenly. "Beef prices, records of sale, a contract with a stockyard…" He had the file open atop the others. Papers slid out to the floor.

Will shoved his chair back just as Jerry said in triumph, "Got it! Let's go."

Wheeler was outside talking to the neighbor.

"Gotta go," Jerry said, and all three men ran for the Explorer, the neighbor's querulous voice following them.

"Ranch? Wayne hasn't run any cattle in years! Why would that no-good boy of his be out there?"

Jerry hit the lights and siren both and screeched away from the curb. Wheeler got on the radio, reporting their route and destination.

"Request second unit."

Dispatch concurred. A patrol officer came on. "We're out past the high school now. Shall we proceed?"

The Explorer rocketed across the Deschutes bridge. All their heads damn near hit the roof, but he took the corner on two wheels.

The two detectives conferred, then Wheeler got back on the radio. "We aren't two minutes behind you. Hold off until we get there. Do not alert suspect. Repeat, no siren or lights when you near the property."

The officer came back on. "We'll hang back at Highway 20 until you get there."

Jerry swore as half a dozen people came out of a brewpub and stepped into the street, laughing and probably drunk and oblivious to the law enforcement vehicle bearing down on them. He had to come to damn near a full stop, Will swearing, every muscle in his body taut.

When they finally reached the highway, Jerry opened it up. He silenced the siren but left the flashers on as he raced east on the flat, dark strip of pavement. Town and its lights fell behind them. Will saw a light now and again out in the darkness at the occasional ranch house. None of them spoke. Instead, they listened to the massive manhunt underway. The crackling voices of sheriff's deputies and ESPD officers reported in as they investigated storage facilities and car dealerships. Nothing.

This could be another dead end. If it was…

Panic smothering him, Will bowed his head and made himself breathe, in through the nose, out through the mouth.

Don't mourn yet.

This made sense. Gavin had hated the ranching life, hated his stepfather. He'd enjoy defiling the ranch and

Wayne Gaines by extension with the blood of his terrified victims.

Trina's blood. It had been too long....

No. Don't think about it. Don't look at your watch again.

She was strong. Trained. She wasn't like the other women, who would have responded with fear, who didn't know how to fight back.

Keep fighting, Trina.

Please, God, let us be right. Let them be there. Let her be alive.

TRINA KNEW she was almost done. She hurt so terribly. On the side where she was shackled to the pipe, her shoulder was dislocated or broken. One eye was swollen shut and from the other she saw through a mere slit. Her lip was split, swollen, her mouth filled with blood. Ribs must be broken; every breath was agony.

Once, briefly, she heard a distant siren and felt the tiniest stirring of what might have been hope. Gavin faltered in his attack. But then the siren faded and she knew it was somewhere far away, outside the bubble that contained the two of them, predator and prey. A speeder getting a ticket. A deputy rushing to the scene of an accident. Not coming here.

No one would come.

"You're a worm," she whispered.

He hit her, over and over, bouncing her head on the rubber mat. He hadn't torn her breast apart with his teeth yet. She thought that must be part of his sexual rage/pleasure, and although he'd pressed his penis to her, it remained flaccid. He desperately, frantically, needed her to submit, to beg, to cry, to fear him.

"Not a monster. Scum."

As long as she hated him, sneered, jeered, she won. Already she'd won, she thought in that detached part of her mind that still functioned. The battle had been so vicious, her body was a petri dish of evidence that would convict Gavin Husby of murder. He wouldn't dare display her after death, and that mattered to him almost as much as the act of raping and killing. He wanted Will to see her, tortured, raped, *obscenely* dead. How could he be satisfied if he couldn't achieve that perfect conclusion?

She spat blood in his face. "Still can't get it up?"

"I'll show you!" he snarled and sprang from her.

She rested, let her swollen eye close. Any small respite. Darkness called, wanted her. She wanted it, to sink in its embrace, for the pain to go away.

But she couldn't let him win.

She pried open her eye and saw him coming back, brandishing the broken handle of some farm tool. A rake or shovel. She'd been prepared for almost anything, but this... Her control shattered and terror flooded her. Despite herself, she scrabbled backward.

He laughed. "So what's it going to be? Me or my right-hand dick?"

THE PATROL UNIT WAITED on the highway verge. Headlights picked out a dirt road, framed by a sagging Ponderosa pine gate, burned with the words *The WG Ranch*. Jerry cut the roof lights and turned onto it, the other SUV right behind him. They rattled over a cattleguard, then followed what was little more than a track through empty, winter-sparse land. They must have gone half a mile before they saw a cluster of trees and buildings ahead.

"There's a light," Jerry murmured.

"Gaines might have sold the ranch."

"I don't think it's at the house."

Another few hundred yards later, he turned off his headlights. Behind him, the second unit went dark, too.

Moonlight faintly illuminated the landscape. Jerry hit a pothole right away, swore. Sagebrush scraped the side of the Explorer and he growled under his breath.

Will stared ahead, his eyes adjusting, now able to make out white light leaking from one of the outbuildings. They were a quarter mile or more away when Jerry said, "Time to walk," and braked.

They closed doors quietly and assembled, listened to a few words from Jerry, then jogged toward the ranch. Jerry puffed and lurched with his stiff-legged gait. Will wanted to hurry, go faster, but Jerry wouldn't be able to.

They might still be wrong. Some rancher might be out tending a sick cow.

But Will didn't believe it.

MUST NOT SHOW FEAR. Unless…one chance. One small chance.

"Please." Tears tried to leak from her eyes. "Don't."

He straddled her, his penis hardening. "Beg, bitch."

She wasn't strong enough to kick. Oh, she wanted to be.

She let a whimper escape her. "Please. Please don't."

Gavin Husby laughed in triumph and tossed the tool handle aside. It clattered on concrete. He dropped to his knees between her legs as she moaned and lay compliant, defeated.

He came down at her, bit her breast, pushed his penis against her.

She made a fist of her hand but for two fingers, held

stiff. And when he lifted his head, blood running from his snarling mouth, she drove her hand upward with everything she had left in her, straight into the soft socket of his eye.

He fell off her, crawled away, curled into a fetal position. She had never heard anyone scream like that.

Trina laughed, then sobbed.

As if in a dream, she heard a sharp, startled, "Son of a bitch!" and they were surrounded by her saviors. In her dream, it was Will himself who knelt over her, crying, promising her forever and a wedding day and a move to San Diego and sunshine if she wanted and if only she would live. For him.

As she fell into darkness, the last thing she heard was the miracle of Will Patton saying, in a broken voice, "I love you, Trina Giallombardo. I love you."

EPILOGUE

THEY DROVE to Salem together, Will, Trina and Meg.

Trina still hurt. She had to move very carefully to avoid jarring her ribs. One arm was in a sling to let her shoulder heal from the dislocation. Her wrist, torn from the handcuff, was still wrapped, the fingers that emerged from the dressing puffy and stiff. Her bruises had gone through every imaginable hue and were now a dirty yellow rimmed with purple. Even after two weeks, her face was still swollen; the cheekbone and her nose had been broken. Her black eyes had been things of beauty. Her words were still a little slurred. And she would always bear scars on her breast.

But she'd won. Not just with her death, but with life.

Will loved her. She was actually starting to believe he did. He'd hardly left her side in the hospital. She'd regained consciousness in recovery to hear his voice. Sometimes at night, she would wake up and find him sleeping in a chair at her bedside.

He'd told her how sorry he was a thousand times. If he'd stayed away from her, this wouldn't have happened. He'd branded her by falling in love with her.

She admitted that she had believed he didn't want to be seen with her in public and now felt stupid not to have realized why Will didn't want anyone to know they'd become lovers. Somehow, she hadn't imagined herself as a target. She was a cop, after all. And maybe more important, she didn't look like Gillian and Amy and Karin.

On this trip across the mountains, Meg drove. Will sat beside Trina in the back, holding her hand, his thumb tracing absentminded patterns on her palm, his gaze tender every time he smiled at her.

At the penitentiary, Meg surrendered her sidearm and they all submitted to a pat-down. They were escorted to a room very like the one where Trina had once interviewed Ricky Mendoza.

They waited in silence, Trina sitting because she still felt so exhausted. Will's hand rested on her shoulder. Meg paced.

At a footfall, they all went still.

Ricky Mendoza appeared in the doorway, his stunned gaze taking them in. Trina heard a shocked murmur from Meg, who'd last seen him as a cocky, handsome young man, not a scarred, wary one.

He took a few steps into the room. "What happened to you?" he finally blurted, looking at Trina.

"The man who put you in here did it."

He stood, apparently stunned, a suddenly frantic gaze shifting from face to face. His voice was hoarse. "What man?"

"The man who has murdered maybe a dozen women or more," Meg said.

"He killed her. Gillian."

"Yes."

Mendoza groped for a chair, his knuckles white as he gripped the back. Finally, he half fell into it. He leaned his elbows on his knees and bowed his head, lank hair hiding his face. When he looked up, his eyes had a sheen.

"Everyone knows I didn't do it?"

Meg smiled at him. "The governor's aide called last night. He's given you a pardon. You're walking out of here, Ricky."

He cried unashamedly. When he finally wiped his eyes on his shirtsleeve and spoke, it was to Will. "I'm sorry. She was a nice lady. A classy lady. I should have sent her back to you that night. I shouldn't have wanted something not meant for me." He swallowed. "I've wanted to say that for a long time."

Will's eyes were wet, too. "It wasn't your fault. None of this was. I wish we could give you back these years."

A ragged laugh escaped Ricky Mendoza. "You're giving me back my life. Shit, that's more than I ever thought I'd have."

Me, too, Trina thought. *Me, too.*

"I'll tell you what, though," he said. "I don't think I'll be coming back to Elk Springs."

They left him expecting official notice and walked back out of the state penitentiary.

The afternoon crisp and cold, Will and Trina waited while Meg went to get the SUV. Watching her lieutenant walk away across the parking lot, Trina said, "Your mom. Is she okay with this? I mean, us?"

Will laughed softly. "Are you kidding? She told me I'm the luckiest son of a gun on earth. I already knew that. You, my darling, aren't just beautiful…"

She couldn't help laughing, too, even though it hurt. She might be many things, but beautiful wasn't one of them right this minute.

"Not just smart," he continued, "not just kind, discerning and gutsy. No, what you have is heart." He laid his hand gently beneath her breast, the one that would be scarred. "Just like all the Patton women."

Her smile wobbled and she went into his arms. Once upon a time, she'd worshipped from afar. Dreamed of who she wasn't and wished she was.

How rare and amazing was it to get to go to heaven on earth? *She* was going to be a Patton. Will's wife. Smart, kind, gutsy.

Maybe even, on a good day, beautiful.

Everything you love about romance...
and more!

Please turn the page for Signature Select™
Bonus Features.

Dead Wrong

BONUS
FEATURES
INSIDE

Getting to know the
CHARACTERS
Meet the Patton Family

ED PATTON, Elk Springs police chief, casts a shadow over his daughters' lives and even the lives of their children long after he's gone. A hard man, he possessed a vicious, cold temper and a streak of cruelty that his daughters knew well.

JOLENE PATTON loved her daughters but wasn't strong enough to stand up for them or for herself to the angry man she'd married. Knowing he'd pursue her forever if she took their children, she fled to save herself, leaving behind the mystery of whether she had truly escaped—or was buried somewhere in Oregon's bleak high country desert.

Their Children:

MEG PATTON, the oldest daughter, fled in turn when her father beat and humiliated her boyfriend, Jack Murray, and she knew he couldn't protect her—or the unborn child she carried. She saved herself and Will, but lived with the guilt of abandoning her younger sisters.

RENEE PATTON, the middle daughter, both defied and feared her father. She's bitter at the desertion by first her mother and then the big sister who'd been her protector. Glad when Ed Patton dies, she can't seem to avoid following his footsteps. She's an Elk Springs police officer, and she continues to live in the Patton family home even though she's afraid to sit in the living room, where she senses her father's ghost.

ABBY PATTON, baby of the family, learned to use charm to wrap Daddy around her little finger. Despite her skill—or perhaps because of it— she's the most emotionally damaged of the three Patton daughters. The only honest relationship she's had as an adult is with Renee. Whether she's capable of having an equally honest relationship with a man is open to question.

MICK SARICH has always known Chief Ed Patton was his father. Neither he nor his mother have ever approached the Patton family, though, and now that his mother is dead Mick is focused on wanting to grow up to be a hero just like his father.

The Men in the Patton Sisters' Lives:

JACK MURRAY, Meg's high school boyfriend, suffered humiliation at Ed Patton's hands and heartbreak when Meg fled, unable to trust Jack to protect her. He's made himself into a harder man than he would otherwise have been, but his defenses may fall when he finds out he and Meg have a son together.

DANIEL BARNARD, rancher, has been haunted by the disappearance of his grandfather, who wandered out the door in a snowstorm and was never found. The bones Daniel's dog brings home open a Pandora's box of secrets—and introduce him to Renee Patton.

SCOTT McNEIL, manager of the enormous ski resort that has transformed Butte County, has never recovered from the loss of his infant son from SIDS. Rescuing a baby girl from an icy winter night on the mountain changes his life again.

BEN SHEA, Elk Springs homicide detective, is a tough guy on the surface, but his greatest satisfactions are the home he's remodeling and his garden. Why he falls for a complicated, prickly woman like Abby Patton is a mystery to him.

The Patton grandchildren:

WILL PATTON grew up as the only child of a single mom, smart, athletic and loved, although he's consumed with curiosity about his dad. He watches his friends' relationships with their fathers with envy, and imagines having the same kind with his. Unfortunately, *his* father doesn't know he exists.

EMILY McNEIL is saved by her mother's courage and pure luck. Rejected by her grandparents as a child of sin, she's adopted into the Patton clan.

MATTHEW JEROME / EVAN McNEIL* is Meg's baby son.

SARA and **RACHEL SHEA** are the young daughters of Abby Patton, Butte County fire marshal.

DILLON and **KATHLEEN BARNARD** are Renee Patton's children.

*You know the blooper reel at the end of movies? Well, authors make bloopers, too. Little Matthew Jerome McNeil metamorphoses from one book into Evan McNeil in later ones, despite the vigilance of author, editor and copy editor.

The Publishing History of PATTON'S DAUGHTERS

When Janice Kay Johnson first came up with the idea, she thought she'd write one big book featuring the three daughters of Elk Springs police chief Ed Patton. But then she and her editors decided PATTON'S DAUGHTERS would make an excellent trilogy. The three stories, *The Woman in Blue*, *The Baby and the Badge* and *A Message for Abby*, appeared in the Harlequin Superromance line over three months in 1999. Once those stories were published it became clear Jack Murray, whose life was so closely connected to the Pattons, needed a story of his own. And that's how *Jack Murray, Sheriff* came to be in 2000. Later that year, Janice was asked to participate in a Harlequin Superromance anthology called *Born in a Small Town*. She decided to go back to Elk Springs to tell the story of Kevin McNeil, brother of Scott, who was the hero of one of the original books *(The Baby and the Badge)* in "Promise Me Picket Fences." Six years later she returns again with the Signature Select Saga you hold in your hands. In *Dead Wrong*, Ed Patton's oldest grandson, Will, is the protagonist. From one idea, six books. (Seven, if you count the reissue of the first two PATTON'S DAUGHTERS in a collection called, not surprisingly, *Patton's Daughters*.)

CHRONOLOGICAL BOOK LIST

The Woman in Blue
(Harlequin Superromance #854, July 1999)

The Baby and the Badge
(Harlequin Superromance #860, August 1999)

A Message for Abby
(Harlequin Superromance #866, September 1999)

Jack Murray, Sheriff
(Harlequin Superromance #913, May 2000)

Born in a Small Town
(Harlequin Superromance #936, September 2000)

Patton's Daughters
(Signature Select Miniseries, January 2006)*

Dead Wrong
(Signature Select Saga, February 2006)

* reissue of *The Woman in Blue* and *The Baby and the Badge*

A conversation with
Sarah Baczewski,
Janice Kay Johnson's Daughter

Sometimes you learn more about a person through what others have to say. Janice's daughter shares with us what it's like to live with this writer mom!

Is your mother, novelist Janice Kay Johnson, a romantic?
You've got to be kidding. Well, okay. She does like some old things, like old roses, quilts, antique furniture. But lace and hearts and flowery fabrics...no. Really. No. I'm pretty sure she'd prefer honesty to lavish compliments. She does like romantic movies, though, and she reads romances.

Does she enjoy cooking and other domestic pursuits?
(Daughter falls to the floor laughing.) (Once she recovers she answers.) An even bigger no! Mom's idea of a domestic pursuit is quilting. She hates to clean house, and home-cooked meals on

the table at five o'clock? A distant memory. She did what she had to do when my sister and I were little, but once we were capable of cooking ourselves, she figured she'd done her duty. Nope, Mom would really, really like a housekeeper who leaves for the day just as dinner is ready to come out of the oven.

Describe a typical dinner table conversation at your house.
All over the map. I occasionally have to squelch her when she gets too enthusiastic about something she's researching. For example, lately it's been serial killers and she started sharing fascinating details about a book on investigating the time of death. When she mentioned maggots, I politely suggested we talk about the movies that had come out that week instead. Mom is always researching something—it could be a historical period, the experience of growing up adopted (for her next trilogy), sexual abuse, private investigators, oddball professions, you name it. She reads widely for pleasure, too, has plenty of hobbies and follows world events and politics, so we actually have pretty lively dinner table conversations—when she cooks, that is.

What do people think when you tell them your mother is a romance writer?

When I was about three and someone asked what my mother did, I told them she typed. They would nod politely. Now that I say *what* she types— mostly they're fascinated. Once in a while you get the slight curl of the lip as they say, "Romance?" Usually, though, people have a pretty good idea how hard it is to write a 320-page novel of any kind, and to have written and published nearly sixty—they're impressed.

Describe your mother at work.

I'd like to say she puts on panty hose and a suit, but really she usually wears jeans and a T-shirt, clogs or slippers (sometimes pajamas, if she's in a particularly unambitious mood). Her desk is a mess—piles of books, magazines and papers everywhere. She gets pretty grumpy when she can't find something. Every few months, she takes a day or two to clear the piles and start a new "system" for organization, which fails a week or two later. As an incredibly organized human being, I can safely say I didn't inherit it from her.

Do you read her books? Enjoy them? Do you ever critique them while she's writing?

Actually, I do read her books and think she's an amazing writer. I don't read all of them, because I'm twenty-two and she tends to write about women in their thirties and family issues that don't interest me much yet. I don't plan to be the mother of a teenager for a long time! I don't usually read them while she's writing, but she does ask for ideas when she's plotting or runs into a problem, and I suggest titles sometimes, too.

Do you dream of being a writer?
It's funny you ask, because, like, *everyone* in my family writes! My granddad published textbooks and trail guides, my grandmother writes books for kids and mysteries for adults and my father published a really funny young-adult novel. I'm a huge reader, so Mom keeps saying I'll end up as a writer. I was a theater major in college and am interested in film directing, but as it happens, right now I'm writing a script for a romantic comedy, so I guess you never know.

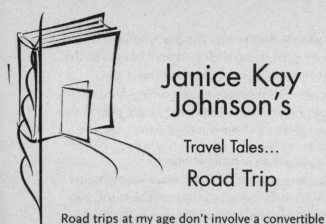

Janice Kay Johnson's

Travel Tales...

Road Trip

Road trips at my age don't involve a convertible with the top rolled down, a cooler of beer on the backseat, a handsome guy behind the wheel, the open road before us. Nope, even an overnight getaway means careful packing (mustn't forget the prescription medications) and the assignment of responsibility while I'm gone. (Who is going to feed the animals? Make sure the garbage gets taken out Tuesday night. Be there when the guy comes to repair the disposal, etc.) Which is not to say that taking off for a couple of days with a friend, thus leaving the responsibilities behind, isn't pretty darned exciting.

There is a reason, of course, that I'm going to tell you about my most recent escape. I went to Portland for two days with a friend who is also a writer, and on the way we plotted two stories, one for her and one for me. Mine was the short story in this volume. I write 330-page books. *Not* short stories.

The atmosphere for plotting was right, because, while ostensibly we were taking the trip to see her daughter, in reality we were on our way to Powell's Books, the grandmother of all bookstores, the city block of room upon room upon room of used and new books mingled under subjects. Researching police procedures? Here's a nice long aisle of shelved books reaching toward the ceiling. Inuit art? Adoption? South American history? Get a bunch of writers in there, and they scatter with incoherent cries of delight. Just try to round them up.

But I live a five-hour drive from Portland, and there we were, Pat and I, with nothing else to do but talk. She's been writing Western historical romance for Kensington, but was plotting a paranormal romance (since sold to Pocket Books). I was faced with the appalling necessity of writing something under twenty pages long. All I knew was that I wanted it to link to the rest of the books in the PATTON'S DAUGHTERS miniseries. For some reason, I kept remembering the recurring thought Meg, Renee and Abby had that "Dad would be turning over in his grave" or was "resting uneasy in his grave."

If we took the words literally... What if the ground was disturbed, and his grave was found to be empty? Given what a hideous man he was and how frightened of him his daughters were, the idea gave me goose bumps. But...why would somebody want his remains (not a pretty sight after fifteen years or so)? What if *he* was there, but was missing a body part? Say, a finger. Yeah, but darn it, why? Honestly, digging the guy up didn't make sense. Defiling his gravestone, for someone who'd hated him...that was logical if twisted. But actually digging him up and opening the coffin—well, that made sense only if someone wanted something buried with him. And it would be a heck of a lot of work, especially given that you'd have to do it in the middle of the night, so you'd have to be majorly motivated.

Pat and I were on a roll. Tacoma passed, Olympia, Mount Saint Helens on our left. We paused at a used bookstore in Chehalis (we're like quilters who know every quilt shop in the state; we know our bookstores), then continued on. By the time we started over the Columbia River, Portland's skyline ahead, we had the story nailed down. The good part was we still had something to do on the way home! Her story!

The perils of road-trip plotting? Well, you know how you get great ideas in the middle of the night, only they don't seem so great in the cold light of day? Sometimes it works like that. Worse yet, another writer friend and I once went to a conference in Eugene, Oregon (another couple of hours down the road). We were pretty tired on the way home, but we were going to plot two books. Ideas flowed. We started getting excited.

We came up with the best plots ever! Trouble was, neither of us wrote them down (she was driving, I get carsick if I read or write while moving). We both returned to the books we were working on. A couple of weeks later, I couldn't remember the story we plotted for me. I called her. She didn't remember mine—or hers! We both still wonder whether those weren't our breakout books, our chance to crack the *New York Times* Bestseller List—or really lousy ideas.

But the short story actually got written, and it might not have if Pat and I hadn't craved a visit to Powell's Books.

ROLLING OVER
IN HIS GRAVE

by Janice Kay Johnson

RENEE PATTON absentmindedly dumped the dregs of coffee from her mug into the sink. She was speaking to the Kiwanis Club today and hadn't planned a talk. Not that she hadn't given a couple hundred of these speeches since she'd become Elk Springs police chief. If she could find her notes from the last time…

The phone rang.

She answered. "Renee speaking."

"Chief, this is George Hillyard out at Mountain Rest Cemetery."

Rotary Club, if she remembered right.

"I hate to bother you at home," he continued, "but I thought you'd like to be informed. I just got a report of a grave being disturbed out in the area where your dad is buried."

"His grave?" Goose bumps rose on her arms. Lord help them all. Somehow she'd always known that Chief Ed Patton wouldn't rest in peace.

"We don't know yet. An attendant reports dirty footprints. I'm heading over myself…"

She grabbed her car keys. "I'll meet you there."

"I can call when I know more…"

Renee had already hung up the phone and was going out the door, the Kiwanis Club forgotten.

She didn't make a habit of visiting her father's grave. She'd hated and feared him in life and often marveled at the fact that, even so, she'd walked in his footsteps, becoming police chief just as he'd been. But she knew right where he lay. She remembered all too well standing at graveside fifteen years ago with her youngest sister, Abby, as the coffin was lowered into the gaping hole. Aware of sympathetic glances, she'd kept her gaze lowered and hidden the relief that had dawned in her breast.

After winding into the cemetery, she parked behind a blue sedan and a worker's pickup, then walked across the springy grass to join Hillyard in his dark suit standing with two cemetery workers, all staring down at the fresh dirt sprinkled on the smooth grass around her father's grave. Clearly, someone had heaped dirt beside the grave. Dirt that had since disappeared.

Without a word, Renee crouched to tug at the grass. Her second yank brought results. The sod peeled off like a bandage from a wound.

Behind her, George Hillyard said a heartfelt, "Damn." Followed by, "I'm sorry, Renee, but we're going to have to dig him up."

"Oh, yeah," she agreed.

She called her sisters, Abby now an arson investigator, Meg a lieutenant in the sheriff's department. Both joined her to watch as workers dug.

Renee kept casting uneasy glances at the dirty trail that led away from the grave. It petered out as it went, not quite reaching the paved road that wound through the cemetery. She told herself the grass had cleaned the soles of the grave robber's shoes. That was the only reason the trail seemed to vanish in midstride.

But finally she said, "Is it just me wondering if he finally pushed his way out of there?"

They both made strangled admissions that the thought had, unpleasantly enough, crossed their minds,

With a clang, a shovel hit a solid surface. More carefully, workers cleared the mahogany lid of the coffin. Finally, one crouched in the hole and pried up the lid.

"Well," George said at last, "thank our dear Lord no one took his body."

Mostly mummified, Ed Patton lay where they'd put him, head on the satin pillow, his uniform having aged better than he had. It was Renee, staring into the hole, who said, "His badge. We buried him with it."

A small tear in the fabric of his jacket gave away the haste with which the badge had been ripped off.

"Why would anyone want it?" Abby asked. She neither expected nor got an answer.

"Now what do we do?" the cemetery director asked.

"Fingerprint the coffin," Renee said.

Eyes narrowed, Meg was studying the shining face of the granite marker. "Do the gravestone, too."

Surprised, Renee shrugged and pulled out her cell phone. "Pete," she said into it, "I need a fingerprint tech."

Meg and Abby left. Only Renee remained, in a vigil that felt symbolic. She'd been the one who'd lived with him until his death, the one who'd maintained the family home long after his death without daring to move a thing for fear his ghost would lash out at her.

The fingerprint technician arrived and dusted the coffin lid with powder. Shaking his head, he said, "I'm finding prints, but I don't think they're fresh. I'm betting your grave robber wore gloves."

Who'd want to open a coffin with their bare hands? "Do the headstone."

"Lookee, lookee," he said a minute later. Right over the engraved letters that said Police Chief, a set of four prints showed clear as day. Just below the letters was the thumbprint, as if someone had rested a hand on the stone in reverence.

"Might not be our robber," Renee said.

"Might be, though," the fingerprint tech added.

She nodded and said to the two cemetery workers still standing by, "Bury him."

She watched while they obeyed, wanting to be sure plenty of heavy dark earth weighted down the coffin lid. They stretched the sod back over the grave and brushed the grass with brooms until the dirt was diffused, the ground appearing undisturbed.

Then and only then did she leave, just in time for her speaking engagement.

THE FAMILY CONFERENCE that night included the three sisters, their husbands and Will, Meg's oldest boy who was now an assistant district attorney for Butte County.

Who and why was the topic.

"Somebody who hated his guts," was an oft-expressed opinion.

"Since that's one hell of a long list," Abby said, "we may have trouble narrowing it down further."

"On the up side, a goodly number of people who hated him will have been fingerprinted," Meg pointed out.

Renee hardly needed to say, "But not necessarily their descendents." After all, the grown son of parents who'd died horribly thanks to Chief Ed Patton's barbaric style of policing had already targeted their family once.

Will interrupted. "But why would someone who hated him dig him up just to steal his badge? Desecrating the grave, sure. Scattering his bones, smashing the headstone, that makes sense. Stealing the badge and then closing the grave up so neatly, that *doesn't* make sense."

Ben Shea, Abby's husband and a Butte County sheriff's department detective, agreed. "What about one of the old-timers who worshipped him and thinks law enforcement in this town will never be the same? Can't you see one of those potbellied bastards polishing that badge and displaying it on an altar to the good ol' days?"

"Could be a kid," Will suggested. "On a dare."

Meg had been rubbing her collarbone, right where Ed Patton had once broken it. She'd confessed that it sometimes ached.

"I say we publicize this. Get the paper to highlight Chief Patton's sins. We can mention that we have leads and believe we will shortly be making an arrest."

24

"Scare the crap out of him." Renee nodded. "I like it."

"If it's a kid, he'll open his big mouth to someone," Renee's husband said.

"I always enjoy an opportunity to remind people what a son of a bitch he was," Abby agreed.

"Why don't we offer him the opportunity to return the badge without consequences?" Will suggested.

"Good idea." Renee looked around the table to see if other comments were forthcoming. When none were, she said, "Meantime, we'll be running those fingerprints."

MICK SARICH spread his schoolbooks out at the kitchen table after the dinner dishes had been cleared.

He waited until the two other kids went upstairs and he heard the television come on in the living room where his foster mother had gone to spend her evening like she always did before he snatched up the newspaper to see if anything had appeared yet.

When he saw the cover story, his heart raced: Police Chief Ed Patton's Grave Desecrated

He hadn't desecrated anything!

Except there was that unpleasant moment when he'd seen the corpse and torn the badge off in his haste to be done and safely home.

He kept reading, the hamburger casserole he'd eaten for dinner turning to cement in his stomach.

Elk Springs police chief Renee Patton reports that investigators are vigorously pursuing several leads and expect the carelessness of the offender to bring about a quick arrest.

Carelessness? What were they talking about? He'd worn gloves, and since it had been three in the morning when he'd started digging, he knew damn well no one had been around to see him. He'd washed the tools and put them back in the garage so his foster mother wouldn't notice they'd been used.

Just below the lead article was a second one, about Ed Patton's years as chief of police. Some of his apprehension fading, Mick started to read.

But he hadn't gotten far when his stomach began to knot again. This couldn't be true. None of it. Ed Patton had been awesome. He was like Batman,

BONUS FEATURE

knocking heads together. A hero. All of this was just crap. Lies.

He shoved his chair back and called, "I have to go to the library," and went to the garage for his mountain bike. Not really his, of course, any more than the bedroom or the clothes the state bought for him were his. But his to use. Borrowed, was how he thought of them.

He peddled furiously along quiet, neighborhood streets, crossing the Deschutes River. At the public library, he left his bike in the rack without even bothering to chain it. Inside, he had to wait fifteen minutes before some fat old guy got up from the microfiche machine and he could claim it.

He started way back, before Ed Patton become police chief. His name kept cropping up in the newspaper. Mostly he was named as the arresting officer. Then Mick came to a front-page story about a teenage boy being shot to death by a police officer. The boy had been breaking into a store, but he'd run when Officer Patton had confronted him. The article said he'd swung around with something in his hand, and the officer had thought he had a gun.

Mick scrolled to the next day's edition, where Ed Patton was named for the first time. A neighbor who'd stepped out on her porch claimed the boy never had turned around and didn't have anything in his hand. She said the police officer had shot him in the back.

Crouching over the microfiche reader, Mick found a follow-up article dated two weeks later. Officer Patton had been cleared. He said one thing, the witness another, but they'd had no reason to doubt that Officer Patton was telling the truth about what he'd thought he saw. The incident was a tragedy, etc.

In an issue dated three months later, Ed Patton made the front page again. A man had shot his wife and kid when the police officer responding to a neighbor's call kicked in the door instead of trying to negotiate. The guy's sister was enraged, saying her brother had been really depressed but he never would have hurt anyone if somebody had just given him an out. Once again, Ed Patton was cleared.

A sick feeling was growing in Mick's stomach. He kept reading, kept finding stories about Ed Patton when he became sergeant, then finally police chief. There were always allegations of brutality, but he kept rising in the ranks. He was "tough on crime," editorials claimed.

Mick had really, really wanted that badge as sort of a symbol. *He* was going to grow up to be like Ed Patton.

But now…now he didn't want to be anything like him. He didn't want the badge. He wished he'd never thought of this incredibly dumb idea.

Mick turned off the microfiche reader and went to the bathroom. Grateful he had it to himself, he dropped to his knees in front of the toilet and puked.

They were going to find him. He knew they were. He'd be arrested and handcuffed and humiliated, and he didn't know how he'd ever been so stupid.

Peddling home, he felt like he had a fever. Chills washed over him. Maybe not like a fever. Maybe like a ghost was near. A ghost who was really pissed because Mick Sarich had dug up his grave and stolen something from him.

I'll get rid of the badge, he thought. He could throw it in the river.

But what if somebody saw him throw something from the bridge, and they dredged, and…

A Dumpster. There were bunches of them in the alley that ran behind the main street with all its shops. Nobody would look in those. Or one of the neighbors' garbage cans.

…vigorously pursuing several leads…the carelessness of the offender…a quick arrest…

He turned into the driveway, then felt terror close his throat when the dark shape of a man materialized between his house and the neighbor's. Mick fell off his bike and left it lying there, racing for the front door. Inside, he was panting when he locked it and turned out the porch light.

Back pressed to the door, he stood there for a minute. Two minutes. Nothing. No footsteps on the porch, no firm knock on the door. No "Open in the name of the law."

The shape had been nothing but a shrub. He *knew* there was a bush right there between the houses. Getting freaked out like this was so dumb.

But he didn't go back out to put his bike away. Instead, he called, "I'm home," and took the newspaper again from the recycling bin where he'd returned it. What had they said about returning the badge?

"HE'LL MAIL IT," Abby grumbled.

Renee shook her head. "I wouldn't. Not if I was scared. I'd worry about fingerprints and my handwriting and the postmistress remembering who mailed that package."

The moon was barely a sliver, casting little light. The cemetery was pitch dark. Abby bumped into a stone and muttered something.

"He'll throw it away."

They were speaking in whispers now.

"It depends who he is." Renee had thought a lot about this. "He worked really hard to get that badge. He might have never seen a corpse before. Part of him might feel bad about what he did. No." She shook her head, even though Abby couldn't see her. "I think he'll return it. And if I were him, this is what I'd do. Sneak back and leave it on the gravestone."

"Maybe we should just let him."

"Don't you want to know who stole it and why?"

"Crap," her sister growled. "Of course I do. I'm here, aren't I? Unlike our beloved big sister."

"Who had an excellent excuse." Her young son was sick, her husband out of town. It was too bad, because she'd been more enthusiastic about the idea of a stakeout than Abby was.

"But what if this guy doesn't come tonight?" Abby grumbled. "Or tomorrow night?"

"What? You afraid of ghosts?" Renee mocked, covering for the fact that she *was* afraid of ghosts. Her father's in particular.

"I appreciate my sleep." Abby sighed audibly. "Okay. I'll hide behind that bush. You can have the tree."

"You're skinnier. You should take the tree."

"This was your idea. I want to sit down."

Grumbling to herself, Renee conceded the point and went to stand behind the thick trunk of an old maple. Actually, she all but plastered herself to it, since she had no idea what direction the grave robber would come from. She was betting he wouldn't turn on a flashlight, except maybe briefly to be sure he had the right grave. Just so she wasn't an obvious silhouette, the tree would provide enough cover.

Silence settled over the graveyard. The late spring chill began to seep through her coat and athletic shoes. Leaning against the rough bole, she began to wish she could see the grave. What if nobody had dug it up? What if, by pure force of will, Ed Patton had

30

pushed up the lid and risen from the coffin, returning to it with the first touch of dawn's light?

Oh, for Pete's sake! She should never watch shows like *Buffy* if her imagination was going to be this vivid! She'd seen his body. He'd been half bones, half mummified. Dead.

That didn't mean his spirit, as malevolent as he'd been in life, hadn't cast off the earthly shell and risen from the grave.

Taking the badge with it? she scoffed. Peeling up the sod and strewing dirt around it?

Don't be an idiot.

Every so often, she cupped her hand over her watch and peered at the faint green face. Ten o'clock became eleven, then midnight. The witching hour. How late should they stay? What made her think this guy was going to return the badge at all? He'd wanted it really bad. He'd recognize all that stuff in the paper as the fiction it was. If he bothered to read the paper at all.

One o'clock. Renee kept expecting to hear Abby declare, "Enough." She was being more patient than Renee had anticipated.

One-thirty. She was freezing. Stiff. She didn't *care* if ghosts wandered the cemetery. She just wanted to go home and crawl into her warm bed beside her big strong husband. He'd murmur in his sleep, and his arms would come around her. Maybe he'd even wake up, and his hands would wander over her while she told him about their futile stakeout, and after a minute she'd forget about everything but him, and his lips, and…

She jolted to consciousness. Her skin prickled. She'd heard something. A sharp breath. A muffled exclamation.

Renee held herself very still and listened. She was just thinking that she'd imagined the sound, or that she'd heard a foraging raccoon, or maybe Abby had stirred, when she heard the distinct sound of somebody breathing. Hard, as if he'd run, or was scared.

She inched around the tree, her back to it. Her eyes had long since adjusted to the dark, and she saw movement. The figure stopped by her father's grave. A circle of light appeared and illuminated the gravestone.

She stepped away from the tree and said, "Put your hands up! This is the police."

The light vanished, the figure bolted.

It didn't get far. There was a thud as a second figure hurtled itself at the first one. They toppled to the ground. Renee switched on her flashlight to see her sister struggling with a man clad in jeans and a black hooded sweatshirt. Renee walked over and planted her foot on the man's back.

"Freeze!" she snapped.

He went still, then sagged. Abby yanked his hood off and shoved him over onto his back.

"Oh, my God," she breathed, and scrambled away.

32

Aghast, the sisters stared down at the teenage boy who lay at their feet. He was the living image of a young Ed Patton.

"Who are you?" Renee whispered.

WITH THE DOME LIGHT on in the car and the heater running, the tall, rangy boy handed Renee the badge. "I'm sorry. I... This was really dumb. I never thought…"

Interrupting his stuttering, she repeated, "Who are you?"

"Mom always said he was my father. You know. Ed Patton." The boy shrugged awkwardly. "Except I can't prove it, 'cause she didn't put his name on my birth certificate."

"But...how old are you?"

"I'm sixteen. Well, almost sixteen."

Ed Patton had been dead only fifteen years. It was possible that he'd fathered a son that late in life… Late. What was she talking about? He'd only been sixty-four when he died. Men that age did sometimes have children.

"Wow." She shook her head. "We'll have to talk to your mother."

He shrank back against the car door. "The newspaper article said I could bring it back and not get arrested."

"I didn't mean that. I meant about your paternity."

"Oh." He was silent for a moment. "Mom's dead. She had cancer. She died when I was ten."

Renee and Abby exchanged a glance. "Then who do you live with?"

He shrugged again, voice full of bravado, face so young. "I'm in a foster home. I keep getting moved, but when I'm eighteen I won't need them anymore anyway."

Abby spoke for the first time in a long while. "You're a Patton, and you've been growing up in foster homes."

"I can't prove he was my dad," he repeated.

"Why did you take the badge?" Renee asked.

He ducked his head again, his brown hair falling over his forehead. Voice nearly inaudible, he said, "Mom talked about him a lot. She said he was like this hero. That I should be proud 'cause he was my dad. I just...I wanted something that was his. You know? I could pretend he gave it to me."

"You did this all by yourself? In one night?"

"Of course I was by myself!" he flared. Then he hunched his shoulders again. "Truth is, I peeled up the sod one night, then laid it back down. So it was faster the next night."

"So why'd you return it?"

He lifted his head, pain flashing across his face. "After I saw the article in the paper, I went to the library and read all about him. He wasn't a hero, was he? I don't want anything of his. He's not my dad. I bet she lied to me! I bet…"

Very softly, Renee said, "He was your father."

He jerked. "What?"

"We can run a DNA test if you want, but I don't think there's any doubt. You look just like him. Wait till you see a high school yearbook picture of him."

His Adam's apple bobbed. "I look like him?" Then he said, "But I don't want him to be my father!"

Abby snorted. "None of us want him to have been our father, but you can't change what is."

"*Our* father?"

Renee smiled at him and held out her hand. "Mick Sarich, I'm Renee Patton."

Mouth agape, he shook her hand.

"Abby Patton."

He shook hers, too.

"We're your sisters," Renee added helpfully.

"But…but you're…"

"A lot older than you?"

"And…and you're the police chief."

"But still your sisters."

He thought about it, then squeaked, "Jeez."

She put the car in gear. "Right now, I'm going to take you home. Tomorrow, you're going to meet the rest of the family. You have another sister and plenty of nieces and nephews."

Appearing stunned, he kept staring at her.

"We'll have to figure out who you're going to live

with," she continued, conversationally. "Do you like horses? Daniel would be thrilled if you did. Maybe we'd be the best choice."

"Hey," Abby protested. "You know Ben would like a son. And Meg and Scott will be putting in a bid, too."

"We'll flip a coin. Or let him choose." As she braked at the foot of the cemetery road, she glanced at her passenger. "Unless you hate the whole idea…?"

Tears streamed down his face. "Why?" he choked. "Why would you want…"

"Because you're family, of course." She reached out and squeezed his hand. "A Patton."

A hot tear dropped onto her hand.

With satisfaction, she pictured her father's dessicated corpse.

Yeah, roll over in your grave, Daddy dear. We've found him now, and he's ours. And there's not a damn thing you can do about it.

36

THE END

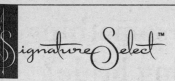

**From the author of the bestselling
COLBY AGENCY miniseries**

DEBRA WEBB

VOWS *of* SILENCE

A gripping new novel of romantic suspense.

A secret pact made long ago between best
friends Lacy, Melinda, Cassidy and Kira resurfaces
when a ten-year-old murder is uncovered. Chief
Rick Summers knows they're hiding something, but
isn't sure he can be objective…especially if his
old flame Lacy is guilty of murder.

**"Debra Webb's fast-paced thriller will
make you shiver in passion and fear."**
—Romantic Times

Vows of Silence…coming in March 2006.

A forty-something blushing bride?

Neely Mason never expected to walk down the aisle, but it's happening, and now her whole Southern family is in on the event. Can they all get through this wedding without killing each other? Because one thing's for sure, when it comes to sisters, *crazy* is a relative term.

The

GOOD KIND

OF CRAZY

TANYA MICHAELS

▼ Silhouette®

SPECIAL EDITION™

BRAVO FAMILY TIES

Stronger Than Ever

THE IRRESISTIBLE BRAVO MEN ARE BACK
IN *USA TODAY* BESTSELLING AUTHOR

CHRISTINE RIMMER's

THE BRAVO
FAMILY WAY

March 2006

The last thing Cleo Bliss needed was
a brash CEO in her life. So when casino
owner Fletcher Bravo made her a business
proposition, Cleo knew it spelled trouble—
until seeing Fletcher's soft spot for his
adorable daughter melted Cleo's heart.

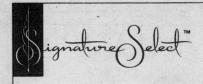

All's fair in love and war...
So why not do both?

BOOTCAMP

Three brand-new stories in one Collection

National bestselling authors

Leslie Kelly

Heather MacAllister

Cindi Myers

Strong-willed females Cassandra, Rebecca and Barbara enroll in the two-week Warfield crash course to figure out how to get what they want in life and romance!

Experience *Bootcamp* in March 2006.